BONE RIVER

BONE RIVER

MEGAN CHANCE

amazon publishing

Text copyright © 2012 Megan Chance
All rights reserved.
Printed in the United States of America.

Published by Amazon Publishing
P.O. Box 400818
Las Vegas, NV 89140

ISBN-13: 9781612184845
ISBN-10: 1612184847

For extraordinary friends

Lynn Beeman, Jo'Ell Catel, and Tammy McMullen

PROLOGUE

SHOALWATER BAY, WASHINGTON TERRITORY

SPRING 1855

———————

IT WAS A SACRED PLACE, AN ANCIENT PLACE. HERE WAS THE confluence of river and bay, of sky and forest, salt marsh and slough, the water stretching its fingers far into the land as if it meant always to reclaim it. Here was a presence that gave weight to the fog and the rain, that lingered in the swollen air, even in sunlight, especially in moonlight. A presence I felt, that I'd felt since my father and I had first come here three years ago, drawn by science, by possibility.

The Indians all said the land was haunted, but Papa built a house and put up a barn without regard for spirits or Indian superstition—almost in spite of those things, as if he meant to insist upon our rationality—and the river rewarded him, spilling its secrets onto the bank, relics from an old Chinook village, detritus from middens long buried or washed away in floods. An ethnological gold mine that kept my father here even as he hated it. He built the house on a rise and glared at the Querquelin River as if he could keep it within its banks by sheer force of

1

will. He saw only science here, and study, and he disdained that sacredness I felt, that sense that spirits hovered always. The land *was* haunted, I thought, but Papa only said, "You have too much imagination, Leonie," and I knew he was right. It was unseemly in a scientist, a flaw I usually fought.

But today I felt those spirits waiting to claim him.

He coughed, and I was at his side in a moment, pulling the chair closer to his bed, reaching for the basin of cool water, dipping the cloth. I wrung it out, but before I could bring it to his fevered skin, he caught my hand to stop me with more strength than I'd expected.

"Are you thirsty?" I asked. "Can I bring you something?"

He shook his head. I let the rag drop back into the basin and curled my fingers around his, bringing them to my lips. His graying hair was sparse against his scalp, his sun-touched skin freckled with dark spots that only served to bring into contrast its ghastly hue. There were dark circles beneath his eyes and stubble upon his cheeks, and his lips were blue, as was the skin around his nostrils.

He beckoned weakly for me to come closer. I leaned down, a corkscrew of blonde hair loosening from my pins to bounce against his shoulder. I saw his eyes follow it. He had always loved my hair. *You have my mother's hair*, he'd said to me once. *Funny, isn't it, how things find their way down?*

I blinked back my tears; he would not want to see them.

"Want…" His voice was hoarse, barely there.

"You mustn't talk. Save your strength."

A bare smile. "For…dying?"

"Please don't say that."

His fingers moved in my hand. "You…must…leave…"

"Leave? I won't leave your side, Papa, not now."

An impatient shake. "This…place."

I sighed. I squeezed his fingers. "Papa, please…let's not talk of this now."

"When June...goes..."

My chest tightened. I had been trying not to think of that, of Junius leaving us, though I knew he would once Papa was gone. My father's protégé was a restless man, always looking for something better, his gaze settled ahead as if the world around him didn't exist. There was nothing to bind him to this place once Papa was gone. "When June goes, I'll still have Lord Tom. He'll stay with me. You know he will. There's nothing for you to worry about."

"No," he said. "June...you marry."

"Marry Junius?"

He coughed. It went deep; he hacked and shuddered, and I put my arm around his shoulders to keep him from choking on his own blood, grabbing a nearby handkerchief, trying not to see the clots, the darkness of the blood, the proof that his lungs were no longer whole enough to keep him here.

The attack went on long enough that I thought it must exhaust him. He closed his eyes and I leveled him gently back to the pillow. I wiped the blood from his lips and expected him to drift into unconsciousness, but he didn't. His hand fell to his chest, searching for a talisman that was no longer there—a pendant he'd lost long ago, though the nervous habit of touching it had never left him.

"Marry...June." Insistent this time, even through his weakness.

"You...you can't mean it. He's *old*, Papa. Why, he must be at least forty."

"Good...man."

"I know that." And I did. But a husband..."I'm not ready. How can I be a wife? I have so much to do..."

"Marry...him." He attempted a smile. "Keep you...safe."

"He won't want to, Papa. He has his own life—"

"He says yes."

I stared at my father with surprise—and yes, a little resentment. "You asked him?"

Papa nodded. "Promise...me."

He was *dying*. What right had I to question him? He'd never hesitated to do what was best for me. He'd been the only parent I'd ever known, becoming both mother and father from the moment my mother died birthing me. He had sacrificed everything for me. He had taught me everything I knew. And what else had I? When Papa was gone, I would be alone. *Alone.* I'd been fighting the thought for days. Now it rose to overwhelm me. What would I do without him? How would I survive?

And in the grip of that fear I said, "All right."

"Promise."

"I promise."

Again, that faint smile. The obvious effort of it tore at my heart.

He closed his eyes.

I stayed there by the bed. He lingered another hour, and then I felt him go, a gasp, a sinking, there and then suddenly...not. I put my head on his chest, listening for breathing I knew already I wouldn't hear, and the stillness crept into me, an emptiness I did not know how to fill. I broke into helpless, convulsing sobs, crying into his shirt, wishing for his arms around me, no matter how clumsy and inept the embrace. He had always been uncomfortable with such displays, but I would have given anything to feel once again his awkward, hesitant patting, to hear his *There, there, my dear. You know I hate to see you cry.*

I sat there for a long time, until I felt the warmth leave him, until the blue of twilight eased through the windows and my father's body was covered in shadow, and then I went to his desk. On the shelf above were his leather-bound journals, on the desk were the relics we'd collected together, the ones that were his favorites: a bone knife from the Dalles, a Chinook horn spoon, a ceremonial rattle, a carved wooden bowl that now held spare buttons and a needle, and a small leather bag of tobacco, so dried out and old now it was mostly dust. I smiled at it, because it had been more than a year since he'd had to give up the pipe he'd loved, and yet that bag was still here, and I knew he'd been unable to throw it away, although he had to have known he would never smoke it. The contradiction of him, so sentimental even as ruled as he was by logic and reason...Oh, I would miss him so.

I blinked, wiping tears away with the back of my hand, and glanced out the window at the deepening blue-gray sky, the fog rising now from the bay, ghostly and beautiful, and two men walking through it, crossing the salt marsh between the house and the mudflats. Lord Tom, the Shoalwater Indian who was like a second father to me, and Junius became more corporeal with every step, solid men finished with ghostly legs, Lord Tom looking for all the world like one of his Chinook ancestors, his long black hair bouncing over his shoulders, a net dangling from his hand, Junius capable and good-natured, laughing at something Lord Tom had said. I saw what my father loved about Junius. His strength was hard and sharp-edged; from here I could not see the gray threading through his brown hair. With a little startle I remembered the promise I'd made my father.

I heard them on the porch, the low murmurs of their talk, their stomping feet, and then the door opening and closing, the soft call, "Leonie?"—careful not to wake him who was already gone. I heard the steps on the stairs.

The two of them came inside, muddy-booted, wet from the knees, bringing cold and the smell of the bay and the marsh into a room that I realized suddenly was already cold. Had I fired up the stove today? I could not remember.

Junius said, "Leonie, why are you standing in the dark?"

Lord Tom said softly, "Teddy *yaka memalose*."

It was a measure of his grief, I knew, that he did not speak the English he knew perfectly well. I did not take my eyes from Junius. "Yes. He's gone."

Junius glanced at the bed and then at me. "Gone? Christ, Lea, I'm so sorry—"

Lord Tom made a little sound. When Junius and I looked at him, he said, "*Mahsh kopa illahee.*" *We must bury him.* He was already backing away, repelled, his people's cultural fear of the dead overcoming even his grief. He could not wait to leave the room, and he would insist Papa's body be gone before he would enter the house again.

"Tomorrow," I said. "We'll bury him tomorrow."

Lord Tom nodded curtly and said, "I'll bring the canoe."

I didn't protest or stop him when he left. Instead, I looked at Junius and said, "He would not want to be buried like an Indian. No canoes. He would want a decent Christian burial. Will you make him a coffin?"

"Yes," Junius said.

"He said you would marry me," I said bluntly.

Junius looked startled. "Yes, but—"

"I promised him I would."

He hesitated. "Leonie, you should know…I…I'm already married. I have a wife. In San Francisco."

I blinked at him in confusion. *A wife.* Which meant he could not marry me, and I would be alone after all. Alone and lonely, with only the spirits for company. I struggled to contain my panic. "Then why did you tell my father you would marry me? And why haven't you ever mentioned her?"

"Because she doesn't matter. I'll marry you, if it's what you wish."

"It doesn't matter what I wish. You're already married."

"She's not important, Lea. I just wanted you to know. I promised your father I would marry you and keep you safe, and I will. Mary and I…we've been apart for…some time. I was young, and…we weren't good together. I left her. She's probably already forgotten me."

"But Junius—"

"We'll be together, you and I," Junius went on quietly. "I'll take care of you as I promised. Mary means nothing to me. But *you*…you do. I'm never going back to her. I'll stay with you."

My fear fled in quick relief. I wouldn't be alone. I could keep the promise I'd made to my dying father. And…I didn't know much about marriage or laws, but surely Junius did. He was so much older. He knew better than I what was possible.

"You'll tell her, though?" I asked. "You'll write her and do whatever…whatever must be done?"

"Yes, of course. I'll take care of everything."

I nodded, relieved. The world had changed around me, and it seemed so sudden, though Papa had been dying for a long time. I'd never dared to think of what would happen once he was gone. But Papa had thought of everything for me, just as he always had. He'd given me Junius.

The spirits in the air seemed to fade and quiet.

"You'll have me then?" Junius asked.

I said, "Well…I said I would."

He held out his hand, and I stepped forward, taking it. I looked into his chiseled face, into his deep-set eyes, and he pulled me into his arms, holding me tight against his chest. I buried my face in his coarse cotton shirt, breathing in the salt-sweat smell of him, the tang of oysters and the bay and the tidal mud. He was solid and warm; I had not known I was cold until I touched him.

"I'll take care of you, Lea," he whispered again into my hair. "I promise."

I felt my father's blessing settle over us like a shroud, gentle and soft and benevolent.

I was seventeen.

CHAPTER 1

TWENTY YEARS LATER

AUTUMN 1875

I HEARD THOSE SPIRITS AGAIN THE NIGHT THE RIVER GAVE up its bones.

I was sitting at the kitchen table with Lord Tom, transcribing the Indian stories I loved, when the storm began, howling through the hemlocks, alders, and cedars ringing the salt marsh, an eerie wailing made worse by the screeching and clattering of branches and the high-pitched whine through the roof shingles.

I shivered and glanced out the window to the darkness beyond. "Junius should be back by now."

"Hmmm," Lord Tom said noncommittally. "No good to be out when the *tomawanos* howl."

I gave him my best quelling glance. "It's only a storm, *tot*"— calling him uncle, as I always did—"not spirits."

He said nothing to that, and I looked back down at my notebook, trying to banish the sense of…suspense, I supposed…that hadn't left me all day, as if something was lurking, waiting. It was the reason I'd asked Lord Tom to tell me the stories tonight, something to distract me. But it wasn't working, and the storm wasn't helping. The air felt shivery and odd, and Lord Tom's talk of spirits only made it worse. I was already too sensitive to this kind of thing. Usually I was better at fighting it. This was only a storm like many others, I told myself. Still, when a gust of wind blew a spattering of rain hard against the window, I jumped.

Lord Tom gave me a knowing glance. "You hear them too."

"Don't be ridiculous. I'm only worried for June."

"That one fears nothing," Lord Tom said. "He's fine, *okustee.* Should I continue the story?"

I nodded and took a deep breath, feeling warm and reassured when he used the nickname he kept only for me. *Daughter.* I drew strength from his calm and resolved to focus. "Go ahead."

"*Chako elip sun wawa Italapas.*" Lord Tom's voice rose and fell, the harsh syllables and consonants of the Chinook jargon set to the time of the flickering lamplight and the scratching of my pen upon the paper as I transcribed the old tale. *Come very early, said Coyote.*

I loved these stories, the tales of the trickster Coyote and the great Thunderbird Hahness and the adventures of the time when the mountains were people. I loved the way they sounded in the old Chinook too, the way Lord Tom told them, that singsong voice that brought me back to when I was fourteen and had just come to this place, not yet used to settling, uneasy at the presence I felt here and my father's impatience with my fears. I remembered one day, when Papa was buried in his cataloging, and Lord Tom had seen my loneliness and taken me salmon fishing. There, he'd begun to teach me the trading jargon and told me the first of many tales, as if he'd somehow understood the joy I would take from them. They helped me understand this strange new place, to make it mine, much to Papa's dismay.

I'd thought once the Indian legends would be the tales I told my children, but, well...some things didn't work out as planned. Now I told myself I transcribed them for the scientific world, preserving a dying culture, but the truth…the truth I never admitted was that they were for me. I was fascinated by them, though they were lewd and primitive and my father had hated them and had forbidden me to listen to them. Junius agreed with my father—he disliked my interest and said the stories were too obscene for a woman to hear. But the nights I spent listening to Lord Tom were some of my favorite times.

Except for tonight. Tonight, the harsh sounds of the jargon played on my nerves, and Coyote's obscene tricks couldn't make me laugh or distract me from the sound of the wind and the voices I heard in it.

Voices? There are no voices, Leonie. It's only your imagination. Do you understand? It's not real. What kind of scientist gives in to such fancies? I heard my father's words and his affectionate sighs of exasperation as if he stood beside me, though he'd been gone now more than twenty years.

Lord Tom said, "What is it, *okustee?*" and I realized he'd been talking and I was just sitting there with my pen dripping ink onto the paper.

"I'm sorry, *tot*, but—"

There was a noise on the porch, and the door opened, bringing a blast of chill wind, the smell of the river and salt mud and Junius with it.

I jumped up in relief. "There you are! I was worried."

"Nothing to fear." He smiled at me, taking off his coat and boots and hat, hanging them beside the door. "It looks to be a bad storm, though. I hope the barn doesn't flood. It's going to be a wretched winter, I think."

I closed the notebook, but not before Junius noticed.

His smile died, but he only said, "You should be drawing those relics Baird's waiting for. I wanted to send them off tomorrow."

I looked guiltily at the bowl on the table, part of our latest collection of Indian relics that I was cataloging and drawing before we sent it off to Spencer Baird, the assistant secretary at the Smithsonian National Museum, who had charge of procuring Indian relics for the Centennial Exposition's ethnological exhibit planned for next year. He'd commissioned us, along with many other ethnologists, to get him the collection he needed, and he'd been anxious and persistent. He was nervous about the exhibit's prospects—if it succeeded, it meant money and fame for the museum, which had not much of either. He'd already sent us several letters urging us to collect more, and to hurry. "I *was* doing that. But then the night got so dark, and—"

"And Yutilma began howling," Lord Tom put in.

I gave him an admonishing look.

Junius sighed. "You shouldn't encourage her, Tom."

Lord Tom turned an innocent expression. "Encourage what, *sikhs*?"

"The two of you conspire against me," Junius said.

"I needed a distraction," I said. "As you were so late."

"You could at least distract yourself with something elevating. There's a Bible right over there. I'll bet you can't even remember who Job is. Your father would have my head."

"My father didn't give a damn about Job. All he cared about was ethnology."

"And raising a daughter who wasn't a savage," Junius said. "A task he left in my hands, as I recall. And look at you, bent over a lamp and listening to Siwash superstitions. Yutilma howling indeed."

"Call it my birthday present," I said.

"That's not until tomorrow."

"An early one, then."

Junius sighed. "You're wearing me out, sweetheart. It was a long day and I'm tired. Now I'm for bed. You coming?"

Lord Tom rose and put aside his coffee—his signal that he was done for the night—and I rose as well and followed my husband up the stairs. The wind sounded louder up here, clattering against the roof, and the dark cold seemed forbidding and dangerous, barely kept at bay by the walls and the roof, as if Yutilma and the wind were only giving us quarter. *I'll leave you safe and warm now, but one day perhaps I won't be so kind.*

Voices in the wind, in the rain. Spirits in the water. I felt spooked and uneasy. That wretched eerie howling...I couldn't remember hearing its like before. I went to the window that overlooked the Querquelin River—translated to Mouse by the settlers, though I preferred to call it by its Indian name. It was too dark to see it, but I heard its rushing and churning, which seemed violent tonight, and as full of talk as the wind.

Junius lit a candle. "You shouldn't listen to those stories."

He sounded as he had in the beginning years of our marriage, when he'd taken over my father's role as teacher, and I chafed a little at it now, until I looked over my shoulder and saw the concern in his eyes. "They're only children's tales. Haven't you said that yourself?"

He was quiet for a moment. Then he said, "It wasn't so long ago that hearing them made you sad."

Sad. Yes, I had been that. But I wasn't anymore. I'd come to terms with things I could not have, what wasn't meant to be. "I'm all right."

"You've been better lately." I heard the reluctance in his voice as he said it—he hated to speak of those times as much as I did. "I don't want you to—"

"You needn't worry," I said firmly, forcing myself to smile. "Truly. It's only this wind. It's so strong and...and it doesn't sound right. It makes me uneasy."

"It's no different than any other storm," he said, though I heard his relief. "But I've been thinking...we could leave this place, Leonie. Before the winter sets in. Go someplace else. Someplace new, where there's actually sun. This rain would make anyone melancholy. God knows I'd be happy to leave. I've been saying it for years."

"Please, not that again. I love it here. You know that."

"I don't think it's good for you to stay."

"I'll be fine."

Junius hesitated. "All right. But...no stories for the next few days, I think."

I nodded, too unsettled to argue, though I did say, "I still think Baird will find a use for them, if I ever get them translated."

"Baird doesn't care about the stories, Leonie. No one does. There's no point in it. No one would notice if you put them aside."

This argument, too, was an old one, better ignored, so I went up to him, putting my arms around him and whispering, "Let's go to bed."

He let the argument go, distracted as I'd wanted him to be. He reached up, taking out the pins in my hair until it fell down around my shoulders, a mass of wispy blonde corkscrews, more than any one man could hold, though, as always, he took it in his hands, squeezing it and letting it bounce back, laughing a little before he buried his face in it, his mouth finding my ear. He pulled me to the bed, and soon we were tangled beneath the blankets, and his hands roamed my body with familiarity and ease, making quick work of it, holding me as tightly as he always did, as if he were afraid I would move and thrust beneath him, and the truth was that sometimes I wanted to, but the first and only time I'd done so he'd been horrified, and I'd learned to do nothing but hold him.

He groaned and collapsed upon me, his lips moving soundlessly against my shoulder. I stroked his back until he rolled off and wrapped his arms around me, pulling me close until I was spooned against him, his hands cupping my breasts, his breathing soft against my ear.

He was asleep within moments, though I never went easy into sleep when we were done, and tonight was no different. My skin felt charged. I felt again those spirits in the air, again that uncomfortable suspense. *Something was coming.* The words went round in my head, twisting with Yutilma's chatter, with the wild creak of the fir and alder and the slap of water against the shore. The house groaned, a loose shingle clattered. I stayed awake, listening.

The storm faded before dawn, before Junius woke for good, in time with the tides as though his body were a clock that told them. He rose, leaning to kiss me gently. "Happy Birthday," he whispered, and when I started to get up, he shook his head and said, "Stay in bed today. It's my present to you. Lord Tom and I can take care of the oysters."

I didn't object. It was cold and dark and the last place I wanted to be was on an oyster bateau in the choppy water after a storm. So I kissed him and fell back into sleep as he readied to go out to the whacks in the dark.

He and Lord Tom were long gone when I finally got out of bed. The world was quiet, but I still felt last night's uneasiness like a whisper against my skin. I went downstairs to find the stove already fired and a pot of steaming coffee. I poured myself a cup and raised it in a toast. "Happy Birthday to me, Papa," I said. "Can you believe how old I am?"

I never felt his presence more strongly than on my birthday, despite the fact that his things were always all around me, cluttering every surface and corner, each holding a story I never forgot: those Bela Coola masks hanging high up on the wall from Papa's last trip north; those stone sinkers found on a day when Papa agreed with me how graceful the pelicans were as they flew low along the water. Wooden Chinook salmon hooks and spindle whorls, and strings of the narrow, cone-shaped dentalium shells the Indians had used as money, called *hiaqua*, piled in coils of clean white and smoky gray and hanging from nearly every knob. Suddenly I missed him so much, and all the hours we'd spent together, digging for relics in the mud, all the ways he'd been both mentor and parent, that twinkle in his eyes when he smiled at some lesson I'd learned particularly well...

How melancholy I was today. Birthdays always brought that out in me, but this year seemed especially bad. It was just the storm, I told myself, trying to shake it off, shoving my feet into a pair of boots and grabbing my old wool coat, along with a pair of thick gloves and my wide-brimmed oystering hat, and going out into the day.

The air was crisp and expectant. The storm had swept away the clouds, and the sun was shining, a brisk, chill breeze blowing off the water, summer's warmth gone for good. Sodden leaves from the alders and maples scattered over the grass, gold and orange and brown. Fallen branches lay cracked and splintered all about. Edna grazed contentedly in the yard, already milked. I stepped through the clutter on the narrow porch, beaten old chairs and piles of nets and an old pair of long oystering tongs, and went down the stairs to the yard.

I was at the river before I realized I was heading toward it. I stared down into the churning water, the long grass of the bank trailing in its eddies, the currents at the shore lapping more roughly with the stirring up of the storm and the added rain. Usually I could see to the bottom here at the shore, but not this morning; it was murky and mysterious today.

It was then I heard the noise that had me glancing toward the mouth of the river where it plunged into Shoalwater Bay. There, only a few yards away, stood a great blue heron, ruffling its feathers—the sound I'd heard. I'd never been so close to one before, and I froze, catching my breath in surprise. The two of us stared at each other, his dark eye and long yellow beak, the shaggy feathered tuft of his chest. For long moments I didn't move, but then, suddenly, he lifted his dark wings. I was so close the air they stirred pulsed against my skin. I watched him fly off toward the bay, and it was a moment before I dropped my gaze again, before I noticed the strangeness of where he'd been standing.

The bank had fallen away. This was not uncommon; the river was constantly eroding the banks. But this cut was large—at least three feet of the shore had fallen into the river, and it looked odd, cleanly shored, as if the chunk had been cut away in one swipe of a knife, not bits and pieces falling and crumbling the way it usually did. I picked up the hem of my skirt—already sodden from the wet grass, as were my boots—and stepped down to see. The sheared clay bank did not look like clay, but something…strange. Beneath a thin layer of clay was something mottled, discolored, with light and dark striations. Hesitantly, I scraped it with my gloved finger. It didn't give at all when I pressed it.

It was narrowly ridged, nothing natural. Something was buried here, and I was on my knees in the mud before I knew it, heedless of my skirts or the river, scraping at it gingerly at first, and then, as my excitement grew, scrabbling like an animal. I could not get at it quickly enough. I bent to dig around it, but there was no *around*. When I scraped away, there was more, and more, a wall of ridges and coils that stretched a foot and a half wide before I decided I couldn't get at it with my hands alone.

I ran back to the house for a shovel and pick, half-fearful that it would have disappeared when I returned. But no, it was still there, no figment of my imagination. I took up the shovel and dug and scraped, as careful as I could be through my excitement, because I didn't know where it ended and I didn't want to do any damage. It began to reveal itself: reeds woven in a pattern of dark and light—an Indian basket—but a design I didn't know. The damn thing was huge, the biggest basket I'd ever seen; there seemed to be no end to it. I was sweating in the chill; I took off my coat and laid it on the bank and kept going. I thought of how that heron had stared at me, *summoning* me to look, as if this was something he meant for me to find.

I was wet to my knees and filthy with clay by the time I had it half-dug out of the bank. I tried to tilt it loose, but it was caught fast, and it felt solid, which told me there was something inside. I tried to rock it, cursed when it didn't budge, and grabbed the pick again. A shadow crossed the water.

"What *are* you doing, sweetheart?"

I glanced up. Junius stood there, hatless, his salted hair blowing into his face, one hand shielding his eyes.

"Look, Junius," I said breathlessly. "Look at what I've found. The bank broke away…there was…a heron…and I found this. It's a basket, but I've never seen its like. I think—"

He jumped down, sliding on the mud, splashing. His rawboned hands ran along the coils. "Damn right it's a basket. Biggest one I've ever seen." He shouted, "Tom! Lord Tom, come here!"

Lord Tom hurried over, peering over the bank. "What?"

Junius grabbed the shovel from my hand, and I stepped back thoughtlessly, too deep. The river spilled over the tops of my boots, and I slogged out, but Tom grabbed the pick and joined Junius, and there was nothing for me to do but watch impatiently as they dug it out. The two of them had the basket mostly clear in the time it had taken me to dig an inch.

Junius threw the shovel aside and rocked it as I had tried to do, and Lord Tom grabbed the other side and shoved, and between the two of them, they had it lifted from its clay bed and shouldered onto the bank. It was half as tall as Lord Tom, coming to Junius's hips. Clay still clung to it in clumps. Junius brushed it away, revealing a beautiful, intricate pattern of geometric lines and figures, a combination I'd never seen, black against what had once no doubt been a creamy pale, but which was now discolored where the clay had leached into it.

Junius glanced at me. "Well, what do you think's inside?" He took hold of the handle, jerking it, but it was lodged tight, held in place with compressed clay.

I pushed him gently aside. "You're going to damage it." I took hold of the looped handle and rocked the lid a little. I had to force myself to go slowly. Finally the mud crumbled; the lid loosened. I lifted it away just as the sun came from behind a passing cloud, illuminating the contents.

"Oh dear God," I breathed.

It was a body, crouched in a fetal position, brown hair that looked almost reddish in the light. I looked up at Junius, who was staring over my shoulder.

"Christ. Who the hell is that?" Junius peered into the shadows of the basket. "Help me tip it over."

Lord Tom shook his head and backed away, murmuring a string of words beneath his breath, none of which I recognized. June and I ignored him. The basket was not so heavy as I imagined, and we tipped it onto the ground easily and gently, and then Junius reached inside, grabbing the body by the shoulders, pulling it out, wincing as it scraped along the side, and I watched in fascination as it emerged, bit by bit, shoulders draped in cloth of a deep saffron color, very fine. She was so well preserved it was astonishing, bare arms and skin shiny and dry and stretched tight over the bones and the color of oak . Not so dark as Lord Tom's skin, nor as pale as my own. A woman, her arms clasped about her knees, which were pulled up to her chest. Feet bare, fingernails and toenails still intact, but changed, too. Not human somehow, but alien, mysterious. Dry as a husk, hair down and flowing but...lifeless. The clothing she wore came away in places, a leather headband was peeling and cracking. A mummy. Unwrapped, but so many of them weren't. She was like many I'd seen during those years Papa and I had traveled from one ethnographic site to another, except she was flawless.

I knelt beside her, pushing back the hair that fell forward to hide her face, and her profile came into view, eyelashes resting upon cheeks that had sunken into the bones, lips pulled back from what few teeth remained, which were brown and crooked, and I felt this strange sense of inevitability, as if the mud and the storm and the heron had all conspired to bring us together, to meet—

The idea startled me. *Meet?*

"Mummification," Junius said, breathing the word as if it were somehow magical, reaching out.

Lord Tom slapped his hand away. "*Kopet cooley.*"

"Why shouldn't we touch it?" I asked in surprise.

Lord Tom was obviously shaken. "Rebury it, *okustee.*"

"Rebury it? After I've spent the whole morning trying to get it out?"

"*Mesachie memelose.*"

Lord Tom was as superstitious of the dead as all his people, but to call this a bad spirit was odd.

Junius ignored that, saying to him, "Did the Chinook know how to mummify?"

Lord Tom shook his head.

"Were there any legends among your people about it? Myths? Anything to indicate the method might have been known?"

Lord Tom looked sick. "No, *sikhs.*"

Junius looked back at me. "No Chinook Indian did this, Lea. Not the Chehalis either. They're all too backward. Do you know what this means? She must be ancient. A people who knew how to mummify...they must have had contact with the Egyptians. She's one of the Mound Builders, Lea. She could be what we've been searching for. Proof."

I looked back down at the mummy. Junius, like my father, believed there had been an advanced culture here before the primitive Indians had supplanted it, though I had never enter-tained the theory completely, and I couldn't really say why. Junius and Papa saw the whole of North America as a great palimp-sest—groups overtaking other groups, never evolving, only new people coming in and wiping out the old. *No Indian made those things. There had to have been people here before them,* my father had told me—a dozen times or more. And Junius had agreed. *A civilized race, killed by savages. One day I'll prove it, Lea. One day...*

But there had not been any proof to find. Not yet. I was not certain this mummy was proof now, though she was proof of… something.

"This is no Chinook design. Not Bela Coola either. Or Kwakiutl, for that matter. I've never seen it before. If this is as ancient as I think it is, and not Indian…Baird will go mad for it. The Russell name will be famous, and—"

"No," I heard myself say.

Junius frowned. "What?"

"We aren't sending her to Baird." My own words surprised me, no less than how fiercely I felt them. "She belongs to me."

"Of course we're sending her. I'll make certain Baird puts your name on it too. He needs this for the Centennial Exposition, you know that."

"I'm not sending her to him."

Junius looked at me as if I'd sprouted a second head. "You can't keep her, Lea. Not something like this."

He was right. She was a rare find. I had no business keeping her. I should send her to the National Museum, where there were ethnologists who had studied many mummies. But I couldn't bear the thought of letting her go. It felt so…wrong. Stubbornly, I said, "I want to be the one to study her."

"You? You've never studied anything like this before. You don't know how."

"Then I'll learn."

"Lea, be reasonable."

I looked back down at her, the reddish hair, the saffron cloth. And I thought of that heron on the bank, looking at me, waiting for me to look down, to see her, that inevitability I'd felt. Studying her was suddenly the only thing I wanted. I could not ever remember feeling so strongly about anything. I didn't know how to explain it and I didn't try.

"I'm not sending her to Baird. It's my birthday, Junius. Give me this. Please. I'll study her. I'll figure out who she is and where she came from—"

"No." Lord Tom spoke so loudly and suddenly both Junius and I started. When I looked at him, he said, tight-lipped, afraid, "You must rebury her, *okustee*. She is bad luck. *Mesachie tomawanos*. She belongs to the dead. Give her back to them."

His words were so solemnly intoned they raised gooseflesh. I forced myself to ignore him and looked pleadingly at Junius. I felt my husband measuring my resolve. He sighed. "I'll think about it. But for now, let's get it into the barn." He looked at Lord Tom. "Will that ease your mind, old man?"

"It makes no difference," Lord Tom said morosely. "The *memelose* will find a way to take her back, wherever she is."

His dark gaze caught mine; again I felt a spooked shiver. But I was certain, too. She belonged to me—and as strange as that feeling was, it was stronger than Lord Tom's warnings about the dead and their intentions, and I chose to forget his words as we took her to the barn.

Once there, I brought out the lantern, and Junius and I spent hours looking at her—long enough that I forgot supper, and we ended up eating raw the oysters he and Lord Tom had brought from the whacks, shucking them over a bucket in the barn, sucking them down like savages. Lord Tom had disappeared almost the moment Junius put the mummy on the makeshift table we'd made from two sawhorses and a plank.

"Moping about *skookum tomawanos*, no doubt," Junius said when I mentioned it.

Powerful spirits. "It's a dead body. You know what his people say."

Junius leaned close to her. "The cloth is so fine. It would have taken a loom of some kind. A factory even."

I winced when he rubbed it between his fingers. *Don't touch her*, I thought angrily, and then was startled that I'd thought it.

"Perhaps they were as advanced as we are," he went on.

"To be wiped from the face of the earth so cleanly?" I asked.

"Not cleanly. We have evidence they existed."

"But not their cities," I persisted. "If they were as advanced as you say, there would have been cities."

"We'll find them," he said confidently.

"I want to explore the bank where I found her. As soon as it's light. Tomorrow. Perhaps there's something to be found there. Something we didn't see."

Junius went quiet and still, his face took on that scolding teacher look, and I wished I hadn't said it. "Lea...you've never studied anything this important before. It's not a few bowls or baskets. This could change everything we've ever known, and—"

"I know that. Don't you think I know it?"

"Baird's got people who are trained to do this."

"But if we send her to them, they'll be the ones who discover where she's from and who she is."

"We'll still be credited with discovering her."

"But we won't *know*, will we? And I...want to know." I took a deep breath and looked down at her, the lamplight shining on that reddish-brown hair, the saffron of her dress. "I can't explain it. I feel as if I'm the one meant to discover who she is."

"Just because you found her doesn't mean—"

"She's *mine*." I said it sharply, too intently; I knew it when I saw Junius's surprise, the way he drew back and frowned.

"It's more than that, Leonie. Baird needs this and so do we. Bowls and spoons, a few baskets here and there—he's got enough of those things to fill ten museums. We have to send him something more important if I'm going to get any recognition at all in that exhibit."

He was right, of course. The exposition's ethnology exhibit was not just important to the Smithsonian, it was important to Junius. His chance to finally have the recognition he longed for, to be seen as an ethnologist of importance.

"I know. But not her."

"Why *not* her?"

I could not bear to hear the words I knew he would say if I tried to explain what made no sense even to me. *You've too much imagination, Leonie.* So I said nothing.

"We're not capable of studying it the way it needs," Junius insisted in my silence. "We're collectors, Leonie, not anatomists."

"My father would have studied her himself."

Junius sighed. "Sometimes I think Teddy did you a disservice."

"He raised me to be an ethnologist, and that's what I am."

Junius gave me a thoughtful, measuring look that said what I'd heard a hundred times before, and not just from him. I'd had an uncommon education. Science, ethnology, collecting—even for men, the work was hard. And I was just a woman, and too sensitive for such endeavors. My father had said it even as he labored to teach me the theories he didn't believe I could learn.

I said, "What if I could get you something else? Something just as big?"

"There's nothing just as big. Unless you find another mummy in that bank."

"What about Bibi's canoe?"

"You know as well as I that she won't trade the damn thing."

Junius had been trying for a year to obtain Bibi Kafkis's canoe—which had belonged to her late husband, called the Duke by the settlers in mockery of his status among his own people, and because his Indian name was unpronounceable, which were the reasons for Lord Tom's name as well. The canoe was huge, a whaling vessel meant for twenty men, and decorated with carvings and paint. Bibi's unwillingness to let it go was one of Junius's greatest frustrations, because it was of great ethnological importance, and it was just rotting away where she kept it upended beneath the overhang of a tool shed.

"What if I could get her to trade it?"

Junius gave me a skeptical look. "She won't."

"Not to you. But I've never tried."

"Well, you're as canny a trader as a Chinook, that's true." Junius made a face.

"If I can, will you let me keep the mummy?"

He was quiet for a moment. Then he said, "I suppose it can't harm to keep it for a few weeks. But only a few weeks, Lea. See what you can discover, but we'll have to send it off eventually. I'll write to Baird and—"

"You can't tell him anything about her. Not yet."

He hesitated, and then nodded. "I suppose if the canoe's on its way, that will be enough for a while."

"Thank you."

He stepped up to me, tugging at my mostly loose hair. "Look at you. You look as if you've been rolling around in mud."

"Not much better than you, Mr. Russell."

He laughed and pulled me close. "Come on. Let's go in."

I pulled away, suddenly uncomfortable, cold to the bone. I glanced at the mummy. "I don't like leaving her in the open. I'd feel better if I could lock her up. Why don't you bring out that old trunk?"

"It will wait until tomorrow." He turned to go.

I grabbed his hand, stopping him. "No, Junius, please. Bring it out tonight. She's too exposed here."

"We'll cover her with a blanket."

I felt panicked. "That's not enough. Anything could come in here during the night—"

"The door's closed, Lea. It'll be fine tonight. I'll bring the trunk out before I go tomorrow."

I knew the tone in his voice. I would not be able to budge him. I said nothing more when he grabbed an old horse blanket from its hook on the wall and draped it over the mummy, but I couldn't shake my discomfort, and I spent the whole evening restless, thinking of her in the barn, cold and lonely and alone.

But of course, she wasn't any of those things. She was a mummy, long dead, long gone. She felt nothing. No more than did those masks on the wall or that basket before the whatnot or those cedar bowls on the table waiting for me to draw before we sent them to Baird. To think anything else was pure foolishness. It was not objective or scientific. Not at all.

I reassured myself of that as I went to bed. But still I was up a dozen times that night, going to the window, looking out at the looming silence of the barn, at the shadow of the cut in the bank, a dark hole now in the night, with the river rushing beyond it shining molten in the moonlight.

CHAPTER 2

JUNIUS WAS UP WITH THE DAWN, MOVING THE TRUNK I'D emptied to the barn. I went with him, watching anxiously as he put the mummy inside.

"Be careful," I cautioned, and he gave me an annoyed look.

"For God's sake, Leonie, I *am* being careful."

"Perhaps…perhaps we should leave her out after all," I said uncertainly. "I could do some work with her today."

"I thought you were going to get to that cut in the bank."

"I am, but—"

"It's going to rain again. If you don't get out there now, there may be nothing left to find."

I knew he was right, but when Junius closed the trunk, suddenly I couldn't breathe. I turned away quickly, nearly running into Lord Tom, who gave me a worried, anxious look, and I realized my hand had gone to my throat. Quickly I lowered it, and his gaze went beyond me, to the mummy.

"You will not rebury it?"

"It's just a body, *tot*," I said, as much for him as for myself. "You talk as if there's some vengeful spirit waiting to pounce upon us, but she's been buried in that bank for centuries. The spirit's crossed over. Why would it be upset? The body looks peaceful enough."

"She is not peaceful," he told me, and then he turned and went back into the house.

His words disconcerted me. I went out to the cut, determined to forget them, but when I stood at the edge of the hole and looked down at the water pooling at the bottom, the river already beginning to take it back, I was arrested by a sense of... of sacredness, I suppose. This was a burial ground, and though I had wanted nothing more than to get to it, to find the answers to who she was that I knew must be there, suddenly I felt as if I were trespassing. As if it were somehow wrong to dig here.

But if one believed the Indians, this whole claim sat on top of an ancient burial ground—perhaps even the one that had belonged originally to her people, though I'd never found anything but Shoalwater and Chinook relics, and I'd never felt this kind of reluctance before, as if something were physically keeping me from stepping into that hole.

A shiver went down my spine; I felt uncomfortable in my skin, as if something or someone were watching me. Carefully, I looked over my shoulder. There was nothing but the house beyond, the trees, branches waving gently in the chill breeze coming off the water. I was imagining things again, and what mattered were facts. *A physical fact is as sacred as a moral principle.* My father used to say that all the time. They weren't his words, but his mentor's—Louis Agassiz, who was a professor at Harvard—but they were Papa's guide and his bible: *It's facts that matter, Leonie. Not supposition. Not stories.*

I let those words take hold and banished Lord Tom's as I went to fetch the shovel and pick and pail, and then I set myself to digging with determination, ignoring everything but the process I knew so well. It was slow work, because every shovelful I put aside had to be raked and gone through by hand. *Observe first*, Papa had always said. *Construct generalizations later.* For now, I concentrated on *finding*, and as I worked, I became myself again, the ethnologist I'd been brought up to be. I broke up clods of dirt looking for anything that might be a clue, something that could be as small as a bead. I found rocks and oyster shells and the odd root, but nothing else. As the hours went on, my back and shoulders grew cramped and tired and my skirt and stockings sodden.

It didn't take long before I knew there was nothing here. My instincts screamed it. But instincts weren't good enough— where did such feelings come from anyway? They weren't proof of anything. One couldn't trust something so nebulous. Junius would laugh if I came inside and said I *felt* there was nothing to be found, so I forced myself to keep going.

I was bent over another useless pile of mud and tiny rocks, sifting it with my hands, when I heard a call from the water. I glanced up, straightening when I saw a canoe coming ashore. I thought at first it was Junius returning from the whacks, but then I saw it was two people. And one of them was a woman. A short, squat woman who stomped through the shallow water and onto the shore without hesitating, her dark calico skirt dragging in the water.

Bibi Kafkis.

I stared in stunned surprise. Bibi never came out here; she rarely left her dilapidated old shack in Bruceport. I thought perhaps Junius had gone in to tell her I wanted to speak with her about the canoe, but I couldn't imagine that would have brought her out. If she wanted to trade, she'd just tell him to send me to town.

I dropped the handful of dirt I still held and climbed out of the hole, pulling off my filthy gloves and dropping them to the ground. I reached the weathered gate at the edge of what passed for a yard the same moment Lord Tom did. He was frowning fiercely, his disdain for Bibi already evident. Lord Tom thought she was a charlatan, and that her play as a medicine woman reflected badly on their people, especially because it had been her father-in-law who'd been the real *tomawanos* man—not even a blood relation. I thought Tom's outspokenness about her fakery mostly a waste of time. Bibi was half-crazy, yes, but she was harmless. His protests did nothing but make her dislike him, which wasn't helpful now that I needed that canoe.

I gave Lord Tom a look of warning just as the man who'd brought Bibi—Michael Johnson, who owned oyster beds near ours—approached, saying, "Afternoon, Leonie, Lord Tom."

I nodded a greeting back to him. "What brings you out here today?"

Michael rubbed his chin. "I was going out to fix the bateau, and she showed up just as I was leaving and asked to come. Said she wanted to see you."

Bibi stared up at me. "*Klahowya, klooshman.*" She was older than Lord Tom by only a few years, but it was enough that she bore the sloped forehead that used to denote high caste among the Chinook, a deliberate deformity that had fallen out of fashion by the time Tom was born. It broadened the plane of her face and made her skull look as if it came to a rounded point at the top of her head, rather like a sugarloaf. Her gray streaked hair was plaited in a single long braid, and she wore a blanket around her shoulders that draped to her thighs—white banded in red. She glanced to Lord Tom, and narrowed her eyes as if she'd smelled something rotten, and then she snapped something in Chinook—not the jargon we all understood, but the language that few knew and fewer spoke. Beside me, Lord Tom stiffened.

Warily, I said, "*Klahowya,* Bibi. I'm glad you're here. I wanted to talk to you about the canoe."

She said, "No *huyhuy.*"

I frowned. "I know you don't want to trade it, but—"

"I have *wawa,*" she said simply.

A message. How puzzling. I couldn't think who would have entrusted Bibi with a message for me. But I nodded and said, "Why don't we all go on to the house then? There's coffee on."

I turned to lead them, but Bibi grabbed my arm hard, stopping me. "No. *Nesika wawa.*"

Only we talk.

Lord Tom made a face. "What has such a *pelton* woman to say? *Cultus wawa. Mamook hehe.*"

A crazy woman. Jokes and nonsense.

Bibi's fingers tightened on my arm.

I said, "It's all right. Lord Tom, why don't you take Michael up to the house and get him some coffee?"

Lord Tom hesitated, but then he motioned for the other man to follow, and the two of them started up the crushed oyster-shell path to the house. When they had gone a short distance, I pulled my arm from Bibi's hold and said, "What message, Bibi?"

She said, "I have a *dleam.*"

I had been curious, but now I realized Lord Tom had been right. This was just more of the nonsense we'd all come to expect from Bibi. "A dream? Was the Duke in it? Did he tell you it was about time to trade his things? You could use a new pair of boots, I think."

"About you." She leaned forward, her dark eyes huge and strange in the broad flatness of her face. "*Mika mesachie mitlite.* In my *dleam*, I see this."

You are in danger.

The hair on the back of my neck raised. Again I felt that strange sense of someone watching. Uncomfortably I glanced toward the cut in the river. "I'm in the middle of something, Bibi. Go get some coffee and I'll—"

"It is about the *memalose kopa chuck.*"

The dead in the river.

I froze. "The *what*?"

She nodded with obvious satisfaction. "Now you listen, *nah*? The *tomawanos* calls for you. What she wants, I do not know, but it is you she wants."

"Wait," I said. "Say that again. What do you mean? What *memalose kopa chuck*?"

"*No klap?*" she asked in surprise. "You will."

"Yes, I found a body in the river. Well, not a body, really, but…but…how do you know this? How do you know about her? I only found her yesterday."

"I have a *dleam*," she said simply.

"Bibi, who told you about the mummy?"

She said again, "My *dleam*."

Said as if it were the only answer to give, regardless of how impossible it was. I sighed in frustration.

She said, "She says to tell you he will come soon. *Kloshe nanitch.*"

Keep watch. Be careful. Again, I felt that shiver. I forced it away. "He? Who's he? What nonsense is this?"

"*Wake hehe, ipsoot klooshman.*"

This is serious, sly wife. Her favorite nickname for me.

"It *is* serious. Which is why I wish you wouldn't say anything about the mummy, Bibi. Please. I don't want the word to get out. I want some time to study her, and—" I stopped. She wasn't listening. Instead, she was digging around in the pocket of her skirt. "Did you hear me, Bibi? Please. Keep it secret. *Ipsoot.*"

She pulled something from her pocket, holding it out to me. "You take this."

What was in her palm was a bracelet, and nothing fine. A few strings of twine—and store bought at that—knotted through five charms, all made of abalone shell, their iridescence flashing rainbows, each etched with some figure, a few lines. A worthless, ugly thing.

"She wants you to wear it." When I made no move to take it, Bibi shoved it at me again. "You must wear it."

"I'm not much for finery—"

"Take it."

There was no point in arguing. The sooner I took it, the sooner I could be back to the river. I plucked it from her hand. "Thank you."

She looked at me for a moment, as if she were trying to read something in my face, and then she turned away with a nod, seemingly satisfied, and trudged down the path toward the canoe without another word.

She didn't look back, and I dropped the bracelet into my coat pocket, feeling unsettled, not knowing what to think. She was a strange old woman, and I was glad she was going. She stood by the canoe now, waiting, and I knew she wouldn't budge until Michael returned to take her back to town, so I strode quickly to the house, hurrying up the stairs. Michael and Lord Tom were standing in the kitchen, each with a cup of coffee, and I called out, "She's waiting to go back, Michael, so you'd best hurry. You know she'll stand there in the cold all day."

"What did she want?"

"She had a dream she wanted to tell me about," I said.

"Siwash mumbo jumbo?"

"Something like." I grimaced. "I'm sorry you had to come out all this way for it."

I left quickly then, before he could engage me in a conversation I didn't want, and I hurried back to the hole, and my digging, and I forgot Bibi's dream and the bracelet and my uneasiness, burying it in mindless drudgery. I didn't even see them leave.

When Junius returned late that afternoon, it was with two men in tow—Adam Leach, who owned the whacks next to ours, and Sydney Dawes, another oysterman. He brought them up to the edge of the hole and said, "Hello, sweetheart."

"Building a dam, Leonie?" Adam Leach asked.

I glanced up. "Do I look like a beaver to you?"

"Well yeah, right now, you kind of do." He laughed, and Sydney Dawes laughed too.

Junius said, "They came out to see the mummy."

I pushed up the brim of my hat and leaned on the shovel handle. I was relieved for a moment—Junius was telling people, and that at least explained why Bibi had known—but then I was annoyed. "I didn't know that you meant to tell the world."

Sydney said, "Ah, Russell, looks like you made her mad."

"I'm not mad," I said, though I was. "You boys go on and take a look at her since you came all the way out, but I wish you wouldn't go around telling everyone you see. It's bad enough that Bibi was out here casting her spells, I don't need any other pretend mystics wasting my time."

Junius frowned. "Bibi was here?"

Adam said, "Where are you keeping this thing, anyway? Let's go see it. I want to get back before it's too dark."

"In the barn," Junius said, waving them off, and as the two men made their way there, he said to me, "Why was Bibi here? Did you talk to her about the canoe?"

"She wouldn't listen. She wanted to tell me about some dream she had." I glared after the two men. "Really, June, did you have to tell everyone? If Baird finds out—"

"How's he going to find out?" he asked. "Who's going to tell him? All these men care about are oysters. They'll take a look at her and go home and forget about it."

"Hey, Russell, we ain't got all day!" Sydney Dawes called out.

I glanced toward them, thinking of how they'd be looking at her as if she were some curiosity in Barnum's museum, how they would stare and prod and touch and laugh, their crude jokes. The thought troubled me and brought back the uneasiness I'd felt at Bibi's visit. "Junius, don't...don't let them touch her. Please."

"We won't harm a hair," he promised, and went off after them.

I watched him walk off to join them and I turned back to the hole. But I couldn't lose myself in the work. I wanted to be with the mummy, not in this wet and muddy hole. It seemed pointless, such a waste of time. So far, my instincts had proved right. I'd found nothing, and there looked to be nothing to find. Why continue?

I took up the shovel and pick and went back to the house, leaving them on the porch as I went inside. Lord Tom was sitting in his customary chair by the organ.

He said, "What did that *pelton* woman tell you today?"

"She'd had a dream. The mummy's *tomawanos* wants me. Junius has told everyone about her, it seems." I couldn't keep the bitterness from my voice. "Now he's out there like some lyceum showman. Too bad there's nothing to unwrap or he could charge admission."

Lord Tom grunted. "Bibi said more than this."

"Yes," I said. "More nonsense."

Lord Tom said, "The *memelose* are tricky, *okustee*."

"And this one's been dead a long time. Her spirit's long since passed over, even according to your Chinook legends. It's not coming back. How can it hurt me?"

Lord Tom looked unconvinced. "*Kloshe nanitch, okustee.* That is all I'm saying."

Kloshe nanitch. Be careful, listen, watch. He'd said such words to me a hundred times. There was nothing unusual in them, and the fact that Bibi had said them to me just this morning meant nothing either. "So you think Bibi's right?"

He shook his head. "That one? No."

"Then there's nothing to fear, is there?" I went to the stairs. "I'm going to wash up. I'm filthy."

When I came downstairs again, it was to find only Junius sitting at the table, sipping a cup of coffee.

"Where are the others?" I asked.

"They headed on back," Junius said. "You want to tell me why the hell Bibi felt the need to come all the way out here to tell you about a dream?"

I shrugged. "She wanted to give me a bracelet to wear."

"A bracelet?"

"A charm, I think. Against the *skookum tomawanos* or something. It's just a bit of twine from Garrett's, with some abalone shell."

Junius laughed. "Yeah. That'll be some powerful magic. What *tomawanos* is she talking about?"

"The mummy's, of course," I said. "I wish you hadn't told her about it, but—"

"I didn't tell her."

I frowned. "You didn't?"

"I wasn't anywhere near Bruceport. I saw Dawes and Leach out on the whacks."

"Then how did she know?"

"No idea. I'm sure she heard it from somewhere. How else?"

How else indeed? *In my dleam,* she'd said. But that was impossible. Wasn't it?

"Johnson said we should start our own museum and charge a fee to see her," Junius said.

"Absolutely not," I snapped.

"I was joking, Lea. But people will want to see her. You might as well get used to it. She'll be a curiosity for at least a while."

"As long as they don't touch her," I said. I saw Junius's quick frown, but I was relieved when he said nothing.

As the night wore on, it grew harder to banish Bibi's dream or her warnings. I felt strangely haunted. I tried not to give in to the terrible urge to go to the barn, to check on the mummy, to look at her, to touch her. Time was my enemy, but surely not so much as I felt, that if I did not go out there *right now* I would somehow be letting the answers slip away. It was foolish, and I knew it. Speed was not my friend when it came to research. I must be slow and steady and complete. I was good at detail, and I was good at it because I didn't hurry, because my father's teaching had been thorough and strict, drawings sometimes done ten times or more before they satisfied him, measurements refigured, words rejected and recrafted. So this need for hurry was strange and new. I fought it—I could not afford to make mistakes, not with her. I sat and wrote down everything I meant to do, step by step. To measure her and draw her, to explore and list every mark upon her skin. Slowly, as a true scientist would, as my father had taught me to be.

But I couldn't focus. What I wanted tonight was a story, to hear Lord Tom tell me something new, but Junius was here to criticize and I didn't want that either. So I went to bed. The warmth from the stove and our bodies had risen, but it hadn't completely banished the cold, and I shivered as I undressed and put on my nightgown and went to the bureau to brush and braid my hair.

I stopped short. There, next to my hairbrush, was the bracelet Bibi had given me, the abalone glimmering in the faint light. I frowned. How had it got there? I had left it in my coat pocket. I hadn't taken it out.

I heard Junius's footsteps on the stairs, and then the bedroom opened and he came inside. Before he could say anything, I said, "That bracelet, June, the one I told you Bibi gave me? Did you take it out of my pocket?"

"Bracelet? No. Why would I?"

I stared at the bracelet, confused and disturbed. I picked it up and let it fall into the carved horn bowl—my father's—alongside loose buttons and a brooch, the only other piece of jewelry I owned. And then I turned determinedly away. It was late, and I was tired, and I reassured myself: it was easy to forget something so small, an action so thoughtlessly taken. It was nothing more than that.

CHAPTER 3

THE SERE GRASS WAS STIFF AND PRICKLY BENEATH MY BARE *feet where I sat on the hill overlooking the valley, a basket of berries at my side, my saffron skirts shifting about my legs with the hot dry summer breeze. I was waiting. Waiting and impatient, and that waiting grew and grew until I was so tense and anxious I did not think I could wait another moment.*

Then I felt him. I turned to look.

Everything changed.

I rose to run, my foot catching the basket, upturning it, and the berries spilled onto the ground, a pool of them like blood, the basket rolling and rolling down the hill, the design woven into it— light reeds against dark—flashing as it rolled, and I could only stare at it, frozen. I could not move. He was here, and I knew what was coming, and I was afraid. I was afraid and I could not run and could not scream—

I woke with a start, sitting bolt upright, sweating, choking, my chest so tight I could not catch a breath. I gasped, panicking, clutching my throat.

"What is it? What's wrong?" Junius's voice, sleepy and alarmed. He grabbed me, and I fought him, unthinking, still caught in the dream, trying to get away. "Lea, stop. It was a dream. It was only a dream." He pulled me hard into his chest, murmuring, "It's all right, sweetheart. It's all right."

My fear faded in the reality of Junius's warmth, the darkness of the room, the moonlight casting a subtle light beyond. I was here, in my bed, in my room.

I took a deep breath, and another, until my heart fell into a regular beat.

"A bad nightmare?" Junius asked.

"Yes," I managed. "Yes. It was...terrible. I was waiting and... and the basket overturned, and it was so...so horrible..." It sounded ridiculous when I said it. Not the least bit frightening.

Junius whispered, "Ssshhh. Ssshhh. It's all right. Nothing to worry about. Just a dream."

I lay back with him, snuggling into his arms. I listened to the rise and fall of his breathing, the beat of his heart, until the dream faded and was gone.

The next morning, Junius said, "That was a bad nightmare you had last night," and I nodded and told him I couldn't remember it, which wasn't true. I tried to forget it as I went about my chores, though I couldn't. There was something about the dream that carried, that made me even more anxious, and it all settled around her. I wanted to see her, to touch her, to be reassured—*about what?* I found myself pausing in the middle of carrying milk to the springhouse, staring at the barn, murmuring, "What trick have you played on me?"

I refused to surrender to such absurdity. Dreams, instincts... I'd fought them all my life. As a child, I'd always been suscepti-ble to bad dreams—I'd awakened to blind fear in the night more times than I cared to remember, running to Papa's room to fling myself into his arms, begging for his comfort. He'd soothed me with whispers, *Ssshhh, ssshhh, my dear, dear girl. It's only a dream. There's nothing real in it*, though in the morning it had always occasioned a lecture—I should not have read those old legends or listened so closely to the songs, or whatever it was I'd done to bring the bad dreams. *Superstition is the enemy of objectivity*, he'd told me often. Science needed facts.

I remembered those words and told myself I would take my time today, do my chores, go out to her when I was good and ready. I was no green girl to run at every change in the wind.

But still, when Junius stopped me as I finally made my way to the barn, saying, "I need those drawings for Baird first, sweetheart. The collection's been waiting long enough," I felt a sinking desperation.

"But I—"

"The mummy can wait. And you haven't got that canoe yet for me, have you? I might have to send it off after all."

That was true. I hadn't kept my end of the bargain. I needed to go into Bruceport and speak with Bibi again, but after our conversation yesterday, I was reluctant. I didn't want to hear her words—I was already uneasy enough. *Without cause*, I reminded myself. Still, Bibi would wait. I'd talk to her tomorrow.

I forced myself to attend to the chore of drawing, resisting the call of the mummy. I picked up the bowl waiting on the table, turning it in my hands, running my thumb along the broad form lines of the salmon carved upon it. Junius, who was going to the stove for a cup of coffee, glanced over his shoulder and said, "A camas bowl, I think."

But I saw skilled hands carving, smoothing, polishing. I saw, in my mind's eye, the bowl sitting at the edge of the fire, the oil it held glistening and pungent. I shook my head. "Oil," I said softly, without thinking.

Junius frowned. "Why do you say that?"

I saw the way he was looking at me, that frown between his eyebrows, the same one I'd seen on Papa's face a dozen times. "The salmon carved on it. And it still smells of oil," though neither was true. Salmon was a common motif. And the bowl smelled like nothing but dust and old wood.

"Ah." Junius nodded and poured the coffee. "Well, write that down too. It's always good to give Baird a story."

I thought he was mocking me, but when I looked at him more closely I realized he wasn't really paying attention, and I felt a quick relief. I'd always had too strong an imagination when it came to the relics. It was easy for me to envision the life they'd lived—dancers wearing those masks that now hung on the wall while the fringe shivered with their movement; sinkers plunging deep into a cold river, holding nets taut; salmon hooks taking shape beneath the blade of a stone knife. Sometimes those stories felt so real…but I thought I'd learned long ago to keep such ideas to myself.

It was the mummy. She was too distracting. And my dream… I tried to shake it away and settled myself to the drawing, hurrying through it, keeping my fancies well at bay, not allowing myself to think of the stories these things could tell, but even so, it was growing dark by the time I finished for the day.

I managed to make it out to the barn, but only for a few moments before I had to start supper. The whole day had escaped me. I didn't even bother to take her from the trunk. I only stood there, holding the lantern over her, watching the light turn her oak-colored skin to honey and glisten on the molasses-taffy color of her hair, and I was struck by a reverence that made me catch my breath. For a moment, as I stared at her, I felt as if I'd somehow brought her alive. I saw the faint rise and fall of her chest, the flutter of her eyelashes upon her cheeks, and I found myself whispering, "Who are you?"

I'd no sooner said the words than I felt how foolish they were—not just because I'd spoken them aloud but because I'd expected an answer. She was no more alive than the straw or that harness hanging on the wall. But when I closed the trunk lid, again I felt that sense of suffocation; it was all I could do to turn the key in the lock and walk away.

I could not stop thinking of her, and it wasn't just questions about her people or how old she was or whether she was Indian—the kinds of questions I *should* have been asking. Instead, I wondered what had brought her here from hills with long brown grass and wind full of the scent of sun and dust. I wondered if those berries had been her favorites and why she was waiting and why that waiting had turned so afraid. *A dream, Leonie. Not real.* But as the days went on and the dream returned, it seemed so. Sometimes I could feel that grass against my feet, and when I took down my stockings and saw the milk white of my own ankles, I was startled that they weren't brown. I thought of those berries spilling into a pool like blood as I spooned red currant jam from a jar. I washed dishes and thought of the black and white on that basket flashing as it tumbled down the hill.

My chores kept me from her aside from a few minutes here and there. I tried to visit her every day—*as if she was an old aunt you feel beholden to*—and it *was* rather like that. I felt I had to reassure her I was here and would remain so. *Soon*, I kept promising. *Soon.* Because there was no time for real study. Drawing the relics took days. Then butter had to be made before the cream soured, and soap, and the garden had to be cleaned out before the weather turned completely. And there was always someone else here too. Every day brought men out to look at her. Sydney Dawes and Adam Leach had done their work well, and Junius had been right when he predicted the barn would turn into a curiosity museum. Much of the time, Junius was so busy showing her off that I had to be the one to go out to the whacks to harvest the oysters with Lord Tom. When I complained of it, Junius said, "You show her then, sweetheart. God knows I'd be happy for you to."

But I couldn't do it. I couldn't stand the thought of answering their stupid questions or watching them look at her as if she were an oddity like a monkey-faced Fiji mermaid or a two-headed snake. It made me nervous, too, so many come out to see her. Baird was certain to hear of her now. Someone would talk, and it would get to some newspaper, and then to him. And once he asked for her, what would keep Junius from sending her away? It wasn't as if I'd kept my end of the bargain. I hadn't gotten him the canoe. But if I couldn't find the time to study the mummy, I surely couldn't find it to get to Bruceport and talk to Bibi.

It didn't help that the dream invaded not just my waking hours, but my sleep, too—not every night, but enough that I came to dread it. It no longer brought horror and panic, but a nausea that was sometimes so bad it was all I could do not to bolt for the chamber pot, to lie still until the feeling passed. I never woke Junius, and I don't think he noticed my restlessness. I said nothing to Lord Tom, though I saw the way he watched me, as if he were searching for something. He knew me better than anyone alive—even Junius—so well that sometimes I thought he must be reading my mind. But Lord Tom didn't question me, and I was grateful for it. I kept thinking, *If I could just get to her, if I could just study her, this would all go away and I would have my life back again.* I would be myself again.

Though really, how was I *not* myself? It was just…that anxiety from the dream seemed to inhabit me. That *waiting* I'd felt since the night of the storm. I was aware of every moment passing, and myself growing older within it, everything I'd ever wanted stretching farther out of reach—but that was so strange, because what did I want that I didn't already have? Beyond children, of course, but…some things you just had to live without. Still, that anxiety pushed and pushed and it didn't matter how I pushed back; it didn't go away.

It was two weeks before I managed to find the time for study again, and only then because Lord Tom and I returned from the whacks earlier than usual. It was still early afternoon, and if there were no oglers, I would have hours with her. When I saw no strange canoes or plungers pulled ashore, I could barely temper my excitement.

I left Lord Tom to tend the canoe and hurried over the hillocks of marsh grass and the shallow little mud flats between them to the path of crushed oyster shells that led past the worn gray pickets of the fence. Wild rose twined about the gate, mostly bare, a few yellow and brown mottled leaves, full, plump hips, the little thorns grabbing at my sleeve as I passed. I meant to go past the house and straight to the barn, when there was a movement on the porch, and I looked up to see a man sitting on the steps.

Another one of Junius's gawkers. My hopes died; my disappointment and anger were so overwhelming I felt the sudden press of tears. He stood when he saw me, brushing his hands against the faded gray cloth of the coat he wore; it looked old enough to be from the War, though I wondered if he had been the original owner—he looked to be only in his late twenties. His boots and trousers were muddied to the knee with the thick, stinking mud of the flats or the sloughs. I smelled it from where I stood. He had a bag slung over his shoulder, and wore a slouchy leather hat nearly the twin of the one I had on now; beneath it his hair was the deep gold of old coins where it waved against his jaw. A handsome face, one I would have remembered if I'd seen it before, which I hadn't.

He stepped down the porch stairs. "Hello," he said, touching his hat in deference, very polite. "I wonder if you could tell me if this is Junius Russell's place."

"It is," I said, unable to keep the irritation from my voice. "I suppose you've come to see the mummy too."

He looked taken aback, and then he smiled in that way men do who know they're attractive, a straight-on gaze meant to charm. He had a large mouth, a face that was all high cheekbones and strong nose and sharply cut jaw. I'd seen men like this before, young and confident, working the beds or the schooners until they "found something better," thinking already that they were meant to rule the world once everything fell into place. I was unmoved, too annoyed to be charmed by a pretty smile.

"I guess I have," he said.

"Well, come on, then. But I warn you, you'll only have a short time with her. I've things to do." I gestured abruptly for him to follow.

He fell into step beside me as I took him over the hillocky yard. I glanced at his filthy boots, the mud-covered pants. "You come through the sloughs?"

He nodded. "From Bruceport."

"No one told you to go by water?"

A wry smile. "No. They did point me in the right direction, though."

"Not much of a direction. You don't have a horse?"

"I walked." He motioned to the mud on his trousers. "Not well, as you've no doubt noticed."

"At least the tide was out. You could have drowned."

"A blessing, I'm sure," he said.

"Well, you'll no doubt find the mummy worth the trip. Everyone seems to."

"I'm sure I won't be any different, Miss—"

"Russell. Leonie Russell."

He frowned. "Are you his daughter?"

Dryly, I said, "Very flattering, I'm sure. I'm Junius's wife." I'd taken two steps before I realized he'd stopped.

"You're his wife?" He frowned, and there was something about that look that was vaguely familiar. I had the thought that I must have met him before after all. But then the expression left him and he smiled—again with charm. This was a man whose smile had eased many difficulties, I realized. "Forgive me, but you don't look old enough to be his wife."

I gave him a polite smile in return. "I assure you I am. Have I seen you about? Do you know my husband, Mr.—"

"No. I just came up from San Francisco. I'd read about him and the mummy in the paper."

"In San Francisco?"

He nodded. "The *Morning Call.*"

It had made the papers—of course it had, hadn't I been expecting it? But that it had made it to San Francisco...that was farther than I'd expected, and more quickly than I'd anticipated. If news of this was in San Francisco, it was only a matter of time before Baird discovered what I'd found.

I hurried toward the barn as if my speed could somehow ease my sudden dread. When we were only a few yards from the open door, I called out, "Junius! June! There's someone to see the mummy!"

No answer.

"I wonder where he's got to?" I asked, even more irritated on top of being upset. I looked at the man beside me. "I'll see if I can't find him—"

"Perhaps you could show it to me in his stead," he suggested.

I wanted to tell him no, but I had no idea where Junius was or when he would be back, and I wanted this man gone.

"Of course." I grabbed the oil lamp from its nail and the matches settled on the edge of a crossbeam. He waited patiently while I lit it, and then I took him over to the sawhorse bed, where the mummy lay covered with a blanket. Not put away in the trunk after Junius had shown her, damn him. The only good thing about that was that it meant he couldn't be far away.

I uncovered her and lifted the lamp to shine over the old leather of her skin, the fine black eyelashes and brows, the browning pegs of her few teeth. I felt that reverence again, that draw. I could not resist; gently I touched her hair, and I felt him go still beside me.

"She looks as if she's only asleep," he said quietly.

"Yes."

"How did he find her?"

"It was me who found her, actually. Didn't the newspaper article say?"

He shook his head. "It said that Junius Russell found a mummy near the Mouse River. Not much else."

"Of course not."

He eased closer, reaching out a hand, and I opened my mouth to tell him not to touch her, but then I didn't say it. There was something about the way he went about it, as if he were afraid to startle, as if he knew it was discourteous and didn't want to offend, and I found myself appreciating the gesture as if it were me he directed it to. "She's quite beautiful, isn't she?"

I was surprised by his words. I looked at her again. Odd, yes. Compelling, certainly. But beautiful? The lamplight made her skin seem waxed. It brought out the reddish hue of her hair. The saffron cloth seemed to glow. "Yes. Yes, I suppose so."

He turned heavy-lidded blue eyes to me. "How old do you think she is?"

"Junius thinks before the Indians. But I'm not so certain."

"*Junius* thinks? How would an oysterman know?"

"He and I...we collect relics for the National Museum. We've done so for years."

"You do?" He looked surprised again. "The story didn't mention that."

"Apparently it didn't mention a great deal."

"I suppose not," he said with a smile. He looked back at the mummy. "But you said you didn't agree with him. About how old she is. Why not?"

"I don't know enough yet. My father was an ethnologist. He taught me to observe before I jumped to conclusions, and I haven't studied her enough yet to form an opinion."

"*You?* You mean—"

"I'm an ethnologist as well."

"But you're—"

"A woman. Yes," I said grimly, wishing he would leave. "Does that shock you?"

He shrugged. "I suppose that explains why the newspaper didn't mention that you were the one to find it. I'll have to set the record straight."

"Set the record straight? What do you mean?"

"I'm a reporter. I've come to do a story on this."

"I didn't realize we had guests." Junius's voice startled us both. I turned to face the open barn door where he stood.

"There you are," I said in relief. "This gentleman has come to see the mummy. He read about it in the newspaper. In *San Francisco*, Junius. He's a reporter from—what paper did you say you were from?"

But the man ignored me. He was staring at Junius as if he couldn't believe what he was seeing. "You're Junius Russell?"

"I am." Junius held out his hand. "At your service. And you are—?"

The young man did not extend his hand. "Daniel Russell. Your son."

CHAPTER 4

THE WORDS FELL INTO SILENCE. DANIEL RUSSELL WAS staring at my husband with something that looked like challenge in his eyes, and when I turned to Junius, stunned and expecting him to deny it, I saw that he looked at the young man—*his son*—the same way, with equal challenge and...and wariness too.

"You have a son?" I heard the rising hysteria in my voice.

Junius cut me off with a gesture. "I'll explain later."

"But—"

"*Later.*" He looked back at Daniel Russell. "Daniel. Well, well. Look at you. How old are you now? Why, you must be...twenty six?"

"Twenty-seven."

"Your mother?"

"Your *wife* is dead." The word was blunt, uncompromising. "Last year."

Wife. Yes, there'd been a wife, I remembered. A vague idea of a person, something I'd put on a shelf long ago, and not thought of since. I felt thrown back in time. *I'm already married, Lea. She means nothing to me. I'll take care of everything.* Yes, I'd known about the wife. But a son...a son who would have been five or six when Junius had left them. He'd never told me there was a son. Why not?

"You know she waited for you. She never stopped waiting. But you never intended to return, did you?"

"But she knew," I broke in, unable to help myself. "She knew not to wait, didn't she?" I looked at Junius. "*Didn't* she?"

Daniel looked at me. "You knew he was already married?"

Helplessly, I started to make the excuse that shamed me.

Junius held up a hand to stop me. "Leonie, please."

But I'd had enough. "God *damn* you, Junius."

I was out of the barn before he could say another word. I ran across the yard, past where Lord Tom sat on the porch. I was inside and nearly to the stairs before I heard the door slam behind me, before Junius caught up with me, pulling me to a stop. I wrenched loose. "Don't touch me."

"Lea, please. Let me explain."

"You've had twenty years to explain."

"It isn't like that."

I turned on him. "Then what is it like, Junius? Why tell me about a wife but not a son?"

He looked helpless and out of control, not the Junius I knew, but I was too angry and ashamed to soften. He said, "It didn't matter. He didn't matter."

"Your *son* didn't matter."

"I knew you wouldn't leave it if I told you. I knew you'd tell me to go back. But you needed me, and…and Mary and I were done, Lea. We were done. I hoped she would think I was dead."

I stared at him. This was not the man I knew. "But why?"

He swallowed, glancing away. "We'd married too young. Her parents disliked me. I was…restless. Couldn't keep a job. We did nothing but argue. I thought they'd be better off without me."

"But…your *son*," I said, and suddenly I was overwhelmed with loss and absence, with the grief I thought I'd come to terms with, that I'd accepted. But that horrible sadness swept back, worse, because now I knew without a doubt that our lack was my fault. Mine. I had not had children, and I had kept him from the one he had.

"Lea," he said softly. "I knew you would take it like this. I knew if I told you, you'd be…"

He was a blur in front of me. "Be what?"

"Don't cry," he said. "Lea, sweetheart. Please don't cry."

"You should have told me," I managed.

"Why hurt you needlessly? I wasn't going back. It would only have come between us." He gathered me in his arms, and I found myself bending, melting into his chest, burying my face in his shirt. He whispered, "I'm sorry. I'm sorry that you found out this way. I'll send him away. You'll never have to look at him again. I'll go out there now and send him back to San Francisco."

I shook my head against him. "You can't do that."

"Why not?"

I pulled away, swiping my hand across my eyes. "You abandoned him. You can't just send him away. You have to find out what he wants. You have to make it up to him. You would have gone back if not for me."

"No—"

"I know you would have. You're an honorable man."

"Lea, for God's sake. It's long past time to make things up. I promise you he's here because he wants something, no other reason. Let me find out what it is and send him on his way."

I pulled away hard, stepping from the circle of his arms. "You talk as if he means to takes something from you."

"Why else would he be here?"

"Perhaps to get to know his father." I could not keep the bitterness from my voice.

Junius let out a heavy sigh. "Perhaps. But I doubt it. Why don't you let me find out what the hell he wants before you start thinking we need to make things up to him?"

"But we do," I said softly, feeling my responsibility and my sorrow like a weight. "He's your *son*."

Junius gave me a troubled look. "You have a good heart, Lea. But there are some people who don't deserve it."

"You don't know that he's one of them."

"You don't know that he isn't." He dragged his hand through his hair and turned back to the door. His shoulders sagged, he looked tired and *old*. "I'm sorry, Leonie," he said again. "You don't know how much."

But I was still angry and guilty and hurt, and I wondered which he was sorry for—not telling me about the son he'd abandoned, or for being caught in the lie?

I followed him out, back into the chill. Lord Tom was still on the porch, his chair angled back against the wall, his hat pulled low. He'd no doubt heard every word.

He tilted his hat back. He was frowning. "Your son is still in the barn."

Junius went down the stairs. As I made to follow, Lord Tom reached out, touching my arm, stopping me. When I looked back at him, he said softly, "Bad luck."

"Don't be ridiculous," I said impatiently, but his words startled me; I looked at the barn, Junius striding toward the young man waiting inside.

Lord Tom said, "*Kloshe nanitch, okustee.*"

"Yes, of course I'll be careful." I pulled away, hurrying after my husband.

At the barn door, Junius paused, and I came up beside him. Daniel Russell was inside, as Lord Tom had said, and he was standing by the mummy, holding the lamp, looking at her with a kind of studious attention that made me pause, uncertain whether to be pleased or troubled. When he heard us, he turned around, lowering the lamp, and I found myself looking for Junius in him, some evidence of blood. He had the same color eyes, I realized, and that alone was enough to make my stomach sink. *Junius's son. Who was not mine.*

Junius said, "I imagine that wasn't the greeting you were hoping for, boy. I'm sorry for it. You…you caught me by surprise."

Daniel glanced at me. He was nearly vibrating with anger. He glanced back at Junius. "I imagine so."

Junius licked his lips a little nervously. "So I…what do you want from me?"

"Junius," I warned.

"He's come with some expectation, Lea, as I said. I just want to know what it is."

"It's all right," Daniel said. "It's a fair question. As it happens, I do want something."

Junius turned to me triumphantly.

Daniel went on, "I want a story about the mummy for the paper I work for."

"A story?" Junius's voice was heavy with suspicion.

Daniel's smile was thin. "A story."

"You didn't come all this way for that."

"My editor says I did. But you're right, that's not the only reason I came. I wanted to see you as well. Now that I have, well…I guess the story's the better reward."

Junius's mouth tightened. "Talk to your stepmother about it then. She's the one studying the damn thing."

Daniel looked at me. I said quickly, "Of course. I'll tell you whatever you want to know. But…well, it could take some time to discover anything of interest, and in the meantime, perhaps you could stay here with us." I said the words before Junius had time to protest.

Daniel raised a brow.

Junius glared at me. I glared back at him. "It would give you and your father a chance to know each other."

Daniel laughed shortly and glanced away.

I felt a swift surge of anger, of dislike. Before it could gain sway, I nudged Junius, who said bluntly, "If you decide to stay, it won't be free room and board. You'll work like the rest of us, but I'll pay you fairly for it."

His distrust was in every word.

Daniel let out a breath. He looked back at me, and then at Junius, and that gaze was assessing and distant, uncomfortably so. Suddenly I was sorry I'd suggested it. I wanted him to say no, to walk away and let me forget he existed. Junius was right; he was a stranger, and one who had plenty of reason to hate us both.

But I could not forget him now, nor my part in why he was here. I felt him as a punishment I deserved when he said in a tight, quiet voice, "All right. Why not?"

And I could not help hearing Lord Tom's words. *Bad luck.*

Daniel was hard-edged, cautious, and in this he was a mirror of his father. They barely spoke to each other as we went into the house, but Daniel wasn't speaking to me either; I saw the way he looked at me, and I knew that he had named me a villain too. I could not disagree with him.

He paused just inside the door, glancing about, calculating in a way that made me think Junius was right about him. I saw him take in the frayed settees and the organ in the corner that only Junius played, the pile of Indian baskets, the crowded whatnot full of carved argillite figures, masks, rattles, and coiled strings of hiaqua.

"These are all Indian relics?" he asked.

Junius nodded.

"So you really are a collector."

"I told you we were ethnologists," I said.

Daniel put aside the bag he carried and picked up a bowl, turning it in his hands. "Do you make much of a living being an ethnologist?"

"It's not the money that matters, but knowledge," I said.

"So they're not worth anything?"

"To the right person they are."

"Museums, you mean?"

I nodded. "And other collectors. But most of what's here I keep just because I like it."

Daniel set the bowl down again and looked at Junius. "Of all the jobs Mama told me you had—and lost—I don't recall collecting being one of them."

"Things change." Junius crossed the room to the kitchen, grabbing a cup, pouring coffee.

Daniel threw a quick glance at me. "Yes they do."

Quickly, I said, "Your father was an ethnologist before we met."

"Was he?" He didn't bother to hide his skepticism.

"He's one of the best," I said defensively.

Daniel said, "Really? Is he famous?"

Junius glanced up quickly. "I will be. As soon as they see that mummy."

No mention of me, of course, but he was only trying to impress his son, who seemed impervious to being impressed.

The tension in the room was unbearable; I could not imagine living with it for long. But neither did I know exactly how to ease it. Uncomfortably, I said to Daniel, "I'll show you to your room."

I led him to the stairs, nervous, and he followed me slowly, looking at everything, and I was suddenly aware of my poor housekeeping, by the relics covered with dust and the dirty stairs, because lately, I'd had little time to keep things neat—not that it was something I had ever thought much about in any event. No other visitor had ever inspired in me this self-consciousness.

We reached the top of the stairs. "There's our room," I said, gesturing to it, "and the storage room. Yours is at the end of the hall." I led him to my father's old room, standing back for him to go inside, which he did, and I felt him there as an invasion. *He is your stepson, Leonie*, I reminded myself, trying to ignore how uncomfortable he made me.

He stood in the middle of the small room, looking around at the narrow bed, the shelf of journals, the dresser littered with relics and the window that looked out on Shoalwater Bay.

"I hope this will do," I said.

He nodded. "It's fine."

"I—I'll leave you then. I'm going to make supper. Come down when you like."

I stepped away and hurried down the stairs. When I reached the bottom, Junius stood there, nursing his coffee. I breathed a sigh of relief.

Junius said, "Regrets already?"

"Not at all."

"Liar." He put his coffee down and reached for me, pulling me close, nuzzling his face in my hair. "I'm sorry I didn't tell you about him, sweetheart. I just—"

I pushed away.

"Lea, I stopped thinking about him a long time ago. I think I almost…forgot about him."

"I can't believe that."

"It was a life that didn't feel like mine anymore."

"And no doubt it was easier to almost forget."

He smiled slightly and reached for me again. "Maybe. I didn't want the past to spoil things. I thought he'd be better off without me. I think he was."

I felt how convenient that was, another way to make things easy, to justify his abandonment, but I said nothing. I felt sick and angry as I swatted his hand away and went to the stove. "Well, he's here now. You'll take him to the whacks with you tomorrow?"

Junius gave me a grim look. "If you insist. But don't expect me to make it back alive."

I didn't laugh, and Junius didn't smile.

CHAPTER 5

THE QUERQUELIN GURGLED AND RUSHED BESIDE ME. I KNEW *this landscape, but the colors were all wrong, muted and off, as if I walked in a yellow mist, and I knew what was wrong was my fault, and that I had to fix it but I felt half-blind, as if the strange colors were affecting me, too, and I knew I had to find it before I couldn't see at all. I must find it. I must... and as my panic grew I became aware of the cries of the gulls, louder and louder, so loud they were all I could hear, and then the birds were swirling around me, a cloud of them, a maelstrom, dipping so close I felt the brush of their wings and saw their angry yellow eyes, their open, wicked beaks. I ran, trying to escape them, flailing at them, panicked and terrified, and then I tripped, falling hard to the ground, covering my head to save myself from the birds.*

And then it was silent. A silence so loud and huge it was more terrifying than the furious cries of the gulls. I felt something beneath my hand, something smooth and fine, saffron-colored cloth. There she was. The answer I'd been searching for, the thing that would put everything right. She was sleeping, one arm crooked beneath a softly rounded cheek, but as I looked at her she opened her eyes, staring right at me, and her gaze was dark and fathomless and terrifying. I scrambled away, screaming, though no sound came out. I'd done it wrong. I'd done it wrong and I could not take it back or get away as she began to wither, her body lifting and twisting as if in the hand of some invisible giant, shriveling, and I knew that if I didn't run I would be next. I would be next and yet I couldn't move or run or scream or—

I started awake, my heart racing. It took a moment for me to realize where I was—in my room, with Junius beside me, and dawn lightening the curtains. Gradually, my heartbeat slowed, but the horror of the dream didn't ease. I felt her watching me; I saw that dark, terrifyingly fathomless eye.

She was tired of waiting.

I slipped from bed, trying not to wake Junius. He stirred, turned over, fell back to sleep, and I dressed quickly. I left my hair in its thick braid trailing down my back. I crept from our bedroom, into the hallway, down the stairs. I took up my notebook from the table along with a pencil, and grabbed the key to the trunk from the basket by the door. I put on my coat, hat, and gloves, and went out into the damp, cool morning. The horizon was a pale light, a fog hovering over the bay, the soft brush of a yellowish mist. I felt the fear and panic from my dream, and I could not keep from glancing over my shoulder as I hurried from the porch to the barn.

I felt a rush of impatience when I saw Edna there, waiting to be milked, something I could not ignore though I wanted to. The dream gathered, anxious, waiting, as I finished the chore and loosed the cow to graze. I felt that horror still; I was half-afraid and urgent as I unlocked the trunk and lifted the lid. At last. At last I was with her.

And then the dream left me, just that quickly. At the sight of her I could no longer remember why I'd been impatient, or the fear that had dogged my every thought since I'd awakened. Slowly, I lifted her from the trunk, laying her on the makeshift table. I forgot everything but my need to discover the truth of her, that same feeling I'd had in the dream, that she was the answer, that if I could find her in time I could save myself.

The thought surprised me. I could only stare at her, motionless, disconcerted. For weeks I'd wanted nothing more than to be right here, but now that I was, I felt at a sudden loss. I was so ill equipped for this. I wasn't certain what to do, how to go about it. I tried to think of Papa, of the rigorous course of study he'd crammed into my head. I would have to draw her, of course, but before that...Skull measurements, I remembered. Morton's *Crania Americana,* the measurement of brain capacity. But no...this was no skull to fill with lead shot, and now it was all about craniometry anyway. Agassiz's eight types, a cephalic index...The words leaped around in my head, confusing. I could not remember the categories, or even how to measure, so instead I satisfied myself by looking, noting my every observation in the notebook: where the skin was cracked or tearing, the number of teeth and their locations, discolorations. Drawing and observing was something I *could* do. I was so completely caught up in it that when I heard the movement at the doorway I jumped, nearly dropping the notebook.

It was Junius. "Here you are. When did you come out here?"

I realized how light the day was beyond him. "Near dawn."

"Didn't you hear Leach shouting? Schooner's coming in. Get your gear. We've got to get going."

The schooner from San Francisco was in Bruceport to buy oysters. There hadn't been one in weeks, and we'd all been waiting. It needed all of us to load the sloop and get there in time— first come, first served, and a late arrival meant perhaps not selling at all. The day I'd planned with the mummy would not happen after all.

Disappointment overwhelmed me, along with the sharp memory of her unflinching, terrifying gaze, demanding my presence, my study. I couldn't go. She wanted me here. But no, that was ridiculous. She couldn't *want* anything, and I couldn't stay. Junius and Lord Tom needed me.

I said to Junius, "I'll be there in a moment," and he went out again, and I turned back to the mummy, thinking I'd take just one more moment. One more look here, at the scraped elbow, and then her clasped hand—

"Leonie, what the hell are you doing?"

I whirled around.

Junius again, furious now. "We're waiting for you. What the hell's taking you so long?"

"I'm sorry, I—"

"Get your gear." He was thin-lipped as he stalked over to me. I stood there like a stone. He jerked his head at me. "Go on. I'll put it away. You're costing us time. Hurry up. Lord Tom and the boy are at the sloop."

The boy. It took me a moment to remember who that was. Daniel. Junius's son. I'd forgotten all about him. I felt caught in a haze, caught in her orbit and my dream, and nothing felt real but the barn. It wasn't until I walked out that the feeling cleared, that I remembered myself. The oysters. The schooner. We were already late. There was no time to do more than grab my oystering boots and my hat and the heavier leather gloves and then race out to where Lord Tom and Daniel were waiting by the plunger.

Lord Tom frowned. Daniel did little more than nod a good morning. He huddled, his hands in his coat pockets and his hat pulled down hard, his face more finely sculpted now in the harshness of the morning light, or perhaps only because he was cold.

Lord Tom turned to the plunger, and I realized that Junius was already behind me, having rushed from the barn. "Let's go," he said, and within only a few moments, the four of us were on our way.

Bruceport was maybe three miles away by land, but no one went anywhere by land, because the way was all hilled forest and salt marsh and tidal sloughs that were full of water when the tide was in, and thick viscous mud when it was out. Impossible to cross, and Daniel had been lucky—it wasn't uncommon for those who tried to get stuck and sometimes drown when the tide came in. This morning the bay was gray and touched bright here and there with reflections from the ever-changing shadows of the sky. The sloop was crowded with the four of us. We'd be sitting on top of each other once the oysters were aboard, but the more hands there were the more quickly we could load, and I knew by the set to Junius's face that I had cost us; we needed those extra minutes.

Junius sat aft to manage the rudder and the mainsail and the jib, and Lord Tom sat to his right. Which meant there was only one seat left, for Daniel and me to share. He leaned away as far from me as he could, his face tight with distaste. Whatever charm I'd seen in him was nowhere in evidence.

I tried to ignore it, to make myself smile despite my rapidly growing distrust. He was my stepson, and I owed him. "Do you know how to sail?"

He didn't look at me, but pulled his collar up further over his chin. "No."

"Junius, you should teach him."

My husband stared at the sail. "What for, Lea? I doubt he'll have much use of it in San Francisco."

"You never know. It's a useful enough skill," I insisted. "What do you think, Daniel?"

Daniel said, "I think it would be a waste of time for everyone."

I went quiet then. There was no point, especially if neither was going to try.

Gulls swooped and cawed, and I shuddered, remembering my dream, and felt Daniel's quick glance, which I ignored. I put the dream behind me—for now, I had to think about oysters, not mummies or finding answers or the strange and unwelcome sense that there was something wrong that I must fix, and she was the key to that. None of it made sense. It wasn't rational; it wasn't real.

Pelicans flew in lines one after the other, their bodies elongated *Z*'s against the full gray of the clouded sky, more graceful than they looked on the ground—scarcely the same bird. Ducks and herons grouped along the shores, the ducks huddled into themselves against the cold. The culling bed was almost halfway between the Querquelin and Stony Point, and once we were there it was only work and hurry, a constant rhythm of shoveling up the oysters, checking them to make sure they were the palm size we needed and that there were none broken, which happened too often, as the Shoalwater oysters were delicate and thin-shelled and the tongs we used to harvest them were crude and too rough.

The water was cold, but at least it wasn't raining. Junius had Daniel and me on the sloop, sorting through the shovelfuls he and Lord Tom tossed aboard. Once I showed Daniel what we were looking for, I left him alone. He was a good worker, quick to catch on, and I was grateful for that, at least, though the silence between us was strained.

The hold was half full before he said, quietly, as if to himself, "Christ, this is miserable work."

"It's worth it. And June and Lord Tom have it worse. At least you're on the boat." I glanced to where the other two stood in knee-deep freezing water as they shoveled oysters from the culling bed onto the deck.

My leather gloves were soaked through, my fingers numb. I picked up a handful of oysters, glancing through them before I dropped most of them into the hold and a broken-shelled one into the bushel we'd be taking home. Nothing to do but eat them.

He said, "So do I have any brothers or sisters? Or did they all run away to avoid this?"

The question surprised me, not just that he'd asked it but because of the stab of unwelcome pain it brought—surely I should be used to this by now. I'd answered such questions a hundred times, but coming from him it felt personal and somehow...accusing. "No," I said shortly. "We've no children."

He raised his gaze to mine, and I said quickly, wanting to stop that conversation before it went any further, "What sorts of things do you need to know for your story?"

He let me change the subject. "Anything you can tell me. Where you think she's from. Who you think she might be."

I laughed a little. "I'm a good ways from knowing any of that, I think. But I suppose that gives you some time to get to know your father."

"I know as much of him as I want. The story is more important."

"It's a long way to come for just a story."

"Well, they'll pay me enough to keep my father-in-law happy for a bit."

I looked up in surprise. "You have a wife?"

He shook his head and threw a handful of oysters a little too violently. "Not yet. A fiancée."

"Oh. Will she mind your staying here for a time?"

"Not if it means we can be married," he said. And then, "So who's the Indian?"

"Lord Tom. He's been with us since my father and I first came here."

"A hired hand?"

"Much more than that."

Daniel raised a questioning brow, and I found myself saying, reluctantly, "Papa and I found him at our door one night. His whole family had been taken by smallpox a few months before, and he was very sick with fever. He had no one else, and there was no doctor for miles, so we took him in. When he got well, he taught us the ways of his people—salmon fishing and smelting and things like that, and he was very good at trading, which was helpful to my father. After a while, we couldn't do without him, and he was devoted to us both. When Papa died, Lord Tom stayed with me."

Daniel nodded. I expected him to say something like, "But he's a savage," or to protest that I kept an Indian so close, but he seemed to accept it without question. For a few moments there was nothing but the sound of shoveling, the clatter of oyster shells falling to the pile. Then Daniel said, "He doesn't like you with that mummy. He spent the whole morning frowning at the barn."

I was startled that he'd noticed it. "Tom's like all his people. They're afraid of dead bodies."

"Why?"

"Because spirits are tricksters. They lure the living to the land of the dead."

"Does he think she's Indian?"

"I don't know what he thinks except that her spirit is powerful and dangerous and will bring nothing but bad luck. No matter that she's probably a century dead at least, and her spirit's already passed over."

Daniel glanced up from the oysters, his eyes the only color in a face washed pale by the cold. Again I thought of how like his father's they were. He frowned. "What?"

"The Chinook believe the spirit passes after five years, and then it can't come back. At least, that's what all the stories say," I explained. "So I don't know why he's so disturbed about this one."

"So what do you mean to do with her?"

"Study, describe, answer what questions I can. Then Junius wants me to send her to Spencer Baird at the Smithsonian."

Daniel tossed another handful of oysters. "What will this Baird give you for her? How much does one make on the dead?"

I didn't like the way he'd worded it; his contempt of me was in every syllable. "I don't know. But I'm certain Junius has some idea."

Just then, Lord Tom brought the last shovelful, and he and Junius came aboard, their boots dripping water as they tried not to slip on the piles of oysters. I lowered the basket of broken shells over the side to keep in the cold water until we returned from Bruceport, and then focused on sorting what was left, glad for the chance to ignore Junius's son for a bit. His questions had been a bit too sharp—it was hard not to think that Junius was right about him. But I told myself that wasn't fair. I hardly knew him, and he had reason to dislike us both. I couldn't blame him for showing it.

We were well under way by the time the sorting was done. I tucked my gloved hands into my armpits to try to warm them. It was useless; they were too far gone, and I was looking forward to a visit to Dunn's saloon once we'd sold the oysters, the warmth of many bodies, no matter how stinking the air.

Once we got closer to Bruceport, the wildlife gave way to bateaus, canoes, a roughly built clinker or two, and other plungers darting everywhere, their sails plumped with breeze as they made their way to Bruceport or Oysterville across the bay or any one of the tiny towns that had sprung up on these shores in the last twenty years, all of them dedicated to the oysters that were our own personal gold rush. Thank God San Francisco loved them so well.

Bruceport sat at the curve of the bay, fronted by mudflats and behind a raft of driftwood, huddled at the base of a forested hill that provided wood for the sawmill the men of the shipwrecked *Bruce* had started when they'd founded this place. There were no wharves—you couldn't build one long enough to reach past the flats when the tide was out—the schooners from San Francisco just anchored out in the shallows and waited for the oystermen to bring them their cargo. And now that we were here, I realized it might be hours before there would be a visit to Dunn's. The bay was full of plungers just like ours, all sidling up to the schooner whose keel was settled deep in the mud. Despite our hurry, we would be one of the last to sell, and there was no guarantee we would even empty the boat. If the schooner filled before they got to us, there would be none of our oysters on it.

Junius swore beneath his breath as he let the sail go slack to take our place in line, and I looked away, not wanting to catch his eye, feeling guilty. I saw Adam Leach's boat at the ship now, loading oysters into the bushel baskets the men aboard lowered over the side. Quickly I looked about, calculating our chances. The schooner would take close to two thousand baskets, and each of the plungers in the bay held the same four hundred ours did. We would be lucky to unload half ours.

"*Wake kloshe*," Lord Tom said quietly.

Junius said tersely, "Not good indeed."

"What's wrong?" Daniel asked.

"We're too late," I told him. "The boat will be full by the time they get to us."

But it wasn't bad luck, I told myself, refusing to look at Lord Tom. There had been a reason for our tardiness, though it didn't make me feel any better to know it, given that the reason was me.

The loading always went quickly; it was only a few hours before it was our turn, and it went just as badly as I'd expected. We'd unloaded less than half the plunger before the men called down that they were full. We'd given them less than two hundred baskets. They threw down a little bag with gold pieces inside—a bit more than three hundred dollars, which wasn't bad unless you considered that we'd been expecting more than six.

Junius emptied the bag out into his hand, and then he held out a fourth to Daniel. "Here's your share, boy."

Daniel stared at Junius's hand. "How much is that?"

"Eighty dollars. It's your—"

"No, how much in all?"

"Over three hundred dollars."

"For two hundred baskets of oysters?" Daniel sounded incredulous. "They paid that much?"

Junius gave him a grim smile. "Don't you know how much oysters are selling for in your own hometown?"

"I know they're for rich men, and too expensive for me. I've never even tried one."

"Well, that'll change," Junius said. He poured the rest of the gold back into the bag and tucked it into his pocket before he glanced regretfully at the schooner. "It should have been more. We'll get here earlier next time."

Lord Tom said, "It will be like this next time too, *sikhs*, unless the spirit quiets."

Junius rolled his eyes. "Well, maybe we'll be lucky and the mummy will be on its way to Baird by the time the next schooner's in. So who's for a drink? I could use one myself. And something to eat."

We beached the plunger and covered the remaining oysters with a wet tarp, and then we all went ashore. Oysterville was the biggest town on the Shoalwater, but Bruceport was next with its two hotels, two stores, and a school. There were about twenty families' worth of houses, and a score of saloons that catered to oystermen and sawmill workers. The streets were packed mud, and watering troughs made of rough-hewn wood and filled with rainwater were here and there, though there were few horses to take advantage of them. A boat was more useful in these parts. A few pigs wandered about, poking at trash piles or the unsavory things hidden in potholes, shooed away by a housewife hanging her laundry or dumping a chamber pot into a cesspool.

Dunn's saloon perched just on the other side of the driftwood raft that separated town from beach, and therefore was often the first to see the gold coins of the oystermen when they came ashore again after selling to the schooner. It was a ramshackle place, gray and weathered, with moss growing on its steeply pitched roof, and it always looked about two minutes away from collapsing in on itself. But it had been there as long as I could remember. Groups of men squatted on the dirt outside, playing monte or the Chinook game *la-hull*, with its disks of wood colored black or plain. It was a favorite among both the Indians and the oystermen who had been here from the earliest days. Lord Tom and I had spent many evenings playing it, but it bored Junius.

Inside was a roughly planed floor smoothed by years of foot-steps, scattered with muddy sawdust and some tables and chairs. The saloon was as full as I'd predicted it would be, gold pieces changing hands so quickly they flashed in the dim light. As usual, I was the only woman there.

Junius brought a bottle of whiskey to the table and three glasses. He poured the liquor and shoved one each to Lord Tom and Daniel before he swallowed his own in one gulp. "I've ordered chowder," he said.

"Your wife doesn't get a drink?" Daniel looked at me. "You work as hard as they do. Seems you should get the same reward."

"It's all right," I said. "I don't want it."

"You don't like it?"

Junius said, "*I* don't like it."

I looked up quickly and said, "I...drink affects me...too much."

Daniel said, "Well, I guess an old man with a young and pretty wife can't want her enjoying herself too well, can he?"

Junius said, "You're on thin ice, boy."

Daniel took a sip. "So how did you two meet, anyway? Let me guess—you were drinking whiskey and this old man actually looked good to you—enough so that you could ignore that he already had a wife."

His tone was light, conversational, but the words were blistering, and I didn't know which I felt more—anger or guilt.

Junius rose. "That's enough, boy. This is none of your business."

"Oh, I'd say it was," Daniel said, unfazed. His eyes glittered in the dimness of the bar. "Given the circumstances."

I looked at my husband. "Sit down, June."

"I won't have him insulting you. He's reduced twenty years of marriage to a crude joke."

"Twenty *years*?" Daniel choked on his drink. "You've been with him twenty years?" He looked at me. "You must have been a child."

I swallowed my dislike and my offense. I reminded myself that he was my stepson, that I deserved at least some measure of his anger and disdain, that Junius did. As calmly as I could, I said, "I was hardly a child. I was seventeen."

Daniel said, "Seventeen?" He laughed as if he couldn't believe it. "No wonder."

"It wasn't like that, boy," Junius said tightly.

"Really?" Daniel raised a dark brow. "It never occurred to you what a good swap it was? A tired wife and a boy for a pretty girl?"

It seemed so dirty and sordid when he said it. The heat came once more into my face. I opened my mouth to protest.

Lord Tom reached across the table before I could say anything, clapping his big hand onto Daniel's, holding him still. "Enough, *tenas kahmooks*. You know nothing."

Daniel looked taken aback. I saw anger sweep his expression, and then it faded, and he gave a short, tight nod. Lord Tom lifted his hand and sat back again.

The bartender called Junius's name, and he and Lord Tom went to get the chowder, leaving me alone with Daniel, where I did not want to be. When they were gone, he turned to me and asked, "What was it he called me?"

"Puppy," I said, too angry myself to soften it.

To my surprise, he only nodded and reached for his whiskey. "The Indian's like a father to you, isn't he?"

Warily, I said, "Yes."

"How lucky you are. Two fathers, when some of us don't even get the one. Why, when you add your husband in, it's almost like three, isn't it?"

"Lord Tom is right," I snapped. "You don't know anything."

His gaze was as sharp as I felt mine to be. "I have eyes, you know. I can see what's in front of my face."

His glance angled up, to behind me. Junius was back, and Lord Tom, carrying bowls of chowder that spilled over the sides onto their fingers. Junius leaned over me, setting the bowls down, pulling bent spoons from his pocket. "Eat up," he said, taking his seat as Lord Tom put down the others. "There's a dance tonight. I'd just as soon go home, but I guess you want to go." He looked at me.

There was always a dance after the schooner came in, and I could never decide if I loved them or hated them. I liked being among people after the isolation of home. I liked to laugh, and there was always plenty of that here. I liked to dance—a little too well, perhaps. But the women of town would be there too, and I was much less comfortable with them. I preferred the company of men—it was what I was used to. Papa had been my only friend throughout my childhood—I hadn't needed others, and we moved so often I'd never learned the habit of making friends. And I soon learned that my strange education, my passion for relics and study, meant I could not be what other women expected of me. Perhaps if I'd had children…but I hadn't. But tonight it seemed preferable to going home, to being locked in silence and resentment, and it was late enough that I wouldn't get a chance to study the mummy anyway. So I said, "Yes. Please."

Junius nodded shortly. "Well, you're lucky to escape the hard work today, boy, but it won't always be this way."

"I'd rather the work," Daniel said stonily, and I did not miss the implication, that work was better than socializing with us.

Junius laughed and bent over his bowl. "I'll remember you said that when you're complaining about the cold and wet."

"How nice to know that there are some things you can remember," Daniel said.

Junius's face went hard. We finished the rest of the meal in silence.

CHAPTER 6

THE ENTIRE TOWN SEEMED TO BE ON THE MUDDY STREETS tonight, despite the darkening clouds that had moved in with twilight, promising rain. Even the children rushed to the dance, dashing to and fro about the street, shouting and chasing each other, their boots, pants, and skirts muddy, their faces alight with excitement, so it made me smile to see them while at the same time I could not keep at bay my sadness that none of them were mine. My melancholy was always stronger here in town, and with it came the realization that Daniel's presence would raise questions I did not want to answer. I wished now I hadn't agreed to come.

As we made our way up the street, dodging potholes and wallows, I heard the music coming from the open door and windows of McBride's Hotel. It was already full by the time we got there, people spilling onto the porch and out the back door, the windows lining the south side all open to cold and wet air growing colder and wetter with encroaching night. There were no streetlamps, but the oil lamps in the windows cast their light onto the mud all around. Through the windows, I saw whirling and dodging, men and women red-faced from dancing. I heard music and talk and laughter, the clop of heavy soled oyster boots on a dusty wood floor.

Lord Tom stayed outside on the porch where there were some other Indians. It wasn't that they were unwelcome inside, at least not overtly, but as the night progressed and the whiskey flowed, it was safer for them to stay out of the way. By then, of course, they'd be drunk themselves, and just as easily provoked as white men, and Tom was no different when it came to that. He rarely drank at home, but tonight we'd have to carry him to the boat.

There were few strangers here, so even if the place hadn't been almost too full to move, we would have been slowed by greetings. With introductions it was worse, but at least Daniel was polite and charming, and Junius managed a smile or two as he introduced his son. I saw the way the women noted and admired Daniel, and he had a ready smile for them—I was reminded again how handsome he was and how easy he was with it. It was vaguely disconcerting to see him smiling and flirtatious; there was no hint of the sharp and angry young man I'd known the last hours.

I heard the expressions of surprise, "A son? Why, Russell, I didn't know you had a son. And such a fine looking man too!" And I saw the way they looked at me, those quick, puzzled glances as they tried to work it out in their minds. I felt their unspoken questions: *What son is this? Did Leonie know about him? Where did he come from?* We were so isolated here, we all felt we knew everything about everyone, but the truth was that most people here were single men moving wherever there was money to be made, and secrets were the coin of the realm. I wondered that people were so surprised to find that Junius had kept them as well.

In the common room there was a large table with bottles of whiskey and a keg of beer, and other women had brought cakes and pies. I felt a moment's guilt—as I always did—for not thinking to bring anything, but these women hadn't been culling oysters that morning, either. One more thing we didn't have in common. I saw them now at the other end of the room, a group of wives talking and laughing, and I knew I should join them.

But then the Jansen brothers began to fiddle a lively polka, and my foot was tapping before I knew it, and I was closing my eyes and swaying with the rhythm. I wanted to give in to it, to give in to the woman who was not Leonie Russell, ethnologist, but someone else, a woman only, who didn't think of relics and study but only of swirling and stomping and tossing her hair and laughing for the sheer pleasure of doing so.

But that was a Leonie that both my father and Junius had discouraged, so I harnessed her when I saw my husband cross the room toward me. He said, "A dance, sweetheart?" and I smiled and nodded as he took me into his arms. When I danced with Junius, it was easier to remember restraint; he made sure of it with the subtle press of his hands, with every look. With other men, without Junius's constant watch, I often forgot and let the other Leonie loose, something Junius hated.

I thought suddenly of the saloon, of Daniel's words: *An old man with a young and pretty wife can't want her enjoying herself too well, can he?*

No, I dared not let her loose tonight, not with Junius's son watching and judging. I did not want to give him more ammunition with which to wound his father.

"That wasn't so hard, was it?" Junius teased when it was over. He pulled me to the side tables, where he grabbed a cup of beer. I followed his glance across the room, to where we'd left his son. I watched Daniel tip his hat to Eliza Brookner, who cocked her head and gave him a pretty smile.

"People take to him," Junius said thoughtfully. "He's like his mother that way. She was like honey to ants. I never saw a woman like that."

I knew he'd married me at my father's urging. To protect me. He hadn't loved me then, just as I hadn't loved him. But to hear such words about another wife after twenty years…I couldn't help the pricking of my vanity or my pride, or the little stab of jealousy I felt. "Is that so?"

Junius put his arm around my waist. "Until I met you, of course."

I pulled away. "You don't have to say that."

He jerked me close again. "It was a long time ago, Lea. Mary was nothing compared to you."

"You shouldn't say that either. She was the mother of your son." I glanced to Daniel again. He had thrown off his hat, and his deep gold hair fell into his face as he danced with Eliza Brookner, and he was laughing, obviously enjoying himself.

Junius said quietly, "Don't get too attached to him, Leonie. He won't stay."

"I'm hardly attached to him. I don't even like him much. But neither do I blame him for being angry. He has a right. And you should at least make an effort to appease him."

"Why?"

"Because he's your son."

He sighed. His hand tightened on my waist. "Very well. But only because you wish it, sweetheart. I think it's a mistake. Just… be careful of him, will you? And…I think it's best if we never leave him alone with the mummy."

I looked at him in surprise. "Why?"

Junius shrugged. "Just an instinct. Perhaps it's nothing. But let's not assume he's trustworthy until he proves it. I told you—he wants something from me, and he's not being honest about what it is."

"The story, he said."

"Hmmm. Perhaps." Junius eyed Daniel thoughtfully. "But I doubt it. It's only blood that links us, Lea. Nothing more. I don't know anything about him and neither do you."

"I know he has a fiancée," I said.

Junius looked at me in surprise. " How do you know that?"

"He told me. He can't be all bad if someone loves him enough to marry him."

"That proves nothing. You don't know that love has anything to do with it. Look at him. Like I said, he's his mother all over. Ants to honey."

"You say it as if it's a crime," I said.

"Just an observation," Junius said.

The music ended amid clapping, and Daniel and Eliza Brookner were off the floor. Eliza was snapped up by her husband—I didn't actually blame him for how possessively he did so. Before the fiddlers started up again, Sarah Estes was stepping shyly up to him. The boy was well able to fend for himself, I thought wryly.

Junius said, with a little nudge, "You planning on avoiding the sewing circle all night?"

I followed his glance to the wives. I could hear their laughter from where we stood.

Another nudge. "You should go say hello at least. Be sociable or they'll think you're snubbing them."

Which was true, I knew. It was also true that I didn't want them thinking it, that in spite of the fact that I'd been avoiding them they had always been kind enough. And it made Junius happy to see me with them. I knew he worried about the fact that I had no close women friends.

"I've nothing in common with them, June," I reminded him.

"You could try harder," he said. "It wouldn't hurt you to come into town every other week or so for coffee and a little gossip."

"There's no time."

"Go on," he said with a smile. "I'll be right here if you need me."

I felt a little surge of panic. Suddenly I wanted to be home, listening to Lord Tom's stories or drawing relics. I thought of her in that trunk, the lid closed, and I couldn't breathe; I felt suffocated and alone and it was a moment before I realized that I wasn't the mummy, that I was alive, and there was no reason to feel trapped or alone, not here. These women were nothing to fear.

As I approached, Jane Mannering looked up with a friendly and welcoming smile that warmed me. Junius was right; it wouldn't hurt me to try harder. "Leonie! How nice to see you. And here with Junius's son too. What a surprise *that* was."

There were questions in every word, though she was too polite to just ask for the story.

I rewarded her with at least a part of it. "He lives in San Francisco. It was nice that he decided to pay a visit."

"What a handsome young man," Elizabeth Jansen said.

I nodded. "He takes after his father."

Elizabeth laughed. "Oh, he does indeed. And he's as charming as Junius too. Don't you think so, Mattie?"

"Oh yes," Mattie Jansen—Elizabeth's sister-in-law—said.

Elizabeth said, "I remember the first time I danced with June. He was so sweet. I was blushing and he teased me, but he knew how to flatter."

Jane laughed. "I remember. He could have charmed the skin off a rattlesnake."

"Well, his son looks to be no different," Mattie said. "Junius must be proud. And the boy's mother, of course."

Whoever she is. Not you. I thought I saw pity in her expression, and all I could do was pretend not to see it.

"Unfortunately, Daniel's mother has passed," I said.

They all tsked in sympathy. Then Jane said, "You'll be going to Charlotte Thomas's tea for the minister, won't you, Leonie? In Oysterville, remember? At the church?"

I thought of what Junius had said, and knew I should say yes. There was no reason not to say yes, and I had opened my mouth to say it when Mattie said suddenly, "Oh! There goes Johnny again in the beer—" and dashed off after her young son.

Jane laughed. "I do grieve for Mattie. That boy will be the death of her."

"If she can keep him alive that long," Elizabeth agreed. "He's not afraid of anything. Honestly, he could give a bit of that fearlessness to Sarah. She stammers at her own shadow."

"I just read of a cure for that," Jane said, and they were off, talking about their children and every latest trouble with them. Lost stockings and playing in mud puddles and eating too much pie and whether the teacher was lax with discipline. The talk I'd dreaded, the talk that kept me an outcast, though I knew they didn't mean to hurt me. It was just that I was something unnatural, a woman without children, and one more interested in dirty Indian relics than in ministers or teas or schools. We had nothing in common, as I'd told Junius, and I didn't know how to bridge the gap between us, or even if I should. How could I bear being around women whose whole lives revolved around their children? That melancholy I'd pushed away eased back, their laughter and confidences only feeding it, and desperately I glanced around, looking for relief—

And saw the widow Kafkis standing near the entrance of the common room, staring at me with the dark, unfathomable eyes of my dream.

I froze, startled. Bibi had never been to one of these dances before. That she was here was more than strange. I thought of the bracelet sitting in the horn bowl on my dresser, her warnings.

She motioned for me to come to her, and I was so surprised I started to go.

But Jane stopped me. "Oh, I'm so sorry, Leonie," and when I looked at her, her smile was soft; I saw that pity I'd expected. "Here we are, talking about things that must just bore you silly. Please forgive us."

Her kindness was genuine, yet no less humiliating for it. I gave them a quick, forced smile. "I really must go. It was so good to see you all," and then I was off before they could stop me again, relieved to escape them and their talk.

But that relief fled as I fought my way through the dancers to the edge of the floor and saw Bibi's smile, which was knowing and a little wicked.

I said, "I'm surprised to see you, Bibi. I hope you've come about trading the Duke's canoe. I'll tell you what: why don't you just say what you want for it, and I'll see what I can do?"

Her gaze fell to my wrist. "You don't wear it."

"Bibi—"

"You must wear it," she insisted.

"It's very pretty, Bibi, but I'm in water half the day. I don't want to ruin it—"

"*Kimtah kloshe. Mika kumtux alki.*"

The music started up again; I had to shout. "What's not good? What will I understand later?"

"You must wear it," she repeated. "*Mika hyas ticky pe mika halo ikta iskum kumtux.*" *You need it or you will learn nothing.*

"I don't understand," I said. "What am I to learn?"

She grabbed my wrist, circling it with her thick fingers, drawing me close enough that I smelled the coffee and tobacco on her breath. "She wants you, eh? You do this." Before I could reply, she went very still. She looked past me. "Who is he?"

I glanced over my shoulder, but I knew before I saw Daniel across the room, watching us, whom she meant. "Junius's *tenas.* His name is Daniel."

Bibi nodded in an odd, self-satisfied way. Her fingers tightened about my wrist. "You wear it. *Hyas wake hehe witka yaka how nah. Pe mika sick tumtum.*" *Very important now he is here. Or you will regret it.*

"Now that Daniel's here? What's he to do with it?"

She only gave me that implacable glance.

"I've had enough of this, Bibi." I yanked my arm away, rubbing at the impression her touch left behind, trying to erase it, unsettled. Her warnings eerily echoed Lord Tom's and Junius's, and I was coming to feel I'd made a terrible mistake in asking Daniel to stay.

But there was no such thing as bad luck, and these warnings and predictions were nothing more than silly superstition, nothing but the messy fancies I'd been warned against my entire life. There was no *proof* of such things as angry spirits, and no bracelet could protect me from a young man's vengeance—assuming it was even what he intended.

"You will wear the bracelet?" Bibi asked.

"Thank you for the warning," I said stiffly. I turned to go.

"*Mika hyas ticky*," she said.

You need it.

But I had heard enough of things I must and must not do, and I left her without another word. When I looked back over my shoulder, she was gone, either melted into the crowd or gone from the dance hall completely, which was what I preferred, though the discomfort she'd left in her wake stayed with me as George Bannock corralled me for a dance, and I could not find the pleasure I usually felt. Instead I felt as I had in my dream—colors not quite right, and the world beyond the dance floor shifting and changing, nothing quite familiar, and the fear I'd awakened with this morning hovered, waiting, the dread come alive.

Lord Tom was falling-down drunk when we rescued him from the porch. He'd lost his English almost completely—either that or he was slurring so badly it was incoherent, though it sounded more like garbled jargon to me. Junius put Lord Tom's arm over his shoulders and lugged him stumbling through the mud to the beach while Daniel and I followed behind. Daniel was quiet, not commenting on Tom's inebriated state, though I supposed there was not much to comment on. As Papa often said, drunk Indians were hardly a rarity.

It was after midnight when we got to the beach and the plunger. The air was cool, tinged with rain, though it was more mist than anything else, and the heavy clouds scudded over the moon and then broke to reveal it again, from darkness to blue light and back again within moments.

The tide was in, so the boat was floating and we had to walk in water up to our knees to get to it—freezing cold, but it felt good on my feet, which were hot and swollen from dancing. Junius said to Daniel, "I'll need your help, boy, to get him in," and the two of them wrestled Lord Tom into the boat. He fell onto the tarp over the oysters, and I winced, thinking of how many shells he'd undoubtedly broken. He passed out almost immediately after. The dance broke up in the distance, the night punctuated with whoops and yells and a celebratory gunshot.

We kept a lamp in the plunger, which Junius lit, and before long we were on our way, cutting through the darkness with the lamp hanging from a hook on the mast, sending a faint glow onto the bay, mostly making it look dark as pitch. The only sounds were the gurgling hiss of the water peeling back from the bow and the rasp of Lord Tom's snores. We'd made this trip at night a hundred times before, and both Junius and I knew the bay well. He didn't need anyone's help to manage it, so there was nothing to do but keep watch. The sense of disquiet I'd felt since talking to Bibi only intensified here, on the nearly silent water, with the moon suddenly making the shadows hard-edged and cold before it disappeared again. I shivered a little, wrapping my arms around me.

"So you have a good talk with the other girls?" Junius asked me.

I glanced at him in surprise. I'd already forgotten it. "There's a tea for the pastor in Oysterville next week."

"The pastor? You should go."

"I haven't decided yet if I will."

"Hmmm. Jack Boone told me tonight about a collection that might be for sale over there," Junius said. "I thought I'd go look into it tomorrow—unless Bibi was talking about trading the canoe?"

Of course he'd seen me with her. I found myself hesitating to explain, and not just because I'd failed to get what he wanted— though I'd been too unsettled to really try. I both wanted his confident dismissal of *that Siwash nonsense* and felt that such a reaction was somehow...wrong. I glanced at Daniel, who sat across from me now that Lord Tom was snoring in the hold, and I realized he, too, was waiting for my answer. I remembered how he'd been watching me speak to Bibi. I remembered her warnings about him. *Very important now he is here,* and I wondered how I could say that, how I could tell Junius that the widow agreed with him about his son while that son sat listening.

"It was about the bracelet," I said finally.

Junius looked confused. "Bracelet?"

"The one she gave me the last time I saw her. Remember? That bit of twine?"

"Oh, yes. What was that about? Some charm, wasn't it? Something about a dream and the mummy."

"Yes. Bibi wanted to be certain I wore it."

"Protection talisman, is it?"

I glanced at Daniel. His watching was so intent and careful that I had to look away, over the side of the boat, into the water foaming back from the bow, pale in the darkness. "Yes, I suppose."

"More Siwash nonsense," Junius said with a disappointed sigh. "But you should wear the thing the next time we're in town, Lea. Perhaps it will soften her toward trading. I need that canoe—and soon. Otherwise..." He let the words fall; I knew what he didn't say. I should have forced things with Bibi. Next time, I would not let her distract me.

We fell into silence. The breeze was light and steady; the sail fluffed, and Junius tightened the line, and we picked up speed again. Then he said, "Did you enjoy yourself tonight, boy?"

His voice was stiff; I felt his effort in it, and I knew he did it for me.

"Well enough," Daniel said.

"Everyone seemed to take to you. The women especially. I've never seen so many worried husbands."

"They hardly need to worry."

"I suppose not, if you've a girl back home. Leonie tells me you do."

Daniel tensed. "Yes."

Irritably, Junius said, "You'll have to help me out a bit, boy. I'm trying to make conversation."

"What have the two of us to talk about?"

Junius threw me a look and settled back into the seat as if he'd made his effort and meant not to make another, and I searched my own mind for something to say and found nothing, because the only things I could hear were Bibi's words and Junius's warnings, and I wanted to ignore them. I wanted to be charitable, to give Daniel a chance to prove himself.

But just then the moon emerged again, and I was drawn to looking at him as if the moon willed it, so I saw him change within its light, pale blue and white and black, full of sharp edges, and it was as if it illuminated something within him, and it felt dangerous and frightening.

Bad luck.

I turned away quickly, back to the water, letting the silence grow, letting it have sway, and I did not look back again, not until we rounded the point and I knew the mouth of the Querquelin was near. But now the moon had retreated and Daniel looked only like any other man, tired and slumping in his seat, half-softened by shadow and the pale yellow light of the lamp hung on the mast, and I was embarrassed at how well Bibi's words had snuck into me.

It seemed a long time before we arrived home, the silence between us tense, punctuated only by Lord Tom's snores. By the time we reached the shore I wanted only to be away from all of them, to put an end to the night. I got out and moved ahead, letting father and son manage Lord Tom, striding through the darkness, tired and mindless and feeling my own dream in pursuit, hiding in the shadows, breathing, waiting—

I stopped in confusion, glancing about, trying to get my bearings, realizing that in my hurry I had gone right past the house. I was at the entrance of the barn, and the inside was dark as pitch, the trunk a deeper darkness within it, and I could feel her there as if she had called me.

"Lea! What are you doing?" Junius's call roused me almost painfully.

I shook my head, trying to clear it, and called back, "Nothing! I'm coming!" I turned and walked away from the barn, stumbling exhaustedly over the salt marsh as I made my way slowly back to the house.

CHAPTER 7

I HAD ANOTHER BADLY UNSETTLED NIGHT. I DREAMED again about the basket rolling and rolling, the berries spilling, and her unblinking, terrible gaze. When I woke, I was afraid to go back to sleep, so instead I lay staring into the darkness, tracking the night as it inched toward dawn. The horizon had barely lightened by the time I got out of bed. I milked the cow and made breakfast, rushing through it, wanting only to get to the barn and her, but before I could, I heard footsteps on the stairs. I thought it was Junius—I would never get out there quickly enough now—and was immediately annoyed, even more so when I realized it was Daniel. He looked soft with morning, young and almost sweet, even pretty. His hair was tousled, his shirt untucked and hanging to his thighs, and he was stocking-footed. When he saw me, he paused.

I motioned to the table and rose. "Good morning. Have some breakfast. Would you like coffee?"

He stopped me with a gesture. "I can get it," he said, going to the stove, pouring his coffee, getting the mush, sitting down. I watched as he doctored the cornmeal with a large hunk of butter, jam *and* syrup, no milk.

He ate slowly and thoughtfully, sipping his coffee in silence, as if I were not there. I'd nearly decided to leave him to himself when he said, "What did she really say to you last night? That Indian woman?"

Whatever I had expected, this was not it. "What?"

"What did she say?"

"I told you already. She wanted to talk to me about a bracelet she gave me a few weeks ago. A sort of Indian charm, like a rabbit's foot, or a four-leaf clover. For good luck."

"Yes, that's what you told my father," he said. "But you didn't tell him the truth, did you? Why was that?"

I was flabbergasted. "Why would you say such a thing? Of course I told him the truth."

He didn't shift his gaze from mine. "I was watching you last night when you were talking with her. You seemed... dismayed."

"You were across the room. How could you possibly have seen anything?"

"Were you talking about me?"

I tried to laugh—it sounded hollow and unconvincing even to myself. "What makes you think we would talk about you?"

He raised a brow. "I felt my ears burning, how else? And then, of course, you gave it away when you both turned to look at me."

I said, "She asked who you were, that was all."

"And it distressed you to tell her I was your stepson?"

"That wasn't what distressed me."

"So something *did* distress you."

I glared at him. "No. It was no more than I said last night, Daniel. She wanted me to wear the bracelet. She wanted to know who you were. Why would either of those things distress me?"

"I don't know," he said calmly. He toyed with his spoon, but he didn't take his eyes from me, and I felt again that disconcerting fear from last night, when the moonlight had hit him so oddly and I'd felt there was something hidden in him, something of which to be wary.

Daniel trailed his spoon through the pale yellow mush, making red ribbons of the jam and glistening tracks of sorghum, raising steam. "Do you know what interests me most? That he didn't notice. You've been together twenty years and he didn't notice you were lying."

"That's easy to explain. He didn't notice because I wasn't."

"Or perhaps it's only that it's a habit. I mean, he was already an old man when he married you, and you were just a girl. What could you have had in common, really? Why, he probably hardly listened to you at all."

I clenched my cup hard in my hand. "That isn't how it was."

"Except when it came to some things, I would think," he went on. "Then my guess is he was all ears. Bedtime, for example."

I stared at him in disbelief and anger. "How dare you—"

I heard the telltale squeak of my bedroom door upstairs, and I choked back the rest of the words, my anger fading in sudden guilt as I remembered the reasons Daniel had to be angry, the reasons he obviously wanted to punish me.

I heard Junius's footsteps, and I looked down into my bowl, trying to tame my emotions.

Junius said, "Good morning," as he came into the kitchen. "How companionable you both look. What gets you up so early this morning, boy?"

"A woodpecker," Daniel said, as easily as if we *had* just been as companionable as Junius said. "At least that's what I think it was. In those trees just beyond."

Junius came over, leaning to kiss the top of my head before he went to the stove, and I was still disconcerted. He didn't seem to notice. I was grateful for that but at the same time it needled me to know that Daniel would see it too, and it would prove his words even more right than they already were. Because I *had* lied to Junius about my conversation with Bibi, and June hadn't realized it, and I was unsettled by his son's sharp-eyed observation.

I rose, taking up my bowl, only half-empty, and my coffee cup, putting them in the wash barrel.

Junius took his breakfast and sat down. "I thought I'd go over to Oysterville after I unload the oysters. Look into that collection Boone was talking about last night. I'll need your help, boy. Lord Tom's still sleeping off the whiskey."

Daniel said, "I'd hoped to take another look at that mummy today. Maybe even lend a hand with it."

I glanced quickly at him. "Lend a hand? How? What do you know about mummies?"

He shrugged. "Nothing really. But I thought I could take notes for you. You'll be doing measurements, won't you? Or have you already measured the skull?"

Again, I found myself discomfited. "Not yet. I thought you said you knew nothing about ethnology."

"I don't, but isn't that the usual procedure? I've read about craniometry, just like everyone else."

Junius laughed. "Like everyone else? I'd forgotten what a store your mother set by education."

"Not that it mattered, given that I had to quit school to work," Daniel said dryly.

Junius seemed unmoved, and I wondered if I was the only one who felt the guilt Daniel meant us to feel. I turned back to the wash barrel. "I'll be fine working alone. I'll let you know what I discover."

"We'll be back before nightfall. If Lea's still at it, you can help her then," Junius said.

I set the dishes to dry and untied my apron, hanging it on the nail by the sink. "I suppose I'd best get to it," I said, trying not to look as anxious to flee the kitchen as I felt.

Quickly I grabbed my notebook and pencil, put on my coat and boots and went to the barn. The key to the trunk was still in my pocket. I took the lantern from its nail and lit it, and then I opened the trunk. *At last.* Her presence enveloped me, bringing with it urgency—that push to find the answers, that sense that I somehow *needed* them. The lamplight played over the mummy's skin; I had that strange notion of flickering movement, a held breath ready to exhale. I put the lamp onto the board of the saw-horse table and then I lifted out the mummy, laying her on the table, pulling the notebook and pencil from my pocket, opening to the page where my notes ended.

And once again, the urge to touch her was impossible to resist. I laid my hand upon her hair, coarse and thick and dry as straw. I parted it, looking at the scalp, searching for injuries, telltale bumps, obvious discolorations that might be unhealed bruises. In my hurry to leave the house I had forgotten the meas- uring tape. By now Junius and Daniel would be gone, but I found myself strangely reluctant to go get it, as if a cranial measure- ment might tell me something I didn't want to know. If she were Caucasoid, Junius would be pleased, but if the measurements said she was Indian, then Junius's theory that she belonged to a more advanced race would be disproved. Unless…she was both Indian *and* from a more advanced culture.

I heard my father's voice in my head. *Impossible.* And Junius's. *An advanced Indian culture? Are you mad, Lea?* They were right, of course. The idea was ridiculous. I would be laughed out of scientific circles if I dared suggest it. But I stared down at her thoughtfully, taking in the skillfully woven cloth, the leather headband decorated with broken porcupine quills, and my dream intruded: brown, sturdy ankles, a softly rounded cheek, hair rustling in a breeze as she lay on the riverbank before the fear had come and the shriveling began…

I shook away the thought and the shiver that came with it, but I couldn't help thinking how alive she'd been once, how she had moved as I moved, felt as I felt. Again, I heard myself whis- pering, "Who were you?"

No, Leonie. Be objective.

I took a deep breath and pulled the lamp closer. I ran my fingers over her skull, the rounded bone of her forehead, the ridge of her cheekbones, the hinge of her jaw, looking for something—I wasn't certain what. Anything, I supposed. Anything that gave me answers, and touching her this way seemed right, as if I were being somehow led to it.

I slipped behind the dried shell of her ear, and that was when I felt it. A cut of some kind, a...rut. Narrow and faint. I paused in surprise, and then carefully, I felt again. I ran my fingers over it, trying to determine where it ended, but it didn't. It kept going, beneath her jaw, her chin, a line that stretched from ear to ear. A slit throat, I thought, and my fingers trembled when I drew them away, when I brought the lamp closer to see what I had not seen before. It was too narrow; a thin cut. This was no slit throat, no knife wound. The light played over her skin, making shadows beneath her jaw that loomed large. I cursed beneath my breath and angled the lamp again, and it was then that I saw what I could not feel. A mark, a deep bruise beneath the mummified skin, something that had pressed so deeply into her throat it had left an abrasion.

She'd been garroted.

I drew back, my own throat tightening, feeling again as if I were being watched. I glanced over my shoulder—no one, nothing, and yet the feeling didn't go away. I heard Lord Tom's words again. His insistence that she had a restless spirit. One that meant harm. It made sense now, in a way, his superstition at last supported by...well, if not reason, then at least motive. This had been murder, and, if one believed ghost stories, murder begat vengeful spirits.

But he could not have known the body was a murder victim. None of us had. Not until today.

I shook away my unease and picked up the notebook. I wrote: *strangulation abrasion running from ear to ear. Bruising. Clearly intentional death. Sacrificial? Or criminal?* I felt suddenly out of my depth. I knew enough about sacrifice rituals to know there were things to look for. Leaves or something else chewed to bring on the narcotic trance and painlessness that most societies dealing in human sacrifice used. But I could not really know without cutting her open to study her stomach contents. It was what Baird and the museum would do. It was what any scientist would do. My father would not have hesitated.

I tried to ease the sudden lump in my throat. I drew back, studying her again, the fetal position, the slight forward tilt of her head that had hid the garroting wound so well. The way her arms were twined about knees pulled nearly to her chest. The position she'd held in the basket, trapped and suffocating while darkness pressed in and in and in…

I blinked, shuddering. No. That was only my imagination. *Facts, Leonie.* Determinedly I pushed aside her hair to see the back of her neck, to feel if the force of the strangulation had broken it. I traced from the knob on the back of her skull down the vertebrae. Her skin had shrunk to the bones, they were easy to feel, none broken that I could tell. So she'd suffocated, which would have been a hard death, perhaps one that involved struggle, unless her executioner had been kind and drugged her.

I looked for bruising, cuts, something to show whether she'd submitted quietly or fought. Now that I knew what I was looking for, I found those things easily. Discoloration on her wrists that could have been bruising. Tentatively, I pushed the skirt up over her legs as far as I could before her arms around her knees stopped me. Her legs were bare. I ran my fingers over the bony cap of her ankle, her sticklike calf. Nothing.

I hesitated, and then carefully I turned her onto the other side so she faced the open barn door. When I moved the lantern close I saw a discoloration on her wrist that matched the other, another on her elbow, one on her bared upper arm, just below the shoulder, where there were three small discolorations in a line like fingerprints. I set my own fingers to them. Whoever had held her had bigger hands than mine, but that she had been held, I didn't doubt. She had been held, and she had struggled. This had been no peaceful murder; she had not wanted to die nor accepted it. But that didn't mean it wasn't a sacrifice, only that it had not been kind.

I stepped away. Lord Tom's warnings, and Bibi's, seemed now to ring in my ears. I tried to ignore them and picked up the notebook again, writing down my observations, and then I felt again that prickling sense of being watched. I looked over my shoulder, into dim shadows filled with the familiar, hay and straw, barrels, a small garden plow. There was nothing else. No one there but her.

But the feeling would not go away, and with it came fear, the same fear from my dreams, time slipping away and waiting and horror...

She wants you. Why, I do not know, but it is you she wants.

I could not stay there another moment. I threw down the notebook and the pencil and hurried from the barn, and the feeling pursued me into the daylight, across the salt marsh, to the porch. It didn't ease until I was inside the house, and the door was closed, and I was leaning against it as if I'd been chased, my heart racing, my breath coming fast.

I pressed my palms flat against the door and pushed myself from it. I tried to laugh it away—hollow, too hearty, edged with the vestiges of my fear. "You're a fool, Leonie Russell," I said—aloud, though it only made me feel more absurd. And now I had left the mummy exposed in the barn, and I would have to turn around and put her in the trunk. I would have to go back.

But I could not make myself turn around. *A few more moments*, I told myself. Just until I had composed myself. And before I knew it, I was climbing the stairs to our bedroom. There was my dresser, with its little horn bowl, and without conscious thought, almost without volition, I dug through the buttons and hairpins until I found the abalone charms on a piece of store-bought twine. I picked it up, dangling it in my fingers, telling myself to put it down again. This was stupid. One of the most absurd things I'd ever done. There could be no magic in this. There was no danger and nothing to watch out for and there was no spirit troubling me.

But still I slid the bracelet on my wrist, and I tightened the knot to keep it there.

I was sitting at the kitchen table when Lord Tom came in through the back door. He looked wan and sick, his dark eyes bloodshot. I was mending instead of drawing or working on story trans-lations—the mummy had spooked me enough that I knew I shouldn't be listening to legends today. I'd gone back to the barn to lock her away. The feelings that had driven me out were gone, but I still felt uncomfortable over what had happened, though now I wondered just what *had* happened. I couldn't grasp it clearly; it seemed so unreal.

"You look terrible," I told him.

He said, "I feel sick."

"It's your own fault. You shouldn't drink so much."

He went to the stove and poured a cup of coffee, sitting at the table again. He glanced down at my wrist. I realized he was star-ing at Bibi's bracelet.

I pushed it beneath my sleeve, hiding it. "Junius thought it might make her happy if I wore it," I explained. "And maybe more inclined to trade."

"She is no *tomawanos* woman. *Halo latate.*"

"I know it's stupid. Still, I—"

"You should take it off. Throw it away, *okustee.*"

"Bibi's as full of nonsense as you are. Bad luck, *mesachie memelose*—"

"Why wear it, then?"

"I...I don't know. Except today I...*Tot*, I discovered how she died."

Lord Tom went so still he seemed to stop breathing.

I went on. "She was strangled. I don't know if it was sacrificial or not, but she struggled. It was...it was a very bad death."

He muttered something below his breath, though I couldn't understand the words.

I looked up at him. "How did you know...? Why were you so sure the spirit had a reason to be vengeful?"

He paused. "It is not good to disturb the dead."

"But she's so ancient—"

"It is best to leave such things alone. Rebury her, *okustee*. Don't trust *kamosuk* given by foolish women. Give the body peace."

I looked down at the twine peeking from my sleeve. "Bibi said that the spirit would not rest until she had what she wanted from me."

"*Okustee*—"

"And I can't rebury her, *tot*. I can't put a discovery this big back into the ground. You must know that. My father would be ashamed of me. I'd be ashamed of myself."

Lord Tom's upper lip thinned almost to invisibility, and I felt his disapproval like a heavy cloak. "It is bad to fight this, *okustee*. *Skookum tomawanos*. It will get worse until you bury her. More *dleams*. More bad luck."

I was surprised at his mention of my dream. Junius must have told him. And then I thought of today, of the menace that had me running, putting on the bracelet. I thought of Daniel—Junius's warnings and Bibi's, and my sense of him last night. *Bad luck*.

"I don't believe in bad luck, *tot*," I said firmly, as much for myself as for him.

He opened his mouth to say something, but just then there was a noise on the porch—Junius and Daniel returned. Junius had a heavy bag over his shoulder. As they came inside, he said, "We got it, Lea. The whole McKenna collection—or at least what he had left of it."

I forgot bad luck and everything else for the moment. "McKenna—you don't mean Robert McKenna? You didn't tell me it was *his* collection." Robert McKenna had made a trip to the Bela Coola years ago, and the rumor was that he'd returned with rare ceremonial masks.

"I didn't know myself," Junius said as he set the bag on the floor and pulled off his boots. "Not till we got there. He's fallen on some hard times."

Daniel closed the door behind them. "He was drunk. It looked to be a common thing."

"Alas, yes." Junius didn't sound the least bit sorry for it as he strode to the stove where there was a pot of oyster stew keeping warm. He ladled some into a bowl. "Sold his whacks to Crellin. Said he was leaving on the first schooner that would take him, but I doubt he'll be sober enough to recognize when that is." Junius gestured toward the bag. "Unfortunately, there's not much there worthwhile. But he did tell me the story of some settler who was in town a few weeks ago. Sanderson or something, up near Stony Point. I guess he'd found a cave full of relics. I thought per-haps we should go talk to him. Maybe tomorrow, if the weather holds." Junius motioned toward Daniel. "Come and eat, boy. I know you're hungry."

Obediently, Daniel did as his father asked. I watched Daniel surreptitiously, trying to read his mood, to discover how they'd got on during the day, if Junius had made any inroads with his son, if he'd even tried. But when Daniel caught me looking at him, I glanced quickly away again. My fingers crept to the twine about my wrist. When I realized it, I let it go.

"Don't you think we would already have heard of a cave like that?" I asked.

"Depends on how well it's hidden, and who doesn't want it to be found." Junius reached for the jar of pickles. He glanced to Lord Tom, who had moved with his cup of coffee to the rocker by the oil lamp. "You haven't even said hello, my friend. Should I take that to mean you've still got the cursed headache?"

Lord Tom glanced at me, and I looked away. He said, "White men's drink *hyas cultus*."

Junius laughed. "Just remember it's no good the next time we go into Bruceport."

He sank into a chair at the table, pushing his hand through his hair. He gave me a careful look and reached into his pocket, pulling out a folded piece of paper. "I had a letter from Baird today. I picked it up in town. They want Indian skulls and skeletons to be procured *without offense to the living*. Especially sugarloaf skulls."

I couldn't hide my repulsion. "Bodies?"

"Not bodies. Bones." He glanced at Lord Tom, who had gone still as stone. "Everyone's doing it, it seems. The prices they're offering are good: five dollars a skull and twenty for a skeleton."

"But...what are they doing with them?"

"Studying them," he said with a shrug. "They're scientific specimens of a dying people."

Lord Tom spat something—furiously angry and in Chinook.

Junius glared at him, saying sharply, "We're trying to preserve your heritage, if you'd but see it."

"Is that why you collect all this?" Daniel asked. "To save his people?"

"To save his *culture*," Junius answered. "His people are mostly gone already."

Lord Tom made a rude sound.

Junius ignored him, saying to Daniel, "All cultures evolved similarly—from savagery to civilization. Tom's people haven't evolved in a hundred years. They're still primitives. By studying them now, before they die out completely, and before their culture is completely corrupted by contact with settlers, we can gain an understanding of cultures that have already disappeared." He glanced again at Lord Tom, who was still bristling. "Dammit, Tom, your people are living fossils. Without us, without museums, there will be nothing to show you even existed."

"But we aren't going to dig up bodies, *tot*," I said quickly, aware of how avidly Daniel was watching us. "Are we, June?"

"It's a direct request," Junius said. "I can't just ignore it. And how would it look, Lea, if I was the only ethnologist in the area who refused? Collectors are crawling out of the woodwork. McKenna says there are some from Germany here, trading with the Bela Coola up north." He threw another glance at Lord Tom. "Baird would find someone else to give him what he wants. Twenty years of collecting would go up in smoke. But"—he took a deep breath and met my gaze steadily—"I suppose if we had something better to send…"

"No. No, June. You promised I could study her. You *promised*."

His lips tightened. "I know what I said, but this was before Baird's letter. If you won't send her, then we're going to have to do what he asks. I don't want to be digging up bones either, but we're going to have to give him something."

"The canoe. I'll talk to Bibi. I'll go tomorrow."

"A canoe isn't a skeleton. It isn't what he's asking for."

Desperately I rose, going to the bag he'd left on the floor. "Perhaps there's something in here that will work."

Junius snorted. "I don't think so. Those masks aren't secret society, no matter what McKenna said."

"Secret society?" Daniel asked.

"An elite group. They dealt in secret rituals. Like Freemasons," Junius explained. "Or the Knights Templar, I guess would be the closest thing. Very ceremonial."

"And hard relics to get," I said, digging through the bag, pulling out two masks—one a thunderbird and one a raven, with articulated mouths, painted in reds, blacks, and whites. But Junius was right; they were nothing special. "Secret society relics belong to the whole clan. No one is authorized to sell them."

"You mean these are stolen?" Daniel asked, nodding toward the masks.

I shook my head. "Not these. McKenna talked a lot about how he'd managed to get secret society masks, but that's not what these are. I suppose he must have had some others."

"How would he have gotten them if no one could sell?"

"Just because you're not *supposed* to sell doesn't mean they don't. There's always someone willing, you just have to find him. Maybe he's just converted to Christianity. Maybe he's run out of money or didn't keep enough food for the winter. Men like that aren't hard to ferret out."

Junius said, "When you see a weakness, it's no crime to exploit it."

"Is that how you ended up with those? Exploiting weaknesses?" Daniel pointed to the wall, to the Bela Coola masks that hung there.

"My father brought those back from the northern islands," I said. "I don't know how he got them. He wouldn't allow me to go with him."

"Are they secret society?"

"He said they were."

"Why aren't they in a museum? Aren't they worth anything?"

"They're worth a great deal," I said quietly. "But I won't sell them. They were the last things he brought back. His last trip."

"There you are, boy," Junius put in. "You're looking at the best trader on the bay, and she's sentimental as any woman."

"It's more than sentiment," I said.

"You like them," Daniel said.

I looked at him, searching for mockery, but his tone was matter-of-fact and I heard no sarcasm. I nodded. "Yes, I do. They're beautiful in their way. So…fierce."

Daniel's eyes narrowed as he looked at them. I knew what he would say, what everyone said, even Junius. That they were primitive and barbaric, unsettling.

But his voice fell to a murmur as he quoted, "'Tell that its sculptor well those passions read, which yet survive, stamped on these lifeless things.'"

And that astonished me. That so few words explained something I had never been able to, the way these masks held the spirits of their creators, how passion and belief, savagery and solace still lived within wood and bone and paint—and that *he*, this young, angry man who disliked me, should understand it, was more than I expected. "What did you say?"

"It's part of a poem," he said. "'Ozymandias.' Shelley wrote it."

Junius sighed. "Your mother's influence, I see. She was reading poetry to you before you could speak."

Daniel glared at him. "It took the edge off hunger."

My husband ignored that. He looked wary as he fished a pickle from the jar on the table and jerked his head at me. "There's only one thing in there worth anything."

I went back to the bag, pulling out several decorated horn spoons, three etched silver bracelets that were worthless—pretty, but made for tourists, hammered from coins. I put them aside and pulled out the rest: two salmon hooks, a wooden bowl rimmed with the broad character lines of a raccoon, a blubber jar of watertight reeds, expertly woven. All good, but we'd sent dozens of things just like this before.

There was something else, deep within the bag. I reached in until I had my hand around it—hard and smooth. Another horn bowl, I thought, and pulled it out.

A skull.

I dropped it in shocked surprise. From behind me I heard Lord Tom's gasp.

"It's Chinook," Junius said calmly. "Sloped forehead, you see? Sugarloaf—just what Baird asked for." He looked at Lord Tom. "And I don't want to hear any bullshit about dead bodies or spirits coming to steal back their dead. This is science, pure and simple."

"Where could he have got it?" I asked.

"Stole it from a graveyard, most likely," Junius said matter-of-factly. "At least now it can go to a museum. A *museum*, Tom, where they'll take good care of it."

Lord Tom's expression had gone rigid, and my revulsion was almost as strong. I tried to tell myself Junius was right. It was only a relic, something worth studying from a dying culture, but—

"You don't mean to keep it in the house, at least," I said.

"I don't want it out in the rain until I can send it off," June said firmly. He rose and took his dishes to the sink. He raised his voice. "And it's about time his lordship got rid of those superstitions of his. We're living in the nineteenth century, Tom, in the event you hadn't noticed. No one believes in ghost stories anymore."

Lord Tom stood. Without a word, he went out the door, closing it hard behind him.

Junius sighed. "Damn him, anyway."

"You can't ask him to ignore what he believes," I said quietly.

"He's been with us more than twenty years. You'd think he'd be more white than Indian by now."

I said, "It's his blood, you know. I don't think you can unlearn things like that."

"Don't you?" Junius gave me a sharp look. "I guess there are a hundred Spencerians who agree with you. It doesn't matter. We need to find more skulls like that, and you know it, Lea. It's either that or your damned mummy. There's no canoe and nothing else worth sending, and this is *science*, for Christ's sake. Hell, they leave the bodies out in the open air in canoes. How much can they care? I'd think they would be relieved to have them out of the way."

"You don't believe that," I said.

He shrugged. "It's research. The Indians will be gone soon enough, but we can at least save something of them."

"I don't like the thought of robbing graveyards."

"What else were you doing when you dug up that mummy?"

I went quiet. I could not argue that.

"Sometimes we must all do things we don't like, Lea. For science. A body is a body. Even Lord Tom would admit the soul is gone. What does it matter whether the bones sit in the ground or in a museum? Your father would agree with me. You know that."

Yes, I did know it.

Junius's glance went to my wrist and he frowned. "I see you decided to wear the widow's bracelet."

I saw the way Daniel's gaze leaped to it as well.

I said, "*You* told me to placate her."

He exhaled and put a hand through his hair. "I guess I did. It's been a long day. I'm for bed. You coming?"

I said, "In a minute. Just let me put all this away."

Junius nodded, and then he turned and went up the stairs. I began putting the collection back in the bag, the horn bowls first. At the table, Daniel was quiet and still.

"You aren't tired as well?" I asked him.

"I've a letter still to write."

"To your fiancée?"

He nodded.

I picked up the raven mask, waggling the articulated jaw, the long beak opening and closing and I found myself saying, "What you said about these…that quote…it was perfect."

"I didn't write it."

"But you knew it. You understood enough to come to it."

"That's what comes of an educated mother." He laughed a little self-deprecatingly.

Then he said, "Why did you marry him?"

The question didn't surprise me. I suppose I'd even been waiting for it. "I liked him. He was a good man."

"But you knew he was already married."

I nodded, feeling guilty again. "He said he would take care of that. I believed him. And I knew he would take care of me. Of this land."

"This land?" Daniel's gaze sharpened.

"It was mine. My father's."

"How much is there?"

"A section. And the whacks—Papa's eight acres of oysters."

"And a pretty little seventeen-year-old on top of it." Daniel made a sound of disgust.

"It wasn't like that," I said quickly. "It was my father who wanted it."

"Your father?"

I turned back to the bag. I picked up one of the spoons, twirling it in my fingers. "He was dying. He was afraid to leave me alone. He wanted...Well, June and Papa were friends, and...my father asked Junius to marry me. To take care of me."

"And out of the goodness of his heart, he agreed."

"Yes." I looked at him. "Your father's an honorable man. I know you don't believe it, but it's true. He wanted to ease a dying man's worry. And then he kept the promise he made."

"But he broke another promise to keep it, didn't he?"

There was nothing to say to that. It was true. I reached for the other mask, the woven jar.

Daniel rose. "He was with my mother for seven years, and he was always itchy. That was what she used to say. That he had itchy feet. We moved nine times from the time I was born until he left for good."

I put the rest of the things in the bag. I felt the scratch of the rough twine about my wrist, the brush of abalone charms.

Daniel went on. "But you've kept him here for twenty years. What keeps a man like him for so long?"

"I don't know," I said. "He doesn't want to stay. He's always talking of moving on. But I don't want to go. So...love, maybe. Or loyalty."

"My guess is that it's something else," he said, and I looked at him, confused until I saw the frank appraisal in his gaze, until I understood his insinuation. He gave me a knowing smile. "So are you that good?"

It was a moment before I could speak, and by then, he was at the stairs. Sharply, I said, "Daniel," and when he stopped, looking over his shoulder at me, I matched his cruelty with mine. "You've a long way to go before you're half the man your father is."

He went still—for a bare moment, less, but long enough for me to think I'd wounded him—and then he turned back to the stairs and went up without a word.

CHAPTER 8

*T*HERE WAS THE RUSHING OF THE RIVER AND THE CAW OF *the seagulls and the chattering trill of squirrels. And then, breaking the noise of the world, was a quiet, "Please."*

Horror came with the word, with a gaze, weighting the air. I was only a yard from the river when I was caught. I struggled and fell to my knees and tried to crawl away, but the hands were too tight. I pried with my fingers, then something twisted at my throat and I couldn't breathe and I was nothing and my life was ending now, and I'd done nothing, been nothing. My hands were shriveling, drying up, losing strength, crumbling. No, no, no, not this. Please not this—

I was hardly aware of waking, only that I was in bed, sweating in the cold, tears streaming over my cheeks to pool in my ears. I reached for Junius, searching for comfort. But he was gone, and beyond the curtains it was morning.

I rose quickly, going to the washbasin, splashing cold water onto my face, feeling it trickle into my hair, to my scalp, and I kept doing it until my trembling stilled, until my heart steadied, and my horror eased into something less threatening—only uneasiness. I put up my hair and dressed, uncertain whether I was glad Junius was already gone to the whacks or whether

I wanted him and his calm certainty. And then was surprised when I went downstairs to find him still there, sitting in silence at the table with Daniel, and I remembered yesterday, the skulls and Baird's letter and the way Junius's son had insulted me, and how I'd insulted him back, and I was exhausted already.

I said, "I thought you'd gone out to the whacks."

Daniel looked up; deliberately I avoided his glance.

Junius took a sip of coffee and shook his head. "Don't you remember what I told you last night about that settler over at Stony Point? I want to talk to him today. So eat something and come on."

"But the mummy—"

"Will wait." Junius's voice was firm. "You're coming with us."

A little desperately, I said, "Take Lord Tom."

"He's still not speaking to me, at least not this morning. And you know how he feels about Stony Point. He won't go near it. And Lea, I think it'd be a good idea for you to get away from the mummy for a day. Think about something else for a change."

"Junius, no—"

"You're coming." Junius rose and put his dishes in the sink. "No arguments."

I let my further protests die on my tongue. I didn't know how to explain why I wanted so badly to stay without sounding half-mad. Junius would only call me superstitious and sentimental, and how could I say he was wrong? My dream still troubled, and—I glanced at the bracelet dangling on my wrist— along with yesterday's...what did one call it? An episode? A waking dream? Whatever it had been, I couldn't loose myself from the fear that had sent me running into the house. I needed desperately to restore my objectivity. A day away would be good, no matter that I felt uneasy at the thought, and impatient, time slipping away and nothing to show for it, nothing that belonged to me...

Enough. I was going.

Stony Point was only a mile or so from the claim, an easy walk along the beach when the tide was out, impossible when it was in, and the water came all the way up to the bluff. We took the canoe. Junius gave his son a paddle and he sat aft while Daniel sat in front, with me in between. Daniel picked up paddling so well he seemed almost born to it. His father's son indeed—the thought pricked; I felt even worse for the insult I'd given him last night. Though Daniel had been unfair in his appraisal of me, I understood he was angry, and he had a right to be. If I meant to atone for my part in keeping father and son apart, I had to forget what he'd said; I had to apologize. It didn't mean that I shouldn't also be wary of him—Junius was right in that. But I could be wary and still be kind.

The sky was broken clouds, the morning streaming through in golden bursts, reflecting off the water so that it was almost blinding, golden sheets crowded with the tiny black figures of ducks, brants, and Canada geese, and a line of brown pelicans that flew back and forth, scattering seagulls that cawed raucously as we passed. It was cold, and my hands were chilled even through my heavy gloves.

I spotted the narrow strip of land well before we got there, the boulders of black rock jutting out three or four hundred yards into the bay, huge, bare stones piled into a rocky base at the foot of a cliff that was about sixty feet high and probably not ten yards wide, crowned thickly with spruce and undergrowth of vine maple and salal.

Daniel laid aside his paddle and jumped out when we came close, pulling the canoe onto the rocks. He offered a hand to me, meeting my gaze deliberately as he did so, as if he meant to communicate that he wasn't angry, which reassured me as I let him help me from the canoe. Perhaps my apology would not be so difficult.

"McKenna said the cabin was about half a mile in," Junius said, stepping onto the rocks and helping Daniel bring the canoe farther ashore. He stood, his hands on his hips, staring up at the precipitous cliff. "Your father found relics here once, you know. Beads. A few brass bracelets—the ones we sent off to Baird earlier in the year for the exhibit."

I'd never heard Papa mention that. "He found them *here*?"

"Along with a few other things."

"What other things?"

Junius looked thoughtful. "There's a reason the Indians call this place sacred."

I didn't like his thoughtfulness, or the foreboding that struck me at his words. Beads. Brass bracelets. The kinds of things Indians left with their dead.

But I said nothing as we followed Junius to the path that led from the bay. It was narrow and tangled with wild currant and brambles, salmonberry and ferns, and Junius took the hatchet from his belt and hacked our way past the cliff, deeper into the forest. Daniel followed behind, and I forgot Junius's words in my anxiety to find a moment to apologize when Junius wouldn't hear. But before I got the opportunity, I heard Daniel's soft, "Leonie."

Junius was a short way ahead. I paused, looking over my shoulder as Daniel came up beside me and said, "I wanted to apologize for last night."

"As do I," I said quickly, relieved. "I shouldn't have said what I did. I had no right."

"I meant to be cruel," he admitted. "I was angry, and I'm not very good at holding my tongue. I never have been. A failing, my mother often said. Regardless, you've been very...obliging, and you don't have to be. I'm not certain I wouldn't have sent me back into the wilderness. And I've repaid your hospitality with insults, which is unforgivable."

"I think you have plenty of reason to be angry," I said.

"Perhaps." Daniel glanced ahead, to where Junius hacked his way through the underbrush. "I don't agree with you about my father, that's certain. But that's no excuse. He's the one at fault."

"I knew he had a wife," I protested.

"But it's obvious you knew nothing of me. You were a child. I'm sorry I said those things."

"Leonie! Daniel! Keep up!" Junius called back.

Daniel exhaled and looked at me, waiting.

I said, "Shall we just call it a misunderstanding and leave it at that?"

His smile was small, self-deprecating, but it was a smile, and clearly he was as relieved as I. He nodded, and then glanced ahead. "Did you tell him?"

"It was between you and me," I said. "There was no reason for him to know."

Daniel hesitated. "Something else to thank you for, I think. He wouldn't have liked it."

"No." So he *did* want a relationship with his father after all. It was the first indication I'd seen. It made me feel more charitable—perhaps Junius was wrong about him. "But there's no harm done. Come, let's catch up."

I turned to follow Junius. The way grew steeper, into the hills that ringed the point, and we struggled past cedar and alder and salmonberry until suddenly there was no more need to make a path, because one was already there. We broke through the forest and into a roughly cleared spot—still dotted with stumps and brown and rotting pumpkin and squash vines. The cabin was rough as well, split logs and zinc plates, with stacked wood beneath the eaves, and a splitting stump with an ax planted firmly in the middle of it. Smoke curled from the chimney, catching in the branches of the trees above.

"Hey there!" Junius called out. "Sanderson!"

The door opened, revealing a short, barrel-chested man with a thick beard and a bald head. He peered at us curiously as we approached, hooking his thumb in his suspenders.

"Junius Russell," Junius said, taking two long strides to reach him, holding out his hand. "This is my wife, Leonie, and my son, Daniel. We live just south of here. On the Mouse."

"Evan Sanderson," said the man, shaking Junius's hand, and then Daniel's, acknowledging me with a polite nod. He motioned us inside. "Good to meet you, neighbor. What brings you out here?"

The cabin was small, a bed built into the far wall and covered with furs, a table built into the side, a fireplace with a poor draft, over which hung a kettle. The table was littered with traps. There was a loft above, a ladder to reach it, and walls studded with hooks from which dangled leather straps and long links of traps and tools I didn't know. The room smelled of a gamy kind of oil and smoke.

Junius said, "I spoke with Robert McKenna yesterday at Oysterville. He mentioned you were out here. I was surprised. Hadn't heard of anyone settling near the point."

"Been here eight months or so," Sanderson said. Junius sat at the table. Daniel and I sat on the bed. Sanderson pulled up the rocking chair that had been before the hearth. "Can I offer you something? Coffee?"

Junius shook his head. "No, thank you."

"McKenna's a good man. Met him out of Astoria last year. Liked the drink a little too much, I recall."

"Still a fault." Junius leaned forward, resting his forearms on the table. "But he said something that intrigued me. That you'd seen a cave with Indian remains."

Sanderson regarded my husband thoughtfully. "You one of those bone collectors?"

"An ethnologist," Junius corrected.

Sanderson shrugged. "Yeah, I saw a cave like that a few seasons back. I was trapping near Toke's Point, back in the woods there along the river about...oh, maybe half a mile in, past these big rocks on shore. You know where I mean?"

Junius nodded. "I know the rocks."

"It started to rain and I was tired of being wet. Just stumbled upon it. Looked like nothing but moss-covered rocks from the outside, but there was an opening and I crawled inside. Wasn't until morning that I saw I'd been sleeping with skeletons." He shuddered. "Surprised I didn't have nightmares."

"What else was there? Besides skeletons? Anything?"

"Old pots, things like that. I didn't look too closely. But I did get this." He rose from the old rocker and came over to the bed, and Daniel and I moved aside so he could reach the trunk he'd stored beneath it. He dragged it out—like the one that held the mummy, it was a large Chinese camphor trunk that had once been a ubiquitous trade item among the Indians, this one painted bright red, studded with brass nails. He opened it, pushing aside blankets and clothing to pull something out.

A small basket woven of reeds in black and white.

The world dissolved around me. *My* basket. Tumbling down a hill, flashing in the sun, leaving behind a pool of berries red as blood, and someone watching, waiting. That terrible, hovering fear—a wave of nausea swept me. I pressed my hand to my mouth.

"Leonie? Lea, are you all right?"

Daniel's words seemed to come from far away. I blinked at him; he was frowning.

Junius was on his feet. "Lea, look at the pattern."

Daniel's frown deepened. His hand came to my arm as if he meant to anchor me, warm and solid when I felt as unsubstantial as smoke. "Leonie, what's wrong?"

I tried to find myself. I focused on his hand, the press of his fingers, until the world righted. It was all I could do to whisper, "I'm fine."

I saw he didn't believe me, but he pulled away. I felt cold, sick, and sad. Not myself at all.

"The basket's not even the best part," Sanderson was saying. He reached into it, taking out a stone knife bound to a cedar shank. He gave it to Junius before he sat again in the rocker.

Junius turned the knife in his hands. "You found this in the cave?"

"Most everything else was broken," Sanderson said. "Every pot had a hole in it."

"They do it on purpose," Junius said. "So no one will steal them."

"Well, they forgot to ruin that." Sanderson nodded toward the knife.

The basket seemed to waver when I looked at it, its edges fading, blurring, as if it couldn't quite keep to its lines, or didn't want to stay. My voice sounded curiously hoarse as I said, "Could I... could I hold it?"

Sanderson handed it to me, and the moment I took it, my dream swept back. Hot, dry grass beneath my bare feet, the smell of sun-warmed dirt. Berries spilling. Rolling and rolling—

Violently I shoved the basket at Daniel.

He caught it clumsily, saying in a low voice, "Are you certain you're all right? You look ready to swoon."

Junius said to Sanderson, "Do you think you can remember where that cave is well enough to draw a map?"

"Certain of it. God knows I won't forget it. Creepy place."

Junius pulled the leather-bound notebook he carried from his pocket, handing it to Sanderson, who opened it and began scrawling out a map. "From Toke's Point here, and then about half a mile due north. There's no path but for the one I made, which is probably gone by now." A few more quick lines, and then he handed it to Junius. "I'm warning you, it ain't a pleasant place."

Junius nodded and shoved the notebook and pencil back into his pocket. "Thank you. I appreciate it. Come on Lea, Daniel. We'll let our neighbor get back to things."

Sanderson reached to take the basket from Daniel, and suddenly I knew I had to have it. I didn't understand how it had come to be here, or why it had been in my dreams, but I knew it meant something. It had something to tell me. Something important.

"We'll give you three dollars for the knife and the basket," I told Sanderson.

"Three dollars?" he asked. He looked uncertain. "I don't know as I want to sell them."

I controlled my own desire with every ounce of strength I had. Trade was my talent, how to win from someone something they had no wish to relinquish, but I knew I wanted this too much, and I was afraid of making a mistake. The dream hovered, that basket called me like a siren. I wheedled, "What would you do with such things, Mr. Sanderson? Keep them in that trunk? My guess is that you could use a…a new pair of boots, maybe. Or a cooking pot. Three dollars will buy at least another trap."

He hesitated. It was all I could do not to give away how much I wanted it. I ignored Daniel's quiet watching, Junius's tension. I said, "How long have you had those things?"

"A few months."

"Have you had any reason to think them unlucky? Any bad dreams?" I was casting about, hoping to land on something, but I didn't expect it to stick. He'd spent the night in a cave with skeletons and felt no *tomawanos*. So I was surprised when he hesitated.

"A few," he said reluctantly.

I struggled to hide my relief and the triumph I knew was mine. Just like fishing with a Chinook salmon hook the way Lord Tom had taught me. All it took was patience. You waited in the shallows, unmoving, until the salmon came by, and then, one quick twist, and it was flopping and dying on the shore. "I see. You know, the Indians would say that the spirits want those things back. They'd say you'll have bad luck until you get rid of them."

"Then why do you want them?" he asked.

"For the museum. They ask me to get them relics, and that's what I do. I wouldn't keep them in the house if it were me."

He had taken back the knife from Junius, and now he stared at it. "You wouldn't?"

"A rational man doesn't believe in bad luck or spirits, but bad dreams...well, that's something else. Better safe than sorry, that's all I'm saying."

Sanderson frowned.

I rose, touching Daniel's shoulder so he did the same. "Well, you do as you wish. It's not my head the *memelose* are playing in." I did not intend to walk out of here without that basket, but I had to at least be ready to do it. People sensed uncertainty and reluctance. "We've kept you long enough, I think."

Junius rose as well. We'd played this game too often; he knew the moves as well as I.

"Thank you," he said. "And thank you again for the map."

Sanderson nodded, but his frown grew bigger, and he was staring at the knife in his hand, the basket. I was so close. One more step. *Give him enough time to think of what he's refusing. Walk to the door.* In moments, it would be mine.

If I'd just stepped to the door, he would have sold it to us. He would have been outside, following us, calling us back, before we'd gone three strides. Three dollars was a lot of money for a couple of mementos. But the moment I walked past that basket, my dream flashed back, and the urge to have it swept me like a storm, over-whelming. I did not even get another step before I said, "I'll give you five dollars for them, Mr. Sanderson. But that's my last offer."

I was horrified the moment I said it. I'd made the mistake I'd been afraid of. I'd revealed how much I wanted it. I'd given it worth. I saw the glint of knowledge in his eyes and the calcu-lations in his head, his realization that I was playing him, that the relics were worth more than I'd led him to believe. He didn't trust me now. There was no offer I could make that he would accept. And bone collectors, as he called us, were not so hard to find. He could sell the things to someone else.

Sanderson smiled. "I think I'll just hold on to them, if you don't mind."

It was gone, just like that. I was struck with horror and despair. I felt tears start at my eyes, and I hurried out so quickly I did not say good-bye. I was so angry and miserable that I was halfway down the path before I realized I'd left Junius and Daniel far behind me.

I leaned back against the rough bark of a cedar and waited for them to catch up, dashing the tears from my eyes, trying to regain my sanity. It was just a basket. It was like the one in my dream, but it couldn't possibly be the same one. I was an idiot, and *damn*, how could I have let it just slip away? How could I have been so stupid?

Junius came around the bend first, and when he saw me, he said, "Calmed down yet?"

"I'm sorry," I said, struggling for composure. "I ruined it."

"I was certain he would deal," Daniel said casually, but I saw the way he looked at me, his burning curiosity. He'd seen too much, I realized. My near swoon and how I'd wanted it. I felt vulnerable and off-balance.

"It's not often you play a hand so badly," Junius said. "What happened?"

I tried to laugh it off. "I…I can't explain it. I was fine and then I…then I wanted that basket so I couldn't think. It was so like hers."

"I was surprised to see that design," Junius admitted. "But the basket isn't what's important. It's where it came from that matters. If there are answers to the mummy to be found, it's the cave that will hold them. We'll find something there, Lea. Something better than a basket."

"I had him, too," I said, unable to let it go. "He was going to sell."

"It was one mistake. Now stop feeling sorry for yourself and come on. There's something else I want to do before it gets too late."

He started back down the path, plunging into underbrush. Daniel gave me a look I couldn't interpret, and then he turned to follow, and I went after, still feeling shaken at how I'd let it slip away.

I didn't notice how far we'd gone until we were back at Stony Point. Junius stood at the bottom of the cliff, looking up at it the same way he had when we'd come in, and I remembered what was undoubtedly up there, what I believed Junius meant to do.

There was a path that led from the beach, curving around, leading up to the promontory, and Junius followed it, motioning for Daniel and me to come as well. The path stopped after only a few yards, overgrown with brambles and wild currant. Junius seemed possessed by some excitement, a kind that filled me with dread, and I forgot about the basket when we reached the top and I saw the canoes—old and covered with moss, rotting on the ground, tangled with vines, fallen from the posts they'd once been mortised to—or removed from them. The Chinook put their dead in raised canoes, along with their possessions, for a year, after which they took down the bones and buried them. This had been an Indian graveyard like the *tenas memelose illahee* island between here and Bruceport, though I'd never known of it.

Junius stopped, breathing hard. "So your father was right. I'm surprised no one else has seen this."

My dread grew. "Perhaps they have," I said tightly. "And they decided to leave it be."

He moved awkwardly through the undergrowth to the nearest canoe. He grabbed hold of the side, which came away in his hands, the wood rotted through. He tossed it aside and put his boot against the rest, pushing a little as if he meant to test the strength of it. It crumbled as easily as an old fallen nurse log in a wet forest.

Junius cursed beneath his breath, leaning over, rifling over the ground. "More likely they did the same thing Teddy did and took whatever was worth taking. Only canoes here now, and they're too rotted to be much use."

Daniel came up beside me. "What is this place?"

"An Indian graveyard," I told him. "But it's old. It looks to have been abandoned for years. Lord Tom never said anything about it. I'd guess his people have forgotten everything about this place but that it's something to avoid."

Junius stepped to the next canoe, and the next, and I said, "There won't be any skeletons left here, June." I started toward him, and misstepped—a hill that wasn't a hill, collapsing beneath my boot, tangling my foot in vine. I stumbled, unable to catch myself, falling into wild currant.

Junius looked over his shoulder. "You all right?"

"Yes. Fine, dammit." I tried to rise, but the wild currant I grabbed broke away and whatever was beneath me crumbled. My hand went through it to my wrist; my fingers met something hard and smooth.

Daniel hurried over, hauling me easily to my feet, and it was only then that I saw what I'd stumbled over was another canoe, completely overgrown, rotting, collapsing beneath my feet.

"What's that?" Daniel knelt, grabbing the edge of the canoe, pulling it, and it broke into pieces and revealed another one, smaller, beneath, and my stomach turned, because as he pushed the pieces aside, we saw what the small canoe hid, what my hand had come upon: the creamy white of bone, two small skeletons, too small to be adults. The bodies of children, lying side by side, piles of beads gathered beneath their wrists and ankles, where the string that had held their bracelets had dissolved.

Daniel looked up at me. I saw the question in his gaze, and it took me a moment to realize what he was tacitly asking, but I paused too long, giving Junius enough time to notice how still we'd gone.

"What is it?" he asked, and then he was tromping over, and Daniel looked away from me just as Junius reached us and let out a low whistle. "Well, well, look at that. I guess not everything's gone, after all." He said to Daniel, "There are two bags in the canoe. Go get them, will you?"

Daniel didn't move. Again, he looked at me.

Sharply, I said, "Junius, no."

But my husband ignored me. He knelt beside Daniel, pushing aside the rotted wood to reveal the bodies more fully. "Go on, boy. Get the bags."

"They're children," Daniel said softly.

"Indian children," Junius corrected. "And they're going to Baird."

"You can't mean to take them," I protested.

Junius sat back on his heels. "Baird asked for these, Leonie."

I could only stare at him, horrified.

Junius's voice softened. "I don't like this any better than you do, but you know it must be done. Without us, they'll just rot away unnoticed. Everything we can learn from them will disappear. There's no room for sentiment in this. And we *need* them." He paused, his blue gaze hammering. "Baird will just find someone else to get him what he wants. Dammit, Lea, you can't have everything. We either send these or the mummy. Which is it going to be?"

I stared down at the bones. I felt Daniel watching me. Junius, waiting. And I knew my husband was right. This was science. These were no longer the bodies of children, but relics. We had an obligation to study them, to learn from them. We were the caretakers of a disappearing past. My father had believed that a sacred charge, and he'd raised me to think the same. This was *necessary*. What was it I had said to Lord Tom about the mummy—that the soul was gone? I wanted to believe that too. And this was no different.

Junius said, "I thought you were more a scientist than this. Your father would not have shirked it."

That was true. Just because my father had been here and taken only bracelets and beads did not mean he wouldn't have returned for bodies had it been asked of him. My sentimentality was a weakness. It made me feel as if all my study was only pretense. *What kind of scientist are you?*

"If you tell me we can send the mummy to Baird this week, I'll leave them," Junius said quietly.

But I could not do that either. I swallowed hard. "No. Go ahead. We'll send these."

"Good," Junius said briskly, and then to Daniel, "Get the bags."

I stepped back, and Daniel hurried back down the path, and Junius slid his hand along the elongated skulls, the sloped foreheads. "High caste, too. Baird will be ecstatic."

I said nothing. I left Junius there with the skeletons and went farther up the narrow precipice, to the edge, where I stood with my hand on a bent spruce and looked out onto the bay. The clouds had gathered more thickly now, there were no longer sunbreaks, and the water was deep gray and chopped, with little whitecaps. The wind blew tendrils of loosened hair about my face, and I pushed them aside. I watched the birds, the crows and the gulls and the pelicans—for how long I couldn't say—and tried not to think of what was going on behind me, because Junius was right. I shouldn't care. Knowledge was what mattered, and I had always believed that. What was happening to me, that a couple of dreams and a mummy had unsettled me so deeply?

I heard footsteps behind me, a rustling of the underbrush. Junius come to tell me he was finished. But it wasn't Junius who came up beside me to stand on the narrow promontory. It was Daniel.

"He says to tell you he's ready to go back," he said.

I nodded. But I didn't move.

He said, "It's beautiful up here."

"It's going to rain," I said.

Daniel said, "All you had to do was look away, you know. I would have pretended I hadn't seen them."

"I know."

"Then why didn't you, if you mind so much?"

"Because I *shouldn't* mind. Those are only bones. I've handled bones before."

"Human bones?"

I hesitated. Then I said, "No. But it shouldn't matter."

We were quiet for a moment. I listened to the wind, the slap of waves upon the rocks below, and he said, "Why did you want that basket? What was so important about it?"

I glanced at him. He was watching me carefully, as if he could read something in my face, as if he waited to catch me in a lie, and I was startled at the urge to tell him the truth. To say: *I saw it in a dream.* But it was too strange. It sounded absurd. It *was* absurd, and to tell him was even more so. So I said the lesser truth, "It had the same pattern as the one the mummy was buried in."

"Ah." He looked again out to the bay. "How badly do you want it?"

I laughed a little. "Too much so. But I suppose Junius is right. If there are answers, they'll be in the cave."

"If you want me to, I'll go back and get it for you." He didn't look at me, but I felt his tension, sharp and still.

"Sanderson won't sell it to any of us now."

"I don't mean to buy it."

I looked at him more carefully. "Then how—?"

"Do you want it or not?"

"But I…" Suddenly his meaning came clear. "You mean to… to steal it?"

He said nothing. His gaze settled on the horizon as if it were locked there.

I was startled. And alarmed at the ease with which he'd suggested it. Junius's words came back to me. *We don't know anything about him. Let's not assume he's trustworthy until he proves it.* I thought of Bibi's warnings, my own sense that he was bad luck, that there was something dangerous in him.

But then I thought of that basket in my hands. The dream. Answers waiting to be found.

My hair blew into my eyes. When I pushed it back, one of the charms of Bibi's bracelet snagged in a tendril as if to remind me forcibly of her words. *You will regret it now he is here.* I stared down at it, at the way the overcast light played upon the iridescence of the shell, green and blue, pink and silver. And I came to myself.

I said, "No." And then, because the dream lingered and I wanted that basket, and if Daniel was willing to take the risk for me, I was willing that he did, and that frightened me more than I could say, I said more strongly, "No. I don't know why you would think I could approve of such a thing."

His gaze caught mine and held. There was something in his that made me uncomfortable—again I felt he saw so much more than I wanted him to see—and I saw the challenge there and felt nervous and uncertain.

He smiled then. Very small, barely there, and looked away. "Actually, that wasn't what I meant to do. It's only that I think I could talk him round."

I knew it wasn't true, but it was a relief to accept the fiction, to pretend it was what he'd meant. "You really think you could?"

"I can be very persuasive when I want to be."

I thought of when we'd first met, the charming smile, the way he'd had those women in Bruceport eating from his hand. "Yes, I imagine so. I saw you at the dance. Honey to ants, your father said."

"Did he?"

"He said you were like your mother."

Daniel's expression shuttered. He turned to go back down the path. I watched him go, and I found myself wondering what had truly brought him here, what made the kind of man who would so willingly...*persuade*. I wondered what made him offer such a service to me, whom he'd made no secret of disliking, apology notwithstanding.

He glanced back over his shoulder. "You'd best come," he said. "Your husband is waiting."

There was nothing to do but follow.

CHAPTER 9

THE NEXT MORNING DAWNED COLD AND RAINING, TOO windy and wet to make the trip across the bay to Toke's Point, and Junius sat at the table brooding over it while he mended a tear in his boot with heavy thread and a thick, curved needle. The two of us were alone; Lord Tom had not yet come in for breakfast, and Daniel was apparently still asleep.

"I told you what McKenna said about those German collectors up north." Junius spoke lightly, but I tensed, already knowing where this would lead, where it had led a hundred times before.

"Yes," I said warily.

"Maybe we should go too. Sell the claim and the whacks. Try something new for a change." He glanced up at me, a soft plea in his eyes.

But I'd seen that expression so often it only left me weary. "Junius—"

"Yes, I know." He sighed. "You don't want to go. Well, you can't blame a man for trying."

No, I couldn't, though his restlessness had always troubled me. *Itchy feet,* as Daniel had said. I had always thought that Junius's continuing to stay in a place he hated was evidence of how much he loved me. But now I heard Daniel's voice, a needling whisper, *"My guess is that it's something else..."*

I pushed the thought away. It had been an insult only, meant to wound. There was no truth in it.

Junius said, "I need to get something off to Baird this week, though I'd prefer to wait to see if there's something in that cave."

"Sanderson said there were only broken pots," I told him, relieved at the change in subject.

"And *skeletons*," he amended. "We've already got the two, and that skull. I don't know if that's enough to impress him. It would be better to send more."

I tried to hide my distaste. I reminded myself that I was a scientist. I drank the rest of my coffee and rose. "Well, I'm going to the barn."

He knotted the thread and bit it off, setting the boot aside. "I'm going up to Bruceport. I'll take Lord Tom and the boy."

I tried not so show my relief, and just for good measure, I leaned over to kiss the top of his head. He grabbed me about the waist, pulling me down onto his lap, kissing me soundly. When I looked up, it was to see Daniel standing at the foot of the stairs, watching.

I was suddenly embarrassed. I said, "Good morning," and tried to pull away from Junius, but he kept a firm hold and glanced over his shoulder at his son. I couldn't believe he was so blind as to not see the resentment in Daniel's expression, but whether Junius did or not, he obviously didn't care.

"There you are, boy. Get some breakfast. We're going into Bruceport today."

Daniel's glance came to me. "You too?"

I shook my head, extricating myself from Junius's hands. "I'm working on the mummy."

"Then if you don't mind, I'll stay behind as well," Daniel said.

I felt a quick dismay. "You don't want to go into town?"

"Well, as compelling as Bruceport is, I'll manage to resist it somehow. I'd like to take another look at her, and to talk to you as well. About how you found her. It's important for the story."

"Go ahead and stay, then. I can get by just as well with Lord Tom," June said, and I thought he seemed relieved.

I thought of yesterday, the offer Daniel had made, my wariness. "It won't be that interesting, I promise you. I'll be drawing mostly. Measuring. I can tell you whatever I discover."

"Then I'll watch. I don't mind it, really."

Junius shoved his foot into his boot and looked it over. "Let him stay, Lea. No sense in him going out to get cold and soaked. At least you won't get any gawkers out here in this weather. And as long as you're staying, boy, I need you to fix the screen on that rain barrel out back. Bugs have been getting into it. A few leaves, too."

"I'll see to it," Daniel said.

Junius rose and headed to the back door, pausing to kiss me before he went outside. "We won't be late. Back before dark."

When he was gone, Daniel said, "Are you ready to get started?"

I looked at him in surprise. He seemed as eager as I was. "Don't you want breakfast? I can fry you up some salt pork if you like. Or there's brined salmon."

He shook his head. "You're not my mother or my servant. And you look ready to bolt out that door to the barn."

"I would like to get to her," I admitted.

"Don't let me delay you."

When Daniel and I went outside, the rain was sheeting from the eaves of the porch, pockmarking the gray surface of the river beyond.

Daniel pulled the brim of his hat down. "I guess we'll have to run for it."

He was off the porch in a moment, sprinting down the steps and across the field, and I grabbed up my skirt and did the same, reaching the barn just behind him, breathless and wet.

I went to the trunk while Daniel lit the lamp. As always, I felt her the moment I came inside, but it was muted today, as if Daniel had somehow muffled it—something I was grateful for, though it was disconcerting, too, and flickers of my dreams came and went, piercing my consciousness in little snippets until I pushed them forcibly away.

I reached into the trunk, lifting her out, putting her on the table, into the circle of light from the lamp Daniel held. As the light played over her I felt that rush of excitement, again the need to touch her, to know her.

"Is that the color her hair was, do you think?" he asked.

"Close to it. It's faded some. It was darker and richer. When the sun shone on it, it was—" I stopped when I realized what I was saying, when I realized I didn't know it for a fact, that it was only an image from my dream, and I looked up to find him staring at me curiously with a little frown. "I mean…I think it must have been. I can't be certain, of course."

"Have you measured her skull yet?"

I reached into my pocket for the measuring tape, grateful for the distraction of facts and numbers. I held it out, letting it unravel to the floor. "We'll do that now. Take out your notebook."

He reached for his pocket, paused, and then with an embarrassed little laugh said, "I've forgotten it."

I teased, "What kind of a reporter forgets his notebook?"

"A very poor one, apparently," he said.

"Run back to the house and get it. I'll wait."

He grimaced and shook his head. "Not in that rain. Give me yours. I'll take notes for you. If you let me look at it again tonight, I'll work from that."

I took out mine, along with the pencil, and handed them to him. I leaned over her. "Stand back. Your shadow's in the light."

Obligingly, he did, and I bent to the work, measuring the length and the breadth in every permutation. I had never done this before, and I had little idea of what exactly I needed, so I tried to get everything. Later I would attempt to interpret the numbers; for now just getting them was enough. I read each one out to Daniel, who jotted them down as any faithful assistant, and I felt as if I were a real scientist with a real assistant, instead of serving perpetually as an assistant myself.

When I was finished I straightened, putting my hands to the small of my back to stretch. Daniel glanced up. "Aren't you going to do the jaw?"

I frowned. "The jaw?"

"From here to here." He touched the end of the pencil to a point below her ear and then to the apex of her chin. "I think you've forgotten it."

I stared at him, bemused. "How do you know to do that?"

He shrugged. "I remember it from somewhere."

It was odd, that he would know something so detailed, and something about his explanation rang vaguely untrue. I thought of yesterday again, and I felt suddenly cold. "I suppose you know how to interpret these numbers too."

He glanced down at the notebook. "I'm afraid I don't. I only remember the technique. I was fascinated by it, I suppose. Nothing like rocks and bones and snakes to pique a young boy's interest."

He smiled, and it was charming, dazzling, distracting. It drew one in impossibly. "You can't have been that kind of boy."

"Why do you say that?"

"Your...the poetry," I said.

"I told you my mother read poetry to me. Not that I enjoyed it."

"But you can quote it."

"It stays in one's head. And I suppose I grew to like it in time. But you haven't told me what *you* think these numbers mean."

I glanced down at her again, caught up once more in the mystery of her. "I don't know yet. I have a copy of the *Crania* in the house. And Agassiz too. I'll have to find them. But even they won't tell me enough."

"Whether she's Indian or not isn't enough?"

I shook my head. "It won't tell me how she lived. Or why she died the way she did."

"The way she died?" His voice sharpened. "You know how she died?"

"She was strangled," I said, shrugging away the prickle between my shoulder blades, the memory of my dream.

A quick glance. "Murdered?"

"Yes, but it could have been ritualized. A sacrifice."

"How would you tell that?"

"Most rituals don't encourage suffering. Victims are offered things to ease the pain. Plants, mild poisons. Things to numb or even to bring visions. Often there's evidence of that. Leaves or something."

"Have you found that here?"

I shook my head. "So I don't know. Maybe it *was* murder. I wish I knew. Her stomach contents would tell me if she ate something, but—"

"So you mean to cut her open?"

I kept my eyes on her, the soft black eyelashes, the browning nubs of teeth, the shine of her hair in the sun, the peek of an ankle beneath a skirt..."It's why Junius wants to send her to Baird. Because he thinks I'm too sentimental. That I can't do what needs to be done. My father wouldn't have hesitated."

"So why do you?"

I met his gaze. "Look at her. If the means of her death was violent, at least she seems at peace now. I can't ruin that."

"Violent?" he asked. "You just said she would have been given things to numb the pain."

"If she was, it didn't work. There are bruises on her arms where she struggled. She was afraid—" I caught myself, swallowing the words. "At least, I imagine she would have been afraid."

"What does my father say about her death?"

"Well...I haven't told him."

He looked confused. "You haven't? Why not?"

I couldn't explain it to him. I couldn't even explain it to myself. Not why I hadn't told Junius nor why I'd told his son instead. "I don't know."

"One can see the way she preoccupies you. Your gaze goes to this barn a hundred times a day. Do you know what it looks like to me? It looks like you're protecting her, but when I ask myself who you'd be protecting her from, the only answer I have is my father."

"Don't be ridiculous."

"I think you're afraid he'll take the things you've learned for himself. That he'll take credit for your theories."

I couldn't help it; I looked at him with shocked surprise. I had not thought those things, but now that he said them, I realized they were true, or at least they were part of the truth. Protecting her—yes, I wanted that. But why? Because I wanted time to form theories of my own? To not let Junius's thirst for recognition force what we discovered to fit his theories, instead of the other way around? Or something else? Something more... emotional? The thought troubled me. I tried to bring myself around to rationality, to what I *should* be thinking and feeling about her.

"I'm right," Daniel said with satisfaction.

I shook my head. "Not really. Or...not just that. It's...June wants her to prove his theories about the Mound Builders, and—"

"You don't want to have to tell him you disagree." Then, at my further surprise, "You told me, remember? When we first met. You said you didn't believe it."

"It's not that I don't believe it. They've found beautiful things in those mounds. And this fabric…it's far too fine."

"But?" Daniel urged gently.

"But I can't look at those winter ceremony masks and think they're anything but beautiful. And…and *not* primitive. The workmanship is too skilled for that, and imaginative. I think…I think she comes from a different culture than Lord Tom's, but do I think it was a superior one? I don't know. Junius would send her off right now and tell the world what he thinks if I let him. And then he'd be made a fool if it turned out he was wrong. I won't let him do that. Baird's approval means everything to him. He wants to be the preeminent ethnologist in the Northwest."

"Even at the expense of his wife?"

"We're partners, Daniel. I'm not sacrificing anything."

His gaze was thoughtful. "I never said anything about sacrifice."

He flustered me. I took a deep breath. "I should get to drawing."

"Tell me first how you found her."

I hesitated. "It was the morning after a storm. My birthday. The bank had fallen away and there…there was a heron standing there as if it meant to call me over…and I…well—" I laughed a little, embarrassed that I'd revealed the fancy, trying to regain myself.

"A birthday present," Daniel said with a smile.

"That's how I thought of her," I admitted. "As if she'd been put there just for me."

"You said yesterday that Sanderson's basket was like the one you found her in."

I didn't want to think about that. I motioned to the basket against the barn wall. "There. She'd been buried in it."

"It looks like any other Indian basket."

"It isn't. The designs on it aren't like any from around here. They're not Shoalwater, neither Chinook nor Chehalis. I don't know what they are." I frowned at him. "Shouldn't you be writing this down?"

"It's your notebook."

"I don't mind."

"I'll remember it well enough. And you're here if I need to ask questions to remind myself."

I nodded and went on, "In any case, by the time I got it half–dug out, Junius and Lord Tom came home and did the rest. That's all. I found nothing else to indicate who she was or where she was from. Just her. And the basket."

"And now you're going to draw her and cut her open."

I winced. "If I don't, Baird will."

"I wonder…" He looked thoughtful. "Have you ever considered sending her elsewhere?"

"Elsewhere?"

"There are places other than the National Museum that would be interested in her, you know. Places that won't destroy her."

I frowned. "Such as…?"

"A curiosity museum, for one," he said. "I imagine one might pay well for something like this. And she'd remain intact."

"A curiosity museum? But…but that's not science."

"It's entertainment," he agreed. "But you've already had plenty of men out here to stare at her, so I don't think you're that averse to it, and wouldn't it be better to not have to cut her apart? With the story you've just told me about how she died, people would be fascinated. If you like, I could make inquiries…I might know of one or two in San Francisco that would be interested."

"But that's even worse, isn't it?" I said quietly. "To have people gawking at her? She's…she's very rare, Daniel. She's so much more than a curiosity."

"But you don't want her cut up."

"It doesn't matter what I want. Science makes its own demands. I wouldn't be able to live with myself if I didn't…if I couldn't…" I trailed off, looking at her, imagining her in a glass case, people pointing and making faces, a show of oddities. It wasn't what she wanted, I knew. "She was alive once. It's…something like this is sacred."

"I thought you said you were a scientist. That you didn't believe in the sacred. You said her soul had passed over."

I said, "I don't expect you to understand."

"I do understand," he said. "She's remarkable. I'd have to be a fool not to see that. And your devotion to finding the truth of her is remarkable as well. I'm not suggesting you give up your research. I just think a curiosity museum might be the answer when you're done."

"Junius would never permit it."

"So you'll send it off and let him take credit because it's what he wants. I wonder…what is it *you* want, Leonie?"

His voice was low and intent. When I looked at him I saw that strange tension in him again, the same I'd seen yesterday, and I was wary. I said, "I think you want the answers to be simple, Daniel. But they aren't."

"I don't think they're as complicated as you pretend, either," he said.

But I'd had enough. I held out my hand for the notebook. "I really must get to drawing."

Silently he handed it back to me, along with the pencil. I looked down at the page, at his handwriting listing my measurements—how neat was his penmanship, clean and precise, the reflection of a well-ordered mind, one where everything had its place, boxed and stacked and labeled. Which was what he was trying to do with me, I realized. And Junius.

Well, let him. He would learn the truth of things soon enough. Twenty-seven was not so old; he had years to discover that there were pieces of one's life that could still surprise, dreams unrealized, regrets one had never thought to keep.

But as I settled down to draw and he leaned back against the barn post to watch, arms crossed, and the silence stretched between us, I felt the questions he'd asked hovering, the conclusions he'd made, and there was an insistence in them that would not fade, even after the minutes passed and I was lost in my drawing and I forgot he was there. I saw only the lines of my pencil, the broad strokes and shading beneath his precisely drawn numbers, her foot taking shape upon the page, and yet the things he'd said remained, whispering in my ear, soft as the brush of abalone charms against my skin.

CHAPTER 10

I WAS BRUSHING OUT MY HAIR WHEN JUNIUS CAME INTO the bedroom, shutting the door softly behind him. The night was very dark beyond the windows, the reflection of the candlelight haloing against the glass, reflecting Junius too, so I saw the dim image of him pausing, watching me as I pulled the brush through the wild, tight curls of my hair, straightening it only for it to spring back when released, forming a cloud around my face.

I asked, "Are you and Lord Tom on speaking terms again?"

He came back to me as if he'd been lost in reverie, slowly, blinking. "Seemingly. Apparently he's forgiven me for McKenna's skull. Thank God he doesn't know about those Stony Point skeletons, or he might be silent a year. How'd the day go with the boy?"

"Daniel is his name. And the day went well." I put aside the brush and began to braid my hair. "He was a good assistant. He has very neat handwriting."

Junius nodded. He unbuttoned his shirt and drew it off, and then he went to the basin and splashed his face. "Discover anything new?"

I felt the words lodge in my throat, the fervency of reluctance.

You're afraid he'll take your ideas as his own.

But my worries were groundless—why should I expect Junius to do what he'd told me he would not? What reason had I? Quickly, before I could think better of it, I forced myself to say, "I've discovered how she died."

Junius straightened and reached for the towel. "You did? And how's that? Disease, as I suspected?"

"She was strangled," I said.

He paused in the midst of drying his face and looked at me over the edge of the towel. "Strangled?"

"Garroted, actually. With something very thin."

"A sacrifice?"

"I don't know. It doesn't look like it. There were bruises on her arms, as if she fought it. I think it was murder."

"Then why mummify her?"

"I don't know that they did, June. Perhaps it was just…a natural…phenomenon."

He shook his head. "Doubtful. It's too perfect. I'm certain there are signs of deliberate mummification to be found. Did you check for holes in the septum? Incisions in the chest?"

"I haven't got that far—"

"Just because they didn't wrap her doesn't mean she's not stuffed with herbs and rags. You can't make assumptions like that until you've cut her open, Lea."

Uncertainly, I said, "No, of course not, but—it seems odd, don't you think, that there were no funerary relics buried with her? There's nothing at all in the ground where we found her."

"How long did you spend out there? A day? There's more digging to be done."

"I was very thorough."

"I'm sure you were, sweetheart, but you haven't the strength to be exhaustive. I'll send Lord Tom out there as soon as the rain lets up. He'll dig so you don't have to wear yourself out."

I felt a little sting of resentment.

"Perhaps you should go through it yourself, then," I said a little meanly.

Junius said, "You're better at sifting than I am. More patience." He put the towel aside and came up behind me, bending to kiss my shoulder. "Your father used to say it, I remember. That there was no one better for detail work."

Detail work. It seemed too little praise, an insult in some strange way, though I knew he hadn't meant it so. And I *was* good at detail. I'd always been proud of that. I forced the thought aside and tried again. "I remember hearing a story about a settler out here who was buried in a trunk. When they dug him up a year later to plant a garden, he was mummified."

Junius laughed. "What kind of a story was it? An Indian myth?"

"No. Someone told me. I don't remember who—"

"It didn't happen." He was so certain. "Trust me, Lea. Cut her open and you'll see. Unless you're too squeamish."

I thought I heard challenge there, a dare. "I don't know that it will be necessary."

"You mean you don't want to do it," he said. He unbuttoned his trousers, pushing them off his lean hips, revealing his long underwear that went dark and wet from the knees down where his boots had not protected him from the water. "It's fine to admit it. You're tenderhearted. No one faults you for it. Women are meant to be sentimental. It's what makes them good mothers—"

"I'm not a mother," I said, too sharply, disbelieving that he'd even said it.

"You're a stepmother," he said, as if that proved his point, as if being the stepmother to a twenty-seven-year-old was the same as raising a child from infancy. "And you're proving to be a good one too, Lea. I would have sent the boy on his way, but you...I should have realized he would appeal to your natural sympathies."

"Why did you marry me, Junius?" The words came out before I was even aware of thinking them.

His gaze met mine in the mirror. "What?"

Now was the time to take it back, to say never mind, to let it go unmentioned. But I twisted to face him. Again, I said, quietly this time, "Why did you marry me?"

"You know why," he said.

"You promised my father," I said. "But you had another wife. You had a child. Why did you choose me over them?"

Junius's face softened, and suddenly I wished I had not asked the question. There was no reason for it, after all. *Land. The whacks. And a pretty little seventeen-year-old on top of it.* I knew Daniel's suspicions for being the worst sort of bias. Junius was the one I knew, the man I had loved for twenty years. I had never before questioned his love for me.

But the question was there now and it could not be unsaid, so I waited.

He motioned for me to come to him where he sat on the edge of the bed, and when I stepped between his legs, he wrapped his arms about my hips, pulling me close, and his expression when he looked up at me was frank. "Why did I marry you? I've told you. Because you needed me, sweetheart, and Mary and the boy didn't. When Teddy died..." He paused, glancing away as if too moved to keep my gaze. "You were so bereft. I couldn't bear to see it, to tell you the truth. And then, when you said you wanted to marry me...well, there was so much hope in your face. How could I say no?"

"You should have," I whispered.

His smile was wry. "Really? Who knows what would have happened to you here alone, prey for every idiot who set foot upon these shores? I wouldn't have been able to live with myself."

"But you could live with walking away from your son."

"I told you, I thought he'd be better off. He had his mother to love him. You had no one."

Megan Chance

"I had Lord Tom."

Junius shrugged as if that meant nothing. "The boy means to make you feel guilty, Lea, but it wasn't your fault. None of it. Let him blame me, if he wants. That's deserved, at least."

His arms tightened about me, pulling me close enough so he could press his face against my stomach. I felt the warmth of him, the heat of his breath through my nightclothes. "Don't let him come between us."

"Why would he? Don't be ridiculous."

He drew away and looked up at me again. "It's not ridiculous. Where are these questions coming from, if not him?"

"I was only wondering—"

"Because he said something to you about it, didn't he? About how this land was worth something, about the oysters, about you being young and pretty."

I squirmed a little. "No—"

"He did. I can see it." He jerked me closer, holding me hard in place. "He wasn't there, Lea. He doesn't know. He's angry and bitter and he has every right to be. But he doesn't know anything about the two of us, and he has no right to make you doubt me."

"I don't doubt you," I said, and in that moment, it was true. I didn't doubt him, and I was annoyed with Daniel for planting those suspicions, and angry with myself for being so susceptible to them, for forgetting so easily and well my own reasons for wariness. *You will regret it now he is here.*

"I wish you'd let me send him away."

"No," I said firmly. I would stay on guard, but until Daniel proved he was unworthy, I would stay the course. "He needs to know the truth of you. I want him to know who you really are."

"For what reason?"

I threaded my hand through my husband's hair and looked at him affectionately. "Because he needs to know. For himself. He's getting married soon, and I think it would ease his mind to

136

know you're not the ogre he thinks you are. And I know you say you don't care, but I think you would rest easier too, knowing that you have a son who doesn't hate you."

He laughed a little and buried his face in me again, his voice muffled as he said, "You know me too well."

And I remembered suddenly the early days of our marriage, his gentleness and care, as if he'd known how sudden was the shift from student to lover and meant to help ease me through it. I felt a surge of tenderness. I leaned to kiss the top of his head, and he took the opportunity to pull me back with him onto the bed, and then he was kissing me gently and sweetly, undressing me with slow deliberation, so I felt how precious I was to him, how much he loved me, and I felt guilty again for doubting him, for allowing Daniel's words to have any heft at all.

The next day, I woke to overcast but no rain. At breakfast, Junius said, "It looks like a good day to go to Toke's Point."

Lord Tom looked up from his coffee. "Toke's Point?"

Junius nodded. "There's a burial cave there. We heard about it from that settler over near Stony Point. He found a basket there that matches the one the mummy was in."

Lord Tom's expression went very still. "I know of the place."

In surprise, I said, "You know it?"

"It has been a story for many years."

Junius fingered his cornbread. "More than a story, I think. This man had been there."

"It's no good to go near any *memalose illahee*."

"Of course not," Junius said dryly. "Would that the weather was as predictable as your dire warnings. But it's the best clue we've got to her origin. And if there are bodies there, perhaps we can find a connection. If they were sacrificed as well—"

"Sacrificed?" Lord Tom frowned.

"Leonie discovered how the mummy died. She was strangled."

Lord Tom's gaze turned to me, intent enough that I squirmed. I expected him to say something about how he'd known already, or how long it had taken me to tell Junius, but he was quiet. The talk turned to our preparations for the journey, but I could not help but notice how discomfited Lord Tom seemed, how restless. When he went to the back door to go out to the lean-to, I followed him, pausing just behind him on the narrow porch before his door. "What is it, *tot*?" I asked. "Is something wrong?"

He hesitated, his hand on the door latch. "Do not go to this cave, *okustee*."

"Because of the spirits? Or is there some better reason?"

"Why not because I have asked you not to?"

"I can't stay away," I said insistently. "The basket this settler had—it was the same pattern. And she wants me to find the answers, *tot*, I can feel it. In my dreams, she—"

"In your *dleams*?" Lord Tom's glance went to the bracelet, and self-consciously I moved my wrist behind a fold of my skirt to hide it. He sighed. "Leave the mummy alone. Let her rest."

"I can't."

"Will you like what you discover, I wonder?" he asked.

"What does that mean?"

He shrugged and twisted the latch. The door to his tiny room swung open, revealing the bed built into the opposite wall, the tangled Hudson Bay blankets, a lamp whose chimney needed cleaning. "You know the stories. Curiosity makes more trouble. Think of Italapas."

"Italapas's curiosity transformed the world. And Junius will go to the cave whether I do or not."

"Yes. But you are the one I promised to keep safe."

"I'm no longer a child. I think Papa cannot have meant you to watch over me forever."

Lord Tom's smile was small and soft. "It is never over, *okustee*."

He slipped into his room, closing the door gently but firmly, closing me out, and I was suddenly fearful. I did not like to go against Lord Tom's wishes. He had been the one who protected me from the dangers of this world—the tricky sloughs and riptides, marshes that tangled one's feet and threatened always to pull one under, spirits and their lies...

But Lord Tom's spirits were only stories, and I could ignore them now, because I felt her there too, urging me forward, and I felt her pleas and her urgency and I knew there was no question: I would go to Toke's Point because I had to, because science said there was a singular truth waiting to be found, an indisputable answer, and I knew I was the one meant to find it.

Toke's Point was about five miles away by water, near the mouth of Shoalwater Bay, on the northern shore of the mainland. The worst of the journey would be when we'd almost reached it, when the bay was no longer protected by the long finger of land that shielded it from the open ocean. The water was gray beneath the heavy overcast, and choppy. Though there was no rain, the air was wet, the sails slack and heavy. Our way was slow, mostly tacking, and before we'd been out an hour, I was freezing. Even the birds seemed huddled into themselves against the cold. I tucked my hands into my armpits and felt the tension between Junius and his son, the way Junius focused on sailing the plunger as if he'd never done it before, Daniel's studious quiet. He hardly looked at his father, but glanced at me now and again as if I were some mystery he was trying to puzzle out, reminding me uncomfortably of yesterday in the barn. I remembered Stony Point, too, and what he'd offered me, and I didn't trust him. So I avoided Daniel's gaze and ignored my curiosity about him that had not faded but only grown.

We were about halfway across, drowning in silence, when I could not bear it another moment. I said to Daniel, meaning to lure Junius into conversation as well, "Have you been working at the newspaper long?"

He gave me a look that said he knew what I was doing, and then he glanced away with a wry smile that reminded me of his father. "No."

"Is it a good job?"

"Better than some."

"Not as hard as working oysters, I imagine."

Again, that smile, along with a shrug. "Not as lucrative either."

I searched for another question.

Junius said, "Not much of a talker are you? Not like your mother."

"I never saw that in her," Daniel said, staring out into the gray. "She was always too tired. Worked out, I guess. By the time I was old enough to help, I think she'd lost the habit."

We fell back into silence. I caught Junius's gaze, and he raised his brow and shrugged. I narrowed my eyes at him, and finally he cleared his throat and said, "This girl you're planning to marry."

Daniel turned his gaze almost idly to his father. "What about her?"

"Tell me something about her. What's her name? Is she pretty? Where did you meet her?"

"Why do you care?"

"She'll be the mother of my grandchildren, won't she?"

Daniel laughed, short and derisive, and then he glanced at me and went sober and thoughtful. "Eleanor. Her name's Eleanor. I met her at a missionary rally."

"You have a religious bent?" Junius sounded as surprised as I was.

Daniel shook his head. "I was on my way somewhere else and got caught up in it."

"So *she's* of a religious bent."

"Her father's a missionary working in Chinatown. She helps him."

"Ah. Charitable works. She sounds a paragon."

"I couldn't like a paragon," Daniel said. "But you'd find no reason to complain of her."

"What did your mother think of her?"

"She liked her well enough. She wished us to be married last year, but..."

"But what?"

Daniel said stiffly, "Eleanor's father preferred us to wait."

"He doesn't approve?"

"His hopes for the future mirror mine."

"Ah." Junius nodded and glanced up at the sail. "Don't have enough money to support his daughter, do you?"

Daniel looked away.

"Well, no man values what he comes by easily," Junius said.

"You're a shining example of that yourself," Daniel said, glancing at me, and I knew he spoke of how easily Junius had gained me, the way my father had handed me and the land over the way one might hand over a watch or an heirloom. The thought surprised me—such a thing had never occurred to me before.

The wind picked up; the plunger sped ahead, its bow slapping against the choppy water. Junius was distracted adjusting the sail and our course. Soon, Toke's Point came into view.

The tide was in, revealing only a strip of sand that gave way eventually to a stony beach leading right up to woods of spruce, alder, and hemlock, smoke rising from the chimneys of the one or two houses settled in the trees. We came ashore, each of us grabbing a bag of provisions and extra clothing and things for camping overnight. I knew Bill McInery lived nearby, and we could stay the night at his place without trouble, but Junius intended to hike to the cave if we could, and spend the night there, skeletons or no, and I knew already I would not be able to talk him out of it.

Perhaps the skeletons Sanderson had seen were already gone, but I didn't want that either, because it would mean the cave would be scraped clean of anything useful.

Junius pulled the rough map Sanderson had given us from his pocket and stared at it for a moment, glancing down the shore. I followed his gaze until I saw the two large rocks on the beach—the ones Sanderson had referred to.

"There," Junius said. He glanced at the sky. With the wind had come heavier and darker clouds, and it didn't look as if the weather would hold for much longer. "If we're lucky we can make it before the rain."

He led us into the woods, the undergrowth of ferns and vines and salal tangling about our feet, making the way hard. Whatever path Sanderson had blazed was long gone; the only one was that which led to the McInery house on the right.

"Perhaps someone who lives here knows of it," Daniel suggested.

Junius shook his head. "If they know of it, it's too late. If they don't, I don't want word getting out."

He led us deeper, past bare huckleberry bushes and redcaps, salal and salmonberry. We had to force our way through, climbing over nurse logs heavy with ferns and thick with moss. I was in the middle, Daniel following behind, cursing softly beneath his breath when a branch whipped his face. We had not gone far before the rain we'd hoped to avoid began. I could hear it more than feel it; we were sheltered by the bare, dense branches of maple and alder and the feathered ones of hemlock and cedar and fir, but the undergrowth was wet already from yesterday, and we were soaked through before we'd gone half a mile.

The woods were deep and barely touched by civilization, though I smelled smoke caught by the rain, forced to hover low in the upper reaches of the trees. The bag of provisions I carried grew heavier, and my hands and feet were so cold I couldn't feel them. My skirt caught on every vine and shrub I passed, and I was weary of yanking it free.

I'd lost track of how long we'd been hiking when Junius stopped so suddenly I nearly barreled into him. He jerked his head to the right. "There it is, I think."

I saw a huge moss-covered maple, a heavily flagged cedar, a boulder dripping water and moss. Salal and ferns were everywhere.

Behind me, Daniel said wearily, "Where? I don't see anything."

Junius strode through the underbrush toward the boulder and Daniel and I followed. Junius put his hand on the rock, which was taller than he was, and stepped around, and I saw it wasn't a boulder at all but a rocky outcropping, the entrance hidden by angles—a rock face jutting before it, a narrow split that widened into an entrance.

Junius disappeared inside. I waited a moment, until I heard his, "Yes, this is it," before I bent to follow him through. There was not much of an entrance, a few feet, sandstone walls wet with water, and then they were suddenly dry. My boot scraped something that scattered—perhaps the remains of a fire—and then the cave opened before me. I felt the space, and heard the size of it in the hollow sounds of our breathing and rustling. But I could see nothing. The daylight, bruised as it was with clouds and rain, did not penetrate far. It was so dark I could not see Junius at all.

Nor could Daniel see me. He bumped right into me, stumbling, so I grabbed him to steady him.

"Sorry," he muttered. "I can't see a damn thing."

I heard Junius rustling about in his bag, the strike of a match against the stone wall, and then a light flickered, sputtering as he held it to one of the candles we'd brought, which caught and took hold, and the cave came into dim view, a faint glow surrounding us, swallowed by the dark shadows at the edges. The floor was packed dirt, the ceiling perhaps six feet high—just tall enough for Junius to stand straight.

"Well, let's take a look around, shall we?" he said, the strange hollowness of his voice flattening and bouncing against stone walls. Junius reached into his bag for another candle and lit it, handing it to me, and then another to Daniel, and now we had three times the light and yet it was barely brighter, as if the cave itself soaked up the light and our breath, which seemed to pulse against the walls.

"It feels like a tomb," Daniel said.

"It *is* a tomb," Junius said. He stepped in a circle, holding the candle out, measuring the depth of the cave. The candlelight played on the walls, which looked water-carved, smooth and cupped in some places, pocked with deeply burrowed holes. It was probably about fifteen feet square, with no other entrances or tunnels that I could see, and no other trace of something living, not spiderwebs or snakes. But then, when Junius turned again, I saw it: the light dashing over a foot, the remains of a shoe woven of reeds, the creaminess of bone.

I gasped. Junius stopped, obviously seeing what I did. He stepped toward it, kneeling, lowering the light, and there they were, the skeletons Evan Sanderson had talked of, three of them, flat on their backs, arms crossed over their chests, the remains of funereal finery—one or two beads scattered in the dirt around them, a hat woven of cedar bark chewed away by rodents, the broken shards of pottery. Other bones too—animal. Deer, perhaps, or elk. But no other baskets or knives. Whatever else here of value had already been taken. Only the skeletons remained. I felt a stab of disappointment, and horror too, that we were intruding, that sense of something sacred that told me to go, to leave them in peace, and I couldn't help shuddering when Junius knelt beside them, running his hands over them as if they were nothing more than cracked pottery, gently lifting, sending his candlelight over them, hollow eye sockets and holes for noses, jaws that held only a few teeth.

"Indian, probably," Junius said. "But not sugarloaf skulls, so I doubt they're Chinook. I'll have to measure them to know for certain. Look at the pottery, Lea—tell me what you think."

I hesitated, but then I went to the nearest pile of pottery shards, squatting to turn over a piece that had been painted. They were all too fragmented to see much of a design. I turned over another piece, and another, and then I began to see where they had once been a single piece, and I fitted the edges together until I had a few inches of border—all geometric, not the broad form lines of the Indian design I knew. It was very similar to that on the basket that had held the mummy and the one in my dream. Still…there was something not right about it. I saw the design and felt…nothing. Nothing more than what one might normally feel scrabbling through funereal remains. The basket, my dreams, her…it all felt so far away, not present. I knew this was not her place, that these were not her people.

My certainty took me aback. It was so strong I could not dispute it, and I knew this was a waste of time, that we would find nothing of her here. But what nonsense was this? *Facts*, I told myself. *You need facts.* But the words wouldn't stay in my head; I felt as if everything I'd known and been taught was slipping away, and fiercely I grabbed and held on, gripping tight. *What kind of a scientist are you?*

"Well?" Junius asked.

"Similar to the basket," I said. "But…"

He shifted to look over my shoulder. "It's very like."

"You think she came from here?" Daniel asked.

I shook my head. "No."

Junius looked at me in surprise. "No? Why not? That design is more than similar. And these skeletons don't have sloped skulls—neither does she."

"I just don't think they're related," I said quietly.

"What reason have you to say that?"

"I don't know. I just…it's an…instinct." I winced even as I said it.

"*Instinct.*" Everything Junius thought about that was in his sigh.

"Is there anything of value?" Daniel asked.

"Only the skeletons," Junius told him.

I said nothing to that. I'd known already that we would take them back with us. I'd only hoped there would be something else here too, something either to dissuade him from taking the bodies or to provide some clue to her origin. But there was neither, and I rose, tilting my head back, stretching a little so the light from my candle wavered and spun across the ceiling, touching upon a deep black mark—

I frowned, bringing the candle higher, bringing into the light the mark—not a straight line but one that curved unnaturally, down and around, forming a back, a leg, an antler—

"What's that?" Daniel asked.

I brought the candle higher, motioning for him to add his light to it, which he did, and then I saw that it was a painting, brief lines, little embellishment, but it was clearly an elk, and beside it something else—another elk and then something that looked like a bear, but very large and…different. A cave bear.

Suddenly Junius was beside us, breathing into my ear. "Drawings. Will you look at that? Sweetheart, I think we've hit the mother lode."

CHAPTER 11

"THE MOTHER LODE?" DANIEL ASKED, HIS VOICE SHARP-
ening. "What do you mean?"

Junius ignored him. "Sanderson said nothing about these."

"Perhaps he didn't see them," I said. "We almost didn't."

Daniel asked, "You mean…drawings like this aren't usual?"

"No," I told him. "These are the first I've seen, though I've
heard of others."

"Lea—this is proof that the mummy's ancient. Her people
did this, and they were no Indians." Junius's voice was keen with
excitement.

"We can't know that," I said cautiously—and I wasn't certain
why I felt the need to say it, except that I was suddenly irritated at
the way he leaped to conclusions. "There's nothing here to con-
nect with her."

Junius studied the drawings. "Nothing except the fact that
the patterns on the pottery look very like those on the basket.
And look at the way these are drawn, Lea. There's something
similar here, too." He pointed to the antlers on the elk. "Here, for
example. The line stroke—these drawings must have been made
by the same people."

Junius was so positive that I found myself suddenly uncertain. I had no reason to disbelieve him except for my own feelings, which I knew weren't to be trusted.

"You aren't looking close enough," he said to me. "Bring up your light—there, like that. You see the similarities now?"

He looked at me, intent, and I peered at the drawings, trying to see what he saw. Perhaps he was right about this. Junius was better at making conclusions than I. I was always so hesitant, so...slow. He was brilliant, and what was I? Only a woman, as Papa had told me a hundred times. *It's not your fault, Leonie. We shall make a scientist of you yet.* I remembered his intensity, the way he'd looked at me as if he could *make* me what he wanted through sheer force of will: *Promise me you'll fight such sensibilities. Logic, my dear. Logic is your only friend.*

Now, that memory kept me silent. I was more aware than ever of my shortcomings, how I'd let dreams and feelings lead me, how disappointed Papa would be in me now if he were here. Because no matter what Junius said, no matter the evidence, I could not make myself believe the drawings had anything to do with the mummy. They were beautiful, but they were not hers, and I could not bury my feelings in logic. My flaw, again.

Junius reached out to touch them, following the curve of the line with his finger. "That's paint, not charcoal. Whoever did this wanted it to be permanent. I wonder if there are any others?" He stepped away, walking about the cave, raising his candle to look, crisscrossing the walls with the dim light.

Daniel said quietly to me, "What does he mean, a mother lode? Are these worth something?"

"Monetarily? I don't know. But in terms of knowledge... they could be very important." I reached out to touch the bear. Candle wax dripped over my gloves, which were thick enough that I didn't feel the heat of it. In the wavering candlelight, the figures almost seemed to move, as if the elk were truly leaping across some field, the cave bear growling as it gave chase. I studied the long, simple lines, the way one faded at the end as if the artist required more paint on his finger or his brush. I was caught up in the drama of the story the figures told, the beautiful simplicity of it. I could not take this ceiling with me, but I knew I would never forget these drawings. "Perhaps these will tell us something to change everything we know about the past," I said quietly. "Perhaps we'll be the ones to discover it. Perhaps not. But these don't belong to anyone. Some things can't be bought and sold."

Junius was still scrabbling about the edges, searching. I knew, though I couldn't say how, that he would find no other drawings here, that these were the only ones. But again, it was just a feeling. I noticed the way the ceiling was blackened a short distance away. Soot, from a fire, and I imagined it: the cave filled with smoke, the flames dancing, someone dipping his finger in a pot of paint, red and then black and white, drawing so quickly in the firelight the elk and the bear looked alive, animated by flame and smoke. Laughter as another described what had happened, hands moving rapidly in gesture and paint.

"It was a hunt," I murmured. "They were hunting elk, and the bear came from nowhere, and here"—I pointed to three parallel lines—"the spears from the hunters. One struck him"—I touched the bear's shoulder—"here. The bear turned on them. The spear wounded him and made him angry, and he was a cave bear three times their size. The elk ran off, and then there were only the two of them and this bear…" I saw him advance, the sharp yellow of his teeth, the rotten scent of his breath, claws like razors and wild eyes—

"And in the end?" Daniel asked.

His voice intruded. I blinked; the vision faded. There was no fire and smoke, no man painting the story on the ceiling while another told it. No laughter. Only a barren, cold cave, the sound of our breathing and Junius's moving about and the patter of rain on the leaves outside the entrance.

Daniel was standing very close, watching me with this look of puzzlement, and I took a step back and tried to smile. "I…I don't know. I suppose they killed it, don't you? Else who would tell the story?"

I reached into my pocket for my notebook. "I'll need to draw these," I said, handing him my candle so I could get the pencil too. "If you don't mind holding the light."

"You're freezing," Daniel said. "Why don't you draw them after we get a fire going and you warm up?"

"I'm fine."

"You're shaking," he said, and I realized suddenly that I was, that I was numb with cold, that I would not be able to hold the pencil steady enough to draw.

"I'll see if I can't find something dry enough to burn," he said, handing me back my candle and leaving the cave.

Junius straightened and sighed. "I think those on the ceiling are the only ones."

I didn't tell him that I already knew that to be true. He stepped over to me and stared up at the drawings. "Make sure you get the detail. The way that one trails off, the exact proximity of each to the other—"

"I know, June."

"This could be important, Leonie. We'll send your drawings to Baird and see what he thinks. Perhaps he's seen others like them. But they need to be exact."

"I'll do the best I can."

He nodded. "I'll help the boy get a fire started."

I was alone, and the cave was very dark now without their light. Only me and my candle, flickering with my breath so the very shadows seemed to pulse in time, as if the cave had somehow taken on my spirit, and it was lurking in the shadows, watching me, waiting, and the thought was so strange and disconcerting that I laughed in an attempt to banish it. The sound echoed in the darkness, more spooky than reassuring. *Will you like what you discover, I wonder?*

I shook away Lord Tom's words and tried to forget that this was a tomb. Instead, I looked up at the drawings and forced myself to focus on them. I opened the notebook, set it in the crook of my arm, and held my candle to the images and tried to draw, but it was too awkward, and I *was* too cold, my fingers too numb to work well, to capture how dynamic these were, the movement of legs as they sped across the stone, the antlers tossing, the growl of the bear...

A clatter at the cave entrance made me jump. I turned to see Daniel returned, unloading the wood he'd managed to find. "Did we bring matches?" he asked.

"In June's bag," I said, and then I tucked the notebook back into my pocket and went over to him. He was right; I would do better when I was warm, and I was suddenly glad I wasn't alone.

He gave me a knowing glance as he dug about in Junius's bag. "Creepy, isn't it? It feels like—what did your Indian call it?"

"*Memelose illahee.* The land of the dead."

"Yes, that." Daniel found the matches, tossing them in his hand as he turned back to the pile of wood. "Not a place I'd want to be by myself. I wonder how Sanderson stood it."

"He didn't know what it was."

"I don't think one has to know." Daniel glanced about and shuddered. "It feels like death. Except for those few moments when you were describing the hunt. I could almost see that. It was as if you'd been there."

I settled myself onto the dirt floor as he arranged a bunch of tiny branches and dry leaves in a small pyre. I thought of the soot on the ceiling, the smoke that had filled the cave, and I was glad Daniel had thought to put the fire near the entrance, where the smoke had somewhere to go. "I have a good imagination. Sometimes too good."

He struck a match and put the flame to the tinder, patiently waiting for it to catch, leaning down to blow on it gently, coaxing the half-wet tinder into flame. He added some thinner branches, feeding it slowly and carefully. "What do you mean, too good?"

"Sometimes I get…too involved. More than I should. More than any good scientist should."

"You see more than just facts, you mean."

"Facts are what matter."

He fed the fire more wood. The flames grew. I held out my numb hands to them.

"I don't know," he said. "People's lives are made up of more than just facts, aren't they? What about faith? Or spirit?"

"Facts as well."

He said, "Really? Is that what you believe?"

I shrugged. "Even belief is quantifiable. All cultures move through the same stages as they progress. So we can tell what earlier primitives believed by learning what the Indians believe now. Facts."

He laughed a little. "All of human experience reduced to a chart. How humbling."

"Why do you say that?"

"Because if such things are quantifiable, as you say, it means that things can only have one meaning, doesn't it?"

I frowned. "I don't understand."

"Well—" he hesitated. "I suppose…take a still life of…of apples, say. A priest might tell you those apples represent the temptation of Eve in the garden. The fact that they're red…well, that's Satan's color, so that means the painting is clearly a warning of evil. Is that how you scientists go about assigning meaning?"

"I suppose that's a good example."

"But what if that wasn't the artist's intent? What if it was a beautiful autumn day, and the apples reminded him of his wife's cheeks, and that was why he chose to paint them? Or perhaps it was his mother's apple pie that he meant to evoke, or the scent of an orchard in the fall, or even the fact that the taste of a good apple can be as perfect a thing as exists in the world? By that interpretation, the painting of those apples is the very opposite of evil. It's…a paean to God. To heaven, even. How can you claim to know which it is?"

"That's why we collect Indian stories. So we can know which it is."

"I've never heard an Indian story. Are they so literal?"

"Well, no. They're quite…symbolic, I suppose."

"How so? Tell me one."

"Leonie should be drawing cave paintings, not telling stories about primitives." Junius came through the entrance, his arms laden with wood, which he let fall with a clatter.

I felt chastened, ashamed again.

Junius went to his bag and rifled through it and mine, bringing out the dried salmon and corn pone I'd brought. He came over to the fire, squatting down, handing out the food while the firelight played over his chiseled face. We ate for a while in silence, and I was thinking over what Daniel had said, about the apples and the interpretation of meaning, things I'd never considered before, and I felt vaguely uneasy, as if there were something there I should have known, should have suspected, as if I'd pounded hard on a locked door, trying to escape, before noticing there was a key to turn.

Daniel said, "Why don't you tell me one of those stories now? While you're warming up, of course. I'd hate to take you from your drawing task."

Junius glanced up. "Stories are for children."

"We're just sitting here. What's the harm?"

Junius frowned. I shook my head and lied, "I can't. I don't remember one well enough to tell."

"Really? I find that hard to believe. You said you'd been collecting them."

I wished Daniel would be quiet. I felt Junius's tension.

"They're a waste of time," Junius said. "The only good reason for them is to preserve the language."

"Just the language? The stories don't matter?"

"Only if you believe the Chinook were formed from eggshells."

"How is that different from God making Adam out of dirt? Or Eve from a rib?"

Junius lifted a brow. "Not much of a churchgoer, are you?"

"If you want to believe that all of the world's knowledge was gained because a woman bit into an apple"—Daniel's gaze flicked to mine—"then by all means, believe it. I can't stop you."

"Does your girl's missionary father know you think this way?"

Daniel ignored him. "It's just another telling of Pandora's Box. Most cultures have some story about the release of evil into the world. Even the Indians, I'd guess."

Junius sighed.

"Maybe it's not the truth," Daniel said. "But who's to say which version is the most true?"

Junius laughed. "Your imagination is a good as your stepmother's."

"I would guess that imagination tells a good story." Daniel's voice was quiet. "I'd like to hear one. Why not let her tell it? What can it harm?"

Junius's jaw tightened. He threw the last bit of his dried salmon into the fire, where the oily skin curled and hissed and crackled. "Go ahead, Lea. I suppose I can't stop you." His tone was clipped. He rose abruptly. "Tell him one. I'll get more wood for the fire." Without another word he left the cave.

Daniel looked startled. "He objects that much?"

I sighed. "He thinks I spend too much time on them. Papa forbade me to listen to them when I was a child. He said they were too indelicate for a girl's ears. June agrees with him."

"Are they?"

"Some of them," I admitted. "Junius is only trying to protect me."

"It doesn't look like protecting to me."

I sighed. "You're very young, Daniel."

"And that was very condescending," he said.

"You're right. I'm sorry."

"You're no old crone yet. You don't look ready to hobble off into the sunset."

"Perhaps not, but I'm older than you."

"But I'd guess I know more of the world than you. That makes us even. Tell me one of your stories."

I shook my head. "I shouldn't."

"Are you so completely his creature?" Daniel asked, and his voice was very soft, gentle enough that my immediate response died in my throat, and I was suddenly caught by the way the firelight gilded his hair and played over his face, shadows and the glint of skin tight over bone, impossibly sculpted, strange and beautiful.

He smiled beguilingly, whispering, "Tell me a story, Lea."

I jerked my gaze away, feeling a sudden heat in my cheeks, and then I realized what he was doing, how he was manipulating me. *I can be very persuasive.* Yes, he could. That charm that led me into irritation with my husband, that lulled me into trusting a man I hardly knew. *Don't let him come between us,* Junius had said, and I suddenly knew exactly the tale to tell.

"A long time ago, back when the mountains were people, and Coyote was changing the world, he came to a hollow tree that opened and closed in the wind. Coyote climbed inside for a nap. When he woke, the tree would not open. He called for help, and the woodpeckers pecked a hole for him to get out. But Coyote was lustful and greedy, and when a pretty woodpecker came close enough to catch, he grabbed her and tried to have his way with her, and after that the birds refused to help him.

"The hole wasn't big enough for him to escape through in one piece, so Coyote took himself apart. He threw out his eyes first, and Buzzard grabbed them, so when Coyote put himself together again he couldn't see. He put rose hips on the end of two long stems to use for eyes, and they were hardly good enough, but they served to get him to a house where there lived an old woman. He decided to fool her into trading her eyes for his."

Here I paused. Very deliberately, I said, "Coyote could be very persuasive, and he charmed the woman into trusting him. He told her about a bug he saw climbing on the ceiling. When she said she could not see it, he offered to trade eyes with her so she could. She thought he was very kind and helpful, so she did. And as a reward for her foolishness, Coyote turned her into a snail with weak eyes on stems who must crawl around with her house on her back. 'You will think you are getting somewhere,' he told her. 'But it will be the same place.' And so everyone now knows the tale of the snail, and knows not to trust charming strangers." This last line was not part of the story, but my own invention. I finished, "*Kani, kani*," and then I looked at Daniel.

He was watching me consideringly, with a very slight smile that I thought might have been a trick of the light. "Is that meant to be an admonition?" he asked quietly.

And I said, equally quietly, "I'm not a fool, Daniel."

"Believe me, I never took you for one."

"Then we understand each other."

Again, that considering look, that strange and gripping beauty in the firelight. He said, "Do we?"

Just then, Junius stepped around the jutting rock face, his arms full of wood, and the moment burst like a bubble. Daniel looked away, as did I. Junius dropped the wood on the other side of the fire and straightened, wiping his hands. "Story over?"

"All done," I said. "You'd like the one I told."

"Would I?" His mouth was tight.

"The one about how Coyote made the snail."

"I don't remember it," Junius said shortly. "I never paid much attention to those things."

"She's a very good storyteller," Daniel said. "A lesson in every word. But I think now I'm going to bed." He rose and went to where the bedrolls had been dropped by the wall, grabbing his, disappearing into the darkness, and Junius looked at me and held out his hand.

I let him help me to my feet before he put out the fire. "Did you draw the ceiling?"

"I will in the morning," I said as the two of us went deeper into the cave. I heard Daniel moving about in the shadow beyond the candle flame, spreading his bedroll, and Junius and I did the same. I took off my boots and crawled into mine, and Junius pulled his blankets close, reaching to draw me into his arms, burying his face in my hair so I felt the warmth of his breath against my skin, and I closed my eyes, trying to lose myself in the familiar comfort of him.

But I couldn't. Junius was asleep within moments, but I was not, and neither was Daniel. I heard him moving against the other wall of the cave, his sigh as he tried to accustom himself to the hard dirt of the floor, and I felt oddly as if he and I somehow shared the darkness. He was not close, but I felt him there, and I was restless and vaguely irritated. I thought of the way he'd looked in the firelight, and then I realized my fingers had gone to the bracelet, that I was stroking one of the abalone charms that had settled in the hollow of my wrist. I dropped it quickly and closed my eyes, willing myself to sleep.

When I did, she was waiting.

Running again, running toward the Querquelin, which sparkled in the sun. Panic and fear, and then hands grabbing, my fingers prying at my throat, trying to get loose, and before my eyes my hands changed, growing wrinkled and gnarled and freckled, joints swollen, the hands of a crone, withering. Shrinking, wrinkling like an apple in the sun, and horror and disbelief took my panic, but not my fear. My hands, saying I was an old woman with no strength and no passion and nothing done. And then, I heard a voice, hers, whispering, Who are you? What do you want from the world? Why haven't you taken it?

I started at a hand on my shoulder, a gentle shake. "Leonie, wake up. It's morning."

I blinked, disoriented, still caught in the dream, and rolled over to see Junius looking down at me, a lit candle in his hands, and I remembered where I was and who I was. I heard Daniel moving about beyond.

"We've got to get going before it gets too late," Junius said. "And there's still the ceiling to draw."

I nodded and sat up, rubbing my eyes. I tried to look at my hands, but they were only pale shadows in the dark. I flexed them, joints a little stiff from cold, but still strong, still my own.

Junius handed me a piece of dried salmon and said, "I'll pack things up. Boy, will you hold a light for Lea so she can see to draw?"

Pack things up. The bones included, I knew, and again I felt that distaste and pushed it away. That was not who I was. This uneasiness was not who I was. I put on my boots, chewing on the salmon, and rose, pulling my notebook and pencil from my pocket, going to where Daniel stood waiting, a lit candle in his hand.

"Good morning," he said, as I stood beside him. "Sleep well?"

I thought of the dream, the words that were an echo of the ones he'd said to me in the barn—*"What do you want?"*—and I looked away, back to the ceiling, at the figures wavering in the faint light. "Could you hold the candle closer, please?"

He obliged, and I took the pencil and began to draw, and there was safety in that—once I was drawing I forgot the dream. I concentrated so intently it felt almost as if I were the original artist, as if it were me dipping my finger in paint, drawing the story again as quickly as I could, meaning to keep up with the teller.

And then Daniel said, "You do that so well. Have you ever given any thought to studying art?"

He was looking over my shoulder as I drew, standing so close I felt the press of him into the space between us. I stepped away and shook my head. "No, of course not."

"Why not? You've the faculty."

Junius said, "It would be a waste of a good scientific mind."

I went warm at my husband's praise, and turned back to put the finishing touches on the drawing.

"I think you've the talent to draw more than relics and bones," Daniel insisted.

I sharpened the antler, rubbed my finger against the paper to soften the bear's back. "What else would I want to draw?"

"Apples, perhaps," Daniel said, his voice very low, meant for me alone, and it had laughter in it.

And though I knew it was only that charm of his again, I could not help smiling at his tease. But I was glad when I finished the drawing and shut my notebook, and Daniel lowered the candle and stepped away.

CHAPTER 12

THE WAY BACK WAS LONG AND HARD. THE THREE OF US had not been enough to fully break a path, and the only evidence we'd been through once before were broken branches, brambles sliced away by Junius's knife. Otherwise it was just as difficult to tramp through. It was not made easier by the bulk of the skeletons—not heavy but unwieldy, the bags Daniel and Junius carried were constantly snagging on branches that tore and whipped and vines that tangled and dragged. And it was raining again, too—the crossing would be miserable.

When we finally reached the beach, it was already after noon. The bay was shrouded in fog and a misty rain. There was an inch of water in the bottom of the plunger, most of which I bailed out while Junius readied the boat for the crossing and complained about the weather. There was little wind, and the mist was deceptive—it made one as wet as a downpour, just more slowly.

None of us spoke much on the crossing; what words we did say were strangely amplified in the fog, and we were too busy keeping watch—it was impossible to see past the bow of the sloop. Junius was concentrating not only on seeing us across without grounding on a shoal but also on keeping sails taut in a bare wind. "We'd go faster rowing," he complained.

Once we were past the mouth of the bay, whatever light breeze there'd been died, blowing itself out on the narrow finger of land separating the Shoalwater from the ocean. I listened to the creak of the lines and the timbers of the boat, the slap of the water, the caw of the gulls, but for the most part it felt as if we were alone, only the three of us in a world cocooned by fog, with nothing beyond, nothing to know or see or hear. I strained to see, serving as much a watchman as I could. But my thoughts were lost in the memory of my dream, the withering of my hands, myself shrinking to nothing, aging and fading, the desperate questions: *Who are you? What do you want from the world? Why haven't you taken it?*

It was nearly dark when we reached the mouth of the Querquelin. The fog had lifted enough by then to see that the tide was out, turning Shoalwater Bay into a series of channels cut into the mud, but Junius knew these channels as well as I did, and soon we were dragging the plunger ashore. The downstairs windows of the house glowed, welcoming and warm, and I was relieved that Lord Tom was there, that we would not be arriving to a dark, cold house.

But as we neared it, I realized that Lord Tom was not the only one there. I heard voices from inside, arguing, and as we approached the porch, a shadow detached itself from the darkness.

Junius stopped short, putting out his hand to keep me behind him. "Who is it? Who's there?"

"William," said a voice, deep and pleasant, pronouncing the name *Willy-am*, and Junius relaxed, dropping his hand back to his side.

"Willy? What the hell are you doing here?" He stepped forward while the shadow stepped down from the porch and was illuminated by the light reflected from the windows. Short, with dark skin and black hair. Bibi's grandson.

Willy nodded a hello to me and said to Junius, "She insisted I bring her out today. Said she had to speak to you right away."

"Bibi's here?" I asked. *Again?*

From inside the house the arguing grew louder. I couldn't distinguish the words, mostly in jargon, I thought, though too indistinct and quick for me to understand. But now I could hear that it was Bibi's voice, and Lord Tom's as well. My hand went involuntarily to the bracelet.

"What did she want that wouldn't wait?" Junius asked.

"Don't know," Willy answered. "But Tom in there don't like it. The two of them have been fighting since we got here."

"What about?"

"Dreams, I think." Willy made a sound of derision. "Or something. Who the hell knows with those two?"

"Well, we'd best find out." Junius strode to the stairs, pausing only long enough to introduce Daniel to Willy, and then we went inside.

The moment the door opened, Bibi and Lord Tom stopped short, gestures frozen in midair, blazing eyes.

Junius said, "What's all this about?"

Lord Tom's glance came to me. "It is nothing. *Pelton dleams.*" *The dreams of a lunatic.*

Bibi barely came to Lord Tom's shoulder, but she was threatening enough when she launched angrily into some protestation—and then I realized it wasn't jargon she was speaking but pure Chinook. She spoke so quickly I made out only a few words, and then only because I knew some from transcribing the stories. *Visions. Spirit. Danger.* The same things she'd said to me only a few weeks ago. The two of them had been arguing about her warnings, about the bracelet. About me.

"*Kwan, chitsh.*" Willy spoke sharply to his grandmother, and Bibi's lips clamped shut in obedience. She glared at Lord Tom, and then she looked at me. I saw the way her gaze fell to my wrist, to the charm peeking from the sleeve of my coat. A satisfied look softened her face.

To Junius, she said, "I have come to tell you something, *Boston-man*, not to fight with your *wake skookum latate.*"

Imbecile. Lord Tom's expression tightened, but he said nothing.

Junius said, "Very well. So tell me."

"*Mahsh mamook canim.*"

She wanted to sell the canoe. I was so surprised I could only stare at her—both because she wanted to sell it now, after her adamant refusal to do so before, and because she wanted to badly enough to come out here. It was odd, and I didn't understand it. But then I felt such an overwhelming relief I didn't care about her reasons. The canoe *and* the skeletons bought me time. Junius would no longer insist on sending the mummy to Baird right away.

Junius looked stunned. "You want...you're ready to sell the canoe?"

She nodded.

He said, "Why, Bibi? What makes you want to sell now?"

She shrugged, but her little eyes gleamed. "I am *lamai. Wake siah memalose.* Time for it to go."

"You're not dying, *chiksh,*" Willy said.

"Not today, no. *By-by.* But this thing I do not need."

As relieved as I was, I knew to be wary. Bibi was too canny and had always been. I tried to tamp down my excitement, to not hope. I said, "Very well. We'll take it off your hands. Five blankets—"

"Two hundred dollars," she said.

Two hundred dollars. It was a lot of money. Whatever reason Bibi had for getting rid of the canoe, she was not going to give us a bargain on it. She would expect me to haggle, and I had to fight the urge just to agree to her terms. I was afraid to push her too far, to lose the canoe. I glanced at Junius, who gave me a quick nod. I turned back to Bibi. "Is it good, Bibi? No holes? No *poolie*? Not *cultus*?

She shrugged. "You want it, you take it. Two hundred."

"You've waited too long," I told her, bargaining. "We have other things to send. *Elip kloshe." Better things.*

She grinned at me, brown teeth that reminded me suddenly and forcibly of those on the mummy. Small and square, stained with tobacco and coffee. She looked beyond me to Daniel and said, "What will you give me for canoe, *Boston-man tenas?*"

Daniel looked startled. I said, "He doesn't want the canoe, Bibi. He's not a collector."

Bibi raised her brows. "No? What does he want?"

"I'll give you one hundred dollars for the canoe," I went on patiently. "And three blankets. And I'll throw in a plug of tobacco."

She didn't take her gaze from Daniel. "*Kumtux yaka mika mamook ticky?*"

Does she know what you want?

Daniel frowned and gave me a questioning look.

But before I could say anything, Lord Tom spoke to Bibi rapidly and sharply. She shrugged. To me, she said, "Two hundred for canoe."

I had no real idea why Bibi wanted suddenly to sell us the canoe, nor what she wanted from Daniel. But I didn't want her to change her mind. "Two hundred then. Junius, get her the voucher. That's all I'm offering, Bibi. A voucher or nothing."

She gave me a satisfied nod, though she'd derided the US government promissory notes Baird sent us for trade as worthless before, and I couldn't disagree. There was no guarantee when she would be paid, or even if she would. So her acceptance now only made me more suspicious. But I had what I wanted, and I wasn't going to ruin it with questions. Junius reached into the inside of his coat and took out a small leather bag, opening the drawstring, pulling out a folded piece of paper. He went to the table, laying it out flat, uncapping the ink, and dipping the pen to write in the amount. Willy watched silently. Lord Tom went to sit stiffly in the rocker. Daniel stood there looking confused, and Bibi was watching him, an unsettling little smile on her face. When Junius finished filling in the paper and handed it to her, I was so relieved it was all I could do not to grin.

"We'll pick up the canoe tomorrow," he told her.

I said, "Will you stay? Have some supper? It's getting late."

Bibi shook her head. She folded the paper and shoved it into her bodice, and then said to Willy, "We go now. *Hyak.*"

He sighed. "Thanks anyway, Leonie. I'd better take her back."

The two of them went to the door. As Bibi passed me, she grabbed my wrist, jerking out my arm as if to make certain the bracelet was no illusion. She glanced over her shoulder at Lord Tom, who frowned, and then both she and Willy were out the door.

"She sold us the canoe." Junius's voice was wondering.

"Now we can keep the mummy," I said.

Junius looked at me thoughtfully. "For now. Assuming the canoe's in decent shape. But we're still sending it off eventually, Lea. When your study is done."

Even that couldn't dispel my relief. It was only talk. Junius wouldn't go back on his promise to me. He never had.

"Did you find the cave?" Lord Tom asked.

"Found it and explored it," Junius said. "It was mostly scavenged, I'm afraid. Nothing left but some broken crockery."

"I said it would be *cultus.*"

"Oh, it wasn't worthless." June smiled. "In fact, we found some paintings on the ceiling. I don't suppose you'd heard stories of those?"

Lord Tom made a face.

Junius went on, "Too advanced for Indians. I think they were drawn by the mummy's people."

Tom looked at me. "And what do you think, *okustee*?"

I had gone to the stove, holding my hands over it, wishing I could just plunge them into the hot water reservoir. "I've never seen anything like them. They were beautiful."

"Drawn by ancient ones?"

"Undoubtedly ancient." But what I didn't say was what I believed, that it wasn't the mummy's people who had drawn them.

"So you brought nothing back?"

Junius said, "There were skeletons there."

"They're outside," I said quickly. "They're not Shoalwater. Junius thinks they might be from her clan."

I expected Lord Tom to object. He surprised me when instead he said nothing, only looked at me thoughtfully.

"What is it?" I asked. "Why do you look at me that way?"

"Nothing, *okustee*. I am only happy to see you returned safely."

"There was little chance of it being otherwise, despite your fears."

"What fears were those?" Daniel asked.

"Lord Tom warned me against going to the cave. Too many bad spirits."

Tom said, "It was not spirits I warned you of."

"Whatever it was, I'm untouched, as you can see."

"Perhaps." Lord Tom looked at Daniel, and then back to me, a glance that confused me and made me want to squirm. He exhaled heavily and got to his feet, crossing the room to the back door. "Good night, *okustee*. *Klahowya*."

I stopped him. "Not yet. What were you and Bibi arguing about? What did you say to her?

He frowned, jutting out his chin. He tapped his finger against his head. "She is *pelton*, that one. You should not listen to her."

"I'm hardly listening to her, *tot*."

"Then why do you wear this?" He grabbed my wrist, just as she'd done, lifting it so it was between us before he let it drop again.

"Lord Tom's right, Lea," Junius said. "Now that we have the canoe, you shouldn't encourage her."

"I..." I didn't know what to say. I thought of the day I'd put it on, that nameless fear that pursued me from the barn, the panic only the bracelet had eased. The thought of taking it off...I couldn't explain why I didn't want to. "I don't want to cross a *tomawanos* woman," I said finally.

Lord Tom made a sound of derision. "She is no *tomawanos* woman, *okustee*."

"What harm can it do?" Daniel put in. "It's just some twine and a few shells. I think it's interesting."

Junius said, "By wearing it, Lea's giving in to superstition."

Daniel went to the settee and sat down. "You'd take everything from her, wouldn't you? You'd leave her with no poetry at all."

"Poetry? What are you talking about?"

"You won't let her tell the stories she loves. You *protect* her from her own imagination. That's the poetry I'm talking about, old man. The things that make life more than a drudgery. There's only so much science and work anyone can bear."

Junius looked startled. "Drudgery? Is that what your life is, Lea? Drudgery?"

"No, of course not," I said. "I—"

"No drinking and one dance every few weeks. Is that all the joy she's allowed? How niggardly you mete it out."

"Daniel," I said sharply. "That's enough."

He said, "I'm only trying to help you, Leonie."

"You're not helping. And you're not right. Please. Leave it be."

His gaze met mine for a brief moment before he shrugged and looked away, sagging into the settee. "As you wish. Be a drudge if you prefer."

Junius's lips thinned. "You'd best watch yourself, boy."

"Or you'll *what*? Give me a beating?"

Junius stepped forward. I said, "June, perhaps you'd best put Edna in the barn. It's dark."

I was grateful when he gave a quick nod and turned on his heel, going to the door and out.

Lord Tom gave me a sharp look. I didn't understand it, and it made me uncomfortable, just as everything tonight had. But neither did he say anything more as he went out the back door.

The house felt suddenly too quiet: the hiss of the water in the reservoir, my breathing, Daniel's presence. He was taking off his boots, wiggling his sodden toes. I still had my coat on. I undid the buttons and took it off, hanging it on the hook beside the door and taking off my own boots. I wanted to be gone, alone in my room, quiet and still. I started past him to the stairs. I said, "Good night, Daniel—"

He grabbed my hand as I passed, stopping me, his fingers tangling in the twine that had slipped to the ball of my thumb. "What was it she said to me?" he asked.

"Junius is right, Daniel. She's just a crazy old woman. You shouldn't give credence to anything she says."

"Then why *do* you wear it?" His thumb slipped over a charm. "If you shouldn't give credence to anything she says?"

"I don't know," I said softly. "Perhaps because..." I paused, but he was watching me, waiting, and I knew he would wait like that until I gave him an answer he believed. "Because I have this feeling the mummy wants me to."

His expression went thoughtful.

"Please don't tell June I said that," I said quickly. "He wouldn't understand. I don't even understand, really, and I know it's absurd, but—"

"What did she say to me?"

I sighed. "'Does she know what you want?'"

He looked confused.

"That's what Bibi asked you. The exact words: 'Does she know what you want?'"

"What does that mean? Who's *she*?"

"I don't know. I told you to pay no attention to it."

He was quiet. His thumb dragged over the charm once again, and then he released me, and I drew my hand back quickly. Once more, I said, "Good night, Daniel."

He nodded. Distractedly, he said, "Good night."

It was early yet. No one had seemingly noticed that there'd been no supper. But I wasn't hungry, and as I went up the stairs, I was overcome with exhaustion. I didn't bother to wash, only undressed and climbed into bed, my hair still in its pins, and then I lay there and listened to my own breathing in the darkness, thinking again of the withered hands in my dream, and the words that circled in my head like a caught song. *What do you want from the world?*

CHAPTER 13

I SLEPT LATER THE NEXT MORNING THAN I HAD SINCE I could remember. When I woke, it was long past dawn, and the dreams I'd had tangled like briars in my head, dark and grasping: the mummy and the drawings on the cave ceiling; Bibi putting the bracelet in my hand; Junius saying, *Don't let him come between us*; and, *Who are you who are you who are you?* I felt unsettled and peevish, and the darkness of the day did not help my mood. Fog hung close to the ground, pounded by a steady rain into a gray miasma, and everything else looked wet and black, the whole world closed in.

I rose, my body aching as if I'd twisted and tossed all night long. I dressed slowly, listening for any sound of life. No footsteps and no voices, and it was late enough that I knew Junius had probably already gone to Bruceport to pick up the canoe. He would have taken Lord Tom with him, and Daniel too, I hoped. I was undoubtedly alone, but still I left my room with a sense of anxiety. Daniel's door was open; when I peeked inside, it was to see the bed made and no sign of him. Downstairs, there was no sign of anyone. There were no boots by the door but mine, and coats and hats were gone. It wasn't until then that I allowed myself to relax. The day was my own, and I knew exactly what I would do with it.

There was cream to be churned into butter, and clothes to wash and mend, lamp chimneys to clean, and floors to sweep, but I did none of those things. I grabbed my notebook and my pencil and I went outside. My thoughts were tangled and distressing; I needed something to focus on. I needed her.

I glanced toward the shore as I came off the porch. The plunger was gone, as I'd expected, the canoe left behind—and I stopped, frowning. It wasn't upended as it usually was to keep the water out. It looked as if Junius had thought to take it and changed his mind. Odd that he hadn't turned it over again, especially in the rain. I should turn it. But I was too impatient; Junius had left it that way, he could tend to it when it was full of rain and heavy. I hurried down the stairs and across the yard to the barn, stepping inside.

And I stopped again, because there was Daniel, bending over the mummy's trunk.

"What are you doing?" I asked—too sharply, startled and a little panicked, Junius's words flooding back: *I think it's best if we never leave him alone with the mummy.*

Daniel jerked as if I'd surprised him. He looked over his shoulder and then he straightened slowly. "You startled me."

"I'm sorry. Why are you in here?"

"I thought I'd take a look at her," he said, so smoothly. He pointed to a covered pail on the table. "I milked the cow, and then…I was curious."

I was not soothed. I felt I'd caught him in a lie. "I thought you were going with Junius."

"No. He and Lord Tom went to Bruceport to see the crazy widow. I didn't want to go. He didn't want me to come either, so it worked out for both of us."

"You should have come to get me if you wanted to look at her. I've the key."

"So I've discovered." He smiled—again, that charm.

I felt it work me too. I thought of the cave, firelight molding his face. Determinedly, I pushed the thought away, remembering instead the story I'd told him, my suspicions, Bibi's warnings about him and Junius's. Coldly, I said, "I don't want anyone but me alone with her."

"I've offended you." He stepped toward me. "I'm sorry. I didn't realize you felt that way."

"Well, I do."

"I suppose I'd feel the same. You can't want anyone interfering with your investigation."

"Exactly." Every word he said was the right one, disarming. There was no reason not to believe him. The pail was full of milk. He didn't seem the least nervous or dodgy. But my suspicion lingered. *Be careful, Leonie.*

Daniel reached into his pocket. "I couldn't sleep last night. I was up early. I went for a walk along the beach. I found this." He put his hand out, opening his fingers, setting on the makeshift table a piece of sea glass the color of the sky—that is, the color of the sky when one could see it. The color of Junius's eyes. And Daniel's too.

I wasn't ready to be assuaged. I was not ready to believe him. "It's very pretty," I said reluctantly.

"Hmmm. You know, it's quite beautiful here."

"It's pouring."

"I don't mind the rain. It's peaceful."

"How different you are from your father."

"I don't mind that either." His voice was wry. "He doesn't find this place peaceful?"

"Peaceful? I'd say not. I told you, he hates it. He'd rather leave."

"But you won't go. I remember that's what you said. Why not?"

I shrugged. "I belong here."

"Because of your father?"

"My father hated it too. He came for ethnology, but he was like Junius, always ready to be moving on. When I was a child, we moved constantly. He was always looking for new things to study, new things to collect."

"That must have been hard for a young girl."

"I don't remember it being hard. I had Papa. It was just...just the two of us then, and that was all I needed. He was my teacher and my friend as well as a parent. I didn't realize there was any other kind of life. Not until we came here and...and he became too ill to leave. Consumption. The weather was no good for him, but he hadn't the strength to go. I was glad of it—oh, not that he was ill, but that we had to stay." I thought of my father, bent over his notebooks in the room Daniel slept in now, the lamplight turning him golden as he wrote, unaware of my watching. How much I'd loved him. "He never understood."

"Never understood what?"

I blinked away the memory. "That I loved it here."

"Or maybe he understood, but he didn't like it."

"What do you mean?"

"It's beautiful, but it's hard," Daniel said. "Especially for a woman. What man would wish his daughter into such a hard life?"

"He wanted me to follow in his footsteps. To be an ethnologist."

"That's different than wading around in freezing water and mud all day. He can't have liked you oystering."

"No, but—"

"Did your father ever see you dance?"

"Yes, of course."

"Then this life isn't what he wanted for you."

I turned to him, bemused. "How can you say that? You never knew him."

"Because I've seen you dance too," he said with a smile, "and no one who's seen that could think you're meant to hide yourself away on a farm and tong oysters for a living."

I did not mistake his admiration, nor my own response to it, my quick flush of warmth, and I realized suddenly what he was doing, how easily he'd turned my suspicions, how well he'd worked me after all. *You're a fool, Leonie.* I said, "I know what you're doing."

He turned a bland expression. "Which is what? What am I doing?"

"I don't trust you."

"Yes, I remember your story." Wryly spoken.

"What do you mean to accomplish, Daniel? What is it you want?" The echo of Bibi's words.

It was as if he'd heard them too. I saw the flash of recognition in his eyes, and the quick way he glanced away told me I'd been right to think it.

I said, "Why are you here?"

"I've told you. I came for the story. And to meet my father."

"No other reason? You don't wish for revenge?"

His expression gave nothing away. "What would it avail me?"

"Satisfaction."

"I don't care enough about him for revenge. I wanted to meet him. I come up here to find he's got a lucrative business—those oysters are a gold mine. I'd be lying if I said I didn't want a part of it."

"And the mummy? What part of her do you want?"

"You know that too. If you discover something important about her, I want to be the writer who tells her story. I want people to know my name. Money and recognition—I suppose I'm more like my father than I'd thought."

"And that's all?" I tried to measure him, but his gaze was unreadable, his stance inscrutable. "That's all you came for?"

"You think I'm lying?"

"I don't know."

"Why would I?"

"I don't know that either."

Daniel smiled thinly. "Have I done something to offend you that you think so poorly of me?"

"Junius suspects you've a hidden motive," I said honestly. "And I'm not certain he's wrong. Bibi warned me about you. What she said last night—"

"My father likes me about as well as I like him. He's been collecting things too long. He thinks everyone's a rival." His voice was bitter, but I heard the hurt behind it. "And I don't know why your Indian woman would dislike me. She sounds no better than a fortune teller. How did she warn you about me? What did she say?"

"That I was to—" I struggled to remember the exact words. *You will need it now he is here.* Not the words so much, but the feeling..."It wasn't what she said really. But she intimated that I should be careful of you."

"Careful in what way?"

"She didn't elaborate."

He laughed shortly. "You know that saying about suspicion? It's like bats among birds, always flying at twilight. This place breeds it. I swear you can feel it in the rain."

It was true; I'd felt it myself. Perhaps not suspicion itself but lingering spirits, the press of the past even when the past was not cities or people but the history of floods and smoke, rain and fog, and trees so tall they blocked out the sun. Dark days, mist and wet, a depth that even sunlight did not penetrate. The brightest summer days made it beautiful but did not disguise it. I'd told my father I'd felt that way once, on a gorgeous summer day, and he told me I had a tendency to the macabre and that he hoped to God I would grow out of it. I never did. I was a little startled to learn that Daniel felt it too. I'd never known any white man who did.

"What is it?" Daniel asked. "Why do you look at me that way?"

"The things you say sometimes...I've never known anyone who speaks as you do."

Again, a short laugh. "You've been dancing in oystering boots too long."

I shook my head. "That's not it."

"Perhaps it's that you recognize the truth in what I say."

Now I laughed. "What you want to be the truth, you mean."

His gaze was searching, unsettling. The lamplight glazed him—I was reminded of what I'd seen in him in the cave, that strange beauty, and suddenly I was seeing him as I had the first time we'd met, when he was just an attractive man and not my husband's son. The moment stretched out. I had to look away.

He said quietly, "I didn't expect you."

Uncomfortably, I said, "I don't know what that means."

"When I came here. I didn't know he had another wife. I suppose I hoped he'd be living in a shack somewhere, some bitter recluse, a drunk perhaps. But then I saw you and I realized why he never returned."

"I said I was sorry for that—"

"I don't want your apology. I'm...I didn't expect you. That's all."

"Then I suppose we're even. I never expected you, either. Not your existence, nor..." I let my words trail off, uncertain what I'd been about to say, suddenly aware of a strange restlessness. A longing I didn't understand. *Who are you?*

I looked at him. I wanted him to go. I wanted not to have to say it.

He hesitated. I thought he would not understand, but I was relieved when he nodded. "I'll leave you to your study, then."

The piece of sea glass he'd put on the table glimmered, as if the lamplight had suddenly hit it, or as if it were illuminated from inside, calling my attention to it again, and I grabbed it up and held it out to him. "Don't forget your sea glass."

He was halfway to the door. He turned. He said, "It's yours. I brought it for you."

He put his hat on his head and turned again to the door, and when he was gone, I looked down at the glass in my hand, a polished round the color of the sky. *Junius's eyes*, I thought. But his weren't the eyes I saw, and I dropped the stone into my pocket.

When Daniel was gone, I turned back to the mummy. I knew she could distract me from the unsettling conversation with Daniel, and I wanted to be lost in her. I felt her waiting for me, and as I unlocked the trunk and took her out I had to fight the urge to apologize for being so long, for wasting time on places that could tell me nothing about her.

I looked her over slowly, wondering where I should begin. I knew I was supposed to be checking for signs of mummification techniques. No brain in the skull, a chest emptied of organs and filled with rags and herbs and sewn back up again. Junius's instructions. I muttered, "Where's the poetry in that, Junius?" and then was surprised at myself for saying it, for *thinking* it. *Where's the* science *in that, Leonie?*

But to find any chest incision, I would have to undress her, and break her. Her knees were drawn up so closely to her chest, and her arms wrapped so tightly about them…there was no way to find an incision without moving them, and no way to move them without tearing her apart.

Can you even bear to do so? Junius's taunt. I did not want to have to admit that he was right, but my reluctance to desecrate her was overwhelming. *Desecrate.* I told myself it wasn't that. This was a body, a husk, only bones. I would not hesitate to break a rock to remove a fossil bone. I was an ethnologist; all I cared about was knowledge.

I forced myself to step away, to get the saw hanging on a nail near Junius's tools. No bone saw, but this would do well enough. When I went back to the mummy I stood there, studying her, looking for the best place to start cutting. The arms first, I imagined. I set the teeth to the joint of her shoulder—

And nearly swooned.

I dropped the saw. It clattered to the floor and I put my hand to my eyes, trying to breathe though a wave of light-headedness. More than that. A sense of wrongness, of intrusion. Her presence was all around me, pushing at me, her horror and her anger, filling me as if it were my own, threatening, terrible, and I was suddenly so afraid I had to fight the urge to run. I clutched the edge of the table, trying to right myself, and gradually the sense of menace faded, and my light-headedness, and I was myself again, and profoundly alone.

Junius was right; I could not do this. It felt less like failure than fear, but my failure was there too, and the fear was still too real to talk myself past, the horror of it lingering. I glanced down at her. "You don't want me to cut you," I murmured without thinking. "Very well. Then what?"

My notebook lay beside her, my pencil had clattered to the floor with the saw. I could finish drawing her, I realized, and not in the pieces I'd intended, a foot or an arm, an incised chest, but whole, as she was. I would not cut into her, not today, *perhaps not ever,* but I could do this. Slowly, hesitantly, I retrieved my pencil, spooked now, waiting again for that sense of menace, but the dimness of the barn was benign, and so was she, and gradually I relaxed, and opened my notebook, and the drawing took over. I became lost in it, and with every stroke of the pencil she became more and more alive to me, her forthright, dark gaze and the saffron skirt shifting about a slim brown ankle and her hair glinting in the late afternoon sun…

The world was already dark when I finally came back to myself, when sheer exhaustion claimed me. I put her away and went to the house. I'd forgotten my conversation with Daniel, but now I remembered it, and I was relieved that I did not see him anywhere about. It felt good to be alone, but I was relieved as well when Junius and Lord Tom returned. Junius's mood was buoyant. He smiled and laughed at something Lord Tom said, and his step was light as he made his way to the kitchen, swooping past the table, wrapping his arms around my waist to nuzzle my neck. "The canoe's in almost perfect condition. We'll be able to send it this week."

"Send it? How? From where? You can't paddle it to Washington."

"No, but we can to Astoria. We'll put it on a steamer from there. Or a train."

I gave him a doubtful look. "That canoe once held twenty men. And you mean to take it south in this weather with only Lord Tom and Daniel?"

"I don't know that it would take all of us," he said, releasing me, stepping back. "I'll send your cave drawings at the same time, I think."

I glanced at Lord Tom, who was taking off his coat and boots by the door, and then to the burlap bags beneath the stairs, the ones Junius had sneaked inside that held the Toke's Point and graveyard skeletons. "What about those?" I asked in a low voice.

"I think they'd best go separately," he said thoughtfully. "I'm still thinking how to do that. Where's the boy?"

I shook my head. "I don't know. He—"

I stopped short at the sound of footsteps on the stairs, and suddenly there was Daniel, looking tousled and drowsy, softly lovely.

"Sleep the day away?" Junius asked.

Daniel raked his hand through his hair and ignored that. He sat at the table, and Junius did too, and Lord Tom came ambling over as I served dinner and the talk turned to the canoe, and I barely paid attention. Daniel said little, and he did not look at me. The fact that neither of us did much speaking did not seem to affect Junius at all. His excitement over finally getting the canoe was evident, and didn't flag throughout dinner, nor after, when he and Lord Tom began to make plans. When I excused myself early to go to bed, Junius didn't seem to notice. Only Daniel looked up and said, "Good night," and I hurried to my room as if pursued. I readied for bed quickly. I left my hair down, and then I snuggled into bed and waited while the lamplight glowed softly gold. I heard the back door close—Lord Tom to his lean-to. I heard footsteps on the stairs—not Junius's, and I deliberately inured myself to their sound, to the walk down the hall, the closing of a bedroom door. When I heard Junius's steps, I was glad. Here, at last, the thing I waited for, and when he came in through the door I let him know I was still awake.

I watched him undress in the dim lamplight—surreptitiously, because he would not like the overtness of it.

He blew out the lamp and crawled into bed. His excitement over the canoe had translated as I'd known it would. He rolled to me, drawing up my nightgown, skimming my thighs and cupping my breasts. I wanted him close; I wanted to know I belonged to him, to undo the buttons on his long underwear and release him into my hand, to lift my hips to him, and hear him moan deep in his throat as he eased into me. I wanted to be overtaken. I wanted savagery. I wanted possession and passion, to grip him with all my strength and rock against him until his thrusting became frenzied. But I did none of those things. He hated it. He'd told me once it was the behavior of a whore. At seventeen, I had been ashamed, and still was, of the untowardness that made me want him that way. And so I let him lift my hips to his, and I bit my lip against the urge to rock and press and churn. His mouth found my throat, his hands tightened.

Junius groaned, and I thought *no no no, not yet*, but he pulled away, and I felt him hot and liquid against my stomach. He collapsed upon me, his breathing heavy and ragged while I throbbed and bit back a cry of frustration, and I was restless again, but I kept myself still. His arm tightened about my breasts. I lay there and listened to him fall into sleep and knew that I loved him, that I was happy. But I heard again the words from my dream, and I felt the brush of the charms about my wrist, the coarse splinter of the twine like a warning.

In the morning I dragged the brush through my tangled hair so ruthlessly it crackled and flew about my head, trying to ignore Junius's whistling and his good humor as he dressed.

Finally, I snapped, "Will you stop? I've the headache."

He turned from the window. "Why? Didn't you sleep well?"

"Yes, I slept fine." I put aside the brush and pressed my fingers to my temples.

Junius went on thoughtfully, watching me in the mirror, "I wish you would reconsider sending the mummy. We could send her with the canoe."

I jerked up. "I'm not done with her."

"But you're not advancing with her either, are you?"

"I am—"

"Have you cut her open yet?"

"Junius, I would have to take her completely apart," I protested, twisting on the bench to face him, trying not to think of yesterday, of my effort to do what he wanted. "Her knees...her arms...I...it's very difficult...and I wanted to draw her first."

"It's been weeks since you did the wash. Butter hasn't been made in days. There's dust on everything—"

"There's always dust on everything."

"You seem preoccupied, Lea."

I frowned at him. "Because I'm not making butter?"

"No, it's not that, it's..." he trailed off with a sigh. "I'll give you until I get back from Astoria. If you haven't cut into her by then, I'll assume you can't and send her to Baird. Is that fair enough?"

In panic, I said, "Fair? No, of course not. You said if I got you the canoe I could keep her. You *promised*."

"For a time," he reminded me. "The truth is, you've been worrying me lately, sweetheart. And I think that mummy is the reason you're not yourself."

"The mummy?" I laughed bitterly. "That's hardly scientific, June. And I'm fine."

"Then prove it. Cut into her."

"All right, I will," I snapped.

"By the time I return," he said. "We'll go as soon as there's a break in the weather. Hopefully in the next day or so. We'll be gone at least two weeks. That should give you plenty of time."

I gave him a mutinous glare, but I didn't argue. I was too angry. I didn't want to say something I would regret.

"I'll leave Daniel here with you. He can help you with it."

"Leave Daniel?" I forgot my anger in dismay. "But…won't you need him?"

"Lord Tom and I should well handle it. And I don't want you here alone."

"I've been here alone a hundred times."

"Yes, but not with the whole bay knowing you've got a mummy."

"There haven't been any gawkers for days. I think they've lost interest."

He stepped over to me. "You said he made a good assistant. Now's your chance to use him. Besides, we're due for a schooner. You'll need help with the oysters. And this will give the boy the time he needs to get his story. Then perhaps he'll be on his way."

"I thought you didn't trust him."

"I don't. Not with the mummy, anyway."

I opened my mouth to tell him about yesterday morning, about my suspicions. But then I wondered what exactly I would say. That I'd surprised Daniel trying to look at her? And perhaps

I *had* misjudged it. He'd seemed so unfazed…I settled for, "Then I can't think why you'd want to leave him with me."

"Because he seems more than willing to protect you." Junius laughed shortly. "Even, it seems, from me. He'll take care of you, Lea. Now I don't want to hear another word about it."

To protest further would make him question me, and I didn't understand myself well enough to answer him. But I could not lose my dread. I glanced down at the bracelet I wore. I thought of Bibi's words: *You will need it now he is here.*

CHAPTER 14

Dark and familiar, close walls and an open door *that let in the smell of sun-warmed grass and dirt. A floor of packed mud beneath my bare feet, a bed of hides and fur that had been pushed aside in the warmth of summer.*

And there, on the floor, a child. Playing and gurgling, drawing pictures on the dirt, and my love for her was full of pride and longing and fear.

Fear most of all.

I felt him coming, a growing storm. I grabbed her up; she squirmed and protested in my arms, and I buried my face in her chubby neck and breathed deep the scent of dirt and milk and knew I must hide her. I must hide her, but there was nowhere to go, and I could not run fast enough or get away. The clouds darkened—the light snapped out. Too dark to see, and I held her so tightly in my arms she whimpered and I murmured Quiet darling, and we'll play a game of hide and seek. Quiet, darling. Quiet. *The wind screamed; the door slammed shut.*

Too late. Too late. He was here.

And suddenly my arms were empty.

She was gone.

I woke to a sadness so full and terrible and pressing I could hardly breathe. It was a weight on my chest, all around me, keeping me awake, staring unseeingly into the night, until Junius finally stirred and rose from bed and dressed. It wasn't until then that I started to cry, and then I could not stop, and he came down beside me, leaning over me as I turned from him, his hands on my shoulders, his voice taut with worry. "What is it, Lea? What's wrong?"

"A dream," I managed. "A dream about a child. She…she disappeared."

"I see." His voice was heavy with exhaustion. His hands left my shoulders. "Lea, for God's sake, not today. There's a break in the rain. Lord Tom and I have to leave."

"Then leave." I sat up, wiping my tears away. "Don't let me keep you."

"You've had dreams before."

"Not like this one."

"You have." His expression was soft and kind. "Just not in awhile. I thought you were done with all that."

I tried to gain control of myself, to harness the melancholy, to push it back into the place I kept it, locked away, solidly hidden. But the dream stayed, the past not so far away, waiting, held in mist. *Just a dream*, I told myself. *Nothing more.*

Junius sighed. "Well, I suppose we could wait another day."

"No," I said, shaking away the sadness, forcing a smile. "No, it's all right. *I'm* all right. Don't let me keep you."

"Perhaps you can cut into that mummy today. That would distract you."

I nodded, though I knew that would only make everything worse. "Yes. Perhaps."

I forced myself to rise, to wash, to dress. I made breakfast with the specter of the dream dodging in and out of my vision— the child there, just over my shoulder, a dirt floor, pictures in the dust. I blinked it away.

Junius said again, worriedly, "We can wait another day, Lea."

I shook my head. "No. You should go."

Daniel frowned. "Is something wrong?"

Junius looked at me as if asking my permission, and I didn't give it, and he looked back at his son with a sigh. "Nothing, boy. Just...keep a close eye on your stepmother, will you? Can I trust you to do that?"

Daniel glanced at me. "Of course."

"Good." Junius's sigh was heavy. "Well then, we'd best be off."

I walked Junius and Lord Tom to the beach. Junius said, "Remember what I said about the mummy, Lea. Don't delay. We won't be that long, and I...I think it will help."

I nodded. I glanced at the sky, clouds gathering upon clouds, all colors of gray. A storm coming in. *Darkness and wind and fear. A door slamming shut.* "Promise me that if it storms you'll get off the water."

"You're all right?" he asked me again. "You're certain?"

"Yes," I said. "I'll be fine."

Lord Tom's gaze fell to the bracelet at my wrist. "*Kloshe nan-itch.*"

Be careful. I nodded and glanced away. Then Junius gave me a final kiss and the two of them started off down the beach. I stood there and watched until they were too small to see, and I was cold and shivering in the wind, and then I turned back to the house.

Daniel was sitting on the porch, staring out at the river. As I came up the stairs, he asked, "Are they gone?"

I nodded.

"Two weeks—is that what you said?"

"Or longer. It depends on how quickly they make it down the coast." I glanced at the sky. "And if the weather holds. And how long it takes to hike back."

"Well, I'm at your disposal. Tell me what I can help you with."

"I'll let you know." I went to the barn, grateful when he did not follow me.

There, I tried to draw her, but my dream kept intruding—when I looked at her, I saw it again, vividly, as if she'd summoned it, and yet—that was absurd, wasn't it? But then I began to remember things, things from the dream, the hair that fell forward to blur my vision as I grabbed up the child—reddish brown, the color of molasses taffy, and my bare feet had been brown and small, not mine. I knew then that the dream was hers, just as they'd all been, that it was her fear and sadness I felt, and she'd wanted me to feel it.

The realization startled me. It was impossible, I knew. Only a fancy. *Not fact.* But it didn't matter what I told myself, my certainty that the dream was hers didn't fade. I didn't understand it. I was afraid, and I didn't know if that fear was hers or my own, and that was the most disturbing thing of all.

Who are you? What do you want from the world?

Not fact. I swallowed hard, looking back at the drawing. Fact was this drawing, the science of capturing her *exactly*. I buried myself in it until my uneasiness disappeared in detail, until I was so focused on getting every nuance of her that I lost track of time. It wasn't until I heard a noise in the doorway that I looked away from her to see Daniel standing there.

He stepped inside. "You know it's getting late."

Beyond him, the short-lived autumn dusk was moving into dark. I glanced back down at her and realized how dim the lamplight was, how hard it was to see. "Oh. I didn't realize."

He came over to me. "May I?" He held out his hand, and I gave him the notebook. He perused the page. "You're so good at this. You've captured her exactly. She looks so...real. Almost alive."

"She's not finished."

"No, I can see that." He handed it back to me, and then he stood there, obviously ill at ease, which was strange. I didn't know what to make of it. "You've been out here all day. Aren't you tired of her?"

"I don't think I could be," I said.

"Have you discovered anything new?"

I shook my head. "No. She's mesocephalic—I know that much—though it doesn't tell me anything really."

"Not roundheaded or long, but in between," he mused.

I was surprised he knew what it meant, and my suspicions rose again. "It doesn't mean she's not Indian."

"Nor that she is."

"Yes." I sighed. "Junius will be disappointed. He wanted certain proof."

"It's good for him not to get everything he wants."

I gave him a sharp look. "He's your father and my husband. I won't hear talk against him. Not while he's gone."

His smile was small. "Does that mean you'll hear it when he's around?"

"He can defend himself then."

"Because you won't defend him."

"Because I don't know how," I said. The melancholy came over me again, and I put my notebook down. "I don't know what excuses will serve, Daniel. And I don't want to be the one to make them."

"That's honest enough."

"And I don't know what you want from him, or what would appease you," I went on. I felt tired, burned out, the dream pressing.

"Perhaps nothing."

I nodded. I touched her hair, smoothing it with a finger.

He said, "What is it you see in her? What fascinates you so?"

"I don't know," I said quietly, which wasn't a lie. "I suppose I feel she has something to say to me. To me alone. And in my dreams—" I broke off, startled at what I'd been about to reveal to him.

"Your dreams?" he urged.

I shook my head. "It's nothing."

"You dream about her?"

I shrugged. "Now and then."

"More than now and then, I think," he said.

That startled me too, that he should see that, that I'd somehow revealed it.

"What happens in these dreams?" he asked.

"I see her life," I found myself saying. "And her death. I told you, I've a good imagination."

He gave me a considering look that made me glance away. I felt like a fool for saying anything at all. I hated how he led me, how easily I told him things.

"You had one last night," he said. "A nightmare, I think."

I looked at him in surprise. "How do you know that? Did Junius tell you?"

"No. It's obvious. You've seemed…sad all day. Though not frightened."

"It was a different dream than I'd had before," I said. "There was a child in it. She had a child. And she was trying to protect it. And it was taken from her anyway."

"No wonder you're sad."

"Yes. And I don't think I can be good company tonight."

He took hold of the edge of her dress, rubbing the cloth between his fingers. I watched him, mesmerized by the movement of his fingers.

He looked up at me, and his eyes were dark in the dim light; I could not read the expression there, but I felt how discomfited he was. "It's late," he said again. "Will you come inside? We can be bad company together."

His words made me smile a little.

"Ah," he said. "There's the first smile I've seen in days."

"Don't do that," I said.

"Do *what*?"

"Try to charm me. I wish you'd stop. It makes me wonder what you want from me."

"What I want," he repeated softly. He looked down again at the mummy, drew his hand away.

I said, "I've been wondering—the other day, at Stony Point— were you serious about stealing that basket? Would you have done it if I'd asked?"

He winced. "*Stealing* isn't the word I'd use."

"Would you have?"

"Does it matter? You didn't want me to."

"Why would you have done it? For what reason? You hardly know me. I don't think you even like me."

His gaze came up, quickly. "That's not true. I do like you. Better than I—" he broke off quickly and sighed. "It's just...I wanted to make things up to you."

"What is there to make up for?"

"It was a mistake," he said quietly. "I'm sorry for it. I wish I hadn't offered, especially as you seemed offended. And now you don't trust me."

"You...interest me, Daniel," I said, struggling for the right words, wondering why I was telling him any of this. But I couldn't seem to stop. "You're so well-spoken. You work hard. And yet you...I feel as if..." I didn't know how to say it. He seemed to understand this place as I did. He seemed oddly to belong here in a way Junius never had. The peace he'd said he felt in the rain, the way he'd taken to the boats and the people, as if he knew both things already. The way he'd felt spirits in the air, in that cave. "I...I wish I understood you better."

"Ask me a question," he said. "Any question."

"I don't think it works that way. I don't even know the question to ask."

"I'll answer whatever you want." His gaze caught mine with an intensity that made me step back into the makeshift table, hard enough that it shifted, rocking off the sawhorse, slanting, and the mummy began to slide. Quickly I twisted around, reaching for her, but the table was in the way, upending, and I succeeded only in latching onto a piece of her dress as the planks clattered to the floor. The gown slipped off her shoulder, and I made a sound of dismay, and then Daniel was there, grabbing her, saving her, and as he did, something slid from the armhole of her dress, slithering over my hand, onto my wrist, and I jerked back again, surprised and startled, thinking it was a spider or a snake, something unexpected. But when I looked down at my wrist, I realized it wasn't anything like that at all.

It was a necklace. A worn and snapped leather thong, and dangling from it was a tooth. A familiar tooth, an inch and a half long, curved. A fossil tooth, one that had belonged to a cave bear, I knew, because I'd seen it before—just this one—and I knew it was the same, because I knew, too, the blue and red patterned beads that bordered it, and the knot in the leather thong where it had broken at least once before. I had seen it a hundred times or more, the shine of lamplight on the tooth, the gleam of the beads where they'd hung around my father's neck.

CHAPTER 15

I STARED AT THE NECKLACE DANGLING FROM MY HAND, confused beyond measure. My father's necklace. He'd worn it every day, and then one day it had just disappeared, and when I'd asked him about it, he'd said he'd lost it. Fallen near the riverbank, he'd said. He'd lost it, and yet it was here, fallen from the mummy's dress, and I could not put the things together; I could not make them coalesce into any kind of sense.

Daniel said, "What's that?"

I held it up to him. The tooth twisted with my movement, shining in the light from the lamp. "It fell from her dress. It's my father's necklace."

"Your father's necklace?" Daniel frowned. He set the mummy back into the trunk, and then turned and stepped up to me, reaching out his hand. I gave it to him, the tooth in his palm, letting the thong fall to pool around it. "Where did it come from?"

"I told you. It fell from her dress."

"I mean, why was it there?"

"I don't know. My father lost it. Years ago. He said it fell off somewhere near the river."

Daniel fingered the tooth. "What kind of tooth is this?"

"A cave bear. Papa always wore it."

"I don't understand. I thought you said she was ancient. Why would this be in her dress?"

"I don't know."

"It must have been in the trunk when you put her inside."

I glanced at it. Before Junius had brought it to the barn, it had been closed up in the storage room upstairs, where my father hadn't set foot in twenty years; even before that, as he left it to me, and never had occasion to go inside. "I'm the one who cleaned it out. There were only blankets. And there's no padding in the trunk for it to have fallen into. Only lacquer. I would have seen it."

"I suppose it must have found its way into the basket then."

"The lid was closed tight. We had to pry it open."

"Then through the weave."

"It was too tightly woven. It was meant to be waterproof."

"What other explanation is there?" He handed me back the necklace.

I let it dangle from my fingers, the tooth twisting back and forth. I felt stupid and slow. "I don't know," I said. "Unless…"

"Unless *what*?"

"Unless he found her himself, once before."

Daniel frowned. "But that would mean he reburied her."

I met his gaze. "Or someone did."

"Who? Why would anyone do that? You said she was an important find. You said she was ancient. Why would he want to hide her away again?"

I looked again at the tooth, dangling from my fingers, spinning slowly in the lamplight. "I don't know. Unless…perhaps she's not as important as we think."

"You don't believe that."

"I'm not the ethnologist my father was, Daniel. Perhaps I'm wrong about her."

"And Junius?"

I shrugged. "Perhaps he's wrong as well."

Daniel's gaze sharpened. "Even I can see that's ridiculous, Lea. You and my father both believe she's special. Surely there have been new theories since your father died. Why would he have known more than either of you?"

"I don't know. But what other reason could there have been for him to rebury her?"

"Maybe your Indian's superstitions got to him."

I laughed shortly. "Not Papa. He thought their superstitions nonsense." I coiled the necklace in my hand, feeling my father in it, remembering how it had looked around his neck, how he played with the tooth sometimes when he was concentrating hard, twirling it in his fingers, rubbing it like a talisman. It had been the first fossil he'd found, he'd told me. Found in a cave in an Ohio wood, along with more recent arrowheads and bones from common black bears all mixed together, an Indian butchering cave, but the cave bear skeleton had been a good find. He'd had the tooth strung for good luck, and he'd not taken it off until he'd lost it. I'd been…fourteen then, I thought I remembered. Or perhaps earlier. Perhaps thirteen. What I did remember was that he had been pained by its absence. His hand went often to his throat as if he were searching for it to rub, a habit that had lasted until he died.

I glanced up at Daniel, who was watching me carefully. "I don't know why he would have done it. I don't know why he would have reburied her."

"You don't know that he did," Daniel said reasonably. "It's useless to speculate. You can't know, not unless he told someone. Or wrote it down."

I thought of the row of leather-bound journals upstairs. "He kept a record of everything. Everything he found. In his journals."

"Those books upstairs? There must be fifty of them."

"I don't need to go through all of them. I only need the years before he died. Just when the necklace disappeared. Three years. Four at the most."

"It might be easier to ask Lord Tom."

"Tom didn't know anything about the mummy," I said, remembering the day I'd found her, his surprise and dismay and fear. "He was there the day we pulled her out. He would have said if Papa had dug her up before. He told me to rebury her."

"Then perhaps he'd said the same thing to your father. Everyone's claiming there's something otherworldly about her. Perhaps he convinced your father that she was a danger."

"He didn't know she was there. I would swear to it." I knotted my father's necklace and put it on, closing the lid of the trunk, locking the mummy away. "I'm going to find out."

We hurried across the field and through the mist and into the house. I didn't pause to take off my coat or boots or hat, but made for the stairs and my father's old room.

Daniel came up behind me. "You're certain there's something to be found here?"

I moved quickly to the bookshelves. "We won't know until we look, will we?"

I reached up to take one down—I had never touched these, not since he'd died nor before—and the shelf was too high; I could not quite reach. Daniel was there in a moment, reaching from behind me, pressing close enough that I caught my breath at his proximity, and I felt him start too, and then he stilled, hesitating before he grabbed three of the thin volumes and pulled them down. He stepped back almost immediately and handed me the books.

"Which ones?" he asked, eyeing the shelves.

"He went through two or three a year." I flipped open the covers of the ones Daniel had given me, glancing at the dates scrawled in my father's handwriting. My throat swelled at the sight of it. So familiar. I had not been able to bear looking through these after he'd died, and then I had to admit I'd forgotten them, caught up in my new life, my own science, my love affair with the man Papa had chosen for me.

For a moment I was lost in memories, and then I recalled myself, focusing on the date—too early, both that one and the other two. I handed them back to Daniel and gestured to the shelf. "We need later than this. I don't know if they're in order, but I suspect so. We'll need some from the end."

I backed away from the shelf before he could step forward again, out of his way, and obediently he put those back and took down two others. When he gave them to me, I opened the covers. One four years before Papa had died, one three. I felt a surge of excitement.

"We'll start with these," I said, handing one to Daniel. I sat down on the bed, scooting back to lean against the wall, opening the first journal, already falling into my father's words.

January 5, 1851—
Traded today: paper of buttons for two wooden spoons, one alder, carved with seal, the second cedar and deeper bowled, perhaps a small ladle (?) and otter emblem.
One blanket for: baskets, 4; woven hat, 2 new; one emblem painted longhouse door...

It went on like that, lists of things he'd traded, things he'd collected, some of which I remembered, most of which I did not, because he'd sent them off to museums or sold them to other collectors. I'd gone through five pages of it before I realized that Daniel was on the bed beside me, propped against the footboard, the other journal open on his drawn-up knees. He glanced up as if he felt me looking at him and gave me a small smile. "Fascinating reading. I'm like to fall asleep."

"It's mostly a record of collecting."

"So I see."

"But he wrote in them every night. I know he wrote about his theories. And certainly if he had found her—"

"Oh, I don't doubt that he would have written about her. If he found her. It's only that we may waste two years of our lives only to discover he didn't."

"I tell you the necklace couldn't have fallen into that basket by accident. It was sealed tight. We had to break the mud to get it open."

"I believe you." He glanced down at the open journal, reading quickly, laughing a little. "Listen to this: he quotes Morton here: 'It makes little difference whether the inferiority of the Negro is natural or acquired; for if they ever possessed equal intelligence…they have lost it; and if they never had it, they had nothing to lose.'"

I nodded. "Yes, Papa quoted him often."

"He goes on to say, 'The more acquainted I am with the Shoalwater, the more I agree with Morton's assessment that the Indian is inferior to *all* races. After hundreds of cranial measurements and phrenological studies, I feel confident in asserting that they are indeed deficient in all areas of arts and sciences, and I must conclude the brain itself so lacking that any attempt at civilization must go awry. But as to whether the experiment itself is so, it remains too early to predict.'" Daniel looked up. "The experiment? What experiment is he talking about?"

I frowned. "When was that written?"

A glance down again. "June 16, 1851."

I would have been thirteen, and working with Papa almost daily, and yet this was the first I'd heard of any experiment. "You're certain he said *experiment*?"

Daniel nodded.

"I don't know anything about an experiment," I said.

"Perhaps he didn't share it with you."

"I was his assistant and his student. He discussed everything with me—who else was there?" I said. "And this would be before he met Junius. I knew everything that had to do with Papa's work."

Daniel raised a brow. "He mentions it again here, three days later: 'a lamentable setback. But I cannot let emotion get the best of me. I must proceed with the experiment as mapped. One cannot stay in this place without experiencing the occasional pollution—too many damn native influences! Impossible to isolate. But I refuse to admit to failure.'"

"It must be something to do with the Indians," I puzzled. "Perhaps it was something he thought indelicate—"

"Indelicate? How so?"

"He was...reticent...about telling me some things. He felt the Indians were immoral, and he disliked speaking to me about it. He...he didn't like that I disagreed with him. He thought my ideas unladylike."

Daniel's gaze went bright with interest. "Unladylike?"

"I didn't think—I *don't* think—the Indians particularly immoral. Just different. For example, they see nothing wrong in having multiple wives."

"A creed my father embraced wholeheartedly, I see."

"Actually, Junius finds it abhorrent."

"He's a hypocrite then."

"Yes. But I have to admit that it always made a queer kind of sense to me. There were political gains to be made, and women were good traders and gatherers. When one has to constantly fight both the elements and the slaving raids of the northern tribes, well..." I shrugged. "Papa hated that I understood them. But I always thought that was our task. He said I took it too far."

"A daughter who understands savages," Daniel mused. "Yes, I can see why a father might have found it frightening."

"He was an educated man. He should have realized it was only intellectual curiosity."

Daniel laughed.

"He was as well-read as you are. Would you have found it frightening?" I insisted.

Daniel's laughter died. "It doesn't frighten me. Just the opposite, in fact. But I'm not your father, and no doubt he found it disturbing to see your interest in savagery when he knew what other men are thinking when they look at you. He could not have been blind to it."

I felt the heat rise in my face and I looked away.

Daniel went on, gently now. "All fathers want to keep their daughters innocent, don't they? I'm not surprised that he kept the more...indelicate...aspects of his study from you."

"I knew about such things anyway," I said, keeping my gaze focused upon the pages, my father's handwriting. "Some of the relics are very...obscene. He thought I didn't understand, but I did."

"Obscene how?" Daniel asked.

"The usual thing. Huge breasts and bellies. Erect...phalluses."

"How very descriptive."

I glanced up, but his expression was impassive, his eyes hooded. I said, "They weren't really. At least, they weren't very detailed. Papa must have believed I would think they were giant sticks or something. I can't imagine he would have had me draw them if he'd thought I knew what they were. Some of them were jokes—Indians have a perverse sense of humor sometimes—but most of them were fertility icons. We had some around the house until Junius sent them away. Not that they helped."

Daniel glanced away. He flipped the pages of the journal almost idly. "You wanted children?"

I tried not to feel pain at his question, to answer lightly. "Doesn't every woman?"

"Not in my experience," he said.

"Oh?"

He gave me a wry glance. "But then again, I haven't spent much time with respectable women, so I'm hardly an expert."

"But your Eleanor—"

"I'm not asking her. I'm asking you. Did you want children?"

"Very much. Once." I smiled weakly, pushing away sadness. "But some things aren't meant to be. I suppose it's for the best. It's given me more time to dedicate to ethnology. My father would be relieved."

"Relieved not to have grandchildren?"

"My mother died in childbed. He was afraid for me. That was part of it. But mostly he wanted me to pursue science, and he feared children would interfere with that. The fact that I was a woman was already a flaw hard enough to overcome. He worried I would abandon my studies and whatever capacity for rationality I had if there were children."

Daniel frowned. "I see," he said slowly.

"I *wanted* to study."

"I didn't say otherwise."

"But that's what you believe, isn't it?"

"What I believe," he said, looking at me, "is that you've spent your life doing what others want. Have you ever asked yourself what the world could be if you did what *you* wanted?"

Who are you? What do you want from the world? His words brought the dream hard into my head, an echo that made me curl my fingers into my palm. "You don't know anything."

"So you keep saying," he said lightly, but his gaze called me out; his gaze said something I didn't want to hear.

For a moment, I stared at him, caught. I *felt* him. For a moment, I felt a possibility that alarmed me, so insistent it was, and I put aside the book and rose, slamming from the room without grace, nothing but panic, downstairs and out again, without thought or volition, racing for peace and calm and reassurance, outside and across the yard and in the barn, and then I was standing over her closed trunk, and there was no reassurance there, either, but the melancholy from my dream returned, that terrible sense of loss, those haunting words, *who are you?* And still I stood, staring down until it became too dark to see.

That night I tossed and turned, and finally I gave up any expectation of sleep. I lit the lamp and felt myself to be a little child braving nightmares, and that little child craved the comfort and reassurance of her father's words—the things that had always comforted me in the past. He was not here, but his journals were, waiting for me.

I got out of bed, pulling on my dressing gown, taking up the lamp. The night was dark as pitch, the sky so clouded there was no moon. I heard the soft patter of rain on the rooftop. The floor was cold on my bare feet as I padded from my bedroom and into the hallway. I glanced nervously at Daniel's door—still closed, no light peeking from beneath it, and I hurried as quickly and silently as I could downstairs, clutched by an irrational fear that I would wake him, that he would come out to find me thus—something I most assuredly did not want.

The journals were on the table. I picked up one and raced back to my room, closing the door gently behind me, a bit too relieved that I managed it unscathed. *Unscathed*—what a strange word to use. To think him capable of scathing me—I laughed, and to my surprise it caught hard in my throat. I was a fool, and I knew it. Scientists did not let emotion rule their thinking. I was, after all, the most evolved kind of being—not a *man*, of course, but still, as Agassiz said, one of the highest and last series among living beings. I did not have to give in to primitive feelings. I was happy in my life. I was *happy*, and here was my father's journal to reassure me of it, to tell me again who I was. Leonie Monroe Russell. My father's daughter. Junius's wife.

The thought restored me, and I went back to my bed and settled the lamp on the bedside table. Then I crawled between the blankets and opened the journal.

February 15, 1852: Argument today with Old Toke. I was looking for a wooden salmon hook, which he said his people did not use anymore, much preferring bought ones made of metal, and he offered one of those, which I refused. When I said my only interests were in those that were authentic and made the old way, he was very offended and said white men cared only for the past, and not for the truth, and I said only the past was the truth. His people will all be dead soon enough, and it is irrelevant and irresponsible to imply otherwise. There is no hope to offer to his people at all. I had hoped to be able to give some solace that environment could change their future, but the experiment has not solved this question for me.

The experiment again. I frowned and continued to read.

The Indians here are lazy—all tribes, even the northern ones. They respect pleasure above all else. But the northern tribes are raiders as well, almost single-minded in their pursuit of slaves. This is a conundrum: their laziness requires they find others to do their work for them, and yet the aggression required to steal such slaves is also necessary. What then sets the aggressively lazy North apart from the pleasure-loving South? The weather is the same. The vegetation and animal life the same. The ocean is the same. Is it biological? At some point, did a member of an advanced culture mate with a primitive and through the pollution of miscegenation instill aggression in later stock? Or vice versa: was there a mixing of blood in the southern tribes that negated that aggressive tendency?

The experiment has come no closer to showing me the truth except that I have seen that tendencies do pass through the blood, and environment can squelch them in some fashion. But what would happen if one were not vigilant? If I were not here to fashion it, how might it go astray?

Whatever this experiment had been, Papa had been obsessed with it, and I didn't even understand what it was. It wasn't what I was looking for, of course—I wanted some indication of who the mummy was and where she'd come from—but I was puzzled and troubled by the fact that this experiment had held Papa tight in its grip and I'd known nothing of it. I had been his favorite companion—how often had he said it? I was his only assistant before Junius came, my hand had been in everything Papa did, and yet he had never mentioned to me the very thing that was the focus of his study, and I didn't know why.

Because he didn't trust you to be able to continue it.

I tried to push the thought away, but it wouldn't go. There were too many others that reinforced it. Papa's fear that the fact of my sex kept me from having a true faculty for study. His constant deriding of my theories about the Indians and their stories, the way he'd forbidden me to listen to them when I was a child. He had told me I had a quick mind and was proud that I'd inherited that from him. But he'd also called me too sensitive and imaginative.

The curse of your sex, I fear, Lea, he'd told me when I was just fourteen and as devoted to him as any acolyte, and when I'd asked him what he meant, he told me, *Women were created for having children. Science goes against your natural abilities—such study may indeed be impossible for your sex, but I have hopes that you might overcome it.*

I will overcome it, I had said confidently. *Tell me how.*

Your mind is highly distractible. A proper scientist does what he must to ensure there will be no such distractions. Perhaps you should consider a life of celibate study.

Like a nun? I had asked, laughing, thinking he was joking.

He only gave me a soberly thoughtful look and said, *No, my dear, I'm not talking of religious isolation, but of a life dedicated to research.*

Well, then that's what I'll do. I don't wish ever to marry, I said.

He smiled gently. *It's not marriage I object to, but perhaps you'll be lucky, my dear. Remaining childless might help mitigate your unfortunate biology. I hope it will. I would pray for it if I were you.*

I had promised to do so, I remembered now, and for a time I'd obeyed, dutiful prayers to God each night, asking that I might be spared the curse of children so I could dedicate myself to study and collecting.

Such prayers had not lasted the summer, but only because I'd been too busy and forgotten them. My father had been struck by the call of the Pacific Northwest Indians, and it was about that time we'd moved to some dirty little town in northern California, and Papa had been so disgusted by the degeneration of the Indians there that we hadn't stayed long.

And now I wondered, had such prayers truly had an effect? Here I was, childless as I'd promised him. Had God listened to the prayers of a devoted fourteen-year-old over the ones made by a woman of twenty, who had hoped for children despite their distractions, who, for a time, had wanted them more than science?

And perhaps that was my punishment, I thought, for ignoring what I was, for having the pride to think I could be both a mother and an ethnologist. I thought of my father, and how furious he would have been at my later prayers. No doubt he'd been at God's side, counseling Him that I didn't know my own mind, bemoaning the lack of dedication that had allowed my biology to overtake my intellect, telling God that, despite all his work, my mind was as feeble as any woman's, and he'd been a fool to think it could be otherwise.

He'd known it always, hadn't he? It was why he'd never shared the experiment with me, because he'd known I hadn't the capacity to continue it. Because I wasn't the ethnologist he was, and could never be, and *that* was why I couldn't see what was wrong with the mummy, why I was blind to the reasons he must have had to rebury her, as I was almost certain he had.

Imagination. Desire and yearning. Sentimentality. Flaws, every one. My objectivity was as substantial as paper melted away in rain, no matter how I tried to gain it. I dreamed about the mummy and drew her instead of cutting her open as anyone else would have done. My father was right. I was no kind of scientist at all. A real ethnologist would have seen right away who she was. A real scientist would already *know* her.

I was drawn more to dreams, to a presence that could not really exist, to imagination instead of fact. I wore an ugly, cheap bracelet because a witch woman had frightened me with talk any thinking man would deride. I was attracted to my stepson—yes, I admitted it—because I sensed an *affinity* with him that I'd never felt for another man. Feelings, all of them. Not facts. Not science.

But there was still time to stop it all. Tomorrow I would finish the drawing and cut into her. Tomorrow I would get rid of this bracelet. I would give Daniel the money to go back to San Francisco. I would even take him to Bruceport myself.

There was still time to return to the Leonie I'd been.

Resolved, I put the journal aside and blew out the lamp. I snuggled into the blankets and closed my eyes and waited for the peace of sleep, the solace of determination.

And the nightmare of her returned, worse than ever. Again the child on the floor, the love and doubt and fear. But this time there were voices added, muffled and changed as if I heard them through water, tones loud and angry but indistinguishable. A man's, a woman's. They were fighting, and it was about the child, and my fear was terrible and all-encompassing, and then again the withering away, an old woman's hand, freckled and spotted, and then skin turning to leather, muscle adhering to bone, then crumbling to dust, crumbling and crumbling and blowing away in a moist south wind, and *you don't know who you are. You don't know...*

I woke breathing hard, tears streaming down my cheeks, shaken and uncertain. The feelings didn't leave me as I rose and washed and dressed, not as I brushed my hair and pinned it up. The echo of that voice stayed with me—*You don't know who you are*—and I thought of the reassurance of my father's words, of my determination to do what must be done to regain my will to be who I was, what the years of my father's training, and Junius's, had made me.

I went downstairs as if set for battle. I made porridge and coffee and went to milk the cow. The wind was picking up—not the south wind from my dream but a northern one, bending the hemlocks, scattering the rain. The perfect day to be in the barn, dissecting the mummy.

I threw a quick glance at the trunk as I left the barn, ignoring the trepidation that swept me, trying to forget the last time I'd tried to cut into her and what had happened. Superstition and imagination and nothing more. Today would be different. Today I would do what I should have done to begin with, and nothing would stop me.

I poured the milk into the screened pans on the back porch and went in through the door there, nearly stumbling over Daniel, who sat at the table just inside. He glanced up, and suddenly I thought of when I'd seen him last, how I'd run away. I felt myself go hot; I saw him notice it in the moment before he looked away, and I felt the tension rise between us; the air charged and unstable as any storm.

I passed by him quickly, going to the stove, pouring coffee with hands I willed to steady.

He said, "Nightmares again?"

I was startled, once again, by his perceptiveness, alarmed by the things he saw in me. I clung hard to my resolve. "Yes, as it happens. But I think I know the cure."

"There's a cure?"

"I'm going to cut the mummy today."

He went still. Then, "You're going to *what*?"

"Cut into her. Cut her apart. It's the only way I can see if she's been deliberately mummified or if she *was* sacrificed."

"I thought you weren't going to do that. You said that she was at peace and you didn't want to ruin that."

I winced. "That's not scientific."

"What does that matter?"

"I'm an *ethnologist*, Daniel. I've delayed too long as it is. There's no excuse for my not doing it before now."

"You're believing what he tells you and not following your own instincts—"

"It's stupid," I snapped, turning to look at him. "It's not logical. These things I feel are ridiculous."

"Why won't you trust yourself?"

I thought of my dream, my father's words, my flaw, and in frustration and desperation, I blurted out the words without thinking. "Because I'm not good enough to trust myself. If I don't do what needs to be done, then this is all a waste, don't you understand? I have to prove I can do this or my *life* is a waste, this... this...barrenness and prayers—it's all pointless." I was horrified when I realized what I'd said, what I'd told him. I turned back to the stove.

He said quietly, "Perhaps science isn't the point, Lea."

I bit my lip against sudden tears. Dear God, I was a mess. I took a deep breath, staring down at the bracelet shivering on my wrist—my other resolution, I remembered. To take it off, to burn the damn thing as Lord Tom wanted.

And then I heard the shout outside.

Daniel said, "What was that?"

The shout came again.

Daniel shoved aside his coffee and rose, frowning. He hurried to the front door, opening it, and I followed him to the porch. From there I could see the plunger near the beach, sails fluttering to slow it. Adam Leach—I recognized the boat.

Daniel went down the stairs and into the yard, and now I heard the shout distinctly, "Schooner's on its way!"

"The schooner," I said, and then, "Wave to show him we heard," and Daniel did, and the sails tightened again; Adam sailed off to tell the others on the bay. I said to Daniel, "We have to hurry. We can't be late as we were last time."

He came up the stairs again; together we went into the house, and I remembered my third resolution last night. Now was the opportunity to tell him to go. The schooner was here; after we sold the oysters, he could be on it heading back to San Francisco and his fiancée. I meant to say it. But now, faced with the reality of it, my resolution wavered. I couldn't say the words. He would want an explanation, and I could not give it to him. I could not voice it, because to voice it made it real. I could not admit to myself why I wanted him to go, and so there was no way to say it.

I went into the house to get my things, and I said nothing of it at all.

CHAPTER 16

I̲T WASN'T LONG BEFORE WE WERE IN THE SLOOP ON OUR way to the culling bed. We were both soaked through before we reached it, and Daniel's lips were colorless with cold, rain dripping from the brim of his hat. He didn't complain; together and silently we shoveled oysters into the hold, synchronized, one shovel and then another, working rapidly, sparing only what talk we needed to get the job done. My hands and feet and knees were aching from cold when we were finished, my teeth chattering. We were off, rain spattering in our faces, the wind filling the sails, the water nothing but chop. Daniel sat silently, his hands clenched together, his eyes very blue in the pale of his face, his eyelashes spiky with rain. Like some sculpture, I thought. So still and pale and chiseled and beautiful. I turned away quickly.

I had long since ceased to feel my hands and my feet by the time we got to Bruceport. The schooner was just coming in, men moving about the deck, blurred in the rain. I let the sail go slack and took our place in line—fourth this time. We would sell all the oysters. Good luck, for a change.

I watched the schooner drop anchor, the first plunger scurry up to its side. Daniel said nothing, nor did I as we watched one boat after another empty its hold, and then it was our turn, and they were lowering the baskets over, and Daniel and I were working side by side, loading them while the rain beat down and the wind began to pick up. He was faster than I was, given how clumsy were my numb hands, and finally he said, "Let me do it, Lea," and I sat down again, putting my hands beneath my armpits to try to warm them, watching him efficiently and easily complete the job.

"Four hundred!" one of the sailors called over the side, throwing the little bag full of coins. Daniel caught it and handed it to me.

"Let's go get warm," he said. "You look like a piece of ice."

I managed to get the plunger ashore without much trouble, though I could not manage the centerboard and Daniel had to lift it for me so we could beach it, and he was the one who covered the hold with an oilcloth to keep the rain out. Then we trudged to Dunn's, me clumsy with the cold, tripping over the driftwood strewn about the beach so that I nearly fell, and Daniel grabbed my arm to steady me. He released his hold almost immediately, abruptly enough that it was obvious, and my nervousness settled back. He should be on his way to San Francisco. But at least there would be others in the saloon. We would not be alone.

The saloon was not yet full, as we'd been among the first to sell. There was a table in the corner beside a small cast iron coal stove, and Daniel pointed me toward it and went to the bar. I didn't argue. I settled onto a bench and leaned toward the warmth. Daniel returned with a bottle of whiskey and two glasses and then went back for two bowls of chowder. I took off my sodden gloves and put my pruney hands around the bowl. I would have jumped into it had it been big enough. Daniel sat down and uncapped the whiskey, pouring some into the glasses, shoving one of them toward me.

I reached into my pocket for the bag of coins, pulling it out, trying to open the drawstring with my numb fingers.

"Leave it," he said, swallowing his whiskey in one gulp.

"You'll need to pay—"

"I already did."

"Then let me count out your share."

"It will wait. Warm up first. I trust you to remember it." He touched my glass with the tip of his finger. "Drink up."

"I don't drink, remember?"

"I remember that he doesn't like you to. But he's not here, and I won't tell. It will help you get warm."

I shook my head. "I shouldn't."

"I hear you say that too often. Who's stopping you? Not me."

"The last time I drank whiskey it was…not good."

"How so? Did you get drunk and sloppy?"

"Something like that. It was a long time ago. I don't remember it all that well." It had been at a dance, and all I remembered of it was how the colors had seemed so vibrant, how everything had swirled together. How I'd danced and laughed, and Junius had pulled me from Duncan Furth's arms and dragged me home. "I made a scene at a dance. I was a little too…free. Junius took me home and I was sick all over the boat. I don't hold it well."

"And he hasn't let you have a drink since."

"It's not like that, Daniel. You think he's an ogre and—"

He held up a hand to stop me. "You said you wouldn't make excuses for him. I like it better when you don't."

"All right."

"At least eat the chowder."

I put the money bag aside and did as he directed. By the time I finished the soup, I was beginning to feel my hands again.

"Thank you for your help today," I said. "You're a good worker."

"So you've said. You pay me well enough to be," he said. He took the last bite of his chowder and pushed the bowl aside.

With deliberate lightness, I said, "How like an oysterman you look. Why, one would think you were born to it. What would your Eleanor think to see you now?"

"I don't think she would appreciate it."

"No?"

"No." He drank his whiskey and grimaced. "This may be the worst whiskey I've ever had."

"Will makes it himself."

"What does he use, lye?"

"Why wouldn't she appreciate it?" I asked. "Eleanor, I mean?"

"She has some idea of me as a gentleman poet," he said. "I suppose I shouldn't have quoted Milton to her."

"I'm certain she found it very romantic."

His gaze came up. "Why do you say that?"

"Don't most women find it so?"

"I don't know. Do you?" His gaze was direct.

I was suddenly flustered. I looked away.

He played with his empty glass, spinning it a little between his fingers. "It's only that she's very…naive. I know she cares for me, but she's a respectable woman from a godly family. Does she really want a man who must work hard for his living?"

"But you've elevated yourself already. Surely the newspaper—"

"Yes, the newspaper." He laughed shortly.

"It's very impressive, you know, what you've done. How you've managed things given…" I couldn't say the words.

"Indeed. Risen from the ashes of poverty." He lifted the whiskey in a mock toast. But he didn't drink it. He stared into it. "I won't be poor again."

"No, why should you be? What with the oystering money you've earned and the newspaper."

"Yes." There was something hard in his eyes that I shrank from. "How strange to find that my father will provide after all."

I was uncomfortable. I had the sense he was talking about something more, something I didn't know that reminded me of Junius's warnings. "You've earned this, Daniel," I said quietly. "You've worked for it. He respects that, even if he doesn't say it."

"I don't think it's hard work he respects."

"Please don't start this again—"

"I think he takes what he wants. I think he always has."

"Daniel—"

"And I think I'm more like him than you know."

He was looking at me so strangely. I shivered—dread again, or a presentiment, but of what I didn't know, and I couldn't grab hold of it.

He looked away. The saloon was full now, men pressed into every nook. They brushed up against us on all sides. It was stifling, close with the scent of oysters and mud and sweat, coal smoke, chowder, and whiskey. Like being inside the basket, unable to move, elbows pressed against reeds, suffocating in darkness—

"Leonie? Are you all right?"

I blinked, coming back to myself. He was leaning forward, a look of concern on his face, and I swallowed and said, "I'm fine. It's only…it's too hot." I was sweating. My face felt red and very warm.

"Let's get out of here." He drained the last of his whiskey, and then he left the rest of the bottle on the table and rose, holding out his hand to help me to my feet. I grabbed it; his fingers closed warmly around mine, pulling me with him through the crowd while I smiled and said hello to those I knew, but I felt a little light-headed, not quite myself, not until we were outside again on the narrow porch, and then into the street, where there was no shelter, and the rain was coming down hard, puddling the street. It was dusk. Already I heard the music coming from McBride's, the fiddlers again, and I thought, *no, no dance* at the same time I yearned for it, at the same time my heart leaped at the music.

It was then I realized that Daniel was still holding my hand. I stepped away, disentangling my fingers, not looking at him. "We should go. It will be dark soon, and in the rain it will—"

"You don't want to go to the dance?" His voice was sharp, hard.

I shook my head. "I think it's best if we go back home."

"You want to dance. I know you do."

"No, I—"

"I won't even dance with you if you don't want. All right?"

There it was, the tacit reference to something I did not want to admit, not to him and not to myself. I did not know what to do with it, or what to say.

He held out his hand. "Come with me?"

I thought of the darkness of the basket, my own hands withering, my sense of time passing, and it was as if I heard her voice whispering in my ear, urging me. I felt her as if she stood beside me. I felt her all around me.

I gave in and let him lead me to the dance.

McBride's was full. There were many oystermen still at Dunn's, but the schooner dances were not restricted to oystermen. Indians were already gathered on the porch, half-drunk, and inside the sawmen—half-drunk as well—and their families were already dancing, women beaming and flouncing their skirts, the pound of boots vibrating, and children dodging their parents and each other. The air was damp and hot and heavy, windows half-open so that the rain splashed in to wet the floor beneath. I had no time to regret coming or to change my mind, because almost the moment Daniel and I went inside Michael Johnson swooped down on us, laughing and saying, "Hello my fine Russells. Thought I saw you on the water today. Dance with me, Leonie?"

I didn't cast the slightest glance to Daniel as I took Michael's hand and let him lead me into a rousing polka. Without Junius there urging me to correct behavior, and with my own confusion distracting me, urging solace of any kind, I did what I was not supposed to do; I became not Leonie Russell but that stranger again, who laughed and spun and flirted and cared nothing for oysters or science but was only a woman. I danced as I wanted to, until I was laughing and my hair was falling into my face. And with that freedom, something else bloomed too, something I did not like or expect, because when the polka was done, I saw Daniel across the room, dancing with Anna Parker, who was a rather heavy mother of four, but he was smiling at her and she looked flustered and charmed—how appealing he could be, how easy it was for him to make women love him. The thought surprised me, but not more than the stab of jealousy I felt. I gave myself back over to the dance, and I tried to keep from searching Daniel out.

But I didn't succeed very well. I knew where he was every moment, and I knew when he was watching me too, and I was conscious of performing for him, of laughing a little too loudly, flirting a bit too obviously. I enjoyed myself, but it was a show, too, and I didn't ask myself what I was doing or why. He did as he'd promised; he didn't once approach me or ask me to dance, and I was grateful for that at the same time I waited for it, both wanting it and afraid of it. As the night went on everything I did became about avoiding him, while at the same time I wanted him to notice me. I did not rest or sit out a single dance, even though I was breathing hard and sweating and my hair was falling from its pins. To rest meant to think, and I wanted not to think. I wanted to feel nothing but the music and my body. I wanted not to be aware of him at all.

And then I saw Bibi.

Twice now she'd come to a dance. And this time, too, I knew she'd come because of me. She stood at the edge of the floor, watching me, though she didn't call me over and I didn't go to her. I didn't want to hear her witch words, not her warnings or her fears or her talk about the *she* who wanted something from me or about the things Daniel did or did not want.

I looked down at the bracelet on my wrist—still there, because when the call for the schooner had come I'd forgotten my resolution. The rain was pounding; I heard it at every pause in the music, the rush of it upon the street, the growing pools of it beneath the windows that slicked the floor when people walked through it, leaving streaks of mud one had to be careful for or slip. When Jackson Anders asked me to dance, I turned deliberately away from Bibi and went into his arms. I pretended not to see her smile.

But with her coming, my awareness of my stepson became overpowering. He was there, talking with a group of men at the table, eating a piece of cake as crumbs spilled from his fingers, and then, dancing with pretty young Celeste Martin, whose husband had just brought her from Yakima two months ago. Dark haired, limpid eyed. Younger than me by nearly two decades.

I stumbled; Jackson tightened his hand on mine and said anxiously, "Did I step on you?"

I smiled up at him and shook my head. My hair fell into my face and I tossed it back, and I was so determined not to catch Bibi's glance that I looked everywhere but her direction, and that was how I caught Daniel's.

He stood at the edge of the crowd, and he looked up just as I looked over, and then I could not look away. It was as if something held me there, some pull I could not release. He went still as well; the moment held until Jackson said something, and I turned back to him.

I did not want the dance to end because I knew what would happen when it did. When the music stopped, and Jackson released me with a little bow, I thought about fleeing. The porch was not so far. Only across the main room. Except that I would need to make it through the crowd without being asked to dance. And I would need to make it past Bibi, who guarded the entrance like some sentinel.

Daniel came as if I'd summoned him. His hair gleamed golden in the lamplight, there was the fine sheen of sweat on his skin. He looked reluctant, uncomfortable, wanting and not wanting in equal measure, and I thought how foolish we both were, how ridiculous. I looked up at him, and he said, "I know I said you didn't have to...just tell me if you don't want to dance with me. I won't insist."

I held out my hand. The music started, a waltz, and he hesitated as if he were surprised. When his fingers closed around mine and I went into his arms, we kept stonily distant from each other. He did not try to bring me closer. It was as if desire had created a wall between us, one neither dared cross, and I saw him fight it even as I did. And all the time, that pull, that irresistible pull, and the music soared and dipped—oh, how good the Jansen brothers were at fiddling a waltz, how sweet it was!—and I closed my eyes and let the music invade me, let it urge me into playing along, let myself sway, and pretended it was not Daniel I danced with at the same time I knew his every movement. And then, suddenly, he dragged me close, almost violently, as if he hated to do it but could not resist, and I was up hard against him, feeling his warmth and mine answering it, and everything shifted. I heard the music and his breath and my own, one body, one motion, a place I fit that belonged just to me, a desire that took prisoners, that took me. I had never felt anything like it, and I knew it was wrong, but I did not want to let it go. In that moment I would have fought the world to keep feeling it, and then the music ended and I looked up at him, and when I saw the way he was looking at me I came back to myself.

I disengaged from him so quickly it was awkward and unseemly, untangling my fingers from his, which did not seem to want to release me. Desperately I looked away toward the door, toward Bibi, who was no longer there. She had disappeared.

I dodged across the dance floor, quickly and purposefully enough that no one stopped me. I had no thought beyond leaving. I was on the porch without my coat or hat before I knew it, stumbling into a group of Indians playing a rather drunken game of *La-hull*, barely avoiding the wooden disks rolling across the planked floor. And once I was there I had no idea what to do or where to go. I crossed my arms over my chest and stood freezing and staring out at the curtain of rain, and a wind that blew it at an angle, not sideways yet, not a storm. The only storm was the one raging in me.

I heard the footsteps behind me. I knew who it was before he spoke a word; I knew also that I would pretend I hadn't felt the things I had, that I would deny him.

I moved to the edge of the porch, beyond the Indians, and he came up beside me. I didn't look at him. I said, "We should think about heading home."

He let out his breath. "In this weather?"

"It's not so bad. We'll only get wet."

"It's going to storm."

I shook my head. "We'll beat it if we go now."

He said quietly, "I asked McBride if there was a room to be had and there is. We should stay here tonight. Go in the morning."

"No!" Too vehement, I knew. I swallowed and said more calmly, "No."

He paused. Hoarsely, he said, "I promise I won't…" The rest died, as if he couldn't bring himself to say the words, and I did not finish the sentence, even in my head. I pretended he hadn't said what we both knew he meant. He went on, "In fact, you should take the room for yourself. I'll…sleep in the hall or…something."

"I'm leaving," I said. "You can go back with me now or stay and make your own way home tomorrow morning."

"Leonie." His voice was very low. "Let's not compound one mistake with another."

"The only mistake would be in staying," I said. "I'm going to get my coat. I'll see you tomorrow."

"I can't let you go alone. Not like this."

Like this. The world felt swollen, ready to burst and change, and I was afraid.

"Then get your things," I managed.

We went inside to get our coats and our hats and say our good-byes. It took longer than I'd hoped, and when we came out again, the wind had strengthened, the rain blowing sideways after all. I didn't hesitate, but went straight into it. I didn't want to give him the time to ask me to change my mind. I was determined to cross the bay, as if home were some safe refuge, and that was ridiculous too because we would only be more alone there, without society to watch the gates. But I refused to think of that. I thought of a closed bedroom door, of Junius's things all around me, of my life all around me, a buffer to remind me of my obligations and my promises.

The wind threatened to lift my hat from my head, and I shoved it down again and bent into the rain, nearly running toward the beach and the plunger. I was nearly soaked through by the time we reached Dunn's, where there was still a crowd, shadows falling across the street from the windows and men in the lamplight. Daniel said nothing but only hurried with me over the raft of driftwood to the plunger. The ropes—the main sheet and that of the jib—whipped in the wind, uncoiling and bouncing against the mast with little thuds. Neither of us spoke a word as we folded up the oilcloth and pushed the sloop out, sloshing through the shallow water to climb aboard. The boat rocked until we were deep enough for me to plunge in the centerboard, and then it steadied. Daniel struggled to light the lamp, and by the third try had it. I raised the sails and he went forward to hang the lantern, which lent so little light through the gray of the blowing rain that it was wasted.

There was a compass stowed away; we rarely used it, but I needed it tonight. I could see no single landmark, and there were no stars. I pulled it from its leather case beneath the seat and held it up to the lamplight to see the direction, and then I took hold of the rudder and pointed us there.

I was cold and wet through already. But we had barely got properly into the bay before the storm that had been threatening hit hard—and I realized what a fool I had been to insist upon this.

The wind howled and the rain came down like thunder. I could see nothing beyond the deck and the sails. The boat rocked in the waves; handling the rudder took all my strength. Without the compass we could have sailed into the ocean; the wind was so fierce I would not have been able to see enough through the blowing rain to know it. I'd raised the jib, but the storm was too much for it, so I lowered it again, but it caught, the sheets snapping and striking out, tangling furiously about the mast, and the wind filled it and the boat heeled so far over we began to take in water. I let the mainsail go slack, but even so I knew the wind was so strong that the jib would take us under if I didn't get it completely down.

I shouted at Daniel to take the rudder, and when he did I tried to climb to the bow to release the jib, but then we were hit by something—a wave, a burst of wind, and the boat went nearly up onto its side, and I slipped and fell. Daniel caught me by my sleeve, jerking me back so hard I fell into him, saving me from plunging overboard. Water splashed over the side, a wave that soaked us both, a mouthful of saltwater that made me choke and sputter. The wind screamed.

"I've got to get the jib down," I shouted at him, but the wind tore my voice away. I tried to get loose, but he held me fast with one arm, his other shaking with the effort of holding the rudder steady.

"Stay here!" he shouted back at me. "What are you doing?"

"The jib!" I pointed to the sail, fat with wind, the sheets slapping noisily on the deck and the mast.

"Let me do it!"

I shook my head. "Can you swim?"

He let me go, and I tried to find my step. The boat jerked again; I grabbed his shoulder to steady myself and grabbed a mooring line, tying it about my waist in case I fell. The deck was slick with rain, and angled so steeply my boots were half in water as I crept around the hold, nearly crawling to the bow. One of the sheets whipped my cheek; I grabbed it only just before it lashed my eyes, pulling myself upright by holding on to the mast, trying to avoid the slapping mainsail. The jib sheets whipped about like snakes, the rain coming down so hard I could barely see. I reached out blindly, flailing. The wind whipped my hat from my head and it flew off into the darkness, and I made another lunge, grasping the rope at last, untangling it so it was free. I reached to pull the jib loose—

A gust of wind, the boat heeled, I lost my footing and slipped, crashing onto the deck so hard I lost my breath, sliding. I grappled for something, for anything. I heard Daniel shout my name, and then I was plunging into the roiling water, the cold like ice, the shock of it taking my breath, blind and gasping while it grabbed my boots and my coat and pulled me down and down and down, and I couldn't breathe or swim or see—it was too hard, and I knew I was going to drown.

Still, I fought it. I struggled against the water, trying desperately to make my way to the surface, making it only to have a swell surge over me again. My skirt tangled about my legs, impossible to get free. The wind and the water were in my ears. My coat was so heavy. My boots...I could swim, but this was impossible. Impossible to fight the wind and the water and my own clothing. Impossible to catch a breath. Surrounded by darkness and cold so I could not see which way was up, and my arms pressing against the sides of the basket and the suffocating and I was so afraid...

And then I felt it. The tug at my waist, the rope I'd tied around myself. I felt it pull at me, dragging me up, dragging me to the surface, and I broke through, breathing air and water, the shadow of the boat in front of me and Daniel leaning over the side, a panicked look on his face, the rope tight in his hands, and I realized I was not going to die, that there was the side of the boat and all I must do was grab for it, which I did, and then he grabbed at me hard and desperately, jerking me onto the deck so I fell into him, and we both crashed back into the hold and all I could do was lie there and gasp.

His hands were on my face. "You're all right?" he asked. And then again, "Are you all right?"

I managed to nod.

His relief turned to brutality. His hands tightened on my face. He screamed at me, "Christ, this is stupid! Why the hell are we even out here?" He nearly threw me from him, jerking back. "You could have died! And all because—"

I grabbed his arm. "I'm...fine." My voice was too quiet, the wind would not let me be heard. The jib and the mainsail flapped ceaselessly, slapping against the wind. I was lying in water, two inches at least.

Daniel jerked his arm away and put his face in his hands, hunching his shoulders. I tried to take a deep breath and coughed up water, rolling to my side, coughing until I thought I would never stop, and then, suddenly I did. Suddenly I could breathe. It was then I felt how cold I was. Colder than I'd ever been. Deep, unceasing cold. I shook so hard I could do nothing else. The boat rocked, buffeted by the waves and the wind.

"Daniel," I gasped. He did nothing. I think he didn't hear me through the storm. I reached out, touching his arm, and then he looked up, and I said through chattering teeth, "You'll have to get us home. I...cannot."

"How?"

"L-listen to me," I managed. "The...compass. We need to go west and then south. Do you...understand?"

"You're freezing." He leaned forward as if he meant to take me into his arms.

I slapped him away. "The *compass*. We have to get...home."

He hesitated, and then he nodded. He grabbed the oilcloth from where we'd shoved it into the hold and then he steadied himself against the wind, pulling me with him as he sat, drawing me between his legs, wrapping the oilcloth around me before he grabbed the rudder and the compass. I told him what to do, pointing out the sheet that managed the mainsail, telling him to reef it, and then I could do no more. I pulled the wet and slimy oilcloth closer and huddled into the vee of his legs, absorbing what little warmth from his body there was to offer, shaking as I laid my head in his lap. The oilcloth smelled of oysters and the sea. I was soaking wet and colder than I'd ever been in my life, though the oilcloth kept off the worst of the rain and sheltered me from the wind. But I was dripping water, sodden. I could no longer feel my hands or my feet or my face, and I could not stop shivering.

After that, I don't remember. I drifted in and out—sometimes I saw only rain and wind and the faint glow of the lamp against the dark and sometimes it seemed as if the storm had cleared and I was watching Daniel's shadow against a starlit sky, and I was warm and the scent of sun-burned grass filled my nose and my mind so I could taste it. It seemed both forever and only the blink of an eye before I realized Daniel was helping me over the side of the sloop, stepping knee deep into water. We were beached, I thought, and saw the boat tip to one side and the sail flap in the darkness, and I could do nothing, move nothing. I could not think, I felt caught in a dream, and I was so tired and so cold, and suddenly he slapped me hard, stinging, jerking me from the dream. "Wake up, Lea. Stay awake, damn you. *Damn* you!"

I stumbled; I could not use my numb and useless feet, I fell face first into the water, feeling the jarring into my shoulders, though I could not feel my hands at all, and then he was lifting me, carrying me, pulling me tight into his chest. I was vaguely aware that he was stumbling, cursing beneath his breath, and then we were there, up the porch steps, plunging through the door into a house cold and dark as the night had been, but with no wind and no rain, and he fell to his knees as he crossed the threshold as if his strength had carried him as far as it could, dumping me onto the floor so hard I groaned—not from pain but from the jolt of it, crashing my bones together, but not my teeth, which were locked hard against the cold.

Through a daze I realized he was jerking off my boots, my coat, wrapping me in that Hudson's Bay blanket on the settee, not warm enough. Then he was gone. I heard clanging, more cursing—the noise kept me from settling into the dream, and then he was there again, pulling me up, pulling me to where I felt the beginning surge of warmth—the kitchen, the stove. Wood and heat, but I felt so stupid. My thoughts would not coalesce. He pulled the blanket from my shoulders, unbuttoning my dress, and I thought *I should not let him do this* but could not remember why. Like a child, I submitted. He peeled the sodden dress from my skin. I let him drag off my flannel petticoat and my stockings so I had on nothing but my chemise, clinging wetly to my skin, and then he cocooned me again in the blanket and rubbed my hands and my feet vigorously. I could see him doing it but I could feel nothing, and then suddenly I could, pins and needles, and I gasped in pain and tried to pull away. He rose then and shoved something into my hands, something hot—a mug. "Drink it," he said, and his voice came to me like a muffled echo, but I did as he said. Tasteless, but warm. It burned down my chest so I gasped, and he took off his sodden jacket and threw it aside, and then he was beside me again, pulling off the blanket and wrapping himself around me, then the blanket over both of us, and I realized with some faraway part of myself that he was shaking too, that his hands were white with cold. I closed my eyes and leaned back against him as the faint stirrings of warmth crept through me—a burning torment, tingling, sharp and painful and I wanted to cry with it, but he held me close, and gradually it faded and I was warm, and this time when I fell into sleep, he did not wake me.

CHAPTER 17

I WOKE TO WARMTH, COCOONED IN IT, JUNIUS WRAPPED around me, drawing me back against his chest, his fingers tangled in the twine of the bracelet, clutching a shell charm. I snuggled deeper into him, and in his sleep he tightened his hold in response. I was so warm, and he was here, and I felt safe—

But then I realized it was no soft bed but a hard floor beneath me, and in drowsy surprise I opened my eyes, staring into the gray of morning and the still warm stove in front of me. I did not know where I was or how I'd got there; I could not orient myself. Then he stirred, and the night rushed back, and with a little shock I realized that this wasn't Junius cradling me so closely but Daniel.

I should move away. I knew that but I didn't do it. Instead I went still, afraid to wake him. I was so warm. There could be no harm in staying here for a few moments longer. He'd meant only to comfort me, to keep me warm, and I was alive and that was due to him and it seemed ungrateful now to jerk away or to wake him, as it was obvious he'd kept the stove going all night long. So I stayed there, listening to the rain beyond the windows, how it beat so furiously upon the roof, though I heard no wind. The day was gray and muted, the morning shadows dark, and I felt drowsy and languid.

I knew when he woke. The change in his breathing, a little startle and then a stillness, as if, like me, he'd remembered where he was and did not wish to come back to who we were and what we should be to each other. He drew his fingers from the bracelet, and I said nothing, did nothing, his conspirator in pretending there was nothing wrong in this. We lay this way for a few minutes, perhaps a quarter of an hour, before I knew I could delay no longer.

The first thing I said to him was a whisper. "I'm sorry."

"For what?" Spoken into my shoulder, the heat of his breath against my skin, close enough that I imagined I felt the touch of his lips.

"For making you go through that. You were right. We should have stayed at the hotel."

"You're alive. That's all that matters."

"I've you to thank for that. I owe you."

"You don't owe me anything," he said. "There was no choice to make. What was I supposed to do, let you drown? Let you die of cold?"

The cuff of his shirt was still damp. He'd slept all night in wet clothes, a sacrifice that touched me, dangerously so. I pushed gently against his arms until he let me go, and then I sat up, my hip and my shoulder aching from the hard bed of the kitchen floor. I twisted to look at him. "You should get into some dry clothes."

"How do you feel?" he asked me.

"Fine, I think. A little sore."

He sat up. He pulled the blanket off his shoulders and handed it to me, and I took it, wrapping it around. He braced his forearms on his knees, giving me a sleepy, soft smile. "You look like a Pre-Raphaelite painting."

"A what?"

"Your hair," he said, gesturing. "Like that painting by Dante Rossetti. *Beatrice*, I think."

"I don't know what you're talking about."

"She has the same kind of hair you do. You'd like the painting, I think. The drama of it suits you."

"I've had quite enough of drama, thank you."

Still, that smile. He said, "Like that poem too—do you know it? *Porphyria's Lover*?—'And spread o'er all her yellow hair—'"

He stopped so suddenly it was a moment before I realized he meant to say no more, before I felt the quiet, words lingering.

"Now I've quoted poetry to you," he said, and there was something painful in his voice, as if he'd done something he hadn't meant to do, and I remembered last night, his asking whether I found such things romantic, and I clutched the blanket more closely about me—as if it were protection enough from my own yearning, from the things he saw in me that I hadn't known were there.

"Daniel, this isn't...We can't..."

"No, we can't," he agreed, meeting my gaze, and I felt that pull again, the same I'd felt at the dance, this sense of inevitability, as if my will were a puny thing in the face of destiny—ah, but what was that but an excuse? Will was only want's minion. And that I wanted there was no denying.

He leaned forward, slowly enough that I knew his intention, that I could have backed away, but I didn't. I let him kiss me, his mouth soft and full, tentative, testing, and then he withdrew, a bare breath between us, waiting a moment, giving me the chance to deny, to say no, and instead I leaned forward too, and he made a little sound and then his hands were on me, pulling me to him, kissing me again, deepening it, and my arms were around his neck and I was answering, drawn without thought or question, desire burning, alive and awake at last.

The blanket loosened; I let it fall and where the air touched me, his hands followed, in my hair and then to my shoulders, down my back to my waist, over my hips, hot through the thin fabric of my chemise, drawing me closer so I felt him hard against me, and then he was falling back, rolling me beneath him, and my shoulder brushed something—burlap. I reached up to push it away. A bag. Bones chittering against each other.

The bag of bones beneath the stairs. Junius's skeletons.

Reason broke over me like the icy water I'd nearly drowned in. Suddenly I realized what it was we were about to do, what could not be taken back or undone.

He was drawing up my chemise, his hand warm against my skin, and I clamped my own down hard on his, stopping him, twisting away from his kiss, saying, "Wait. Daniel...no. Wait."

It was as if he heard me through a dream. He drew back, blinking. I saw the desire dark in his eyes. His breath came hard, as hard as mine. Hoarsely, he asked, "Did I hurt you?"

"No, but we...we can't do this. We have to stop."

He looked ready to protest. His hand tightened on me as if he meant to continue, to deny.

"We can't," I said again.

He looked at me as if he couldn't hear, as if he didn't understand. I saw him try to shake it away, and then I saw his dawning awareness of what we were doing, of what we'd almost done. His jaw tightened, desire suddenly banked; he pushed off me. "Christ. *Christ*." The words were bitten off, violent. He drew up his knees and buried his face in his arms.

My heart was racing, desire not abating, throbbing and twisting, and I wished...what, that I had said nothing? That even now he was...I swallowed hard and sat up, pushing down my chemise, pulling up the blanket, drawing it close, protection from him, from myself.

I reached out to touch his shoulder, thought better of it, drew back. "Daniel—"

"One moment," he snapped.

I heard his anger and his frustration and I understood it; it was all I could do to keep from saying, *I want you. I don't want to think about anything else. I want to lie with you.* I fingered the charms of the bracelet around my wrist—*You will need it now he is here*—and I laughed wryly.

Daniel looked up. "Something amusing?"

"Nothing," I said, and then I held out my wrist. "This. Bibi's bracelet. She warned me to be careful. She told me it was a protection."

"Against the mummy, you said."

"Against *you*," I told him. And then, bitterly, "And you can see how well it works, can't you?"

"Protection against *me*?" He looked a little stunned. "She told you that?"

I nodded.

He ran his hand through his hair distractedly. "I shouldn't have come here."

"No one could blame you for wanting to meet your father."

"It was too much a...temptation." He went on as if he hadn't heard me. "All of it. As if it had been set there just for me. Everything I wanted. The mummy. My father. I thought I didn't care. I'd been looking for him for so long I didn't want to find him anymore. I wouldn't even have read the paper that day, but there was a wind that blew it up against the dock, and I was picking up a feather that had caught in it and I saw his name."

"You were picking up a feather," I said slowly, remembering the heron on the riverbank, its yellow beak, its questioning eye.

He glanced up at me. "It was a pretty color. Blue-gray. I'd meant it for..."

"Eleanor," I whispered.

He swallowed. "Your widow is right, Lea. You don't know anything about me. And I can't...This"—a gesture, me, him, the two of us—"is not what either of us should want. I should have gone back with the schooner last night."

His words filled me with dismay, though it had been what I wanted, too, what I had not been able to ask of him.

"It was all...too easy," he went on. "I should have realized. I did realize. I just didn't want to admit it."

It was as if he were speaking in a kind of code. I could not quite grasp him. I frowned. "What do you mean? What was too easy?"

"Finding my father. The mummy too. It was just...It's all right. I'll find something else. Don't worry about me." And then, bitterly, "I always land on my feet."

I found myself protesting, delaying. "At least wait until Junius returns."

"I can't stay that long." He gave me a frank look. "You know it too. He's only been gone a few days and already we...I couldn't bear a week or more."

I was quiet. I wanted to beg him not to go; I wanted him to leave that moment. I looked down at the blanket clutched in my hands, the green and red bands against the white. I fingered the soft wool. When I looked up again, Daniel was staring at me.

"I'm afraid to stay," he said. "And I'm afraid to go. I'm afraid of what you'll become if I leave you, Leonie."

I tried to smile. "What I will become? What a strange thing to say. I'm already *become*, Daniel. Dear God, I'm nearly forty. I'm happy. I am. I've told you that."

"You almost died last night. You almost died, and what then? What have you done that was your own? You've wasted your talents. Don't keep wasting them."

"You're wrong about me, Daniel," I said. "And I—"

Drowning.

I faltered. Daniel frowned. "What? What is it?"

I was suddenly cold. Freezing. The plunge into icy water, unable to catch my breath. I felt the lap of water at my bare feet, and I shivered and drew them up closer beneath the blanket. "I'm so...cold."

He was on his feet in a moment. "I'll put more wood on."

I put my hand out to stop him. My head was reeling. I began to shiver. "No, I...it's—"

Fear. I was falling beneath the waves, choking. A memory of last night. The water rising and rising, tangling my skirts, pulling on my coat, drawing me under, and yet...not me at all...

"What is it, Leonie?"

I struggled for breath. I struggled to see past the fear. *You must come. Come now.*

I leaped to my feet, letting the blanket fall. "The mummy," I said. "The water's rising. The river—" I rushed to the door, grabbing my coat, still wet, and pulling it on over my chemise, shoving my bare feet into my sodden boots. My hat—no hat, it was lost to the Shoalwater.

He asked no questions, but put on his own boots. He was dragging on his coat as we went out the door, and then we both halted, stunned. The river *was* rising—it had already risen, the wind I thought I hadn't heard whipping it to a frenzy. Not overflowing its banks yet, but it was a matter of half inches. Edna stood at the barn entrance, lowing and crying, udder full and bloated—I'd forgotten she even existed.

"Oh dear God." I was off the porch, running toward the barn, slipping and sliding through a marsh puddling and swamp-like with the heavy rain. I heard Daniel sloshing beside me.

"The mummy first," I gasped to him as we made it to Edna.

He nodded. I lurched through the door; the trunk was there against the wall, closed and locked, though not watertight. The dirt floor was wet already near the walls, a growing pool of water, the lap of the river beneath the trunk. Daniel took one side and I took the other, hefting it—thank God it was so light.

"Where to?"

"The porch."

The barn was too close to the river, and it had flooded time and again, but the house was on a rise and safe, even if the river kept rising. But the salt marsh was more like a bog now, and the trunk, though light, was unwieldy, and we struggled. We got the trunk to the porch, and then I ran back to Edna, grabbing her halter, pulling her toward the house, where I tethered her to the porch.

I glanced toward the springhouse, which was at the bend, and saw it was half-submerged already, milk and cream spreading into the water, a murky light cloud. How easily the river took what it wanted. I couldn't help but remember what Lord Tom had said the day I'd found her. How the spirits would find a way to take back their own. But the barn was still upright, and it had never fallen in a flood, and soon the rain would stop. It always had.

Edna lowed piteously. Daniel started. "Are we safe here?"

"I think so."

He nodded. "Then I'll milk her."

He left me there. I watched the river for a moment, churning and murky with silt, a fast current, too fast and too high. But there was nothing to do about it. I had no way of stopping it.

I looked away, glancing over my shoulder at the trunk. The porch was already wet from the storm; not a safe place to keep her, so I grabbed the handle of one end of the trunk and pulled it to the door and then inside, hearing Lord Tom's words as I did so, trying to banish my own discomfort. There were already skeletons in the house, how was this different?

I closed the door, kneeling beside the trunk. I took the key from my pocket, turning it in the lock, opening the lid, dreading to see if there was water in there with her, if she had been damaged in any way, relieved to see her there, still in one piece, though up hard against the side as if she'd been thrown there. Daniel and I had not been gentle getting the trunk out of the barn.

But the water had got in—the bottom was wet. She could not stay in it until I dried it out again. I reached in to lift her, pulling her out as if she were a small sleeping child, bending to lay her on the settee as if comfort mattered. I looked at her, her hair draping over the edge of the settee, her arms drawn up, lost in dreams.

Daniel came up beside me. As if he sensed my thoughts, he said, "She almost looks alive there. As if she's only sleeping."

"You're the only one," I said quietly.

"The only one *what*?"

"The only one who thinks of her as I do. The only one who doesn't think of her as something to sell or hide away."

He was quiet for long enough that I looked over my shoulder at him. He had turned to stare out the window.

"Do you think they would have made it to Astoria in this storm?" he asked. "You don't suppose they drowned?"

"If it began to be a danger, they would have beached the canoe and taken shelter. Lord Tom grew up on these shores. He knows what to do."

"How certain you sound."

"I am certain. He and Junius have traveled in weather worse than this."

"And he thinks nothing of leaving you here alone. With flooding rivers."

"There was no fear of that when he left," I said softly. "And he didn't leave me alone. He left me with you."

He turned to look at me. "What a fool he is."

"He trusts me," I said. "And Daniel...I'm not going to give him a reason not to."

Daniel took a deep breath and nodded. He glanced out the window again. "The water's rising quickly. Perhaps we should make for higher ground."

"It won't come this far."

"Why not?"

"It never has before." I could not say why I was so certain, exactly, except for the reason I had told him, that it had never happened before, as many times as the river had flooded. And the mummy was part of my certainty too, though I would not admit it even to myself, this sense I had that she would keep us safe, that she wanted me to find the answers and the river would not take her back until she was done, and she was not done.

He turned to look at me, and in that look was this morning, and I thought of the kitchen floor and the way he'd kissed me and the strength of my desire. I said, "Don't look at me that way."

"I can't help it," he said.

"You have to try," I said. "For my sake, if not for your own. I'm married to your father."

"Married? You're not married to him, not really."

"I made vows."

"Not binding ones. He was already married."

"They felt binding to me. They still do. I meant them, Daniel. I've been married to him in my head for twenty years. How can that be nothing? And...and you have your Eleanor."

He sighed. "Yes. Eleanor. I used to dream about her, you know. Every night, I dreamed of touching her, of...ah, never mind."

I felt the sting of jealousy, though I had no right. None at all. "I imagine it must be hard to be away from her for so long. You must miss her. And here...we're so isolated..."

He skewered me with his gaze. "Now it's you I'm dreaming of."

I was shaken, warmed, aroused. "You love *her*, Daniel. It's only that I'm here, and you're lonely."

"That's not the reason," he said quietly.

"You're affianced. You've made a promise you have to keep. I think you should make yourself think of her. I think you should—"

"Would she want me to keep such a promise now, I wonder?"

"Of course she would. And you must anyway. This is...a passing thing. We won't give in to it."

"She was my mother's choice for me," he mused. "I was happy about it, but now I...I wonder if...if perhaps I only loved her because my mother demanded it."

"Do the reasons matter? You *were* happy about it. And your mother knew you best. I've no doubt she wanted only your happiness."

"My mother was trapped in her own misery. What she wanted for me was not happiness."

That startled me. "How can you say that? She was your mother."

"Because I knew her," he said, his eyes fierce. "Because I listened to her hate him every day. Because I watched her up to her elbows in lye soap and scalding water, saying one moment that he would return and save us, and the next that I must find him and take vengeance for both of us. I know why he left her, Lea. I know because I loved her but every day I wanted to leave her too. And I feel her there, in my head, urging me always—" He bit off the word and turned away.

I stared at him, surprised by his words, feeling a sinking in my stomach for what his father and I had done to him, for the hatred that lingered in him still. "Urging you to do what?" I asked softly.

"To hurt him," he said. "To give her peace."

I felt sick. I remembered now, too late, that I wasn't to trust him, that I *hadn't* trusted him. "I...see. So...I'm to be your revenge?"

He looked at me. The fierceness in his eyes died. They were only blue now, and weary. "Lea...the very first time I watched you dance I wondered what it would be like to be your lover. I've never stopped wondering. I can't sleep for wanting you. You're not my revenge, and this isn't an act. It would be better if it were."

His words silenced me. I felt naked before him, unbearable heat rising, this wretched confusion, this bewitchment of yearning. I didn't know what to say. Daniel did not look away, but only watched me with a haunting stillness, as if I were a curiosity in a museum that he expected to animate at any moment—would I run? Would I stay?

"I've frightened you," he said. "I didn't mean to tell you any of that."

"It's all right," I said, and my voice sounded high and breathless, not like mine. I swallowed, trying to right it. "Truly it is."

He said nothing. His smile was small and self-deprecating, and I felt absurd and comical.

"I...I think I'll make us something to eat. We haven't even had coffee," I said, needing desperately to escape him, to right myself.

He raised a brow as if he knew it and said, "By all means. Coffee fixes all ills."

I fled to the kitchen.

CHAPTER 18

ᴅANIEL WENT TO HIS ROOM, AND I BUSIED MYSELF WITH stupid tasks. I listened to the drenching rain and the roar of the river and was aware that I could be wrong about how far it would rise, that it might overtake the house and we would have to find a way to escape it, and yet I baked bread and made a meal as if the world depended upon how elaborate it was. An oyster pie and a dried berry buckle and squash made sweet with molasses. I set out pickles and fried up brined pork and put coffee on to boil, and each of these things settled me more firmly into who I was, until by the time I called up to him that it was ready, I felt myself again.

He came down, holding one of my father's journals, looking surprised at the bounty I'd laid upon the table. "There's enough here for a party." He glanced toward the settee and the mummy. "Were you planning to invite her to join us?"

I smiled at the joke, and it broke the tension between us, as he must have meant it to do. While we ate, I kept the conversation deliberately light, and he seemed determined to help me to do so. We talked of the rain and the usual course of the winter weather, and he told me of the fog in San Francisco and how cold even the summers could be while I said it had been a good summer for harvesting and the vegetable garden had produced well, and fortunately Edna gave enough milk that the loss of what had been in the springhouse would not be too bad.

There was an hour, perhaps a little longer, where I felt things to be comfortable and safe between us, as if we were some long-together couple, and I found myself thinking of how things might have been if I'd met him first, and the unexpected thought flustered me, so I broke off in the middle of a sentence and looked down into my coffee.

He said nothing. He poured himself a cup of milk and took a sip, comfortable and easy as if we were the couple I'd imagined, so when he grabbed the journal from where he'd set it on the table, opening it to a place he'd marked, I could look at him again.

"You found something?"

He shook his head. "Only…it's become rather interesting. In the same sort of way watching a fly is interesting, you understand. Boring and mesmerizing at the same time."

I smiled. "Indeed. Go on."

He smiled back and cast his gaze to the pages, reading aloud, "'L has formed a gross preoccupation in Old Toke's tales.'" He glanced up. "Who's Old Toke?"

"One of the Indians who lived on the bay when we first came here," I told him. "He was an old man then. Toke's Point was his place. He was sort of a leader among the Shoalwater, and he was the best storyteller. I think Lord Tom learned some of the legends from Old Toke."

"So the L is you."

I nodded. "I've told you Papa hated that I liked the stories."

Daniel nodded and looked down again, reading on, "'Not the same, but all primitives are like. Superstition and weakness! I am disquieted—all is naught.'" He frowned. "Do you understand it?"

"Not a bit." I reached for the book, and he pushed it to my hands—how careful we were not to touch. I glanced down at the words.

"What does he mean—'not the same, but all primitives are like'?"

"He found all Indian stories equally primitive, even when they weren't about the same things. And he always equated Indian superstition with weakness." I fingered the tooth on its thong, remembering how my father's fingers had gone to where it had once hung around his neck even as he lay dying.

"All beliefs are a fiction more or less," Daniel said with a shrug.

"How you must horrify Eleanor's missionary father."

"Well, it wouldn't be wise to tell him I think that, would it? I play the image of a model son-in-law."

"It is only a role, then?"

"One among many." He met my gaze. "I say that as one actor to another."

I glanced away. Determined not to rise to the bait, I said, "Was…your mother very devout? Did she realize how you felt?"

"She did when I refused to go to church any longer. Before that, she made me go every Sunday. But once I was bringing in three quarters of our living, I felt I should have a say as to how I spent my time."

"How old were you?"

"Thirteen." He reached for the squash, then pushed it away again as if he'd thought better of it. "What about you? Did your father drag you to church?"

I played with the edge of my cup. "Science was Papa's religion. He read the Bible to me sometimes, not because he believed it, I think, but because he felt he ought to. But we never stayed anywhere long enough to go to church and when we finally came here, there was no church to go to. Not until they built the one in Oysterville. Before that, a circuit preacher came round every few months. He's the one who married Junius and me."

"I wonder what that preacher thought of a girl marrying an old man?"

I snorted inelegantly. "That history repeats itself, no doubt. It isn't that unusual, you know. And it was either marry us or let us live in sin together. What was he to do? I was alone."

"Did you never think that it might be better to be alone?"

I nodded. "I told Papa so. I told him I didn't need to marry. That I had Lord Tom. That I would do just fine on my own."

"What did he say?"

I smiled thinly. "He was most insistent otherwise."

"So you did as he ordered."

"He knew best."

"Perhaps you thought so at seventeen. Do you still believe it?"

I looked up at him. "What good is it not to? I promised. I married Junius. It all turned out. I think Papa would be pleased."

Again, Daniel said, "Do you still believe it was best?"

"Yes," I said, and then, more insistently, "Yes. Papa knew me very well."

"Did he? Then why forbid you what you most loved? The stories?"

"A true scientist looks at facts, not imaginings," I defended.

"Your father's words, I think. What about the story you told me in the cave about those drawings?"

I hesitated. I thought of Papa, of the lessons he tried forever to drill into my head: *Where did that story come from, Lea? Do you know it to be true, or is it just fancy? Is there some savage here to tell it to you?* "Imaginings, Daniel. I don't *know* that's what happened."

Daniel leaned forward. "You have a gift for imagining what other lives must have been like."

"Not a gift, a flaw," I insisted.

"I heard you in that cave, Lea. The things you said…I believed that you knew who had painted those things and why. I believe the things you say about the mummy and how she died. It feels… right. We can't know everything. Instinct matters."

"It *is* a flaw. Papa was right. A real scientist would care only about the facts. It's why I can't understand what he saw in the mummy that I can't see. Why would he have reburied her?"

"You don't know that he did that."

"It's the only explanation. There's something about her that's wrong. He knew it, and he put her back, and I *don't understand.*"

Daniel sighed and rose, picking up dishes, taking them to the sink.

"Leave them," I said. "I'll do them."

"You made dinner. Leave these to me. Stop punishing yourself for what you can't know and go do what you were meant to do. Go draw your mummy."

And so I did. The rain poured and I could hear the roar of the river, but it didn't seem to be rising further, so I sat on the floor before the settee and listened to Daniel clean up, and I drew her. I still meant to cut her apart as Junius had demanded, but once I did that, this drawing would be the only thing I had of her, so each detail mattered. Again, even more so now, I had the sense that she and I were entwined, that the mystery of her would solve the mystery of who I was, even as that thought puzzled and bedeviled me. I knew who I was, didn't I? *Didn't I?*

I glanced up. While I'd been lost in drawing, the day had faded. It was already dark. I'd been aware vaguely when Daniel finished cleaning. At some point, I heard him go out and come inside again, the thud of another pail of milk, the splash of it into the milk pans to set until the cream rose, the clang of the stove door as he fed the fire. He'd lit another lamp, and now he sat in Lord Tom's chair, my father's journal in his lap, his head bowed so the lamplight shone upon his golden hair. He looked up at my movement. "Finished?"

"Not quite. I want to get every detail."

"And then?"

I took a deep breath and set my notebook aside. "And then I cut her open. Junius has given me until he returns to do so."

"We'll keep reading your father's journals. We'll find something there. But don't hurry to tear her apart. Not on his account."

How did he know so clearly the things I wanted, when I hardly knew them myself? How easy it was to talk with him, to listen to him say the things I wanted to believe, to be *known*. The temptation to keep doing so was hard to resist, but I forced myself to remain silent. Because I was tired. My ordeal last night had left me weary, and now that my pencil was set aside, distraction gone, I was aware of him as I had never been aware of any man. I could not stop thinking of the kiss we'd shared, the thing we'd almost done. And I knew I hadn't the strength to withstand him tonight if he should make the effort.

Better to take the sanctuary of the bedroom I shared with my husband, to hide behind closed and locked doors. A wall I could not cross and that required no effort to erect.

I rose, pushing my loosened hair back from my face, still stiff with salt. It needed to be washed, but not tonight. I said, "I'm tired. I think I'll go to bed."

I was tense, expecting him to make some comment, to say something suggestive, to play to my desire. He had to know it was there; it must be in my face as clearly as was his.

But he only nodded and looked back down at the journal. "Good night."

And I was—what? Disappointed? Relieved? I didn't know. I could not decide. The sanctuary I'd longed for seemed suddenly not a sanctuary at all. I hesitated.

He looked up again. "What is it?"

"Nothing," I said, and went to the stairs. "Good night."

Her sandaled feet shushed and crunched through the long grass, a breeze without the scent of ocean or mud, blowing her hair back from her face, drying the sweat at her temples. I felt these things at the same time I watched her from a distance, the grace of her movements, the saffron of her skirt tangling about her legs, molding to her body, wide hips, full breasts, and then falling away again.

She came closer and closer to where I stood, and I watched her come close, even as I saw myself through her eyes, my own blonde hair loose, falling over my shoulders and down my back, haloing in the sun. I put my hand to my eyes to shield the glare and saw myself do so. I felt her smile as my own. I felt her happiness, and just when she reached me, I saw myself disappear, no longer there. I was only her, inside her head, and she kept walking, and then I was myself again, watching her go.

And then I was beneath the water, flailing in a storm, swallowing salt water, trying to find the boat or its shadow but it was too dark and I was twisting and struggling and with no breath to be found, no way to save myself or fight it. I could not find the boat. I could not find him. Choking, drowning, paralyzed with cold, tangled as if in a net, pulling me down and down and down, never ending, falling into disappearing, into nothing.

You almost died, and what a waste. What a waste, what a waste, what a waste...

The salt taste of the Shoalwater was in my mouth when I blinked awake, the words still ringing in my ears. Everything was so sharp. Instead of the darkness of night I saw myself reaching for the rope and flailing, plunging into the water. Instead of the sound of the river I heard the rush of the Shoalwater hard against my ears, and my own choking. I was freezing, my skin goose-pimpled beneath a slick layer of cold sweat.

I had almost died. Another moment and I would have. I would have given in to that nothingness. There would have been no Leonie Russell, nothing of me left but a house full of relics and notebooks with half-translated Indian tales. Nothing to remember. No children—but that hadn't been my purpose, had it? My purpose had been research and study, and yet here I was, and suddenly the sadness I'd felt in the dream, when she'd walked away, was overwhelming. *Who are you? What do you want from the world?*

I wrapped my arms around myself, digging my fingers into my skin, trying to gain hold of my emotions, which were so tangled I could not decide what I felt. Fear and despair and then...

Then I felt her.

One moment not there and then there the next, the way the air changes just before a storm. I stared about the room in confusion; once again her presence was so strong I expected to see her standing before me. But there was only darkness, and in it anger, the terrible menace that had frightened me once before, that raised the hair on my neck, that had me whispering in terrified panic, "What would you have of me? What do you *want*?"

I stared into the darkness. And what came over me then I couldn't explain. My fear disappeared; instead I felt peace, or no...something bigger than that, something that didn't calm or soothe, but lit a flame instead, tiny and flickering, hope and fear and anticipation all together. And in it, I heard her voice.

Live.

CHAPTER 19

THE STORM WAS OVER. THE BRIGHT OVERCAST OF EARLY morning lightened the curtains as I stretched, wincing at the soreness in my arms, at my waist, muscles strained, and it was a moment before I remembered what had caused it. The last vestiges of my near drowning. Then I remembered my dream, the way I'd awakened in the middle of the night, the voice I'd heard in my head.

Live.

I frowned, pushing back the blankets and rising, bare feet on the cold floor. I washed and dressed quickly. I opened my bedroom door slowly and quietly, preparing myself to see him, and then I went downstairs, into the smell of frying salt pork and coffee. Daniel was at the stove, and on the table was sliced bread and butter, the leftover dried berry buckle from last night. "Good morning," he said, looking up from the skillet he was managing with a comical wariness.

"You're making breakfast," I said in surprise.

"Barely. This is about the extent of my skill."

I smiled, going to sit as he took the salt pork off the stove and set the sizzling skillet on the table, releasing it hard, as if the pan was hot enough to burn through the towel he'd wrapped around the handle. The fat spattered a little onto the table, and he gave me a rueful grimace and sat down. "Sorry. As I told you, limited skill."

"I'm not complaining."

He poured a cup of coffee for me and then for himself, and speared a piece of the salt pork onto his plate. "We'll have to wait until the water's gone down enough in the springhouse to clean it, but that's the only damage I can see." He paused. "I was reading the journals last night. I couldn't sleep."

I looked away quickly, feeling the telltale heat in my cheeks, and when I glanced at him again, he was smiling into his plate.

"I didn't find much," he went on, reaching for one of the journals, opening it to a page he'd marked with a slip of paper. "Mostly lists of what he'd been collecting, and some measurements—you know he'd been measuring skulls and sending the results to Louis Agassiz?"

"Agassiz was a mentor to Papa."

"Well, that explains it. Your father sent the results along with some theories as to what he thought about the possibility that the Shoalwater overtook a more advanced race."

"I thought he agreed with June that they hadn't."

"Here he says, 'One can see by the characteristics of the skulls, not just the width, breadth and depth, but by the prominent and regular location of various cranial bumps, that these people were well possessed of such phrenological aspects as secretiveness, destructiveness, and cunning—which is borne out by their behavior even into the present day. They are unsurpassed in trade strategy at the same time they show a lamentable tendency toward the animalistic and an unparalleled (at least in my experience) instinct to self-destruction, which needs only their obvious enslavement to alcoholic spirits to illustrate. The Shoalwater and Chinook do not exhibit obvious warlike behavior, their lack of any skull development in the more refined areas indicates an inability to evolve sufficiently to overtake a more advanced and developed culture. However, I've discovered that the tribes to the north have more developed cranial areas of combativeness, and such tendency is borne out by their frequent slave-raiding trips down the coast. Had an advanced culture once existed upon these shores, it would be the northern tribes who decimated them.'"

I paused in surprise. "He said that?"

Daniel tapped the page. "It's all right here."

I buttered a piece of bread. "What else does he say?"

"'I was shot at today while trying to retrieve a skull. The natives are jealous of any attempt; they have become very watchful and it is perilous now. But I need the measurements to compare. Some I have found with decided bumps in the more exalted areas, which I do not understand. I had hoped for more proof otherwise. I had hoped blood would overcome...I cannot be indifferent, although I try. There is an epidemic ranging among the village now, and soon there will be more skulls. I do not rejoice in it, as to see their grief is very hard—such primitive wailing and crying—but it is convenient.'" Daniel finished with a murmured, "How very practical."

I frowned. "He thought them like children. Unable to control their emotions. He didn't like to see such displays."

"Even in grieving?"

I said thoughtfully, "He believed such things should be more dignified. I remember we were at a funeral once, for one of the oystermen who drowned. We barely knew him, but we went, and it was very quiet and solemn. Afterward Papa said that it was the proper way to mourn, and that I should remember it, because women especially should be contemplative and serene."

"That sounds boring. And not the least bit like you. What did he do when you cried?"

"Oh, he didn't like it," I said softly. "But I think it was the comforting that distressed him more. He wasn't very good at it." I remembered his awkward embrace, as if he wasn't certain what to do or was afraid of doing it the wrong way. "He tried, but he was not a demonstrative man."

Daniel raised a brow.

I said, defending Papa, "Well, many men aren't, are they? But I never doubted he loved me."

"I'm certain he did," Daniel said with a small smile. "Who wouldn't?"

I looked away quickly, and he rose, taking dishes to the sink. He said nothing more, and I took up one of the journals, opened it, and began to read, ignoring Daniel as he continued to clean up. Soon I became lost in my father's words, because, though many of the entries were lists, I remembered nearly every relic he mentioned; I had helped him trade for many of them. He rarely mentioned me. A few times, as in

L has learned the jargon fluently; her capacity for language is remarkable, nearly as if she was born to speak it...

and

Two salmon hooks found near the riverbed. L says one of them was very well used and therefore it must have been 'successful' and she thinks its owner was probably enraged to lose it. Such understanding is becoming distressingly more common.

But for the most part, it was my father's trading that held sway here. And then, after an hour or so of reading, I came across

I have told J of the experiment. I feel he can be trusted and he has promised to be vigilant."

I frowned. J? Junius? I looked up, searching for Daniel, who was sitting in the old chair, poring over another journal. "Junius knew about the experiment."

He glanced up. "How do you know?"

"Papa says it here. 'I have told J of the experiment. I feel he can be trusted and he has promised to be vigilant.' Who else can it be but Junius?"

"What's the date?"

I glanced back down at my father's handwriting. "November 16, 1853. Yes, it must be June." I did not say what troubled me more—that I had not been trustworthy, but apparently Junius had.

Daniel said, "Ask him about it when he returns."

I glanced out the window. Encroaching darkness, just into dusk. I'd been reading for hours, and now the whole idea of Papa's experiment was distracting—better to put the journal aside, to look for talk of the mummy when I wasn't so busy wondering what my father had thought fit to tell my husband but not me. One more insult—and then I paused, startled at the vehemence of my thought. I closed the book and went to make supper. I was aware suddenly of the stiffness of my hair and the smell of the bay that still clung to my skin, no matter that I'd washed. A bath seemed just now the closest thing to heaven.

Daniel went out to milk the cow, and when he returned I made the simplest thing I could think to cook—salmon chowder. I needed most of the pots to heat water for the small tin tub beneath the stairs; the hot water from the reservoir on the stove would not be nearly enough. Then, when the water was ready, I spread a square of oilcloth to protect the floor, and asked Daniel to help me move the tub onto it. He did it without comment, though I was nervous expecting one, and wordlessly he helped me fill the tub with the water I'd heated and then fill the pots again to heat water for him. But when it was done, we both stood there, one on each side, staring down into the steam.

I was the first to step away. I ladled a bowl of the chowder and handed it to him, along with a spoon, and said, "You can take this to your room."

He took it and motioned to the settee, to the mummy. "You don't mind her watching?"

"I'll pretend she's sleeping," I teased. "It should be easy enough, as her eyes are closed."

"I'll close mine."

"I don't think I can trust you," I said.

"Probably the best course," he admitted.

"I'll call you when it's your turn," I said, pulling a towel from the trunk beneath the stairs. He started up them. I hesitated. "Daniel…"

He stopped, turning to look at me.

"You promise you won't…"

"I won't come down until you call me," he agreed.

I smiled, relieved that he was making this so easy. "Thank you."

I waited until he'd gone up the stairs and I heard the close of his door, and then I unbuttoned my bodice and slipped off my dress, a flannel petticoat, my stockings, and my chemise. I unpinned my hair, letting it fall to my waist, and then I stepped into the steaming water, slowly, closing my eyes at how luxurious it felt, how soothing sinking into it.

The tub was small; one could not uncurl in it, but it was relaxing nonetheless. I let my hands float, the abalone charms of Bibi's bracelet bobbing gently in the slight current of my movements. I reached for the soft soap and washed carefully and slowly, and then I washed my hair, bending my head so it floated around me like seaweed, seeing a piece of sea lettuce floating in the water, translucently green, that had been caught in my hair. I cupped it in my hands, thinking of how it had got there, and I remembered my dream, and let the seaweed go again quickly, as if keeping hold of it were a danger, but it was too late. The memory was already there. The dream and the waste of my life tangled with everything else I wanted, the stories and the drawing and the way he'd carried me to the house, his hands rubbing mine, his warmth settled around me, seeping into my muscles, reviving me. And then…his kiss.

I closed my eyes. I imagined I felt his hands, his fingers tracing down my spine, a soft and even pressure, sliding through the wetness on my skin, slowly, easily, and then up again. I felt his thumbs pressing gently at the nape of my neck, massaging the base of my skull, fingers splayed over my shoulders, the faint brush of them against my collarbone. I put my own fingers at the hollow of my throat, pretending they were his, the slow caress, tracing the path of the leather thong around my neck, down and down into the valley between my breasts, pressing the tooth into my skin and then slipping lower and lower—

From upstairs came the sound of a chair drawn violently across the floor.

I started, jerking my hand away, my whole body flushing red, guilty at what I'd been imagining. I still felt the lingering touch, a tingling on my skin. My imagining had been so real I expected to see him there, kneeling beside the tub, watching me with desire in his eyes.

But no, I was alone. I was alone and in the bath and this was how it should be. I could not think of those things. I must not.

Quickly I rose from the cooling water, grabbing the towel as if I meant to hide from prying eyes when there were none. I dried in a hurry, suddenly desperate to be dressed, pulling on my chemise before I'd bound up my hair, so the muslin was wet the moment I put it on. I ignored that, wrapping my hair in the towel and taking up the clothes I'd abandoned, holding them to me as if for protection, feeling chased as I hurried up the stairs. It wasn't until I was safe in my room that I opened the door and peeked around the edge and called, "Your turn, Daniel!" and then I shut it again before he could answer.

I pulled on my dressing gown, buttoning it and tying it, and it was only then that I felt safe again. I heard his door open and his footsteps going down the stairs and breathed a sigh of relief. I sat at my dressing table and dried my hair and took up my brush, and I told myself I was not thinking of him downstairs in the bath, or of how his skin must glow, wet in the lamplight, or the dark gold of his hair. I was not thinking of how real his touch had been in my imaginings.

I tugged the brush almost viciously through my hair, stinging at my scalp, watching myself in the mirror, my impassive expression. How hidden away I seemed, lost even to myself, no sign of the tumult I felt, the tumult he'd caused, no sign that I lived at all.

Live.

The voice came so loud in my head that I looked over my shoulder, expecting to see her there. I dropped the brush into my lap. I heard the faint splash of water lapping against his skin—though it could not have been that. No, it could not have been. Not from downstairs, not through closed doors. But then, impossibly, I heard his soft sigh. And then I felt warm water against my fingers, moving up my hand and then my wrist, the floating of the twine and the charms as I slipped beneath the water to touch him, and he was silken and hard against my palm, unbearably hot, though it was a heat I wanted, and I curled my fingers around him and heard him gasp. I stroked him until he was throbbing and I heard his moan in my ear and my own longing rose like a wave set to drown me.

But I was alone. I was in my room, and I was alone, and this was only an imagining. It was not real.

I picked up the brush again, gripping it hard in my hand, hard enough that it bit into my palm. I would not think it. I would not feel it.

I went back to brushing my hair.

CHAPTER 20

My dreams were restless. Drowning and dry grass and withering, and I woke feeling as if I'd spent all night in struggle. When I went downstairs, Daniel was already there, the stove fired, coffee brewed. He had a cup in front of him, and he looked as tired as I felt, shadows beneath his blue eyes, his hair tousled as if he either hadn't brushed it or had run his hands through it. The collar of his shirt was unbuttoned, revealing his underwear. His gaze came to me and then away.

"I've already been to the springhouse," he said. "The water's down. I'll clean it out."

"You don't need to—"

"I need to be outside today," he said shortly.

The reason was clear, though he didn't say it. He had no wish to be in close proximity with me, and though I should have been relieved—wasn't that what I wanted as well?—I felt oddly hurt.

"Thank you." I sat down.

He stood up so quickly his chair rocked, which reminded me strangely of the sound of his chair scraping back last night, and then the bath, the things I'd felt and imagined.

I bent my head before he could see me coloring.

He said, "I'll get started then."

Once he was gone, I ate a quick breakfast of bread and jam and picked up my father's journal, but I couldn't concentrate on the entries. I was still angry with Papa over his precious "experiment" and the fact that he'd shared it with Junius and not with me, and that mixed with the things Daniel had said yesterday, the things that would not quite leave my head though I wanted them to desperately. *Do you still believe it was best?*

And along with those things, there was the dream, drowning and withering and *What a waste, what a waste...*and the things I wanted burning like salt in a wound, the feel of him against my palm and his fingers trailing over my collarbone...

No, I could not concentrate.

Instead, I drew the mummy. It was easier to focus on her, to focus on drawing and shading, to lose myself in the story of her that I told with paper and pencil, rubbing here to smear the lead, a highlight there. And again, as if she loved the attention, she drew me in, and I forgot everything but the accuracy of the line, everything but depicting each peg-like tooth with as much detail as I could, each strand of hair, the shell-like husk of her ear and the thin, nearly indiscernible scar of an unhealed wound, the mottling of bruising beneath skin coloring to umber.

When the door opened again, bringing with it a rush of cold air, I jumped, startled.

Daniel came inside, his boots coated with mud nearly to their tops. He drew off Junius's old and cracked leather gloves. "It's done," he announced. "All set to rights."

"Thank you," I said again, gripping my pencil hard. "I shouldn't have let you—"

"Oh, I know you feel you should have been the one to do it," he said. He was tense already, his full mouth tight. "My father has you trained as well as one of the Bela Coola's slaves."

"Daniel, must we really have this argument again?"

He hesitated, and then he shook his head. "No. Forgive me. I had a difficult night." He took off his coat and hung it, and his hat, then bent to pull off his boots.

"We both did, then," I said.

"You had nightmares again?"

"No, but...sometimes it's worse than nightmares. At least with nightmares one's sleeping."

He set his boots aside and dragged his hand through his hair. "I suppose that's true enough." He glanced at the notebook in my hand. "Anything new?"

"I decided to draw instead."

"Are you going to leave her there on the settee forever? Not that I mind it, particularly, except that your Indian won't like it when he gets back, and the barn floor's dried out. You could put her back."

"She doesn't want to be in the barn," I told him without thinking, and then, in puzzlement when I realized what I'd said, "I don't know why I said that."

"I wouldn't like it in there either. It's cold and dark."

I couldn't help smiling. "If you were Junius, you'd scold me for my imaginings."

"I don't want to think about the things I'd do if I were my father," he said shortly. He seemed ill at ease, aimless. He went to Junius's organ, pulling out the bench, seating himself there, jerking up the keyboard cover, plunking one finger down on a key. The tone reverberated through the room. He hit it again, and then another, a dirge-like "Hot Cross Buns," slow and menacing, before he pulled away from the keys and stared at the organ as if he'd never seen one before.

"You play?" I asked in surprise. "So does Junius."

He nodded. "I know. It was one of the things I remembered about him." And then, before I could absorb his bitterness over the reason he had learned to play, he twisted away from the keyboard, opening the glass-fronted cabinet that held my argillite collection. The black stone statuettes were worth next to nothing, monetarily or scientifically, because the Indians made them for the tourist trade. But I loved them, and couldn't resist buying them when I found a good artist. Restlessly, Daniel touched one and then another, and then grabbed the salmon. He rolled the smooth, polished stone in his hands, turning it this way and that, and then he said, "Tell me a story about this fellow."

His mood was strange; it matched my own and made me wary.

He held it up so I could see it, the hook of its nose, the stripe along the back. "A fish of some kind, isn't it?"

"A salmon," I said.

"Tell me. Just a story this time, Lea. Not a scolding."

I smiled, remembering the tale I'd told him in the cave, and I tucked the pencil into the spine of the notebook and closed it, laying it on the settee beside her. "Long ago, the South Wind, who was called Toolux, was making his annual journey to the north, which he did every spring. He came upon the giant ogress, Quoots-hooi. Now, Toolux was very hungry, and he asked Quoots-hooi for food, and she gave him a net instead and told him he must catch his own fish. But he was impatient, and he did not like waiting to eat when he was so hungry, so when he caught a small whale in his net and Quoots-hooi told him that he must only cut the whale lengthwise, and must use a shell knife to do it, he ignored her. He cut himself a large steak. It was a terrible mistake, because the whale transformed instantly into an enormous bird—Hahness. She flapped her great wings, blotting out the sun, and the world shook with thunder. She was the Thunderbird, and she flew north, while Toolux and Quoots-hooi chased after. The attempt was futile; they could not catch her.

"It was some time later when Quoots-hooi was looking for berries on Swallalochast, which is known to us as Saddle Mountain, and she found a great nest filled with eggs. This nest belonged to Hahness. Quoots-hooi was hungry, and so she sat down to eat the eggs, tossing the shells down the mountain as she did so. These shells turned into people, the Chinook people, and it was how they were formed.

"Hahness was furious when she found what Quoots-hooi had done to her nest. She sought out Toolux to help her find the ogress, and each spring, the Thunderbird and the South Wind come north to find her.

"And this is why one must only ever split the salmon lengthwise when it is cut, because otherwise they won't run, and the Chinook people will go hungry. *Kani, kani.*"

"'*Kani,*'" he repeated. "What does that mean?"

"It is. It lives. Loosely translated," I said.

Daniel nodded. He was staring at the salmon in his hands, stroking its smooth surfaces, and I thought of last night, of the feel of his fingers on my skin, and my mouth went dry. I said, "Those masks on the wall. One of them is Hahness."

He glanced at them. "Which one?"

I stood, going over to it, reaching up to take it from the nail it hung upon. It was quite large, nearly the length of my arms outspread. A bird face, carved of cedar, with a huge sloping beak, spread wings on either side. "This is a fine one, but I've seen better. My father sold one where the beak opened to show a human face, and the wings were longer even than these." I ran my hand over its curved beak, painted red. The cedar bark fringe decorating the top of its head and the wings shivered. The inside of the mask was smooth, stained with smoke and human sweat; the mask had been well used. I fit it to my face, breathing deep the scent of smoke and cedar.

"You look fierce wearing it," he said.

I lowered it and made a face at him. "It seems it should be heavy, but it's not. They had to dance wearing it."

"Do you know the dance?"

I shook my head, fingering the finely shredded fringe. "Only men dance it. My father knew it. He'd seen it once when he was up north and was invited to a winter ceremony. He described it to me. I can imagine it quite well."

"I'd guess you can. Dance it for me."

I looked at him and shook my head. "I hardly know it."

"I'll bet you could imagine it if you tried."

I should have laughed and put the mask aside. But the way he looked at me urged me to it, and…more than that, I wanted to. *Do what you want*, her voice said, and I put the mask to my face and closed my eyes and fell into my imaginings. Men gathered around the fire in the center of a longhouse, smoke rising to the hole in the top but not well. Filling the room with a gray haze. The clicking, nasally talk and laughter, and the scents of tobacco and the smoked fish hanging in the rafters, strings of dried clams, sweat. The sound of a drum, music made by voices, grunting and rhythmic, and the dancer, coming into the circle now, half-bent, the ball of one foot tapping and then the other, outstretched arms to mimic the wings on either side of his face, his eyes shining through the slits in the mask on either side of the great beak. Dodging and soaring, tipping wings at those sitting in the circle, arching back to let out a whoop, and then the other foot down, one and two and one, and the drums beating loud in my ears, the *nah-nah-nah* of the voices joining and harmonizing, and the story of Hahness and Toolux and Quoots-hooi and the creation of the tribes played out before them. My heart beating fast, hard to breathe against the mask, sweating. One and two and soar, and from somewhere an organ beating out the tune, raw and a little desperate, and I twirled round and round and round until I was dizzy, until the vision fled and I was myself again, there again in the great room of my own house, turning in a circle, laughing at the joy of it, and there was Daniel, matching the organ to my steps as if he saw the whole thing with me, and that seemed right as well, as it should be.

I collapsed onto the organ bench beside him, the cedar fringe pulling strands of my hair with it as I lowered the mask. I pushed them back, breathing hard, still laughing, and he twisted, smiling, to look at me.

"You belong in a cave somewhere, brandishing a spear," he teased.

I laughed. "Yes, well, don't tell anyone. I'm quite certain it would be frowned upon."

"No wonder. A dance like that...we're not so civilized as we like to think, are we? We're only apes wearing clothing. Steps away from savagery."

I said, "I'm not certain I like the sound of that."

"You can thank Herbert Spencer and his theories for it. He's made us afraid of ourselves and each other. He can't banish the emotions that rule us, but he can make us hate ourselves for having them." Daniel met my gaze.

I drew back, disturbed by what I saw in his eyes, by the conversation beneath the surface, the words he was saying without saying them. "If we don't rule ourselves, we become no better than the Indians."

"But you don't believe that," he whispered. "I know you don't believe they're savages."

"No," I managed. "I don't believe it."

"To be civilized means we must hide who we are," he said. "But then we don't really live, do we?"

I did not know what to say. I could only stare at him, and he kept my gaze for a moment before he looked down. He took my hand, uncurling my fingers, laying them out flat in his while he pressed the tip of his finger to the hollow of my wrist. I shivered, and then he touched one of the bracelet charms, tracing the symbol upon it, a feather-like touch.

He didn't look at me, but only twisted the twine about his finger, tightening it so I felt its bite, then letting it unwind again, and then he touched the vein in my wrist, slowly moving upward, up my arm to the cuff of my sleeve.

I pulled my hand gently from his grasp, curling my fingers into my palm. I could not find my voice.

He raised his gaze to mine. "Last night, I"—he swallowed convulsively—"when you were in the bath…" He reached out. Two fingers touched the leather thong at my neck, slid to the pulsebeat in my throat, and then, as if he couldn't help himself, he traced the leather until it disappeared into my bodice, the same path I'd made. His fingers stopped there, burning against my skin, and the vision washed over me again. The way my own fingers had traced down to the tooth, slipping lower, fingers I'd imagined were his, and my palm itched. I remembered the rest of it, upstairs in my room, the way I'd felt him in my hand, the way I'd stroked him—

And he saw it. There was no possible way he could have known or understood, and yet he did, I knew it with a kind of knowing that was impossible as well. Yes, impossible, but the connection between us pulsed and flared, and that was impossible too. That I should feel him so intently. That I should know him. I reached up to take his hand from my collarbone, but instead of pushing him away I found myself clutching his fingers, afraid to let go.

He closed his eyes. He whispered, "Leonie—"

I dropped his hand, leaping to my feet, putting out my arms as if I meant to stop him when he didn't move, when he only opened his eyes and watched me.

Live.

The voice echoed, so loud in my head I was surprised he didn't start at it. "I can't," I found myself saying desperately. "I don't know how."

And then I ran.

I stayed in my room for hours. I locked myself in, locked myself away, hearing Daniel's words: *if we hide who we are we don't really live.* I sat in the cane rocker at the window and watched the sky darken, and still I stared. I heard him come upstairs. I heard the close of his door, and I pulled my dressing gown more tightly about me and told myself to go to bed. But I didn't. I saw the moon come up, white light on the bay beyond, and the wind blowing the clouds across it.

I was drowning, again. Choking and struggling, flailing and swallowing seawater and falling down and down and down into a void, a blackness I could not escape, and there was his voice speaking to me, echoing across it: We don't really live, do we?

And there I was…there she was, watching me, slow and steady, assessing dark eyes, a face beautiful and familiar, though I couldn't say why. Suddenly her eyes hardened, and I was withering, my fingers turning to claws, nails still growing, and my skin adhering to my bones, my skin drying to umber but not stopping, not ending. Just drying up and drying up, withering and cracking and shrinking until I was a seedpod, blown about by a hot wind over prairie I had never seen, and then it died and I was swayed lightly to rest upon the sun-burned grass, and suddenly she was there, standing beside, and I cracked open, my fear cast up out of me like a spirit, a wisp of smoke through a hole in a longhouse roof, gone, dissipating into the clear sky beyond, and her voice ringing in my ears: Go to him. I brought him for you. He was meant for you.

I opened my eyes, staring into darkness striated with moonlight blown by the wind, a chill kaleidoscope of shadow and light. The dream had its fingers in me still, clutching and soundless, a longing so swollen I could not be still. I felt the press of it, its insistence. I heard the words she'd spoken, my own desires given voice. And the pull…the pull was irresistible.

And the fear that had made me a coward was gone. What was in its place was a terrible desire—to live, not to dry up, to be whatever and whomever I was meant to be.

I went to the door, turning the key, unlocking myself, opening it and stepping into the hall. I heard the river as if it were right behind me, not muffled by walls and windows. All around me. I hesitated, putting a trembling hand to the wall beside my bedroom door, feeling as if I'd just emerged, cold and choking, from the Shoalwater. *Don't do this,* I thought, oh, but it was vague and faraway and I felt half-caught in the dream, and there were Daniel's words too. *We don't really live, do we?*

I went to his door, resting my hand upon it for one bare moment before I turned the knob and pushed it open, blinking in the dim light that greeted my eyes when I did so. A lamp turned down low, and he was still awake in the middle of the night, sitting at my father's desk, writing.

He twisted in the chair to look at me, surprise and quick concern. "Lea? What is it? Is something wrong?"

I closed the door softly. "Nothing's wrong."

He went very still. I saw the moment he understood, and it was then that I untied my dressing gown and let it fall. I unbuttoned my nightgown, and he watched my fingers with a rapt greediness that made me go slowly. I wanted to swallow that look; I wanted to feel it all through me. He did nothing and said nothing, only watched as I undid one button after another, as I pushed the gown from my shoulders and let it pool at my feet and I stood there naked before him but for the leather thong and beads around my neck, the cave bear tooth nestled between my heavy breasts.

He swallowed and rose. He stepped up to me slowly, as if to savor every moment, and then he boxed me in, his hands on either side, pressing me back against the door with his hips, and he bent to press his mouth to my neck, my ear, my jaw, the hollow of my throat, and then down to between my breasts, his lips following the path my fingers had given him, pressing the tooth hard into my skin, hard enough that I felt its point, and then he took it between his teeth and it was as if he took me. I arched against him uncontrollably, and he looked up at me, so deliberate, and I shuddered with recognition and inevitability, and he let the tooth fall from his lips to thud gently against my skin, warm and wet from his mouth. He straightened, his hands at the small of my back now, pulling me close. I opened my mouth to him when he kissed me, and tore at his shirt, jerking it so roughly from his shoulders that I heard it rip, desperate as I was for the feel of his skin against mine. I undid the buttons on his long underwear and pushed it away, running my hands over his bare chest; he was muscled and lean and perfect, hard, sweet youth, a kind I'd never touched, and I slid to his trousers, inside. I felt him hot and heavy against my palm, so familiar. I knew him already.

He made a sound deep in his throat and pulled me from the door, pushing me—not gently—so I fell upon the bed, shedding the rest of his clothes. I reached for him and he came to me, and his kiss then was rough and desperately needy and I could not keep from twisting beneath him; I could not keep still and he did not ask me to. Instead he urged me to it, permission to be savage, to be who I was: "*Yes*, Lea, *yes.*" I was burning beneath him and I felt alive in a way I never had, and I could not get enough of him. And I knew that she was right, that he was meant for me, and the danger of him roared in my ears along with the river and I let myself drown.

CHAPTER 21

I WOKE TO THE LATE MORNING LIGHT COMING THROUGH the window over my father's desk, the curtains open to reveal the bright overcast, the trees blowing lightly in a breeze, the river coursing.

I felt Daniel's warmth against my back where we were spooned together, where his arm was flung over me, his hand cupping my breast, his face buried in my hair. The memory of last night washed over me, the way I'd come to him, the fierceness of the way we'd taken each other, and I let myself think only of that, of nothing else. I had done things with him I had never before thought to do. I had been…not myself, and at the same time more myself than I had ever been, and he had been my match in passion and desire, so we had been unable to stop even in exhaustion, and the hours had been filled with *not yet, not yet. I want more.*

I felt both sated and starving, as if I'd suddenly discovered something I hadn't known I craved. And along with that came a reckless joy that took every consequence and flung it away to wisp into the clouds like smoke, to disappear.

Daniel stirred, murmuring whispers into my hair, and I turned to face him. He pulled me with him as he rolled onto his back so I lay half on top of him. I traced down his throat, his chest, letting my hair fall forward to cascade over us like a waterfall. He stroked it idly, tangling his fingers in it. I smiled and kissed him.

His other arm, tucked around my waist, tightened, his hand splayed flat against my hip. "I thought you were a dream last night, when you came through my door."

"I was surprised to find you awake."

"You meant to take me like some succubus?"

"Hmmm, I don't know. What is that?"

"A demon in a woman's form, come to seduce a man in his sleep."

"Like in the Indian legends. Spirits who play tricks on men in their dreams."

"Tricks," he repeated, smiling. "I like that. Spirit, play more tricks upon me."

"Angel or demon?" I teased. I dug my nails into his chest and leaned close to whisper, "Which spirit do you want me to be?"

He grabbed me, twisting me around so I was on my back again, holding me down, teasing me in kind. "You're a bewitchment. Is that what you want to hear? I've never wanted a woman so much."

"Yes, it's what I want to hear," I said, laughing. "You sound tormented. Perhaps I should lift the spell."

He pressed closer. His mouth was a bare whisper from mine. He took my arms, stretching them above my head, weaving his fingers through the twine of my bracelet. "Don't lift it. Make it stronger. Bind me."

The tease was gone. He was fervent, his eyes burning. I shivered and answered in kind. "I would. I would bind you if I could."

My words lingered like an incantation. His hands tightened, his fingers pressing into my skin, fetters lashing his wrists and mine. He said softly, "I'll hold you to that, you know. You promise you won't release me, whatever happens?"

I loosed my hand and pressed my finger to his mouth. "Ssshhh, no promises. Not today. Today let it just be…this."

He moved away from my finger. "Leonie—"

"Just you and me in the world," I murmured. I arched a little against him, my hips to his. "No one else. Nothing else."

I felt his sigh against my breasts, and I twined my fingers in his hair, pulling a little, bringing him to meet my kiss, gentle at first, and then, when he deepened it, fierce and possessive, rousing that fever in me again, and willingly I went into that wilderness with him, where there was no other existence, where the promises we made to each other were the only ones that mattered.

It wasn't until much later, when I heard Edna lowing outside, that the world encroached again. I lay there and watched him as he dressed, hastily pulling on trousers, a shirt. "I'll milk her and be back," he told me. "Don't leave this bed."

I stretched and smiled. "I'm too lazy to leave it."

He leaned down to kiss me quickly. "I won't be long."

He was out the door, racing down the stairs as if he suspected that more than a few minutes could be disastrous. I smiled to hear it, and stretched again, feeling swollen and ripe, aching and glazed with sweat and sex and with no other will than to have him.

I angled my arm beneath my head and my glance fell upon the papers on the desk that Daniel had shoved aside, my father's relics pushed to the edges, and it seemed strange to see the two things together, the two halves of myself.

I sat up, pulling the sheet up around my naked breasts, looking at what remained of my father in this room, the relics and the journals. Daniel had taken it over so completely, and yet my father's spirit was so strong it seemed to permeate the very walls. I felt it grow even as I thought it. And that, of course, opened the door to recriminations, to promises made that I'd broken, to the future my father wanted for me that I'd just thrown away.

There could be nothing but pain from this point on; there was no way to continue without hurt and anger, and yet…could I make myself go back? Could I even be what I'd been before?

And that was how Daniel found me when he returned bearing a pitcher of milk and some bread. He came inside, and I looked at him, and he set down what he carried and said, "I took too long, didn't I?"

Suddenly I was crying; he came to the bed and pulled me into his arms, and I felt his kiss on my hair as I buried my face in his chest. He smelled of cold air and cow and milk; he smelled of me.

He whispered, "We'll talk of all this later. I promise we will. But not today. Just you and me in the world—that's what you said, isn't it? Nothing else. No one else."

I said, "But that's a lie."

"The world runs on lies," he said. "What's another day?"

I shook my head against him and he eased away, pulling off his shirt, taking my hand and pressing it to his bare chest, and I shivered at the desire that leaped through me and felt him shudder in response and marveled that such a simple touch should have such an effect. "You see?" he asked softly, muscle flexing beneath my hand as he raised my chin so I must look at him. "I don't understand it either, but I can't deny it. We belong together, Lea. You know it too. Why make ourselves suffer?"

"Because it's wrong."

"What's wrong is everything else," he said. "We did things… we made promises before we knew each other."

"But we did them, we made them. They're real."

He smoothed my hair behind my ear. "The first time I saw you I felt as if I were waking from a long sleep. Don't tell me you didn't feel the same."

"If I did, it doesn't matter—"

"This is what's real, Lea. The rest is the dream. What's between us—you can't want to throw it away."

"I don't want to. Believe me, I don't. But Junius will come back and—"

"He's not back yet. We have days to ourselves."

"We can't ignore this, Daniel."

"Yes we can. For now, we can. We have these days, Lea. Let's at least take them. There will be time enough for the rest later."

And my reason melted away. I wanted what he did, to not think, to not decide. I wanted to pretend that there were no promises to keep, that he and I were both free. I wanted to keep feeling as I did when I was with him, that stinging awareness, that knowledge that the world was alive and I was alive within it. He was right; I'd been sleeping before I'd found the mummy and she had brought him here to show me I was dreaming, to show me that the real Leonie was the one who danced. And now…now I wanted to be awake.

We stayed in bed for days, leaving only to milk the cow or get something to eat. Chores went undone, everything in my life falling away. I did not think it was possible to be sated with him. I'd forgotten my distrust and my fear; I wanted to know everything about him, and he obliged with a laugh.

"I helped my mother with the laundry from the time I can remember. My job was to stir the pots of lye and soap, and pull clothes from the water because they were too heavy for her so she could wring them and hang them to dry. At twelve I had to get a job. I sold newspapers because I could still attend school. At thirteen I first kissed a girl—she was an orphan who lived on our street, and my mother used to feed her sometimes, like a stray cat. She became a whore, and so…well, you can imagine what happened between us. I worked the docks at fourteen. Fifteen, a printer's devil at the *Call*. Then back to the docks again, doing whatever I could. Shall I go on?"

I ran my finger over his mouth. "Yes."

"I can't concentrate when you're doing that."

Obediently, I removed my finger.

He smiled and went on, "From there...too many jobs. I can't remember them all. I worked for a blacksmith for a while, and a lithographer, which I had to quit when my mother turned ill. When she was well again, I took a job working for a set builder at one of the theaters and ended up working the circuses that came through town—hauling things for them, mostly. Cleaning up elephant and dog shit and watching to make sure customers didn't get too familiar, kicking them out when they did. There were women, enough of them. No one the least bit respectable; there wasn't time for it. Actresses and whores, a contortionist at Selling's Circus—that was interesting—"

"I imagine," I said dryly. I let my hand drift down his chest, to his stomach.

His grin was quick and fleeting. "Mostly I worked. I took whatever job I could, whatever someone would pay me to do. Sometimes I worked two or three. By the time I was twenty, my mother had to quit taking in laundry. We had to give up the house. I moved her into a boardinghouse—the best I could afford, which wasn't much, but the landlady offered to watch over her, and I couldn't afford to hire someone to do it, and so...The room was tiny and we had to share a bed, which was fine until she became too sick, and sometimes I was working late hours, or hours in the middle of the night and it disturbed her sleep too badly. So I slept on the floor. My life...my life consisted of taking care of her and working. She liked to be read to, so I obliged. Poetry and novels. Dickens and the like. Some philosophy, though in her last days she was too busy railing against the world and my father and it only upset her."

"She must have been happy when you got the job at the newspaper."

"I can think of better things to do than discuss my mother," he said, leaning over me, kissing me.

I said, "I want to know you."

He laughed. "There's plenty of time for that. A whole life-time."

In that moment, I believed him.

After a time, we began to move about. The world didn't stop for us, though it felt sometimes as if it had, and I kept reality carefully at bay, as if by not thinking about it I could make it non-existent. So we did chores and I told him Indian stories; we read my father's journals and made love, and I went back to drawing the mummy. Now, capturing her seemed even more important, something I could do out of gratitude—she had given me Daniel, after all.

The day I finished the drawing, I felt an astonishing satisfac-tion. It was the most perfect one I'd ever done.

I said, "I'm finished," and Daniel glanced up from where he lay on the floor beside me, reading my father's journal, which had seemingly captivated him. He brought himself up to look at my drawing.

He kissed my shoulder, my bare skin, where my dressing gown had half fallen. "It's beautiful. Your talents are wasted on science, Lea."

"Have you found anything else in Papa's journal?"

"Only more about this experiment of his," he said. He opened to a page and read, "'I would have preferred a more quantitative measure for this experiment, but such things are impossible given the circumstances. I can only watch and evaluate; I cannot gain access to thoughts or feelings, but can only make assumptions about them. Phrenology is a great help in this regard. Palpitations show cranial bumps not so pronounced in the animalistic areas, but for one exception: vitativeness and also disturbingly so in amativeness. Very pronounced in perceptiveness areas, particu-larly tune, time and individuality. Also spirituality and benevo-lence, therefore perhaps some may cancel out others.'"

"So the experiment was human."

"He doesn't say that."

"But whatever it was, was alive. He says it: 'We can't gain access to thought or feelings.'"

"Nor could he if it was a corpse," Daniel pointed out.

"But in other places, he says he hopes blood overcomes. So it must be a living thing."

Daniel murmured an agreement. He sounded distracted and lazy. He was playing with my hair, which I hadn't pinned up since the night we'd spent together. He liked it down, his Pre-Raphaelite painting come to life, he'd said, and I obliged him because I liked feeling that we walked at the very edge of control always, that our desire was an entity with a will of its own, and it took almost nothing to ignite it.

"You're not paying attention," I accused.

He pulled me down with him. "I'm enchanted by your hair. Have I said it to you?"

"Almost every moment," I told him.

He laughed, his chest vibrated beneath my hand. "So many colors of yellow," he mused, combing a strand through his fingers. "What blond children we would have."

I froze.

He went still, as if he'd just realized what he'd said. "I'm sorry, Lea. I didn't mean it. I was just…thinking out loud."

I made myself smile. "Is that what you want? Children?"

"No." His arm tightened around me as if he were afraid I would flee. His voice was so careful it squeezed my heart. "I've never cared much about it. It doesn't matter."

"You're young still. You'll have them. A dozen, I should think." I tried to keep my voice light.

"Don't say things like that."

"I'm certain Eleanor will make a wonderful mother."

"Lea, don't—"

"And you would be a good father, I think."

He gripped my arm, squeezing it almost painfully. "Stop it. Stop torturing yourself and me. It's not what I want. Not unless it's with you."

I tried to draw away, managing only a few inches before his grip stopped me. "It won't be."

He hesitated. "Are you so certain? I haven't…I've taken no precautions."

"There are precautions?" I asked in surprise. "You mean you could…keep a woman from getting with child?"

He looked equally surprised. "You didn't know that? Well, no, I suppose there's no reason you should. I forget what an innocent you are."

"I'm hardly innocent," I said.

"About some things," he agreed with a grin. "You've an uncanny instinct. It's why I forget. Yes, there are things I could do so you wouldn't conceive. But I haven't done them. You could be—"

"No. There's no need for precautions."

"Have you ever—with him, did you ever think—"

"A few times," I said tersely. "But it never amounted to anything. I can't have children, Daniel. I used to think perhaps it was Junius. But now…you exist and…well, it's obvious it's not him, isn't it?"

"He's an old man. He was old when he married you."

"It's me," I said gently. "I'm sorry."

"Don't be sorry. I told you I didn't care."

"It's not as if it matters, in any case, does it?" I pulled away again; this time he let me go. "It's not as if you and I…"

"Lea, please," he said, sitting up, reaching for me again. "Don't make more of this than there is."

I felt bereft and sad. "I suppose…it was better this way, really. It gave me more time for…for study, and…and one can't have children stumbling over skulls, can one?"

"You did," he said gently. He wrapped his arms around me, bringing me down with him again. "Your father had you stumbling over all kinds of things to hear you tell it, and you suffered no ill effects."

"It would only make things harder than they are. I already suffer because I'm a woman. Do you know of a single famous ethnologist who is also a mother?"

"I don't know any famous ethnologists at all. Much less any who are mothers. But artists...that's another matter."

I laughed at his persistence. "You are so different—"

"Don't say it," he whispered. "Comparisons are odious. I already suffer for it enough in my own mind."

"You do? How so?"

"The usual things," he said wryly. "Has he ever heard you cry out in pleasure? Does he touch you as I do? Have you ever served as his succubus?"

I was burning. "You shouldn't think such things."

"I know. But I do."

"The answer is no," I said, meeting his gaze. "No to everything."

He smiled. His hand came to my cheek, his thumb caressing. "You've no such questions for me? You're mercifully free from jealousy?"

"You said you've never wanted anyone as you want me."

"That's true."

"Even Eleanor?"

"I did want her," he said thoughtfully. "But it was the kind of wanting you feel before you know what wanting really is."

"Did you ever kiss her?"

"Ah, now you sound jealous."

"Because I know your kisses," I said.

"Not this kind. Of course I kissed her. We were betrothed. But I was very respectful. Gentlemanly, even."

"Really?"

"Her position...there are rules."

"Did she respond? Did she want you?"

He looked uncomfortable. "Yes. I thought so, anyway. But now I wonder how true it was. If perhaps she didn't feel the same pressures I did."

"Don't make excuses."

"Perhaps they're more than that. Our parents...My mother had this notion that I needed a wife, that when she was gone I would have no one to take care of me, which was absurd, because I was the one taking care of both of us. She hated knowing that my only feminine companionship, besides her, was...well, what it was. She had wanted a respectable kind of life for me, a respectable wife. It became rather an obsession. She wasn't well, but she kept dragging herself to church, above my objections, and that led to Eleanor's father, and suddenly my mother developed a bizarre interest in the welfare of Celestials—whom she hadn't batted an eye over before, by the way, except to call them vermin who should learn to speak the language of the country where they lived."

"I see."

"Yes. She wasn't at her most pleasant then. It was when she began to beg me to find my father. That and this idea that Eleanor and I were somehow meant to be together became all she talked about. I ended up working with the pastor on one or two things—helping collect men from opium dens and that sort of thing, where it took more physicality than praying. He liked me. Eleanor liked me—or found me unobjectionable, anyway. We talked, we reached an understanding, and...I was engaged, with every expectation that when we married I would join Eleanor's father in his ministry. My mother was beyond happy at the idea that a minister might bring her son in from the pasture and keep him fenced. It was her dying wish for me, just as your father's was for you. Why do we give dying wishes so much weight, do you think? What if it was simply some passing thought they had, like, 'Oh, by the way, I'd like you to bring me some cherries?'"

"You know it's not," I said.

"Yes. But had she lived, I might have fought it. Not right away, but perhaps I would have when I realized…" He paused. "What about you? Would you have fought your father if he'd lived?"

"Probably not. He raised me to be a dutiful child."

"A dutiful child with a wild heart," Daniel said with a smile.

"It would pain him to know that," I whispered. "What about Eleanor? You said she might have felt the same pressures."

"Why are we talking about her?"

"Because I need to know."

His gaze slipped away. "Her mother was dead. Her father didn't like her ministering in Chinatown—a young, unmarried woman—but he needed her help. Marriage solved many problems. His worry was over my ability to provide for her. It's not as if the ministry gives much of an income, but she wasn't used to privation either."

"But he agreed to your marriage?"

"On the condition that I manage to find enough money to keep my lovely wife. He gave me a year to accomplish it."

"And so you came here," I said.

"Sent by your south wind, Toolux," he said with a self-deprecating laugh. "Providence in the form of a newspaper report and a pretty feather." He brought me to kiss him. Soft and gentle, the kind of kiss one gives a lover of long standing, more tender than desirous. "I thought it was fate, and it was. But I don't think it was Eleanor I was sent for."

I brought him for you. He was meant for you.

I glanced over my shoulder at the settee, the mummy, and then back to Daniel. My desire rose like a tide. His collar was open; I traced the ridge of his collarbone; I pressed my fingers to the pulsebeat at his throat. I wanted to gather it up, to hold it close, to keep it for myself—Eleanor and Junius the rest of the world be damned. I moved my fingers and pressed my lips where they'd been, murmuring against his skin, "Does it bother you, to be fate's servant?"

His hands dug into my hips, pulling me closer, not a space between us.

He said, "Not anymore."

CHAPTER 22

I WAS NOT READY FOR THE WORLD TO RETURN, BUT IT DID so anyway.

The window of my father's room faced the bay, and I heard the shout clearly that afternoon and recognized it, and all my intentions flew, everything I'd been telling myself I would do, gone in that moment, in the sound of his voice. I remembered our life together, how I'd loved him, and I was suddenly afraid of the change I'd told myself I wanted.

I sat up, pulling from Daniel's arms. "Junius."

Daniel froze. "It's just the call for the oyster schooner, isn't it?"

"No, it's Junius." I scrambled from the bed, grabbing for my clothes, which were strewn throughout the room. No time to wash or to compose myself. No time for anything.

Daniel said, "Leonie—"

I turned to him as I clutched my dress to my naked breasts, glaring, panicked. "Get dressed, damn you, or he'll know."

He crooked his elbow beneath his head. "Isn't that what we want?"

"No." I shook my head, dropping the clothes I held, pulling my chemise over my head. I could not control my panic or my dread. "Not now. Not yet. I need to…Please, Daniel. Please…I can't…"

"Can't do what?" His voice was cold; his eyes had gone stony.

My dress next. My fingers shook as I tried to do the buttons up the flannel lining of the bodice. "We need to talk about this—"

"We certainly do."

"—But not now. I thought we had more time, but…please. For now, please just get dressed."

He hesitated; I thought he would argue and my panic increased. I glanced toward the window. I saw the gliding shadow of the canoe coming ashore, someone—Lord Tom—jumping out, splashing into ankle-deep water.

"Daniel, please. Please just hurry. They're coming ashore now."

He pushed back the blankets. Naked, he came to me. He pushed aside my shaking hands and did up the buttons of the inner lining, so calmly, so easily, and then the buttons of the outer bodice. I thought he would kiss me, and I pulled away a little desperately, batting at his hands, reaching for my stockings, putting them on.

"He'll know anyway," he said.

"Not if we don't tell him," I said, tying my garters.

"Leonie, he has to know."

I stopped and gave him a pleading glance. "We'll discuss this later. We'll decide what to do later. But for now please just…don't say anything. Please, Daniel. Please."

"You aren't staying with him."

"For God's sake, get dressed."

He let out his breath and reached for his long underwear, and I was so relieved I felt tears start. I blinked them away, forcing myself to think, to be calm, to act as I always did—what was it I always did? How did I act when Junius came home from a long trip? Would I have missed him? I tried to remember other times, other greetings, and could not. I could not remember how I'd been, or what was the last thing he'd said to me, or how I should greet him now, and for a moment I was paralyzed by indecision and uncertainty. I could only sit there watching Daniel—my stepson, I thought suddenly, with a sense of unreality, something I'd forgotten—as he put on trousers, and I felt as if I sat there in a dream, sleeping again, when I had been so very awake…

Daniel glanced over his shoulder, to the window, as he pulled on his shirt. "He's coming across the yard."

I rose. I could not feel my own skin. Daniel glanced at me. Softly he said, "There's no need to panic, Lea. I'll do as you want. I'll do whatever you say. For now."

His voice broke through the dream. I nodded. I went to the door and out, down the stairs, hearing him behind me, following me as he buttoned his shirt. At the bottom of the stairs, he stopped me. "Your hair," he whispered, and I put my hand to it and realized it was down. I turned to him in shock, paralyzed again, and he said, "I'll get your pins," and raced upstairs again, and it seemed forever before he was back, holding a handful of them, giving me one at a time as I scrambled to gather my hair—how odd it felt, to have it up again after weeks, to feel the air on my bare neck, the heaviness of the chignon at the back of my head, but it was also what restored me. I suddenly felt myself again, the Leonie Junius would know, the one who had him as a husband and liked it. And yet…how strange. I was not this woman any longer, and I felt an imposter.

Daniel whispered, "You've disappeared."

Again I felt tears. I wiped them away viciously, hurrying to the door, shoving my feet into my boots, and then I was outside, racing down the porch steps, because I remembered how I'd always greeted him, and this run across the yard was it, the way he dropped the bag he held and opened his arms, catching me, holding me tight—the smell of the sea and smoke and unwashed skin. He held me away long enough to kiss me hard, and then he was smiling and his eyes were glowing and I felt how much he loved me in a deep, deep ache.

Junius released me, his eyes crinkling. "That's the kind of greeting that makes a man glad to be back," he said—the same thing he always said. He bent to retrieve the bag he'd dropped, and I looked at Lord Tom, who was coming up beside him, and who was watching me with this careful look, and I thought, though I had no reason to, *he knows.*

It made me nervous; again I felt that edge of panic, and I told myself Lord Tom couldn't know, that it was only guilt that made me think it. I smiled and said, a bit too brightly, "I'm glad you're home. I've missed you both. How was the trip?"

"Long and arduous," Junius said, walking again, and I fell into step beside him. "Getting that canoe on a train was a misery. It wouldn't fit on a single car. We had to cut it in half."

"In half?" I didn't have to feign dismay.

Junius nodded grimly. "But it's off now. Good riddance." He glanced up as we approached the house. "So he's still here?"

I followed his gaze to where Daniel stood beside the doorway in his stocking feet, his arms crossed over his chest, looking belligerent already.

I glanced away and said as casually as I could, though my heart was racing, "Yes, of course he's here. I would have been lost without his help."

"Is that so?" Junius went up the stairs. I held back, letting both him and Lord Tom go before me. Junius paused at the door, looking at his son, saying, "So my wife tells me you were a help."

Daniel's eyes flickered to me, then back to Junius. "That was your command, wasn't it? Do as she directs—isn't that what you said?"

"It was." Junius reached for the doorknob. "I'm just glad you remembered."

"I remember everything," Daniel said, and though he was looking at Junius, I knew those words had been meant for me. I thought of how we'd been only moments before wrapped in each other's arms, drowsy and satisfied, and to my dismay I felt the blooming heat in my cheeks.

Thankfully, both Junius and Lord Tom were ahead of me, and I didn't think either of them noticed. But Daniel did. Junius opened the door and stepped inside, and Lord Tom followed, and as I went to follow, Daniel grabbed my hand, pressing it hard— only a moment, not enough for anyone to see—before he let me go again. I didn't look at him; I could not.

I felt him come in behind me, closing the door. Junius bent to take off his boots, and then he stopped short, saying, "What the hell?"

Lord Tom froze, muttering something beneath his breath, backing away so hard he ran into me. He looked horrified.

Junius said, "What's *that* doing in here?"

It was a moment before I realized—the trunk in the middle of the floor, its lid open, the mummy inside.

I hurried over to it, closing the lid, trying not to feel the way it closed her in darkness. "The river was flooding," I said quickly. "It got to the barn. We had to move her—" I motioned for Daniel, who stepped over obediently. "We'll put her on the porch, *tot*. Don't worry." I glanced at Daniel.

Daniel lifted one side of the trunk while I lifted the other.

Junius said, "The river's not high now. Put it back in the barn."

I felt a moment of horror as strong as that evidenced on Lord Tom's face. "We'll put her on the porch for now," I said firmly. "You just got back. The barn can wait for later."

Daniel and I took the trunk outside. He pushed aside the old chair, kicked a few pails to roll between the railing slats and fall to the ground below, and then we set her carefully against the wall. I glanced at the roof overhang above. "Do you think she'll be safe here?"

"As safe as anywhere." He straightened; his gaze made me feel naked and vulnerable. In a low voice, he said, "Christ, this is untenable already."

I shook my head at him. "Not now."

He looked as if he might protest, but then he nodded, and together we went back inside. Lord Tom was staring at me, again I felt uncomfortable in it, and I said, "I'm sorry, *tot*. I…I wasn't sure when to expect you."

"The tides were with us," Junius said. "So we took the Unity stage across the beach. Borrowed Wilson's canoe in Oysterville. It all probably saved us a day. Maybe even two. Which was good, given how wretched it was getting down there."

"We thought of you," I said. "Didn't we, Daniel?"

"Wondered if maybe you'd drowned," he said, sitting on the settee hard, every movement clipped and angry.

"Well, that would have satisfied you, no doubt," Junius said wryly, going to the stove. "But you didn't get your way this time, though it seemed like you might once or twice. No coffee?"

"Oh, I…I was so busy I forgot," I said.

"You forgot coffee?" Junius gave me a puzzled smile. "What had you so busy you did that?"

There was no insinuation in his words; of course not. Still I had to look away, avoiding Lord Tom's eyes too, scrabbling for the best excuse, settling on, "The springhouse flooded. We spent nearly the whole day cleaning it out. Well, Daniel did most of it."

"I see." Junius reached for grinder, opened the drawer, and scooped out coffee into the pot. "The schooner come?"

"We sold about four hundred bushels." I told him.

"Good. And I think Baird will pay well for that canoe, too. It's a good specimen, even cut in half. I told him it was for war parties and slave raids. He'll like that."

"Bibi said it was for whaling," I said.

"He won't know that." Junius put water in the pot and set it on the stove to boil.

"You'll make Baird think the Shoalwater are warriors."

"What of it, Lea, if he pays more because of the story?" Junius ran a weary hand through his hair. "Even Lord Tom doesn't care if I lie about it a little."

Lord Tom said wryly, "You white people respect war."

"You see? Better than saying the truth, which is that they dig clams and drink whiskey." Junius laughed lightly. "We've made his tribe noble. With any luck we can rehabilitate them into a proud, resilient people—though actually, I think the savage barbarian story is what draws crowds, don't you think, boy?"

"How would I know?" Daniel asked.

"Because you work for a newspaper, perhaps?" Junius needled. "I'd think you would have an idea of how best to get the attention of your reader. Which reminds me; finished the story on the mummy yet? When are you planning to move on?"

"*Junius*," I said, and Junius laughed again, but it was thin.

"Just joking with you, boy. No harm done." He pulled out a chair and sat down, patting his leg for me to come sit on his lap. He had made such a gesture a hundred times before, and I felt a little sting of resentment and wondered that I hadn't noticed how like calling a dog it was. But neither had I ever ignored it, so I went to him now, seating myself, trying not to stiffen as he wrapped his arms around my waist and pulled me close, breathing deeply of me.

He pulled away, frowning. "You smell different."

"The springhouse, no doubt."

"Maybe." His frown deepened. He glanced down, then reached for my arm. "You're still wearing this?"

The bracelet. I snatched my arm away. "What's the harm in it?"

"It looks ready to fall off."

I glanced down at it. It was true. Over the last few weeks the twine had begun to fray and unravel. Some of the charms looked held on by the merest thread, ready to snap or drop. I'd grown attached to the thing, to the way Daniel touched and tangled it, his fascination, and now I felt a little panic at its decay—which was odd, wasn't it, because now I remembered what its purpose had been. To protect me from Daniel. It was such an obvious contradiction that I was confused and disoriented suddenly, *I brought him for you* and *you will regret it now he is here* rubbing uncomfortably against each other in my head.

Daniel was off the settee, now settling himself against the wall at the bottom of the stairs. "It's been through a great deal," he said. "I'd say it's a miracle it stayed on at all."

I sent him a warning glance, which he ignored.

Junius frowned more deeply. "What are you talking about, boy?"

"Lea nearly drowned while you were gone. Taking your oysters in. The storm hit when we were coming back from Bruceport. She slipped and fell off the boat. She won't tell you that. She thinks it nothing. But she didn't see how close it was, neither the drowning nor the cold."

Junius looked at me. "Is that true?"

I made a face. "Yes, it's true, but it turned out all right, as you can see. I'm here. Daniel kept his wits about him and pulled me in."

My husband glanced thoughtfully at me, and then turned to Daniel. "I suppose I have something to thank you for then, don't I? For saving my wife's life."

Daniel shook the thanks away, a negligent flick of his hand. "We shouldn't have been out there at all. She shouldn't have been. The oysters would have waited until you came back. They would have waited for the next schooner."

"I didn't mind going," I said quickly. "I never mind it. There was no way of knowing—"

"How many usually take the oysters in?" Daniel asked, ignoring that. "Three? He had to know how difficult it would be for just the two of us to do so—and one with little experience and none for sailing."

"What are you accusing me of, boy?" Junius asked. His hand tightened on my waist.

"He's not accusing you of anything." I glared at Daniel, pleading with him. "Are you?"

Daniel's mouth tightened. He glared back at me, and I thought he would say something more; I braced for it. But he only shook his head. "No."

Junius was still tense, but his fingers eased. "I didn't think so."

I pulled away from my husband, rising from his lap, forcing cheerfulness. "Well, I suppose I should start supper. The two of you must be starving."

I felt Junius watch me as I went—I was too sensitive, too guilty; I had the notion that my guilt showed in my every movement. I went to the stairs, meaning to go into the storage room for something—just a chance to disappear for a few moments, to compose myself—and there was Daniel, leaning against the wall, blocking access. He backed away, almost too quickly, and clumsily I went past him, up the stairs, stumbling when I reached the top and saw his bedroom door open and where we'd been only minutes before, what we'd been doing, rushed into my head. I went quietly to the door and closed it before I went into the storage room, and then I stood there, staring at strings of onions and dried salmon hanging from the rafters, barrels of flour and cornmeal, brined pork and salmon, a keg of salt, a covered basket of dried berries, and a wrapped cone of sugar. This room was mine alone, the only place in the house where everything put into it had been of my doing, and I stood there in the dimness lit by a slanted window and closed my eyes, breathing deep the scents of onion and salmon and dust, the fullness of my own intentions and deliberations, the future I'd put into this room.

I heard the low voices downstairs, deep and steady, men's voices, but not angry ones, and I imagined what they discussed. The weather and the trip, the coffee and who would have milk. Junius's resentment of the son he'd abandoned in his every word, Daniel's anger over being abandoned. They would never come right, I knew. It had been naive to think they might, and now whatever chance there might have been was gone.

Your fault again, I thought. My fault that Junius had never gone back. My fault that my own lack of self-control had put one more thing between them.

It was a moment before I realized I was fingering the bracelet, twisting a charm that was already only fragilely held. I let it go, staring down at it, remembering my suspicions and Bibi's words. But whatever spell she'd woven into the charms, whatever she'd meant, hadn't protected me from my own desire. And now everything was as much at risk as she'd predicted. My whole world teetering, tilting, and the promises in this room settled heavily around me, suffocating, my own will manifest in food preserved for a future I no longer wanted, a woman I no longer was.

Junius was a good storyteller. After dinner we lingered at the table, and he told of the trip, how he and Lord Tom had been halfway across the Bear River portage when the storm hit, and how they'd taken refuge in the woods, thinking it would be only an hour or so before they could start off again. The tarp they'd taken with them had blown away, and in the end they'd turned the canoe over and taken shelter beneath it while puddles formed under their feet and the cold settled into their bones. After a day and a half of this, they decided to press on, mud up to their knees, little streams turning into great currents, and then the ocean proper— "well, it was a whaling canoe, wasn't it?" Junius said with a laugh— but the two of them could barely control the thing, and had nearly capsized twice, losing all their supplies the second time.

To hear Junius tell it the struggle had been epic, man against the sea, huge and melodramatic; his hands gestured, his eyes were bright. Even Daniel was captivated by the story, I saw, and Lord Tom laughed once or twice and didn't try to correct my husband. Junius's charm on full display, and the habit of warming to him returned; I was laughing too, and asking questions, falling back into who I was and my place in this household so easily it was as if the last weeks had never been.

But it was only an interlude, and when Junius finished with a flourish, I glanced up to see Daniel watching me, a thoughtful glance, as if he were noting something he'd never before seen, and I was suddenly who I'd been with him, my longing a sharp and bitter taste in my mouth.

I stood—too quickly—claiming exhaustion. I saw the way Lord Tom looked at me, that knowing expression that made me uncomfortable, and I avoided both his glance and Daniel's, though I felt how tense Daniel went, how much he hated this, and I felt so tightly wound it was hard to breathe. I hoped Junius would not follow me right away, and he didn't. He waved me away and said he would be up shortly.

Once I was upstairs, I undressed quickly, pulling my night-gown over my head and trying not to think of how I'd unbuttoned it for Daniel, how it had fallen, pooling at my feet. Had Junius not returned, I would be in Daniel's bed now, arching beneath him—*Has he ever heard you cry out in pleasure?*—my skin tingling and my blood coursing, and I was a fool to not tell Junius the truth this moment. But my mouth went dry at the thought. Not yet. He'd been back barely an evening. I could not hurt him yet.

I climbed between sheets that were damp with disuse—days spent not in this bed but in another—and closed my eyes, trying to relax when I was so tense listening for footsteps on the stairs that I could not even pretend to be asleep.

It was not long before I heard murmured voices, good nights vibrating through the floorboards, the thudding close of the back door. And then the footsteps I dreaded: Junius's. Heavy and labored, and that was a relief. He would be tired. The journey had been a long one. He would collapse into bed beside me and be asleep within moments. There would be no excuse to make him believe when I had never before made one. I tried to think: had there been a time in twenty years that I had said no? Had I ever refused him when I'd always wanted so much, when

I'd leaped at a touch, when I hadn't even realized what I'd been striving for?

I never had.

The door opened; he came inside and whispered, "Are you still awake, sweetheart?" and I stayed silent, though that silence felt too still, false, and I could not calm my breathing enough to effect the lie.

He said nothing; perhaps he didn't notice. He didn't light the lamp again, but rummaged around in the dark. I heard the shush of his clothing as he removed it, the way he let out his breath at the cold. He stumbled a little going around the bed, as if he'd suddenly forgotten the layout of the room, as if nearly three weeks away had blurred twenty years of habit. The bedstead shook a little as he grabbed the post, and then the blankets came away, a rush of cold air, the dip of the mattress, the creak of ropes. He pulled the blankets over and settled in, his cold leg against mine, and I couldn't help myself; I eased it away, a mistake, because it told him I was awake.

He rolled onto his side. His hand came unerringly to my breast, molding to it through my nightgown. I reached up to push his hand away. "June, I'm tired."

He laughed a little. "You're not the one who paddled all day."

"I thought you took the stage."

"Well yes, but that's just as bad. Tom and I had to pack luggage over the dunes when the wheels got stuck." His thumb swept my nipple, then his fingers crept up to the buttons, loosening one, then another.

I grabbed his fingers. "I'm half-asleep."

He ignored me and disentangled himself from my grip, stroking my jaw, then sweeping down my throat, skipping across the leather thong, pausing. "What's this?" He pulled at it, bringing up the beads and the tooth from where they'd been nestled between my breasts.

"My father's necklace," I said.

"Is this a tooth?"

"It belonged to a cave bear." I closed my eyes, refusing to think of the way Daniel had taken it between his lips, how hot and heavy and wet it had felt falling back to my skin.

I felt the tug on the thong as Junius explored it, as he turned the tooth between his fingers.

"A cave bear?"

"It was one of his first finds. He'd worn this necklace since I could remember."

"But you've never worn it before. I've never even seen it."

"I just found it," I explained. "It fell from the mummy's dress."

Junius went still. "What? What are you talking about?"

"The necklace had been caught in her dress."

"How did it get there?"

"I don't know," I said. "It disappeared one day. Papa said he'd lost it out by the river."

"It must have got in the basket somehow."

"That's what Daniel said. But I don't think it could have. The lid was so tight, June, remember?"

He was quiet, still rubbing the tooth between his fingers. "Some other way, then."

"I think he found her before," I said.

"He found her before?" Junius was surprised. "Then why didn't we know about it?"

"Because he saw something was wrong with her," I explained. "It's the only thing I can think of. He dug her up and saw something and reburied her."

Junius let go of the tooth. It fell to my collarbone with a little thud. "That's ridiculous. Why would he have done that? There's nothing wrong with her. He had to know what a find she was."

"I don't know why. I'm trying to find out. Daniel and I have been reading Papa's journals, and—"

"Daniel?" Junius's voice was sharp.

"He volunteered to help me find the answer. It would help him too. For the newspaper story, remember?"

Junius was quiet, and I went on quickly, rolling over the suspicion I thought I heard in his silence. "He's very clever, you know. Like you. He's good at seeing things."

Junius drew back a little. "You sound as if you've taken a liking to him."

Now was the time to tell him. *Tell him now.* But I couldn't. Twenty years, and in the last three weeks, I'd forgotten the *who* of Junius, I'd forgotten that I loved him, that I'd been happy. To leave him had seemed so easy—how startling to find now that it was not the least bit so. I managed, "Of course I have. I've tried to...for your sake."

"I told you not to get close to him. I told you we couldn't trust him."

His words annoyed me suddenly. Sharply, I said, "Then why did you leave me with him for three weeks?"

It was not the kind of thing I usually would have said. Not the kind of thing I would have even thought before. I heard the echo of Daniel in the words, and I felt Junius jerk, as if I'd taken him aback. "Because you needed the help with the oysters."

"But he was right, wasn't he, when he said we should have waited for you to get back? It was hard for just the two of us."

"Are you angry with me?"

I swallowed hard. "No, of course not."

"I'm sorry it was so difficult. You've done it a hundred times before. How was I to know you would fall off the boat?"

"We shouldn't have gone at all. I saw the storm was coming, and I—"

"You've been listening to him."

"What was I supposed to do, ignore him for three weeks?"

"I told you he would try to come between us."

"You shouldn't have left him." I felt stiff and angry, at odds both with him and myself. Blame was easy to embrace because it alleviated my guilt. Blame for the way Junius had been so desperate to be out from under the yoke of his son that he had left me too. Blame for not understanding my vulnerability. Blame for his selfishness that had led to my culpability. Slowly, as if he didn't really want to know the answer, he said, "Which do you mean? That I shouldn't have left him here with you? Or that I shouldn't have left him before?"

"Both."

"I wanted to be with you, Lea. I wanted to take care of you. You were so young and…and helpless—"

"And you wanted me in your bed."

Again, I felt his surprise. "You *have* been listening to him."

"Isn't it true?"

He hesitated. His hand came to my hair, hesitant, cupping my head. "You wanted me, too. You must admit that. The way you looked at me—"

"Don't blame me for this. You made the decision."

"We made it together. You knew about Mary."

I turned my head away, jerking from beneath his hand. "You said you would take care of things with her. And I was seventeen."

"A woman grown. Do you really mean to blame this all on me? Lea, he's using you. He sees your kindness and he's trying to win your sympathy. He knows he can turn you against me. He knows how that would punish me."

"Would it?"

"Yes. Christ, yes, it would. You know that." Junius gathered me into his arms, pulling me close, and I let him, unresisting but not helping either, not complicit. I felt like a doll in his arms, pliable and unyielding at the same time. He kissed my jaw, my cheekbone. "I see it already, the way he's planted doubt in you. Don't let him do this. Twenty years…we have twenty years together. He doesn't know anything about me. He hates me. Why would you listen to him?"

My guilt was enough that when Junius reached for the buttons on my nightgown again, I let him unbutton it. I let him bare my breasts and press his mouth to them. I let him ease up my nightgown and come between my legs. He panted into my ear and rocked against me, and I went still in habit and distaste, feeling as if I betrayed them both, father and son. I waited patiently until his thrusting became faster and more frenzied and he pulled out to spend himself against my stomach, and I realized for the first time—now that I had something to compare—that he did that often, and I wondered what pleasure he strived for, what I hadn't the experience to know.

My longing for Daniel rose, and along with it came terrible guilt that only grew when Junius gathered me close in his arms, resting his head against my breast, loving and content as if nothing had changed—and I knew that for him nothing had. I was still the woman he loved, the woman he'd cared twenty years for, staying in a place he hated because I wanted it, keeping the promise he'd made to my father—the promise I was breaking.

Junius was a good man, and in his arms I felt my betrayal as an aching regret I could not get past. I did not know how to tell him the truth. As he'd said, this would punish him, and what had he ever done to deserve such punishment? How could I hurt him this way?

If I said nothing, if I sent Daniel away, Junius would never know what had happened. He would never be hurt, and I would not have thrown away my father's hopes for me; I could pretend I'd never given in to the Leonie Papa had been afraid I would become, the nature he'd warned me to be wary of.

Or I could tell Junius the truth. I could go with Daniel and leave this place I loved and give up everything and walk into a future uncertain and strange. I knew I loved him. I knew I wanted him. But the Leonie I had been told me the three weeks I'd just spent with him were nothing but a fever dream, and one did not throw an entire life away for something so new, no matter how exciting. Because excitement faded. Passion and lust gave way to affection and common interests—this I knew, because I'd once felt such desire for my husband, hadn't I? And when those things were gone, what had I to give to Daniel? Whatever his protests, he was young enough to want children someday, to start a new future, and I...I was thirty-seven. Too old to start over again. What I'd had with Daniel was something to put aside and forget, to take out and think of only now and then, in my most private moments.

Rationality was a bitter thing. I thought of Daniel and his golden hair and the way his body felt against mine. I thought of watching him walk away, and my vision blurred in sudden tears. I did not want to let him go.

But to make such a sacrifice, to hurt everyone I loved, to break every promise I'd made...in Daniel's arms, with no one else around, the choice had not been difficult. But now that Junius was here, I questioned myself. Now that Lord Tom looked at me with his fathomless eyes, I felt the wrongness of what Daniel and I had done. The truth was that I barely knew him. I had been suspicious of him myself. Junius did not trust him. Bibi had warned me of him. Lord Tom did not like him. I was uncertain and afraid—perhaps I was not seeing clearly. I knew already how dangerous were my yearnings; my father had been relentless in telling me so.

I remembered a time when Papa had come back late from a collecting trip to find me at the fireside with Lord Tom and Bibi's grandson Willy and his sweetheart Melia, who was teaching me a Chinook fishing song after an evening of storytelling. I remembered how soft was her voice to start, how it had grown louder and the others had begun to pound in rhythm and the whole thing had crept so beautifully into my blood that my own voice had raised as well, my own hands beat time upon a log. I felt wild and free and happy that night, and Papa, emerging from the darkness, had seemed to me at first a strange spirit from one of

Lord Tom's stories, and I'd shrieked in surprise and terror until I realized who it was.

When the others had gone, Papa told Lord Tom to unload the canoe, and when Tom gave him a worried frown, saying, "*Sikhs,*" in this warning voice that made my father bristle, Papa had snapped roughly, *We've no need of you just now, Tom.* When Lord Tom left, Papa took both my arms hard, forcing me to look at him. *You are not a savage,* he'd said brutally.

Of course not.

Then why are you acting like one?

Papa, it was only singing.

Only singing. He made a small laugh. *Only singing. With such small things does it begin.* He'd relaxed his hold, looking so disappointed my heart ached. *Leonie, you are too immoderate. You know this. But you must guard against it, or you'll become like them. Savagery and licentiousness are always waiting. If we give in to them, we become little better than animals. Is that what you want?*

No. No. I'm sorry. I won't do it again.

He'd sighed and released me, and I threw myself into his chest, hugging him tight while he stood there awkwardly. After a moment, he put his arms around me, stroking my hair, murmuring, *You are my daughter, Leonie, and I love you.*

I felt his forgiveness then, and I vowed never to give him another reason to fear for my degeneracy. But as hard as I tried to fight such things, I'd given in more than once. Not just to singing, but to my sensitivity and my fancies, to my fondness for dancing. I had an excessive nature; this interlude with Daniel had only proved it. I knew Papa and Junius were right. Who was I to question those who knew me best?

I had been content once; I could be content again. Couldn't I?

The question went round and round. I could find no answer I wanted to keep.

It was a long time before I slept.

CHAPTER 23

I WOKE EXHAUSTED, QUESTIONS STILL IN MY HEAD AND NO
closer to a decision. Junius was up already, pulling on his
trousers, and when I stirred, he looked over at me and said,
"We'll have to return Mac Wilson's canoe sometime in the
next few days."

A quick hope flared, the thought that perhaps I could have
another day to think, a day without either of them. I said, "Why
not today? You can take Daniel with you. He can follow in the
plunger."

"He's not skillful enough."

"He managed it during a storm."

"With you directing him, no doubt," Junius said. "I want
to check things over today, but we'll all make the trip later this
week. I know you'd like the chance to go in to town."

"I've so much to do here. The mummy—"

"Not cut into yet, I see."

"No, not yet. I've only just finished drawing her."

He gave me a reproachful look. "It couldn't have taken you
three weeks, Lea. You had days while I was gone. What the hell
else were you doing?"

In pure defense, I snapped, "It took me some time to recover from almost drowning. And just because you aren't here doesn't mean your chores don't need to be done. And there were Papa's journals to read, too. To see if he'd said anything about her."

"You shouldn't waste your time with those."

I frowned and sat up, pulling the blankets with me against the cold, ignoring his comment. "There *is* something in Papa's journals that's interesting, June. Not about the mummy, but... he keeps talking about an experiment. Do you know what he means?"

"An experiment? What does he say about it?"

"Nothing I can put a finger on. Something to do with the Indians, and whether environment can overcome blood. Mostly cryptic remarks, but he did say he'd told you about it and that you promised to stay vigilant."

Junius put on his shirt and buttoned it. "You know your father. He was always prattling on about some theory or another."

"Yes, but this one seemed important. And he refers to it over and over again."

"Hmmm. Something about skulls, maybe? He was doing a lot of measuring back then. Phrenological stuff."

"Yes, he mentions all that. But I had the impression this was something...living."

Junius let out his breath. "Well, I don't remember it. Hell, it's been twenty years, Lea. You can't expect me to remember all his crazy nonsense. I'm sure it's nothing to worry about."

"I don't worry about it. I just find it curious."

Junius nodded, obviously distracted. He said, "When I sent the canoe off to Baird, I sent a letter with it telling him about the mummy."

My father and his experiments fled my thoughts. I pushed back the blankets and rose from the bed. "You did? But we agreed—"

"We agreed you would cut into her before I got back," he pointed out. "I thought you would be finished with her by now."

"Junius, you promised her to me. You should have waited."

"It's not my fault you took so long," he said. "You should have had the boy help if you're so reluctant. I'm certain he wouldn't be."

"I'm not reluctant."

"Then no harm's done, is it?" Junius gave me a stern look. "Baird probably already knows about it, in any case. If it was in the newspapers in San Francisco, word's undoubtedly got to him by now. So do your job, Lea. Cut the thing apart and be done with it. Then we'll send it on to Baird."

My legs felt unsteady; I sat on the edge of the mattress.

Junius came over, patting me on the shoulder. "We'll send your notes with it. Give them to me as soon as you can, and I'll write everything up."

"You'll tell him it's *my* study, won't you?"

"Of course. Didn't I say I would?"

But there was something so facile about the way he said it, and I wasn't reassured—though that was foolish, I told myself. Junius loved me; we were in this together. It was only Daniel's resentment putting words to my own.

I swallowed my anger and watched Junius leave and then I got dressed. But the conversation had only for the moment put aside the questions I'd struggled the night with, and I wished it were possible to lock myself away in this room, to not see anyone or do anything or feel the struggle within me, and the moment I pinned up my hair I thought of Daniel saying "You've disappeared." I knew it was true; I felt it. A strange bifurcation, two halves of myself.

Who are you? The mummy's voice drifted into my head. *Who are you?* and *I brought him for you*, but now, away from Daniel, I wasn't certain I trusted the voice. It was my too-vivid imagination, the one that only told me what I wanted to hear, the one that

made right everything wrong I'd done, that justified an immo-
rality I knew I should feel more intently than I did.

I lingered until one moment more would cause questions,
and then I went downstairs, my chest tightening, wondering what
I would say when I saw him, what I would feel. But Daniel was
not there, nor was Junius. Only Lord Tom, sitting at the kitchen
table, looking through a book. It was a moment before I realized
it was my notebook, the translated stories, and he had it opened
to a picture I'd sketched one night while I was alone with Daniel,
the story of the Chinook tribe's creation, illustrated with Quoots-
hooi cracking eggs and throwing them down the mountainside,
one transforming into the legs and arms of an emerging Indian.

Lord Tom looked up slowly, as if he could not bear to tear his
eyes away from the book. "When did you do this?"

I stopped short. "Oh, I was only playing. I know they're not
very good, but—"

"It *is* good," he disagreed. "Though Quoots-hooi is rounder
and uglier."

His praise warmed me. "I was remembering her from that
mask Papa had."

"Not a good one. A lazy artist. You are much better."

Nervously, I said, "You should put that away, *tot*. Before
Junius comes back in. It will only annoy him."

He ignored me, leafing through the pages. "There are no
other pictures."

"Only the one. I was telling the story to Daniel, and I—" I
broke off, glancing away, not wanting to say why that story in
particular had stayed in my head, why I'd chosen it to draw.

Lord Tom closed the book and pushed it aside, back to where
he'd found it, beneath my father's journals. "Your father's writ-
ings are here."

I nodded, disconcerted at the change in subject. "Yes. I've
been reading them. I was looking for some clue to the mummy. I
thought he might have written about her."

Lord Tom frowned. "Why would he have done so?"

"I think he found her before I did."

Now he looked vaguely alarmed. "Why do you think that?"

"Because of this." I pulled the leather thong until the tooth and beads of the necklace I wore emerged from the neckline of my bodice, and held it out for him to see. "Do you remember this? Papa used to wear it all the time."

"I remember."

"I found it in her dress. I don't know why it was there. Junius says it must have fallen into the basket, and I'm not sure Daniel doesn't think so as well, but I think Papa found her once before. I think he found her and—"

I stopped. Lord Tom's expression had frozen. He looked carved as a totem sitting there, staring at the tooth as if it paralyzed him.

"*Tot?*"

He blinked, coming back into himself again. "You must put her back, *okustee*. Bury her."

I sighed in exasperation and let the tooth drop. "Not this again. Is it still bad luck you're worried about? Because I've been researching her for weeks and nothing's happened—"

"He says you nearly drowned."

"But I didn't. She's not bad luck, *tot*."

"If he had not been there, you would have drowned."

"But he *was* there. And it was the mummy who brought him."

Lord Tom frowned at me, obviously confused.

"It's what she told—" I stopped short. My imagination again and dreams. *It's not real, Leonie.*

"What she told you?" Lord Tom finished slowly. "In a *dleam*?"

I nodded slowly. "Yes. A dream. I know it's not real, but…it seemed so."

Lord Tom's voice was urgent when he said, "Spirits will lie to you, *okustee*. It is what they *do*."

"But…what if she wasn't that kind of a spirit, but a…a guardian spirit? What if she's *my* guardian spirit?"

He looked doubtful. "Spirits lie."

"Then why…?" I foundered. The whole conversation was absurd. My father would never have countenanced it. Junius would condemn me. Only Daniel felt for her what I did. He seemed to understand the strange…connection I felt for her, but now, without him here, those feelings seemed ridiculous, impossible to explain. I should not even *want* to explain them. But Lord Tom had been the one to teach me about the spirits. I knew I could make him see. I wanted him to understand. "If she's bad, she's good too, *tot*. I…I wish I knew *what* she was. I wish I knew why Papa reburied her—"

"Reburied her?"

"That's what I think happened. How else would the necklace have got there? I think he dug her up, but he knew something about her wasn't right, so he buried her again. But I can't see it. I can't find the reason, and—"

"Because she was a *mesachie tomawanos*."

"Papa didn't believe such things," I said impatiently. "He wouldn't have reburied her because she was a bad spirit."

"Some things cannot be known. Some things *should* not be known. Put her back."

"I *can't*. Even if I wanted to, I couldn't. Junius wants to send her to Baird, and—"

"What if they find something you don't want to see?"

I frowned at him, puzzled. "Why do you say that?"

"Things are not always what they seem, *okustee*."

I said a little desperately, "Junius wants her gone too. But I…I'm not done with her. I can't explain it, but…Bibi said she wanted something from me. That the mummy wanted something from me. And I feel that too. I think…"

"You think *what*?" Lord Tom asked gently.

I met his gaze. "I think that if I could discover the truth of her, I would know what to do."

Lord Tom was quiet. I felt him searching my face. I felt him looking for something. I thought he would ask me to elaborate. I thought he would say, "About what, *okustee*?" but he didn't, and that troubled me, that he didn't ask it, that whatever he saw in my face seemed to satisfy him, because he only sighed, and tapped my notebook. He said, "Make Quoots-hooi uglier. Then you should draw the stories."

I was disappointed, feeling as if I stood on the edge of something, as if the answers were just out of reach, and he held at least some of them. "Yes. All right."

He opened his mouth to say something more, but just then the door opened; a burst of cold, wet air, and I was annoyed at the interruption, ready to snap at something, when I saw it was Daniel, and at the sight of him everything left me—I was possessed purely and simply by desire. I thought, *How can I let him go?* at the same moment I felt Lord Tom watching me.

I gripped the back of the chair hard and forced a composure I did not feel and said, "Good morning."

Daniel glanced at Lord Tom, and then gave me a short nod. "Good morning." He took off his coat, slowly and carefully, as if he found the task of unbuttoning crucially important.

I felt Lord Tom's gaze, piercing, as he took in Daniel, and then me, and then he said to me, "Do you remember the story of Loowit, *okustee*?"

And I knew then for certain. I knew he understood, because the story of Loowit was the story of how the Indians came to have fire, but it was more than that too. She had been the only one to have fire, and she had run from those who tried to steal it from her and gone to the great Tyee Sahale across the Bridge of the Gods and told him how cold the Indians were. He gave them fire and rewarded her daring with eternal youth and beauty, so much so that chiefs from many tribes wanted her, and when Loowit would not choose between them there started a war which angered Sahale so that he had destroyed the Bridge to the Gods and separated the tribes from one another.

Loowit would not choose, and that refusal destroyed everything.

I swallowed hard. I pretended I didn't understand his message. "Yes, of course I remember it."

But Lord Tom knew me too well, and I saw that knowledge in his eyes now. "Perhaps you should draw the picture," he said. He pushed back his chair and rose, going to the back door, easing out. I heard his footsteps on the back porch, the open and close of his door.

Daniel said, "What was that about?"

"He knows," I said miserably. I sagged back against the sink and looked away, confused and upset.

He came into the kitchen. "He won't say anything. Not until you do. He loves you."

He was so perceptive. I said, "Yes, but he doesn't like it. He disapproves."

"Do you think so? I'm not certain of that at all."

He stepped closer. When his hand trailed down my arm, his fingers brushing the twine of Bibi's bracelet, I felt again that leap between us, passion and desire, that sense that he was where I belonged, and yet...I remembered also last night, my rational self, my reluctance to hurt Junius, to change my life, and when Daniel leaned in to kiss me, I turned my head away and said, "Don't. Not here."

"Lea, I've gone nearly mad waiting for you this morning. I couldn't sleep—"

"Daniel, please."

"He's in the barn. Lord Tom's in his room. Who's to see if I kiss you?"

"I can't—"

"You can't *what*?" His voice was low and urgent. "What's wrong, Lea? What have I done? Don't tell me you've changed your mind."

"No, I…I just need time. To think."

"About what?" he demanded. "What is there to think about? I love you. You love me. Tell him and let's be done with it."

I shook my head; I could not meet his gaze. "I'm not so certain—"

"You're not uncertain, you're afraid," he accused. "What else must be proved to you, Lea, before you see that you're meant to be with me?"

"You don't know," I said. "You're so young. You don't know how things fade—"

"You think what's between us will fade?"

"I don't know. I…with Junius, it changed, and—"

"Because you don't love him the way you love me. What has he said to you to turn you this way?"

"He hasn't said anything." I pressed my hand flat against his shirt, meaning to keep him at bay, but it was a mistake. He was so warm; I wanted him so much. I let my hand fall again and looked miserably away. "It's what I know. I'm ten years older, Daniel. I know you think it doesn't matter, but you're just beginning your life, and—"

He laughed shortly. "And yours is ending? Is that what you're saying? I'm telling you it's just beginning. He doesn't know you the way I do."

"He does, in his way."

Daniel bit off a curse. "You'll wither away with him. Why don't you see it?"

Images from my dreams. Old woman's hands, shriveling up, crumbling—but no, it was only what I wanted to believe. It wasn't true.

"I thought I knew what I wanted but now…please, you must understand. I've been with Junius twenty years."

"It doesn't bind you to serving twenty more," he said bitterly. He pulled me up hard against him, saying almost desperately. "Come with me somewhere. Right now. You must know a place where we can be alone for an hour. Just...let me make love to you. Let me remind you of what we are."

The temptation was there. To do what he wanted, to let him make the decision for me, because that was what would happen, I knew. I would go with him and the passion between us would blind me and possess me. I could not be rational when I was with him. A life with him beckoned too enticingly. But it wasn't real. It was only a fantasy.

I whispered to him, "You've berated me for doing what everyone else wanted me to do, for being what my father wanted and what Junius wanted. Now you're asking me to do what *you* want. Do you still wish me to choose for myself? Did you mean that? Or did you only mean that I should let you take their place?"

He released his hold, obviously dismayed. "No, of course not."

"Then let me decide. Please, Daniel, just...let me decide who I want to be. You know I want you. You know if I went with you I would do whatever you wished. You would...overwhelm me. But I need to think more clearly. I love this place. There are things I don't want to lose. I don't want to regret it if I choose you. I can't believe you want that either."

He ran a hand through his hair as if to calm himself. "No, I don't want that." His voice was hoarse, banked desire, battened will.

"Thank you," I said.

"But"—a deep breath—"but you can't expect me not to fight for you, Lea. And you can't expect me to wait forever."

The front door opened, a stream of cold air cutting through the warmth of the kitchen. Junius. Daniel stepped back, putting space between us, composing himself so quickly that I was startled at the apparent ease of it. I was not so fast. My heart was beating like a wild thing's; I tried to smile as Junius came into the kitchen. He glanced at Daniel, and then at me.

"What's wrong, sweetheart?" he asked, frowning. "The boy troubling you?"

"Not in the least," I said, turning to the stove, willing my hands to stop their trembling as I poured a cup of coffee.

"The springhouse looks good," he said. "You couldn't tell there'd been a flood."

I couldn't think what to say to that, so I took a sip of coffee.

Daniel said, "You seem surprised."

"You're a good worker, boy, as I think I've said before."

"A lifetime of practice," Daniel said.

Junius gave him a narrow look. I felt the tension between them, with myself as the fulcrum—whether Junius knew it or not. "Well," he said. "Something else to thank you for." And then, before I could do or say anything, my husband's arm snaked around my waist, pulling me to him so hard I spilled my coffee. His kiss was possessive and unyielding—I realized with dismay that he must sense my role in that tension after all. When he let me go, he said wickedly, "I'm still thinking about that greeting you gave me last night," as if Daniel wasn't in the room, but I knew he'd done it for Daniel's benefit. I was afraid Daniel would say something. But when I glanced at him I saw he would not, that he was abiding by his promise to me, though his jaw had gone hard and his mouth tight.

He went to the back door, wrenching it open with an almost vicious twist, and then he was outside, coatless, hatless, letting the door slam shut behind him. I heard his boot steps on the stoop and then the short stairs to the yard.

I jerked away from Junius.

He said, "Wonder what's wrong with him?"

"You shouldn't have done that in front of him."

"Why not? What's wrong with kissing my own wife?"

"Nothing. Except that you did it to embarrass him."

Junius gave me a careful look. "Did I? Now, why would I do that?"

I looked away. "I don't know."

"The two of you were talking pretty close when I came in," he said.

"We were arguing," I said quickly. I put down my coffee and turned away from him, to the sink. The water in the wash bucket was cold and skimmed with grease, but I scooped out a handful of soft soap and went to washing the dishes there as if nothing was wrong.

"About what?"

"About you, as it happens." Close enough to the truth that I hoped he wouldn't hear the lie of it.

"Me?"

"I'm trying to make him see that there's good in you," I said, and now I looked at him over my shoulder, mustering self-right-eous anger. "It doesn't help that you don't make an effort to show him that yourself."

Junius's expression softened. He came up to me, pressing to my back, his hands on my hips. "Lea, Lea," he said quietly. "How many times must I say it? You're wasting your time. Let the boy go. It will never be right between us. There's no point in trying."

I looked down into the sink. "Well, I can't help myself."

He gave me a quick squeeze and stepped away, already dismissing it, letting it fall away the way he let everything go. Easy and without malice. He said, "I appreciate that you want to do this, but it's no good attempting the impossible."

"How do you know what's possible if you don't try?" I asked.

"It's not the trying," he told me. "It's the knowing when to stop. The boy's no good, Lea. It's time you opened your eyes and saw that."

"I think he would surprise you," I managed.

"I think it's you he'll surprise," he said.

CHAPTER 24

April 23, 1854: I find myself thinking again of the 16th century's plastica theory. Not because I believe remotely in the possibility that God first modeled creatures in stone to test them for viability before he generated life within them, and left for fossils those forms he found unworthy, but because I find myself entertaining a version of such a plastica theory when it comes to the development of man. I wonder if perhaps God, like an artist sketching the same thing over and over again until he reaches perfection, must have created the various human groups in experiment, trying out his vision of man in lesser forms before he settled on the last and best. While degenerationism explains why such a divide exists between peoples, I cannot accept the idea that God would allow his perfected man to degenerate into something low and vile. And so, God plays in the mud: his first test the ape-like Hottentots and Australian aborigines, which would have offended, and then next the clearly subhuman efforts of the Negroes and the Indians. We proceed in lightening clay and forming more perfect features and intelligence, through the

Mongols and Arctics until one reaches the clearly superior Caucasian.

And so, given this, interbreeding is so clearly an insult to God that it cannot be tolerated, even if it means ultimately that such interbreeding might elevate the lower types—because this comes at too great a cost. I have seen this for myself, that while the attributes of the upper orders can have some effect on mitigating those lamentable tendencies of the lower orders, so their blood too does tell. It is NOT erased. We must be vigilant—God could not have meant for our clearly superior faculties of compassion, mercy and charity to pollute his own efforts in creating a more perfect Being. To mix with the lower orders only results in the destruction of our own. Does a dog mate with a lion? So too should not those so clearly resembling orang-utangs mate with man. They may seem fully human, but...my experiment proves this not to be true. No matter my efforts, it persists in its constant degeneration. I fear to hope for any future, as it seems more and more obviously that such a thing defiles both man and God.

And yet those more tender aspects in my character, those attributes God must have struggled to create in his last, best order, means I cannot but strive despite my fears. Can it be a flaw to hope, when God so clearly intended such faculty, when I can be only the creature He made me?

"You're wasting your time, sweetheart," Junius said.

I looked up to see him bending over me. He grabbed the corner of the journal, lifting it from my hands before I knew what he was doing.

"Don't," I said, reaching as he dangled it beyond my grasp. "Junius, please! I'm reading that."

He tossed it aside. It skittered across the floor, sliding to a stop beneath Daniel's feet, where he sat in the chair by the lamp. He was reading one as well, and he glanced up. "Let her read it," he said, leaning down to pick it up. "What are you so worried she'll find?"

"Worried?" Junius asked. "I only dislike her spending hours on something that won't avail her anything."

"She can decide what's worthy of her time herself, don't you think?" Daniel asked. "Or are you making all her decisions for her now?"

"Daniel," I warned.

"*Daniel*," Junius repeated, mockingly. "Let him say what he thinks, Lea. You sound like his mother."

"She could not be less like," Daniel said, and I wondered if Junius heard that tone in his voice that I heard, the one that made me have to look away.

Junius sat beside me on the settee, close, putting his arm around my shoulders, drawing me into his side. Daniel watched impassively—how bland he was; the only thing that revealed his agitation was the flex of his jaw, something I only saw because of how well I knew him.

I said quickly, trying to ease the tension, "Papa was talking about the experiment again. I wish I knew what it was. You're certain you haven't any idea, June?"

"None at all." He sprang up again, restlessly, as if something were prodding him. He went to the organ, shoving up the cover over the keyboard. "How about a sing-along?"

"A sing-along?" Daniel asked.

"You can sing, I take it? I'd be surprised if the Russell talent eluded you."

"I didn't know there *was* a Russell talent."

"There is. Singing," Junius said. "What are your preferences? Ballads? Hymns? Bawdy tunes? Opera? We've got them all."

"None of them," Daniel said. He looked back down at the journal he was reading. "You go ahead without me."

"Not acceptable." Junius reached for the folder of music. "Come now, boy, I'm trying to make amends, as your dear stepmother wishes."

Daniel bristled. "You've no real desire to make amends, and I've no wish to accept them."

"Ah, you see, Lea?" Junius spread his hands in a gesture of resignation. "I'm surprised at how willing you are to disappoint her, boy."

Slowly, Daniel closed the journal. Very deliberately, without looking at me, he said, "Not at all. I am devoted to her every happiness."

Junius laughed and looked at me. "Well, well, how fine. You hear that, sweetheart? He is *devoted* to you. No doubt the ladies line up to hear such talk, boy. Women love poetry. I imagine it's worked to your advantage a time or two?"

"Once or twice," Daniel admitted. I felt his glance, and I refused to meet it.

"Well, I know Lea appreciates it. It's good for her to hear some pretty words now and again. Lord Tom and I don't possess the faculty for such romance, I'm afraid." He glanced at Lord Tom, who sat at the kitchen table, silently watching us as he mended a net. "Isn't that so, Tom?"

"Junius," I said with difficulty. "Please."

"Please *what*? What's wrong? I'm trying to get along with the boy, just as you asked."

"You're baiting him."

"It's all right, Lea," Daniel said quietly. "It's not as if I can't manage it."

"You see, sweetheart? He's a tough one. Why, look at all he's done with his life. Working hard, taking care of his mother, saving my wife from drowning…Is there nothing you can't do, boy?"

"I can't save her from you, it seems," Daniel said.

"Is that right?" Junius asked, and now his false joviality was gone. His expression went hard. "Have you tried?"

"That's enough," I said, launching to my feet, my voice too loud. "You're being ridiculous, Junius. And you too, Daniel. It's late. I think it's time we all went to bed."

Junius raised a brow and gave me a half smile. "It's not that late. And I wanted a sing-along, remember?"

"This mood you're in…"

"What mood is that? I thought I was being friendly. I'm only trying to get to know my son. Isn't that what you wanted?"

"Not this way," I said quietly.

Junius shrugged. "It's only that you think him admirable, and I'm not so certain. I can't help but wonder why he showed up when he did. It seems a bit too coincidental to me."

I frowned. "What do you mean?"

"We find the mummy and suddenly here he is too."

I brought him for you. I looked at Daniel, who was watching his father warily, and I said, "He's working on a newspaper story. It *was* the mummy who brought him. You know that already."

"Ah yes, the newspaper story." Junius nodded. "How close are you to finishing that, boy?"

"I'm waiting for more information," Daniel said carefully.

"I see," Junius said. "Or is it just that you're finding ways to prolong your stay? Pretending to help her by reading journals, looking for some reference neither of you will ever find."

"We will find something," I protested. "I'm certain of it."

Junius ignored me. He looked at Daniel. "Well, the thing won't be here for much longer. Did she tell you that? We're sending it off. And I would think you'd be in a hurry to get back home. You've got a fiancée waiting for you, don't you? Time to move on with your life, boy, and leave us well enough alone."

I managed, "Daniel's been very helpful to me, June."

"I imagine." Junius's voice was dry. "But he's got a fiancée, Leonie, and no doubt she'd like him back. You're not being fair to keep him."

Junius was right, I knew. I'd known it last night. My rational self. The Leonie who wanted to keep the promises she'd made. The Leonie who was content. I should let Daniel go.

I looked at him, uncertain, afraid.

As if he knew what I was thinking, Daniel shook his head. Nearly imperceptible, but I saw it. He said to Junius, "I'm in no hurry. Not if Lea wants me."

Wants. Not *needs* or *wishes* or any of those words that had no other meanings. *Wants*, and suddenly I was back in the kitchen and he was pressed against me, speaking low and urgently in my ear. *Come with me. Let me make love to you. Let me remind you of what we are.*

Junius said, "I'm certain she doesn't wish to keep you."

Daniel's smile was very small, "I'm certain she knows her own mind well enough not to require your certainty."

Junius frowned. He looked at me. "Well, Lea? Should we send the boy on his way?"

"Junius, this is ridiculous—"

"Does he go or stay?" My husband's face was hard.

I knew what he wanted me to say. I felt the demand of it. But I couldn't. I said, though I knew I was a fool, "I want him to stay."

Junius stood abruptly, shoving the folder of music back into its place, slamming down the lid on the organ.

Daniel said, "You mean there's to be no sing-along?"

Junius glared at him. "I find I'm more tired than I'd thought. I'm going to bed. Stay up and sing hymns to yourself if you want." He strode over to me and held out his hand. "Are you coming?"

I said nothing, but when he took my hand, I didn't protest or draw away. His fingers gripped mine hard, and I saw the way he looked over his shoulder at Daniel, I felt the way Junius took ownership of me, the way he laid claim, and instead of feeling angry or misused, I felt...sad. Impossibly sad and tender, so I went with him to bed. And I tried not to think of the expression on Daniel's face when I'd gone. As if he'd been both reprieved and punished in the same moment.

She ran, and I ran after, chasing glints of saffron that blurred in the glare of the sun, dark hair gleaming with red. My heart pounded, my breath came hard and fast, but she was always just beyond my reach. She turned and beckoned, haloed by the sun behind her, her edges shimmering and dissipating, the glare of the sun moving to her center until she was not quite real, but only an illusion born of heat and light. I could not see her face, but I heard her voice in my head, no voice but more a feeling. I was too slow. I must hurry. I sped, hoping to catch her while she stopped, but she turned and ran off again and then she was gone, disappearing into the light of the sun, and I halted and put my hand to my eyes, searching for her in a limitless plain, nothing but grassy hills and dust, but she was gone, and a terrible sorrow swept me. I sank to my knees, and suddenly I was falling, sinking fast into a stormy sea, cold to my marrow, frozen and fighting the waves and the current and the storm, strug-gling to breathe, to reach the surface, my legs tangled in my dress and my boots pulling me down into blackness, my lungs bursting. You almost died, and what a waste...*I could not reach the top. I was shrinking and withering, my breath gone, nothing but cold and blackness all around, and she was in it. I felt her there, angry and demanding, menacing.* What do you want from the world?

Dawn broke on a cold and wet morning, the air gathering as if it meant to storm, but when I left Junius's side and rose, the air seemed to snap and dissipate—not a storm after all but only the aftereffects of the dream that left me shaken and sad. I had not had a nightmare like this for weeks. Not since...not since I'd been sleeping in Daniel's bed, and what that meant I wasn't cer-tain, nor was I ready to contemplate it.

But my discomfort grew, increasing with the tension in the house, Daniel and Junius circling, my own desires battling good sense and habit, Lord Tom's thoughtful glances. I was glad when they went about their chores and left me alone, and I sat at the table and opened my father's journal and dedicated myself to the reading of it.

August 3, 1854: Such weakness is in man! Moral principles, common sense, rationality…how easy it is for the passions of the body to rule us instead. Such force of will it requires to live a life unsullied! Do any manage it? Or are such offices given only to Christ and His saints? I can only believe that our God-given intellects are strong enough to overcome our lower emotions—else for what reason were they given? But it requires great intellect, study, and reason to live blameless and pure, and when such things are marred by the very worst of bloods! Oh, how I see it and despise it. What my own weakness has wrought! What does God mean by instilling within us passion and desire along with intellect and rationality? Such contradictory things—what cruelty to ensure that we all must fight such a war within us, and how I suffer and lament the fact that there is no hope for those who do not have the capacity for higher thought and reason. For the superior man, it is difficult enough. Those animals who live on the bay have no hope of it, for they do not possess intellect in vast enough amounts to overcome the will of their senses. The only fortunate thing is that they lack the sense to understand their shortcomings. They cannot suffer what they do not know. But the suffering that is given to one who does know it!

They cannot learn. They cannot be taught. But to leave it as it is, to not try…what is that but compounding my own sin? Surely I owe God my most earnest attempt.

The suffering in my father's words was profound, and I was more confused than ever, my own decisions clouded by the things he said. I had not thought him so encumbered. I remembered what Daniel had said, how we were all just apes wearing clothes, hiding what we really were, and I was afraid. Of my father's written suffering, which I didn't understand, and how it tangled my own war with passion and rationality. Because I had lived both sides, and I knew contentment with one and liked the ease of it. To be content was good. But could it compete truly with that feeling of being so truly alive? How was it possible to fight it? Should one even try?

And that was where rationality told a truth I knew. Such things could not sustain themselves. They burned themselves to ashes, and then what was left? Was it worth throwing everything else away?

The sadness from my dream pricked again, and I felt melancholy and strange, removed from myself, as if a part of me had gone with Daniel and not thought to return. I fingered the edges of my notebook, thinking of Loowit and Quoots-hooi, the pictures that formed in my head like images in smoke, and then I was opening it, flipping the pages until I came to the half-translated story of Loowit. My phonetic spelling of the native Chinook, then the jargon, and my translated English version. I picked up a pencil and began drawing in the margin—the Bridge of the Gods, the fire, and Loowit herself, and her face was so clear to me. Dark eyes and red-brown hair, and I realized I was drawing her from my dream. The dress she wore was the same, and I'd drawn a deerskin headband decorated with embroidery of porcupine quills. And then her transformation, because Sahale had turned her into Mount St. Helens to punish her—a beautiful, perfect ice-covered cone of a mountain with a volcanic heart of fire.

I forgot my father's journal and my nightmare. I thought only of the story, of drawing the pictures that chased themselves in my head, and when I was done I stared at the drawings I'd made. The story was there, the pictures telling it better than had the English words I'd tried to find, and I felt a satisfaction that bubbled inside of me like joy, and I was smiling when Junius came inside, bringing with him the smell of rain and smoke.

My first impulse was to slam shut the notebook and push it away. But I found myself resisting the urge. I left the book open; I did not put down the pencil I held.

Junius said, "What are you doing, sweetheart?"

I swallowed and told him the truth. "Working on the translations."

Junius paused in taking off his coat. "The *what*?"

"The Indian legends," I said.

"The legends? Lea, you know I think those are a waste of time."

"But I don't," I told him. "I love these stories, June. You know I do. They mean something to me. I don't know why, but they do. They always have." Without thinking, I pulled the notebook closer to me as if to protect it. I saw he noticed it. His jaw tightened.

He went on, "Half of those stories are obscene. They're not meant for a respectable woman's eyes. They're savage, Lea."

"And you think they'll turn me savage as well, is that it?"

"I'm only worried for you. Your imagination—"

"I should think you'd prefer a little savagery in me, Junius," I forced myself to counter. "Most of us feel passion and desire. Don't you?"

He stared at me as if I'd sprouted wings.

I went on, "Even my father fought it, I've discovered. He despaired that he could ever overcome passion with intellect. But do you know what I think? I think it made him feel more alive."

"You don't know what you're talking about," Junius said tightly. "Your father knew such things to be the province of savages."

I felt my blush, but I didn't stop. "Why must it belong only to them? Do the rest of us not get to feel something so sublime? Why then do we own it, if not to feel it?"

"It's our eternal battle. Our struggle with the devil. To overcome such base things is a triumph. It shows God which of us is worthy."

"I don't believe that," I said evenly. "I think He gave it to us for a reason. I have desired you, Junius. Is that wrong?"

He went as red as I felt myself to be. "It's inappropriate in a wife."

"Or perhaps there's nothing more appropriate."

"Why are you talking this way? This is what I mean about those stories—"

"The stories only make me see what I already feel," I said quietly. "And they're something I can *do*. I'm good at this. And sometimes I don't feel as if I'm good at anything else."

He went quiet, his anger muted by sudden thoughtfulness. "You're a scientist."

I waved it away. "I don't think I can be the scientist you are, or my father was."

"Of course you can. There's no one better at detail work."

"That's not science, Junius. It's drawing," I said patiently. I tapped the notebook. "But I think this is my real talent, to illustrate these stories, to help people understand that world."

"Understand it? They'll find it obscene and barbaric. You'll be ridiculed. Even shunned. Respectable women don't *do* this."

"But I *want* to."

"Isn't it enough to draw the relics? What you do is essential, Lea. These tales…they're the meaningless ramblings of a culture that's nearly gone. We've got Lord Tom and those who are left to tell us what things mean. We don't need these. Your father agreed with that. He'd be horrified to hear you now."

"My father believed a lot of things I'm not certain I agree with."

Junius looked stunned. "You don't mean that."

"All these things I'm reading about this experiment of his. How it's wrong to feel passion or desire. How he thinks the Indians subhuman for not just feeling those things, but for surrendering to them—"

"You've never disagreed with that."

"I have. You just never listened. And neither did he."

"You should hear yourself. You sound like some…some… not who we raised you to be—"

"*You* didn't raise me," I said, bristling. "You're not my father, but my husband. I'm no longer your student—in anything. Listen to me, Junius: what you and Papa wanted—I don't think that's who I am."

"Then who are you, Leonie? A researcher of obscenities? An intemperate woman who dances like a whore?" He leaned forward, slamming his hand flat on the table, so hard it shook the papers there, and I jerked back in alarm. "You're my *wife*, goddammit! You're not one of them. You're not an Indian. I won't let you become one."

I stared at him in surprise. "Of course I'm not. That's not what I'm saying at all."

He turned on his heel, storming away from me to the door, jerking it open. He was out on a waft of turbulent air that shuffled the papers on the table and rifled the pages of the open notebook in front of me, so it looked as if Loowit were flying into the mountain she became, her spirit lost in snow and ice, a heart that burned with fire.

CHAPTER 25

THE NEXT MORNING, I WOKE TO JUNIUS'S TERSE "WE'RE going to Oysterville today to return that canoe." And then, before I could protest, "You're coming. Get ready. We're leaving as soon as we can."

Oysterville was just across the bay, on the Shoalwater side of a peninsula made mostly of sand and dunes that stretched nearly twelve miles from Unity on the southern end to Leadbetter Point at the northern tip. Oysterville was nearly a direct crossing for us, and the tide was in, so there was no navigating the channels that crisscrossed the bay to get there, and we just went cleanly across. Lord Tom and I took the plunger, while Junius took Daniel in Wilson's canoe. The bay was the color of a zinc plate and just as smooth, and Junius paddled like an Indian, displacing almost no water, cutting through it as if it were butter, nearly soundless. From my vantage point it looked as if the two of them barely spoke to each other, and I watched them with my heart in my throat and my own confusion a misery. I spoke little to Lord Tom myself, too aware of his watching, of what I knew he saw. I concentrated on the sails, on catching what little breeze there was, on not thinking about the last time I'd been in the sloop or what had happened to me there. In my head it had become the moment everything changed; there was before and there was after, though I knew the truth was not quite that.

Finding *her* was the moment. Suddenly she was there again, her presence so strong that I turned, startled, thinking to see her behind me, and Lord Tom caught my gaze and frowned.

"What is it, *okustee?*"

"Nothing," I told him, disconcerted. The sails flapped. I tightened the sheet and pretended I didn't feel her, that nagging connection, those dreams again, where I was both her and myself.

I felt Lord Tom's gaze, and I glanced at him again, snapping, "What are you staring at?"

He smiled a little and looked away. "The wind is shifting, *okustee*. Time to come about."

It was annoying to realize he was right; the sail was flapping again, and I had been too lost in my thoughts to see the shift. Determinedly, I refused to think of anything. The canoe with Junius and Daniel was far ahead. I concentrated on catching up.

Still, by the time we reached the salt meadow that separated Territorial Road from the bay, Junius was already waiting impatiently for us. We would moor the boat here, and Junius and Daniel would paddle us in. I took down the sails and Lord Tom and I anchored the boat, and then boarded the canoe. Daniel took my hand to help me step from the plunger. I did not look at him, and I thought he was careful not to look at me, but I felt the caress of his fingers, the smooth stroke of his thumb in my palm, and a shiver went through me that I was at pains to hide.

The tide was in almost to Territorial Road, the salt meadow turned into grass-topped muddy islands. The bay was full of bateaus, but no men—the tide was too high for oystering. I could see the homes and stores nearest the bay, wooden structures built on pilings and floats because sometimes the tide came in so far it would flood anything on the ground, turning wells brackish and the streets into knee-deep mud, but to be so close meant better access to the oysters, and Oysterville, like Bruceport, was a town founded on making money.

Junius took us as far in as he could, until the islands turned to mud and Territorial Road was just before us. We got out, and he pulled the canoe ashore and said, "Let's tell Wilson his canoe is back and get something to eat," and we followed him into the town proper like little ducks following their mother, single file, over the sodden ground.

The buildings became more clustered; there were more houses, the office of the newspaper, a boatwright's workshop, the Methodist Church with its gilded cross that looked like something from a Catholic cathedral—as out of place in a town where the sidewalks were made of single planks of sawn lumber as silk among calicos. One could hear the ocean from the weather beach on the opposite side, its roar muted into a constant, rhythmic murmur by the line of forest running the center of the peninsula. Men lounged in front of Clark's Store, one or two women carrying bags and hauling children by the hand stepped out, and we got a few waves and hellos from those we passed, but Junius didn't pause until we were in front of the Pacific House, which, along with the Stevens Hotel, the jail, and the fact that it was the county seat, made Oysterville more of a town than any other on the bay.

The Pacific House was across the street from the church, and the largest hotel in the county, two-storied, with a porch for lounging and a saloon in one wing. During court week the place was usually filled to bursting, despite the Temperance Billiard Hall just down the street, the four other saloons in town, and the dance hall above Espy's store, which held dances twice a week during the court term, and whose floors I'd trod often enough before. But I knew as well as Junius that the Pacific House was where we could find Mac Wilson when he wasn't out on his whacks.

Junius went up the stairs and we followed him through the door and inside.

"Wilson in the saloon?" Junius asked the man at the desk, who nodded and jerked with his thumb, and we turned and went into the saloon, which was better than any in Bruceport, and bigger too, with a long bar against one wall, and oil lamps in sconces on the walls.

The place was half full with men drinking and eating—I was the only woman in the place, and people turned to look as I came inside. But I was used to that—I wasn't the only woman in Bruceport who went into Dunn's, but I was the only woman who went in with the oystermen. I saw Mac Wilson at the bar, and Junius went up to talk to him while we sat at a table near the door. Daniel took the chair beside mine; I felt the press of his leg and I moved mine stealthily away, trying not to look at him—or at Lord Tom, for that matter.

When Junius came back to the table he had a bottle of whiskey and three glasses. He poured whiskey all around. "I've ordered stew and bread. I hope that sits well with you." He looked at Daniel as he spoke.

Daniel nodded shortly and leaned forward, reaching for a glass. "We planning to stay here long?"

"For a bit. Why not? Look around you. It's the closest thing to a town we've got in these parts. My guess is that Lea will want to do some shopping, too. It's not like San Francisco, of course— when did you say you were heading back there?"

"I didn't."

"You've been writing to your fiancée, I hope."

Daniel drank his whiskey in a single gulp. "She knows where I am, if that's what you mean."

"You haven't received a single letter since you've been here."

Daniel regarded his father—his expression was a bit hostile, a bit challenging, but not enough for Junius to take offense. "She's not much of a correspondent. But I've a letter to post to her today."

I looked at him in surprise, jealous in the moment before I realized I couldn't show it. He avoided my glance.

"Well—good. I'd think she would be worried about you up here." Junius fingered his glass. "Most women like to keep a man nicely harnessed—isn't that so, Lea?" He didn't wait for an answer, but went on with, "She must be certain of you. Not worried that you have itchy feet, is she?"

"Because of my family history, you mean?" Daniel asked wryly. "You think it runs in the blood?"

Junius leaned back in his chair, bringing his whiskey to his lips, sipping slowly, as if it were something to savor, instead of the cheapest whiskey Carruthers could sell without making his own, as Will Dunn did in Bruceport. "I hope her trust in you isn't misplaced."

"Junius, please," I said.

Daniel said, "You sound as if her opinion worries you."

"Oh, it does."

"You've ignored me for twenty years. What makes you care so much now?"

Billy Griffin came to the table carrying a tray laden with bowls of stew and a loaf of bread, interrupting the conversation, and I was relieved. Billy was young and given to drinking and carousing, and I saw him as often in Bruceport as I saw him here. He gave me a big smile as he set a bowl in front of me and tossed back a heavy forelock of hair. "Good to see you. You especially, Miz Russell. I was afraid I might hear you'd capsized and drowned when you left Bruceport after that dance a few weeks back. That storm came up so quick."

"We made it in one piece, as you see," I said.

"Barely," Daniel put in.

Billy smiled. "Well, I guess you was in good hands." He clapped Daniel's shoulder hard enough that the spoon Daniel held clacked against the bowl of stew. "You'd a been proud of him, June, taking care of your interests as if they was his own. We all commented on it."

I felt myself grow cold. Junius raised a brow. "Is that so?"

"Hardly left her side the whole dance. Why, I would've thought he was her husband 'stead of you if I hadn't known better."

It wasn't true; I'd only danced with Daniel the one time, but that time…Though I sensed no malice in Billy's description, I knew what he'd seen, what had colored his perception of the evening, and I knew how Junius would take it.

"Well, it's good to know I can trust him to do what's right," Junius said, lightly, casually, but I heard what was beneath it.

"Well, you all enjoy your stew," Billy said, clapping Daniel once again on the shoulder and giving me a smile before he left. It was all I could do to keep my eyes on my bowl, to eat, though I tasted nothing, and my appetite was completely gone.

I felt Junius's eyes on me. I felt Daniel waiting, waiting to see what I would do, wondering. When his leg brushed mine, I dropped the spoon; it fell to my bowl with a clatter and a splash.

Junius said, "You all right, Lea?"

I picked up the spoon again, forced myself to look at him. "Of course. Why wouldn't I be?"

"I don't know. You seem a bit rattled."

I made myself smile. "I'm cold is all."

"Cold? You're red as a beet."

"Leave her alone." Daniel's voice now. Steady, unmoved. "It's me you want to provoke anyway."

"Really?" How icy Junius was, his face like a mask, his eyes blue stones. "Why would I want to provoke you?"

"Because you want me gone. Because you're suspicious of me."

"Why shouldn't I be suspicious, given how *well* you've taken care of my wife?"

Daniel's expression was unreadable. "I was only following your orders."

"A bit too well, I'm guessing."

Now anger flashed in Daniel's eyes. "How little it takes to make you distrust her, when she's been your faithful slave for twenty years—"

"That's enough," I said, sharply enough that they both looked taken aback. "This is ridiculous. People are watching."

"The way they watched in Bruceport?" Junius asked.

"Daniel saved my life, Junius."

"And just how did you thank him, sweetheart?"

My anger erupted. I grabbed Daniel's whiskey and downed it in a gulp, smiling meanly at Junius's shocked expression, and then I pushed back my chair hard enough that it screamed on the floor.

I was out of the hotel before I knew I was going, barely seeing the people on the planked sidewalk before me; when they were in my way I dodged them to slosh through the mud of the street. The whiskey churned in my stomach—I wished now I hadn't drunk it. I'd meant just to show him I had a mind of my own, but it had been a mistake. I felt sick and unsteady. It wasn't until I got to the salt meadow, to the swollen tide, that I felt better, that I began to feel myself again.

The parade ground fronted the bay, and I went to lean against an old cannon that had its place there and stared out. The cold sunlight peeked between a break in the clouds, quick and piercing, its light riffling on the water like little sparks before it disappeared again. One or two seagulls circled and flew away again, waiting for the shift in tides. The cold air felt good on my face, with its smell of smoke and tar and the stink of salt mud.

No one came after me, for which I was glad. I didn't want to see Junius; the lie of who I was now felt heavy in my mouth. I didn't want to deny his accusations, nor to admit them either, and I was angry at his mistrust at the same time I was guilty of his suspicions. I wanted desperately to see Daniel, but I was afraid of that too.

I couldn't make sense of my thoughts or of my confusion, and I stood there until they chased themselves away and all I was doing was watching the tide recede and the gulls come back, the pelicans skimming the waves just beyond, looking for the schools of fish that came with the change, feeling this place seep into me until I felt a part of the bay, until it seemed I might sit out here on this cannon forever, watching the play of light upon the water and the birds who came close because I was so still.

The weather began to turn, clouds coming in, darkness reflecting my mood, a wind rising that felt like the start of another storm. Then I heard them, Junius calling, "Leonie!" from some distance away. I glanced over my shoulder; they were down the street, walking in formation the way geese flew, Junius at the apex and Daniel and Lord Tom following behind on each side. I turned away again, letting my annoyance rise to cover my confusion, to cover the fact that I didn't know what to say to Junius, to any of them.

Then they were behind me, and Junius's hand was on my shoulder, and he was leaning close, kissing the top of my head, saying, "Done with your temper tantrum? Ready to go?" as if I were a child, and I was angry all over again, shrugging off his hand, jerking around to glare at him—and then at Daniel, who at least had the grace to look chastened. The only one I wasn't angry with was Lord Tom, but he was the one who gave the look that chastened *me*, that brought my guilt to the fore so I was the one who had to look away. It was impossible to face the knowledge in his expression, that knowledge that I was to blame for this, that Junius and Daniel were only acting the way men acted when there was a woman at the center, and my actions had made that possible.

No one spoke much on the way back. I stared stonily ahead, refusing to look at any of them, not responding to Junius's few attempts to speak with me, leaving them to talk among themselves in terse, clipped sentences—"tighten that sheet," or "the mooring line's dragging, Tom." Daniel said almost nothing.

When we reached home, Junius said to me, "You and Lord Tom go on. I'm taking the boy with me."

It surprised me, and frightened me as well. "Where to?" They were the first words I'd spoken to my husband since the hotel, and he set his jaw and shook his head.

"We won't be late," he said.

I glanced at Daniel, who did not seem the least surprised, and then back to Junius. "But June, it's going to storm—"

"Go on to the house, Leonie," he said. "We'll be back tonight."

I was suddenly very afraid. "Where are you going? Why do you need Daniel?"

"He's going to help me with something. Go on now."

Lord Tom took my arm. "Come home, *okustee*," he said, pulling me gently with him.

"He's your son, Junius," I said—uncertain why I said it, what I thought.

Daniel said gently, "It's all right, Lea. Go on."

Some agreement between them, then, but still I felt the threat of it. I went with Lord Tom reluctantly. I watched Junius push the sloop back into the bay, and turned to Lord Tom as Junius and Daniel sailed off. "Where are they going?"

"He would not say," he told me—and I wasn't certain if it was a lie.

The house was cold when we went inside, and I tried to keep from thinking about the two of them, of where they were, of what Junius intended, of the fear I felt, and busied myself with the stove. But once I had it lit, I sat in a chair at the table, staring into space, not thinking to cook or do anything else. I picked up my father's journal finally, turning to the place I'd left off, but my mind was restless, wandering, returning over and over again to Junius and Daniel as I read over lists and trade agreements, nothing until August 24, 1853, where was written only:

This could ruin everything.

I frowned at the page, reading it again—my father's handwriting was sometimes hard to decipher, but this was very clear. I glanced again at the date. I'd have been fourteen. Just after we'd come here, before my father had met Junius.

I scanned down the rest of the page. Nothing. A new collection. A few bowls, a Nez Perce necklace—which was odd. How would a Nez Perce necklace come here?—but then again, perhaps it wasn't so odd. They were only on the other side of the mountains, and trade was brisk between them and the Upper Chinook. But I didn't remember it, and I remembered most of the things listed in these pages—or at least I remembered the stories I'd told myself about them.

I looked further—no other mention of ruin. Nothing new. I turned the page. It was dated August 26, 1853. Two days later.

> *Thankfully, the experiment is unaffected. I have made everything right and there will be no repeat, which is the only thing that matters.*
>
> *"Where no law is, there is no transgression." God surely forgives a man for protecting himself against lesser creatures.*

I frowned again at the page and turned it. There was nothing more. Nothing about the experiment or whatever threat there was to it, and I came to the end of the journal without discovering a single pertinent thing. But by then the night was full-on and it had begun to rain hard, the wind gusting against the windows. I heard voices in it, the presence of this place whispering, and I listened and let the journal fall to the table and waited, playing with the tooth hanging around my neck.

I was worried enough that I did not go to bed. I felt a dread I could not banish, and I stood at the window, looking down on the closed trunk of the mummy on the porch just outside, seeing nothing beyond that, only her and then the rain and wind-filled darkness past the halo of light cast by the oil lamp. So when I did see movement, they were already at the porch, coming up the steps, both of them, and I felt a rush of pure relief—I had not realized how much I had expected only one of them to return.

The front door opened; Daniel came in—the quick flash of his gaze, heated, rushing through me so I was breathless—and Junius just behind. They were both filthy and wet, and Junius carried a very large burlap bag that clacked and jittered in a way I knew too well. Bones. He was carrying a sackful of bones.

My relief turned to dismay. "Junius, what have you done?"

He gave me an irritated glance. "No, 'you've returned, my love,' or 'I was worried, it was so late?' How nice to be accused the moment a man walks through his door. Don't you feel the unfairness of it, boy?"

Daniel shrugged and winced. He said to me, "He made me with go with him to another cemetery."

"A cemetery? But…what cemetery?"

"The only one around here," Junius said grimly. He dumped the bag on the ground with little ceremony. "The *tenas memelose illahee*. The island. Where else?"

I was stunned and sick. "You didn't. Junius, you didn't take the bones from there."

"We've got five bodies in here, give or take a skull or two."

I glared at Daniel. "You let him do this?"

He pulled off his boots slowly, as if it were difficult. "I didn't have much choice. He was testing me."

Junius laughed. "The boy doesn't lack for courage. He didn't bat an eye when the shooting started."

"Shooting?" My voice rose. "Who was shooting?"

"I don't know. Never got a good look at him." Junius looked at Daniel. "Did you?"

"It seemed too dangerous to investigate," Daniel said.

There was something between them, some kind of collusion, an air of negligent risk, shared danger, something that left me out and bound them together, and though that's what I had wanted and what I had hoped for, to see it now—Junius's casual bravado and Daniel's nonchalance—was disconcerting and distressing. Neither man was who I knew him to be. Together they were something else, something I didn't like at all.

"What happened tonight?" I asked coldly.

Junius put aside his boots and took off his coat. "Just what I told you. We went to the *tenas memelose illahee*. I didn't think anyone would be there in the rain. I thought you would appreciate my effort to get to know my son."

"Not a sincere effort," Daniel put in. "I think he was hoping to get me killed."

"I told you to run, didn't I?" Junius asked. His mouth quirked; again I felt that vibration within him, the thrill of the chase, the thrill of danger escaped.

Daniel pulled off his coat and winced again. He looked wryly at his arm, where a streak of red colored his shirt. "I thought I felt something."

I had crossed the room to him before I realized I was moving. I reached for his arm, and he pulled away with a small shake of his head. "It's all right, Lea. Just a scratch. I'm not hurt."

"Such motherly concern," Junius said dryly.

I ignored them both. Tersely I said to Daniel, "Take off your shirt. I want to get a look at it."

"It barely hurts."

"Take off your shirt."

"Best do as she says, boy," Junius said. "If you die of infection, I'll never be forgiven."

I waited, tense, worried. Daniel gave a short nod and unbuttoned his shirt and then his long underwear, shrugging both off his shoulders, and I tried not to look at him; I tried not to think of how it had felt to touch him. I felt Junius watching, and I pretended to be what I was not and had never been. *Motherly*, he'd said.

I licked my suddenly dry lips and bent to look at Daniel's arm. The bullet had only grazed, but it was more than a scratch, and it was bleeding and dirty, a diagonal scrape across his arm just below his shoulder. I said, "You'd best sit down. I'll need to clean it."

He nodded and went to the settee, and I glanced at Junius, who was watching us with a curious expression, one that made me uncomfortable at the same time I didn't understand it. I hurried to the kitchen for warm water and soap and the rags I kept just for this purpose.

I sat beside Daniel on the settee and tended to him, concentrating only on the wound, cleaning it—he flinched once, and I glanced up and met his gaze, which was carefully blank. "I'm sorry," I said.

"Just get it done. Please."

"Most men would appreciate such tender ministrations," Junius said. He was sitting on the organ bench. "What is it, boy? Is she not gentle enough for you?"

"It's fine," Daniel said.

"Put some affection into it, Leonie. Perhaps you could kiss it and make it better."

Daniel jerked away. "That's enough. It's all right."

I grabbed his arm back. "Let me finish tying the bandage, at least. Ignore him."

"Yes, by all means, ignore me." Junius said. "Pretend I don't exist. You've already had some practice with that, I think."

I had barely finished tying the knot when Daniel was on his feet, stepping away. He glared at his father. "I've had enough of your little word games and your ridiculous tests. What is it you want from me? What is it you're accusing me of? Just say it and be done with it."

I went cold. "Daniel—"

"I'm not accusing you of anything," Junius said, ignoring me. "And I don't want anything either. Why would you think it? It sounds to me as if you have a guilty conscience. Shall I play the confessor for you?"

Daniel didn't move. I felt him struggling for control, and I was frozen, waiting, afraid. I didn't know what to say, how to stop anything. I knew he would tell Junius what only his promise to me had kept him from revealing the moment Junius returned.

But Daniel said nothing. His chest rose and fell hard, and then he said in a voice so clipped it sounded as if each word was a struggle, "I'm going to bed. It was an exhausting night." He gave me a short nod, flicking his fingers at the bandage around his upper arm. "Thank you." Then he went to the stairs, and up. I heard his bedroom door open, close, and I was sitting there with my husband, a bowl of soapy, lukewarm water on my lap, a wet rag striped with blood and dirt floating within it.

Junius clapped both hands on his thighs. "Well, that's that. Why do you think he got so angry?"

Playing games. A smile, though his eyes were cold. I forced myself steady. "Why did you take him with you tonight, Junius? What did you think to accomplish?"

"I wanted to see what kind of man he was. I wanted to see if he *would*."

"What did you discover?"

"That he's game for anything. That he'll do whatever best avails him. The boy has no morality and no sentimentality, Lea. I wish you would see that."

"I think you're wrong."

He sighed, and suddenly the bravado was gone, and the chill, and he was just the man I knew, the one I'd known for over twenty years. He raked his hand through his hair, and I was struck by the familiarity of the gesture—not in him, though I'd seen him do it a thousand times before, but because in that moment, Daniel's likeness to him was pronounced. The same gesture, done the same way—were such things passed through the blood as well as eye color or build?

Junius said, "He's wound you about with pretty talk and poetry. He's beat me with things I could never do."

I looked down into the bowl, my guilt so intense I could hardly breathe.

Junius sighed again. "I see my youth in him, Lea. I know I must seem an old man to you now, but there are things about him that remind me of what I used to be. I don't know if you remember those things. I don't know if you ever saw them. You must have thought me old already when I came here."

He sounded sad, pensive. It broke my heart. "Junius, I don't see you that way. I don't."

"You're still young," he said softly. "I see the way men look at you, Lea. I see the way *he* looks at you."

I said nothing. I couldn't give him the lie he wanted. My guilt rose so it consumed me, but I couldn't say *He doesn't look at me that way* when it was so obvious he did. I couldn't say *I don't feel his youth* when he made me feel so alive. But Junius's sadness burrowed into me, and I hated it. I hated that he felt it, that there was a need, that it stemmed from me.

I put aside the bowl, water sloshing gently on the floor, and I went to him, holding out my hands, taking his, and he pulled me onto his lap, burying his face between my breasts, holding me tightly, as if he were afraid I would fly away if he let me go.

CHAPTER 26

I IGNORED THEM BOTH THE NEXT MORNING. JUNIUS TOLD me he was going up to Bruceport to pick up some things and check the mail. I was glad he was leaving, but not so glad that he meant to leave Daniel behind. "He's milking the cow and cleaning out her stall. I've told him to help you cut into that mummy when he's done," he told me, and I knew it was a test. If I didn't do it, he would know not to trust me. I would be the woman he'd accused me of being.

He left Lord Tom behind, who asked me, "What will you do, *okustee*?" His question echoed my thoughts, though I knew he was asking what I would do *today*, not with the rest of my life.

"I want to know where she came from," I said to him, because it was something to distract me, a question I could possibly answer when everything else in my life felt so upended. "I want to know who she is."

"It no longer matters," he told me.

It did, but I was tired of explaining that. I stared out the window at the barn, thinking of Daniel out there, and I heard myself asking, "Was it Daniel you and Bibi argued over that night she came out here?"

Lord Tom looked up. His expression showed no surprise. Deliberately he finished tying a knot in the net, and then he said, "No."

It was not what I expected. I remembered the things she'd said to Daniel, the way Lord Tom looked at him. "No? What then?"

He jerked his head toward the window. "*She* is what we argued over."

"The mummy?"

Lord Tom nodded. Somberly, he said, "Bibi is no *tomawanos woman, okustee*, though she would have you believe it. She knows nothing of the spirit. She says it comes to her in *dleams*. She says it wants you to see. But she can't know."

I said, "What of what she says about Daniel? Do you think she and Junius are right?"

Lord Tom said, "Which one? They do not think the same thing."

I looked up again, puzzled. "They've both warned me that he's not to be trusted."

"Have they?"

"Yes. Bibi said that I would regret he was here. And Junius doesn't trust him at all. And you...I don't think you like him either."

"Perhaps you should look again."

His answer was cryptic, but I never got the chance to ask him about it further because at that moment, the front door opened and Daniel came inside, flushed from exertion in the cold, a rush of chill air and the smell of the river. It was still raining hard—it hadn't let up all night, and his coat was dark with wet. He glanced at Lord Tom and then at me and his expression gave nothing away as he said, "I'm done with the barn. My father said you had some use for me?"

Some use for me. I went hot at the image those words conjured. I put aside Papa's journal and rose, trying not to think of anything, not even the words I spoke. "He wants me to cut into the mummy today. He thinks I could use your help."

He looked surprised. "Cut into her? You can't mean to."

"If I don't, it will be Baird who discovers what's important about her."

"Or that there's nothing at all," he said. "Leonie, she's worth more whole."

"Worth more?"

"I've told you that."

"Oh. Yes. A curiosity museum."

"You should consider it."

"If I don't cut into her, that will be her only worth," I said bitterly. "I can't see what it is my father thought about her. I don't understand what he saw."

"Whatever it was, he saw it without cutting her open," he countered.

"It doesn't matter. I'm ready to do it now," I said, a pure lie; I was feeling sick again at the thought. "Would you fetch me the saw?"

Daniel took a deep breath. "Yes, of course. As you wish."

He turned and went back outside, down the porch steps.

Lord Tom had been watching our conversation with interest. I said, before he could tell me what he thought, "If I don't do this, I will have failed the test."

"Who is testing you?"

My father. Junius. The world. It was too big to answer, so I ignored him and put on my coat and my boots. I went out onto the porch, feeling the key in my pocket. I thought of her walking through the long grass, a child on a dirt floor, love and pride and fear, her hair glinting in the sun. I felt a surge of despair—how could I do this thing?

But I pushed those things away. I knelt and unlocked the trunk. I was opening it when Daniel came striding back up the stairs, the saw in his hand. He said, "I wish you'd reconsider this."

"If I can't do this, I'm not the ethnologist my father meant for me to be."

Daniel stepped up beside me. "Old promises, Lea," he said quietly. "I thought perhaps you'd put them aside."

I let the lid fall back. It clunked against the side of the house.

He said urgently, "I've been thinking. I know you love it here. I know you don't want to leave. What if we didn't? What if we stayed—the two of us?"

I looked up at him, frowning. "But...what about Junius?"

"What about him? We'll tell him the truth. You said he hated this place."

"And you think he'd just walk away?"

"It's the noble thing to do, isn't it?" Daniel asked tightly. "He wants to go anyway—that's what you said, that he's tried to go a dozen times already. Why not give him the chance? Why must you be the one making the sacrifice? He's gained a great deal from twenty years with you. He could give you up. He *should* give you up."

I laughed shortly. "He won't."

"How do you know? Perhaps he loves you enough."

"What if he doesn't?" I asked. "We've betrayed him, both of us. What if he refuses—what will you do? Overthrow him like Tiapexwasxwas?"

"Who's that?"

"A giant who was killed by his son. But not before that son slept with his father's wife—his own mother—first."

Daniel said impatiently, "You're not my damned mother, Leonie. For Christ's sake, what are you waiting for?"

I looked down at the mummy. "I'm waiting for her," I said softly, and then I slid my hands beneath her, meaning to lift her out. Something crumbled against my skin. Something like...dust or...no, something gritty. In confusion, I drew back my hand. It was covered with umber flakes. I stared at it for a moment, disconcerted, before I realized what it was.

Daniel said, "Lea, whatever you think you'll discover—"

"No," I said. I ran my hand down her arm, dislodging flakes, her skin coming off on mine. "Oh no, no, no."

"What is it?" Daniel asked. "What's wrong?"

I barely heard him. All I could say was "No," and "No," again, and my dream filled my head, drowning, my body crumbling, withering, swept away in dust, and panic had me clutching her. "No, please. Not yet. You can't! I'm not finished. Please, I'm not finished."

"Lea, what is it?" Daniel dropped the saw, kneeling beside me.

"She's decaying," I managed. I held out my stained hand to him. "Look! The water…I didn't keep her dry enough. She's falling apart, and I'm not finished. I need her to stay. I need her to stay." I could not control my panic; I was trembling. "She's dying."

"She's already dead." He was soothing, reasoning. "Whatever soul was there is long gone."

I shook my head. "It's not. *She's* not. I feel her all the time. I dream about her. And you…she wants you—"

"Wants me for what? I don't know what you mean."

"I can't decide without her. I need her." I was crying now. He grabbed my hand, trying to draw me close.

He looked afraid, I thought, but his voice was so calm. "She doesn't look to be too badly damaged. Perhaps we can save her."

I shook my head. Useless. Nothing to do. She was disintegrating and I knew it would continue. I'd seen it in my dreams. I felt it to be true. She was leaving me, and I had not done what she wanted—I still did not *know* what she wanted.

"We'll put her back in the barn," he insisted. "She was fine there. Perhaps it's because she's on the porch. The rain…"

I looked at him in dismay. "It won't help. It's too late. She'll keep crumbling and crumbling—" *washed away by water, drawn down and down and down, withering and splitting, a seed pod borne away by the wind.*

My throat tightened, the dream was so strong that for a moment I couldn't breathe.

"You'll find a way to stop it."

"There is no way. I'm a fool." I touched her again, the saffron cloth, the dust of her discoloring it at the edges. I looked at him, "How could I have not seen—?" and stopped, because the look on his face surprised me. It was relief, as if a burden had been lifted from him, one that had troubled, and I frowned and said, "You're happy about this."

His expression shuttered. He shook his head. "No."

I was on my feet in a single motion. "How can you be happy? This is all wrong, all of it. I don't understand what she wants from me, and now I'll never know."

"Leonie, you're not making sense." He rose, reaching for me, his hand sliding down my arm as I tried to jerk away, his fingers catching in the bracelet at my wrist, and the fragile, worn twine snapped—not even a sound, just a feather brush of feeling, and I looked down to see it fall as if it were tumbling through water, almost floating, the charms twisting, shining pink and green, blue and silver, until it hit the porch, where it held, just barely, and I made a sound of dismay, I tore from his grasp, falling to my knees to reach for it, but I was too late. It slipped through a crack between the boards and disappeared.

"Let it go," he whispered. "All your talismans...they mean nothing. Trust me, Lea. Let it go." He pulled me to my feet, and I was stunned and uncertain, disbelieving, unresisting as he wrapped me in his arms. My wrist felt too bare without the bracelet, and the mummy was slipping from my grasp, all protections gone.

And then I heard, "What a tender moment. Pardon me for intruding."

Junius.

Daniel's arms dropped from me; he stepped away so quickly I swayed without his support, and without thinking I reached out again, clutching his arm. I saw the way Junius noted it. His blue eyes were cold and stony. He was soaked. Beyond him, the rain poured relentlessly down.

I said, "The mummy—"

He raised a brow; my words died in my throat. Misery and regret and guilt and fear—they were all there. I could not pick one above the other.

"The mummy's decaying," Daniel put in. "I was only trying to comfort her."

"How well you do it," Junius said. "Why, it looks almost as if you've done it before."

I released my hold on Daniel's arm and said as calmly as I could, "I was upset. He was only trying to help. She got wet when the river rose and I...I didn't see it until now. We were going to cut and...and..." I held out my hand uselessly, pointlessly, to show him the umber dust on my palms.

Junius ignored that. He stepped up the stairs to the porch. He barely looked at her. He looked at Daniel, and there was a funny smile on his face, something that raised my dread and my misery. He said, "You haven't told her the truth, have you?"

Daniel went still. "What truth? I don't know what you mean."

"Oh, I think you do." Junius reached into his coat, taking a folded piece of paper from an inner pocket. His gaze came to me. "The reason I went to Bruceport," he said, waving it in his hand. "I've been waiting for it."

Warily, I said, "What is it?"

"A letter, of course." He leaned back against the railing negligently. "From San Francisco. I still have friends there, you know, boy. Or perhaps you didn't realize it. Actually, I think you must not have, else you might have covered your tracks better."

I didn't like the cruel edge in his voice, nor did I like the way Daniel had gone so still—there was a trapped animal feel about it, and I was afraid. "What are you saying, Junius?"

"He's not a reporter for any newspaper," Junius said brutally, though he didn't look at me as he said it, but at his son. "He worked as a printer's devil at the *Call* once, what—seven years ago or so? Do I have it right, boy? The editor there barely remembers him."

I was confused. I looked at Daniel, who very carefully wouldn't meet my gaze.

Junius went on, steady and cruel. "He works for a curiosity museum."

"A curiosity museum," I heard myself repeating—as if from far away.

"Everson's Hall of Curiosities. He's on a mission, as it were, or so the owner was kind enough to tell my friend. Everson made a deal with him—Daniel here would procure the mummy for a split of the profits. He's here to steal her away from you, Leonie. It's why he's come. Not for me, not for any 'story.' He's here for the mummy."

I felt stunned and sick, disbelieving.

Junius went on, "I suspected it from the first. But what I don't know is why he's waited so long to take her. How hard is it to just paddle her away some night when everyone's asleep? What were you waiting for, boy?"

There was silence. Daniel looked at me, and what I saw in his eyes told me it was true. Guilt. And too, a plea for forgiveness. "She's more valuable with a provenance." He said quietly. "I needed the story of who she was."

"Ah. That explains it. And here I thought it was just that you were enchanted by my wife."

I sagged back upon the railing, feeling it shake a little with the suddenness of my weight.

"Lea," Daniel said, reaching for me. "I'm sorry. I'm sorry—"

"Don't touch me." My voice sounded distant; there was no force in it, but he jerked back again as if I'd hit him. Everything, every disparate little thing that hadn't seemed right about him fell into place, all the things he'd said, all that talk about curiosity museums, everything that should have told me. He never worked on any newspaper story. He'd worked for circuses and sideshows. He had too much knowledge about the mummy, about what must be done. The day when I'd come upon him in the barn with her and the canoe readied instead of upended. His willingness to steal. *You will regret it now he is here...*I should have known. I'd been a fool. I said weakly, "Was any of it true?"

"Lea's always enjoyed a good story," Junius said.

Daniel glanced at him, then back to me, quickly, as if he were afraid I had suddenly disappeared. "All of it," he whispered. "Everything I said except for...the reason I was here."

"There was no feather. No newspaper."

"That was true. Your Toolux—"

"Don't." My throat was tight. I felt tears again.

Daniel let out his breath. Woodenly, he said, "It was what happened. It seemed too good to be true. My long-lost father"—spoken bitterly—"and a mummy. Two birds with one stone. Vengeance and...and I needed money."

"For Eleanor."

"Yes," he said impatiently before he took a step toward me and then stopped again, wary. "But Lea, I...I didn't expect you."

The words held echo and force. I remembered the first time I'd heard them, the first time he'd said them.

Junius said, "How touching."

Daniel snapped back, "Go to hell."

"Get off my land."

"It's not your land, it's hers," Daniel said. "And I'll go when she tells me to."

"She's my *wife*," Junius said.

"Only if she wants to be. You weren't free to marry her. Your marriage is a joke. She's less tied to you than I am."

"Tell that to the sheriff."

"The sheriff?" Daniel let out a laugh. "Is there one? Go ahead. Bring him out. Do you really want the whole place to know the truth of what you did?"

I stepped forward, forcing my voice through a throat that felt swollen. "That's enough. Please. Enough."

"Tell him to go, Leonie," Junius said.

Daniel looked at me. "Don't let him do this, Lea. Please. I love you."

"Quiet." I held up my hand, uncertain, unsteady. "Please just be quiet. Both of you."

Miraculously, they were.

I didn't know what to do, or what to think. My thoughts chased themselves like moths, dodging, here and gone. The mummy and the pull of him, and her voice in my head saying *I brought him for you.* Bibi's warnings and June's and now she was decaying and everything dissolving, and I felt as if I stood on the verge of something I wasn't certain I wanted, too afraid to go forward, unable to go back. I found myself rubbing my wrist, searching for the twine, the charms that were no longer there. No protection and only myself to trust.

I said, "I don't know what I want. Neither of you, perhaps."

Daniel exhaled sharply. Junius looked angry.

I left them on the porch and walked into the heavy rain, toward the Querquelin, toward the place where I had found her, and I sat on the bank and watched the water churn and tumble and course—too much rain, the river was rising again. If it kept up, it would flood. But I didn't move. I sat there in the rain until the night came on, and there was nothing more to see, and still I sat, so cold I could not feel my hands or my face, shivering and drenched, voices churning through my head, every one an attempt to define me: *Science needs a more logical brain than a woman's...Where did that story come from, Lea? Is there some savage here to tell it to you?...An intemperate woman who studies obscenities and dances like a whore...You're not a scientist, you're an artist.*

But her voice was no longer among them, and so I could not find myself.

CHAPTER 27

WHEN I FINALLY LEFT THE RIVER, THE NIGHT WAS SO black and the rain so hard it felt I was moving through a void toward some distant, beckoning light, drawn almost without volition, made eerie by the music that floated on the air, organ music, something slow and quiet like a hymn, but I didn't recognize it. When I went inside, Junius was still playing. Daniel was in the kitchen, leaning against the pie safe, a cup of coffee in his hands. Lord Tom was not there, and he was the one I wanted. The comfort of my adolescence, words that didn't toss me to and fro.

Daniel glanced up quickly when I came through the door, and Junius stopped playing abruptly, twisting on the bench to face me. "You look chilled to the bone," he said sharply.

"I need to go to Bruceport tomorrow," I said, taking off my sodden coat. "I need to talk to Bibi."

"To Bibi? What for?"

"I just do. I can't explain."

"I'll take you."

I shook my head. I looked at Daniel, who had stepped into the room, who stood silently by the settee, waiting. I said, "I'll take Lord Tom."

Junius frowned. "Why? You're angry with me? What have I done but show you what a liar he is?"

"Nothing," I said quietly. "You've done nothing. But I'm taking Lord Tom."

Daniel said, "Don't believe everything she tells you, Lea. Please just…just speak with me before you condemn me."

Junius laughed. "Yes, by all means. Give him the opportunity to lie to you further."

I said nothing. I went to the trunk beneath the stairs and took out blankets, bringing them back into the main room, and Junius said, "What are you doing?"

"Making a bed."

"I'm not sleeping here, goddammit. You're my wife. I won't just hand you over to this…this—"

"It's not your decision, June," I said quietly. "And it's not you I'm making a bed for. It's me."

He looked as if I'd struck him. "Lea. Sweetheart. I don't understand. *He's* the one who lied."

I sank onto the settee, the blankets still in my arms. I felt cold and tired, and I could no longer be anything but honest. "I've been having an affair with him, Junius. We've been…together. You know this already, or you at least suspect it. You can't just pretend it hasn't happened. I can't."

I heard Daniel's expulsion of breath behind me. I didn't look at him, but kept my eyes on Junius. His expression turned bleak—he had known, of course. Every word he'd spoken since his return had said it. There was no surprise in his eyes, only a deep hurt that was a pain in my own heart. I could not keep his gaze; I looked down into the blankets.

Junius said, "I forgive you. He seduced you. You were vulnerable—I should have taken more care."

I shook my head.

He went on, almost desperately, "I won't let you go. Twenty years, Lea. You can't mean to throw that away. You can't mean to leave me for him. He's done nothing. He *has* nothing. He's a liar and a thief."

"And you've taken advantage of her for years," Daniel interjected. "You don't appreciate her. You barely know her."

"Stop. Please, Daniel," I said. "Please. It doesn't help."

"You're in love with me," he said, almost as desperately as Junius had spoken. "You know you are."

"What do you know of love, boy?" Junius asked. "What about your *fiancée*?"

"Eleanor will be relieved."

"How convenient. How easily you justify a broken promise."

"Shall we talk about broken promises, old man?"

"Stop it, both of you!" I shouted. And then, when they went silent, I said softly, "Go to bed. Leave me to myself. I'm tired. I'm going to Bruceport tomorrow."

Junius rose from the organ bench. "I won't let you go."

Daniel only looked at me. But I heard the words he didn't say: *Promise you won't release me, whatever happens.*

I closed my eyes for a moment. Dully, I said, "I understand. Please, June, go to bed."

"When *he* does. I don't want him alone with you."

I nodded. "Go, Daniel."

"Promise me you'll speak with me," he said. "After you see Bibi. Promise me."

"Yes, of course." I waved them both away, exhausted, despairing. I waited until I heard them both on the stairs, the close of one room door, and then the other, and I knew they'd be listening for each other, and that was my best assurance that neither would come to me tonight. I was as alone as I wanted to be, but I wasn't relieved as I spread the blankets on the settee, as I undressed to my chemise—nearly transparent with rain, clinging to my skin—and crawled into my uncomfortable, too-short bed. Daniel had lied to me and I should not have trusted him, and the mummy was leaving me and I was afraid. The world felt too big for me suddenly, and this place, this house at the meeting place of the Querquelin River and Shoalwater Bay, was the bastion of safety I'd always known.

I was not sure I would sleep, but…

Water, tumbling and freezing, taking my breath, a tornado of water, spinning me about, drawing me down, tangling me while I choked and struggled and fought, filling my nose and my lungs, roaring in my ears, tearing me apart. I grabbed at my throat, choking and struggling, crumbling like rock dashed by the waves, pieces of me gone, disappearing quickly beneath the sun, burning hot and withering into nothing, drying up, and I felt myself drying with it, my muscles clinging to my bones, skin adhering, stiff and motionless and the sun did not stop burning and the wind rising, dust and wind battering, flaking away skin, sweeping me into its whirling cloud, ashes to ashes, dust to dust…

I woke abruptly, as if someone had shaken me, blinking into moonlit darkness. I heard the wind in the trees outside, a wind from the south—Toolux. The mummy's voice in my ear, as if she stood beside me: *You must come. Come now.*

The call was uncompromising, a command, and I rose from the settee, grateful that she had not abandoned me after all but afraid of what she meant for me to find. The room was cold; I shivered as I put on my still damp coat and shoved my bare feet into my boots, and then I went outside. The rain had eased, but it was only a momentary lull in the storm, the clouds briefly parting over a crescent moon, a heavy gathering of darkness lurking over the bay, biding its time. The river was full and dangerous, pushing at its banks. Everything seemed marked in light and shadow, black and white, like a sharply rendered sketch, lines abruptly clean, shadows darker than any pool of ink. I heard the creak of bare branches, and the shush through the cedar and the fir. I stood there for a moment, hugging myself against the cold, wondering why she'd brought me, why I was here, not yet doubting, still touched by the dream.

I went to the trunk, unlocked it, opened it. She was there, still and sleeping in a pool of shadow. She was still there and it had only been a dream. Her voice, her call, only a dream. I closed the trunk again, turning the key in the lock, putting it back into my pocket. And then, led by something I didn't understand, I went off the porch and toward the river.

I don't know what made me turn and look toward the bay. A sound, a movement, and there he was, the shadow of a man against the moonlight playing on the water, walking along the riverbank. He was hatless, and the moonlight glinted in his hair, making it look bright gold instead of the darker color I knew it to be. He stopped short when he saw me. He was like some alien creature standing there, gilded by moonlight, limned by shadow, all the softness in him cast away, leaving him hard-edged, as sharply beautiful as a forest after an ice storm—danger and damage disguised by sublimity—and my need for him rose mindlessly, until I felt I was drowning in it.

I brought him for you.

But he was a liar, and he had betrayed me, and I was afraid of my own desire, of what I feared he was. I turned away, moving quickly toward the house, breaking into a run when I realized he was coming after me. He was on me before I was halfway to the porch, grabbing my arm, swinging me back to face him, and I tried to jerk away, but he was too strong. I pounded against his chest with my other hand. "Let me go, damn you!"

He caught my wrist and pulled so I fell into him, and then his mouth was on mine, relentless and demanding, pleading without words for what he wanted: forgiveness, redemption. The scent of him—cold night air and the river, salt and wool—was in my head, on my skin, the taste of him bitter and sweet. I fell into the kiss. My fists went slack. When he drew away, I was crying. I buried my face in his coat, and his arms came around me, holding me close, letting me cry.

When it was over, I didn't move, and neither did he. The night was not quiet, a rising wind, the ceaseless rush of water, our breathing. He said softly, "I meant to leave you alone, as you asked."

I heard the rumble of his voice in his chest, and I pressed my cheek harder to it. "You lied to me."

"Yes. I'm sorry."

"Would you ever have told me the truth?"

Hesitation. Then, "I like to think I would have, eventually. But I don't know. I've been looking out for myself a long time. This—what I feel for you—it's new. It takes some getting used to."

Honest enough. I asked, "That day I found you with her. You meant to take her that day. In the canoe."

He flinched. "Lea, I—"

"You did."

A sigh. "Yes. What he said was true. There was a bargain. A share of the profits."

I leaned my head back to look at him, but I did not move from the warm circle of his arms, nor did I back away from how closely I was pressed to him. "I believed you understood."

"I do understand, Lea," he said tiredly. "Better than you know. I know what she is to you and…it's why I delayed so long. Because I was falling in love with you, and I couldn't see a way to take her without hurting you."

"Am I to believe that?"

"It's the truth."

I didn't want to say the next words. "Was it really what I felt that dissuaded you? Or was it something else?"

"What else would there be?" How carefully still he was.

"The whacks, perhaps? The oysters are a gold mine. That's what you said. You said you wanted a piece of them. And then, today, when you said we should stay—"

"Because you don't want to leave," he said, and I heard desperation in his voice.

"I suppose it's all worth seducing an older woman for," I said.

The words settled in around us, louder in their past, in having been said, then any other sound. "Is that what you think I've done?"

"I don't know," I said, pained by the admission, burying my face in his chest again, afraid of what he would say, of another truth. "You said you took what you wanted. Like your father, you said."

"I can't blame you for thinking it," he said. "But it isn't true. I know you've no reason to believe me, Lea, but—"

"None of it worked out as you wished, did it?"

"Not as I'd *planned*, no," he clarified. "But I didn't know you, did I? How could I have foreseen this?"

I pushed on. "And now she's rotting, and she's useless to you."

He looked at me. The moon had lit him, and now when he bent to me it shadowed his face so I could not see his expression. "You were right when you said I was happy about it. I am, for my sake."

"The loss of all that money—"

"I don't care about the money."

"But you cared enough to mean to take her before yesterday, didn't you?" I asked coldly. "What we were to each other—"

"Please don't put it in the past tense."

"—wouldn't have stopped you."

"It *was* stopping me, Lea. I was delaying. Waiting for the story was just what I was telling myself I was doing." He sighed. "In any case, it's done. It's over. Whatever decision you make about us, I've made one of my own."

"A decision?" I didn't try to hide my alarm or the quick fear that came with it.

"I'm not going back to San Francisco, even if you decide you don't want me. I don't want that life any longer. I've already sent Eleanor a letter—and her father too—breaking our engagement."

I drew back, surprised, but his arms tightened to keep me there. "You've done *what*?"

"I was writing it the night you…came to me. I knew it then, even if nothing ever happened between us."

"The letter you posted in Oysterville," I said.

He nodded. "I want to live my life my way, not as other people have planned it. My life. My decisions. Just as your life belongs to you."

"It's not so easy as you make it sound."

He shrugged. "My mother thought I could be a respectable man. She thought I could become a *minister*, for God's sake, when I'd already spent a lifetime proving I didn't care about God. She was wrong, but it took me until I met you to see it. I wanted to live as she wanted, but I'd already spent twenty-six years doing that. You've done the same, Lea. I wish you would see it."

"I've made promises, Daniel."

"Promises to the dead. What if now that they're gone they realize they were wrong? How would they tell us? We have to live our own lives, Lea. Others haven't the right to dictate it for us."

I pulled away from him. This time he let me go. The night air was cold; I wrapped my arms around myself, shivering a little. "I don't know. Perhaps that's true. But what do we become if our promises don't matter?"

He crossed his arms over his chest and glanced back at the river. We were both quiet for a moment. Then he said, "What does Bibi have to do with anything? Why are you going to see her?"

"Because I need to know if the mummy's spirit is real. I need to know what she wants from me. I need to know if it's all just my own imagination. If these are only my own desires."

"Do your own desires mean nothing?"

"I don't know what they mean. I've never…I've never felt anything like them before. I…I'm changing, and I'm afraid. I need to understand."

"And you think the widow will give you the answers."

"I hope so."

Very quietly, he said, "Lea, you can't stay with him. You'll become no better than that mummy. Is that what you want? A living death?"

The way he echoed my dreams…it was uncanny and strange. It made me shiver. I looked away. "I was doing fine before you came along."

"Were you? You can't have it both ways. It can't be *both* fate and coincidence that brought me here. Which is it?"

I didn't answer that. I didn't know what to say. I turned away from him and walked slowly back to the house, up the stairs to the porch. He didn't follow me, and when I got to the door, I turned back to see him, still standing there, silhouetted against the moon.

CHAPTER 28

THE NEXT MORNING, WHEN I TOLD LORD TOM WHERE I wanted him to go with me, he said, "Why do you want to see that *pelton-woman?*"

"Because I want to know what she knows," I said.

He gave me a long, slow nod and said nothing more, but I knew he thought I was a fool.

Daniel and Junius came downstairs just as we were leaving. Junius stepped to me, kissing me quickly, another show of possession, which annoyed me. "Hurry back."

I glanced at Daniel as I went to the door, and he said nothing, only gave me a thoughtful look that made me remember everything we'd spoken of, and for a moment I was afraid of what this journey would tell me. But I went outside. The wind was increasing, my skin prickled with the charged air of an impending storm—not just the rain I'd sensed would return. The river would flood; it was already too high. For a moment I remembered the last storm, the fall into icy water, drowning. But I could not delay, not another moment. It was time to decide, and I needed Bibi for that, so Lord Tom and I went to the canoe and pushed off into the silver bay, choppy and stirred, dark gray clouds scudding over the overcast, double-layered clouds, the firs creaking and singing.

The wind was strong enough that it was hard to talk, words seized the moment they left our lips and blown away. The tide was out, and we followed the deeper channels crisscrossing the flats, and I felt the strength in my arms as I plied the paddle, the smooth, easy pull of my muscles, motions I'd made a hundred times before, and I felt consoled and comforted by the bay; I felt my own soul expand to absorb it. My father's voice: *You only think you love this place because it's the longest we've ever stayed. You don't remember the others. You liked them too.*

He'd never understood. Junius didn't understand. I wondered if Daniel truly did, or if it was only something he said, if the poetry he saw in this place was only for my benefit. And then I thought, *What if I were alone here?* Just me and Lord Tom and the world consisting only of the Querquelin and the bay, and I realized this place could encompass me. That I could be alone here, that I would never be lonely. The spirits of the world surrounded me—and that made me laugh, to think what my father would have said to that, how he hated it when I spoke that way. *You've spent too much time around the Siwash. I'd take you away from here if I could.* As if he could determine who and what I was.

But he had tried, hadn't he? And he had set my feet to my future path, one I had trod blindly, so sure of him, and yet—he had wanted to bury the parts of me he didn't like. He had wanted to exorcise them.

I paused in my rowing, overcome by a resentment I could not remember feeling before, and Lord Tom called out, "What is it?" and I shook my head and went back to rowing.

We were in Bruceport before I knew it, rounding the bend and there it was, plungers and bateaus that had keeled on the mudflats in the minus tide, the deep swallow created by the hulls of the big schooners, Dunn's saloon tottering on the edge of the beach and a slew of houses turned driftwood gray. We took the canoe as far in as we could, and then pulled it ashore several yards—the tide was coming in now. We traipsed awkwardly over the flats to the barnacle-covered rocks and the maze of driftwood on the beach proper. The wind had come up more strongly. I still had not replaced the hat I'd lost, and it blew my hair loose from its pins to whip around my face.

I did not pause or hesitate as I made my way to the far side of town, to the salt marsh crossed by a slough where Bibi's dilapidated shack sagged. The drive to know was too strong, even in the face of Lord Tom's obvious reluctance.

When we arrived, I pounded on the door. I heard creaking inside, the straining ropes of a bed or a table bearing a sudden weight, and the door opened, and Bibi looked at me without surprise or concern. I said, "I have some questions for you, Bibi." When her glance went to my wrist, I held it up for her to see. "The bracelet broke yesterday. I wore it until then."

She nodded and glanced beyond me to Lord Tom. "Then it is good. It has done what it was meant to do."

I was puzzled. "What it was meant to do? But...you said it was to protect me from Daniel. It didn't do that at all. It—"

"Did I say that?" Her brown eyes were limpid as she turned them to me. She frowned. "That cannot be right."

"You did," I insisted. "You said I must wear it. That I would regret it now that he was here. Those were your words—"

"The words of a *pelton-woman*," Lord Tom put in from behind me.

"*Mika kahkwa pelton-man*," Bibi spat back. "*Mika wawa halo delate wawa.*" *You are a foolish man. You deny the truth.*

"*Klaksta delate wawa?*" *Which truth?*

"*She* knows, *nah? She* tells me." Bibi poked her chest with her thumb, her oddly flat face screwed with vehemence. "*Nika kumtux itka mika mamook.*" *I know what you did.*

I listened to them in confusion. Now I turned to look at Lord Tom. "What is she talking about?"

His face had gone stony. "Foolishness, *okustee*."

I looked back at Bibi. "I want to know, Bibi. I *need* to know. What it was all for. What this spirit said to you in your dream. The bracelet didn't work. It didn't protect me from Daniel. It… and…you said she wanted something from me. What does she want? What is she asking of me?" My words came out too fast; I heard the desperate edge to them.

But Bibi just turned a bland expression to me and said, "Do you see her? In your *dleams*, do you hear her?"

"Yes. Yes, I do. All the time. I dream of her nearly every night."

"She shows you *delate wawa*."

"What truth?" I asked desperately. "And why did she want you to warn me away from Daniel? Was it only that he was lying, or was there more?"

"Warn you away?" Bibi looked puzzled. "Why would she want this? She brought him for you."

The same words from my dream. Hearing them come from Bibi's mouth settled them hard in my chest; I went suddenly cold, goosefleshed, as if someone somewhere had walked over my grave. I could barely manage, "But…the bracelet."

"To open your eyes," Bibi said, touching her own with two fingers. "Not to keep you blind. Now do you see, *ipsoot klooshman*?"

"See what?"

She reached out, laying a finger against my abdomen, a touch that startled me. She went still, as if she was listening, and then she said with satisfaction, "He has done this, *nah*? *Mitlite tenas kopa yaka belly*. It is good."

I felt myself pale and I stepped back, away from her finger, from that lurid smile, forgetting the step, coming down hard on the one below. Lord Tom grabbed my arm to steady me.

"Don't be ridiculous." I could hardly hear my own voice. It seemed to come from very far away. "I'm not pregnant. It's impossible."

"*Mamook kloshe mika self.* It is what she means for you. *Hahlakl seeowist. Skookum tomawanos.*" *Prepare yourself. Open your eyes. This is powerful magic.* Bibi jerked her head at Lord Tom. "*Mamook okoke kahkwa pelton man wawa delate wawa.*" *Make this foolish man say the truth.*

The words pelted me; I could barely interpret them, still so stunned by the thing she'd said, the satisfaction in her gaze.

Then she said, "*She* knows you, *okustee.* You are all she sees."

I turned helplessly to Lord Tom. He still held my elbow, his fingers were tight, pressing through my heavy coat. "What does she mean?" I asked him. "What truth? What is she saying?"

"Foolishness," he said again, more roughly than before. "Come, *okustee.* It is time to go."

He pulled me down the stairs, and I went without thinking, my heart beating fast, the things she'd said ringing in my ears. She'd called me *daughter—okustee*—and there was some significance to that, I knew. Bibi had called me many things. Clever Wife, Sly One, Quickmouthed. But she had never called me daughter. And her words…impossible, and yet…I pressed my hand to my stomach, feeling only the wool of my coat. Nothing. Only flat and it couldn't be. There couldn't be…

I've taken no precautions.

There's no need.

My legs went weak; I stumbled. Lord Tom kept me upright, taking me away from Bibi, from the shack, back to the road, to the beach. I was in a daze; for a moment I could not think where I was. *This is what she wants for you. She brought him for you.*

I stumbled over driftwood and fell, and Lord Tom helped me up again, but this time instead of pulling me to my feet, he sat me on a piece of wood and squatted down to look into my eyes. "A storm comes, *okustee.* You must pay attention."

"She said I was pregnant," I said.

He nodded.

"I'm not. I can't be."

No expression.

"She said the mummy brought him for me. That's what I hear too, *tot*. In my dreams, she says it. And I—they can't be real, can they? They're only…dreams."

He nodded. Then he stood, offering his copper-brown hand. I could only stare into it.

"What truth did she mean, *tot*?" I asked him. "She said she knew what you did. What was she talking about?"

"Nothing I did," he said. *"Pelton-woman."*

But I saw the way his gaze slid away, and I grabbed his hand, hard, and held it. "What was she talking about?"

The wind rose, a gust blew the rest of my hair loose. It fell onto my shoulders, the last of the pins clinking on the driftwood before it buried itself in the sand. I pushed my hair back with my free hand and dug my nails into Lord Tom's hand. "Nothing you did. What then?"

My hair whipped against my face, stinging, twining about my throat. I was thrown back into my dream. *Running and running. Footsteps pounding, hands on my arms, jerking me back, yanking me by my hair, twisting me around. I reached up to claw at him, my nails streaking down a stubble-covered cheek, a curse, and my fingers caught on the leather thong around his neck, hard enough to break, and it fell, the tooth sliding into my dress, caught at the sash beneath my breasts, then a jerk so hard backward that my arm wrenched, and tears came to my eyes, and then the sting about my throat wound tighter and tighter, and I was choking—*

"Okustee!" Lord Tom's voice. His face hovering over mine, worry in his eyes. I stared up at him, unseeing, feeling the tooth now between my breasts, the sharp point pressing into my skin.

"Where no law is, there is no transgression." God surely forgives a man for protecting himself against lesser creatures.

"He killed her," I said.

Lord Tom froze.

"The mummy," I explained. "The woman. He killed her, didn't he? Papa killed her."

Lord Tom stepped back, worry replaced by fear. *"Okustee—"*

"It was why his necklace was caught in her dress. Not because it found its way in there, not because he dug her up and reburied her, but because he'd buried her the first time. He killed her and he put her in that basket."

He said nothing. He didn't have to. I saw the truth of it in his face, and I felt nauseated and horrified.

"But why? What was his reason? Was she the experiment? Did something go wrong? He said it was almost ruined. That the experiment was almost ruined. Why? What did she do?"

Lord Tom pulled his hand away from mine and bent, pressing his hands against his thighs, an attitude of dismay and hopelessness. His dark hair came forward, half hiding his face. "I did not know," he admitted, such sad reluctance. "Not until it was done. He wanted help to bury her."

"You knew. You knew what she was and you didn't tell me. It was why you thought she was a vengeful spirit. Because she was murdered. She isn't ancient at all. That fabric...it was woven in a factory. That was why it was so fine. How could I have not known? Why didn't I see?" I rose, grabbing his arm, forcing him to look at me. "How long ago?"

"Twenty-two years," he said.

"Who was she? What was the experiment he was doing? Something about blood and environment, I know, but what?"

"I know nothing of an experiment," he said.

"Who was she?"

Lord Tom's gaze was bleaker than I'd ever seen. His voice was a whisper when he said, "I don't know her name. I never met her or saw her before that day. Before she was already dead. But he said...he said she'd come for her child and he could not give her up."

"Her child?" A dirt floor. A child playing. Love and longing.

"I think that child was you, *okustee.*"

My legs went weak; Lord Tom caught my arm before I fell, but still I wavered, and he helped me sit again on the driftwood. Awkward, rocking beneath my weight, anchored by him.

Gently, he said, "She was Nez Perce. He called her a savage. But her spirit was very strong."

My mother. I thought of everything Papa had told me. How graceful she was, how pretty. I'd imagined parlors and pianos and watercolors. I'd thought once that any talent I'd had for drawing had come from her, lessons in a finishing school…oh, the stories I'd once made for myself before it ceased to matter, before she became irrelevant.

But she had never been irrelevant, and everything I'd thought about her, everything I knew about myself, was a lie. Nez Perce. The tribe beyond the mountains. Sun-burned, grassy hills that felt impossibly familiar. The smell of dust and shadows of clouds moving across the land like spirits.

And my father was a murderer. He was a murderer who had killed my mother because she loved me and wanted me, and everything else was a lie.

I could not reconcile it. None of it. My stomach heaved; I tore away from Lord Tom long enough to retch into the sand, and gently he kept my hair back from my face. When I was done, his hands came to my shoulders, heavy and reassuring. He said, "Do you want to go home, *okustee*? Or should we stay? The storm is coming."

I blinked, putting the world in focus again, looking out at the bay, the rising chop. I could not think, and I did not want to be here. I wanted to be at home. My crook of the river, the bank where I'd found her.

"I need to go back," I said. I took his hand and he helped me to my feet, and I tried to quiet my mind as we made our way out to the canoe, as we sank in the stinking, ankle-deep mud of the flats. I tried to think of nothing. Not what he'd done or who else had known—*Junius. No.* Nothing but pushing the canoe to deeper water, picking up the paddle, my muscles moving without conscious thought. The little splash as it dipped into the water, the thwap of the chop against the sides. Lord Tom steered us true; he required only that I keep paddling, and that I could do. The clouds darkened, hovering low; we weren't halfway there before it began to rain, hard enough to pock the water's surface, wetting my hair so it lay flat to my scalp, dripping over my shoulders and down my back. Too much rain. The river would not hold. The water surrounded me, and I thought again of my near drowning, slipping on the deck, plunging overboard, the tug of the rope around my waist, and then I was crying so that my tears mixed with the rain and I could see nothing but gray all around me.

But all of this was as if I watched from a distance, because I was not Leonie Monroe Russell, but someone else, someone who had once sat on a dirt floor while my mother watched. Someone who had known the sun-burned smell of prairie grass. Someone whose father had murdered her mother, and not well—painfully and in a rage, yanking her by her hair, hair that he'd no doubt run his fingers through once. *You have my mother's hair. Funny, isn't it, how things find their way down?*

He had loved me. This I knew. This I'd never doubted. But to discover this…to know what he'd done…How could I forgive him this?

And she had meant for me to know it, to discover it. Wherever she was, whatever she was, she had come to me, and now she was decaying; I felt her leaving me. I felt her satisfaction blanketing me in rain. *There is no science that proves an afterlife.* There was nothing but my own sense of what had happened, of the truth of it, and yet…what was I to do with it now?

I was shivering when we came ashore. Shivering and wet, cold to the bone, but I felt this all with some part of me I couldn't grasp. Lord Tom gave me a worried look as we started up the broken shell path. *"Kahta mika, okustee?"*

I said, "How can I be all right?"

We went past the gate. There was a light burning in the window. I glanced behind me, to the cut in the Querquelin where I'd found her, taken back by the river that had given her to me. The rain was coursing, the tide rising and spilling, the wind howling through the trees, boiling the river, whitecapping, churning.

We went up the porch stairs, and I saw it there, the trunk, splashed by rain, and I froze—so strange to think of what she was, and what she meant to me. So strange to think of how I'd studied her, how I'd drawn her. The pegs of her teeth and her skin crumbling onto mine, and my legs went weak again. I stopped Lord Tom with a touch and went to her, brushing the rain off the trunk as if it would stay away.

Lord Tom said, "Come, *okustee*."

I obeyed because otherwise I would not have moved from there. He opened the door and I stepped inside to warmth and the smell of salt pork, and there was Daniel at the stove and Junius on the floor, the burlap bag they'd brought back from the *tenas memalose illahee* opened, and he was surrounded by skulls and bones, and I stopped short—the pain in my stomach so hard and fast I gasped, and then I vomited there on the floor—nothing but water and bile, splashing over the floorboards and onto the rug. Junius jumped to his feet and Daniel raced from the kitchen.

I clutched Lord Tom, who held me tight and managed, "Get those out of here."

Junius looked confused. He glanced behind him to the bones, skulls laid out in a line, and then back to me, and then he stepped up, reaching for me, meaning to take me from Lord Tom's grasp, and I pushed him away, shaking my head, saying again, "Get them out of here."

"But it's pouring outside."

"Do as she says, *sikhs*," Lord Tom said.

Junius said, "For Christ's sake—"

Daniel pushed past him, his expression a mask of worry. "What is it? Leonie, what's wrong?"

Lord Tom's grip eased, offering to let me go, to release me to whatever other arms I wanted.

"I'm fine," I said. My voice shook. "I'll be fine."

"Leonie, what is it?" Daniel asked.

I let go of Lord Tom's arm and pushed past Daniel and Junius, stumbling to the settee, putting my head in my hands. Lord Tom strode to the kitchen for a rag and began to mop up bile. My hair dripped, soaking and lank, and I dug my fingers into it, into my own scalp, the bumps there, *spirituality and amativeness, veneration and ideality.* I felt the horror of what was on the floor more than I ever had. My mother's blood. Indian blood. "Get them out," I murmured. "Get them out, Junius. Please."

"Leonie, be reasonable. Don't give me that look, Tom." Junius sat on the settee beside me, putting his arm around my shoulders. I felt his touch like a weight, a burden. I wanted to shrug him loose, but I couldn't bring myself to move. "I'll take them out after the storm. They'll be no use to Baird if they're rotting and crumbling away like that mummy—"

I jerked away from him. "Don't say that. Don't call her that."

Junius frowned with surprise and then made a sound of disgust. "For Christ's sake, Leonie, you need to stop thinking of her as human. She's a relic—hell, the boy will tell you that. He was willing to sell her to a curiosity shop."

"I think you should stop talking," Daniel said.

"Can't stand to hear the truth of it, can you?"

Daniel snapped, "Will you *look* at her? She looks ready to fall apart. What happened, Lea? Tell me. What did the old woman say?" His tone gentled with the questions, though I heard wariness there too. He'd been afraid, I remembered. Afraid of what Bibi would say about him.

I looked up at him. "Is there anything else you want to tell me? Have you any other secrets?"

Again, that wariness, but there was confusion there too, as if he were trying to think of whether he'd failed to reveal something important, and that was when I knew he told the truth. There was nothing to fear from him, but I'd known that already. Nothing to fear but change, a new life I thought I might be too afraid to take. But then I realized he might no longer wish to offer it. The words for what I was were ugly in any language. Half-breed, *sitkum siwash, sitkum Boston.*

He shook his head. "No. Nothing. What did she tell you?"

I looked at Junius, sitting beside me. "My father respected you above all others."

He put his hand on my arm. "Sweetheart, you're shivering. You're soaking wet. Dry off. Go to bed. Whatever you mean to say can be said later. I think you're half sick."

"I need to ask you a question."

"Come on." He rose, pulling on my arm, trying to pull me to my feet. "I'll come to bed with you. I'll keep you warm—"

I jerked away so hard he fell back. "Everything's changed! Why can't you see it?"

"Because I don't mean to relinquish you to this cub," he shot back angrily, glancing at Daniel.

"I'm not yours to keep or give away."

He frowned. "You are my responsibility. Your father gave you to me."

"Like an heirloom," I said, laughing shortly, half crying.

He kneeled beside me, his voice pleading, "Lea, it's an infatuation. Lust. When it's over, what will you have? I'll forgive you this mistake. I've been your lover for twenty years. Does that mean nothing?"

I said, "Did you know who my mother was?"

He looked confused. "Your mother? What has that to do with anything?"

"Just tell me. Did Papa ever say anything of her to you?"

"Lea, you're speaking nonsense. I—"

"Did he tell you that that he killed her? Did he tell you that he murdered my mother?"

Junius froze.

Daniel frowned. "What?"

I ignored him for now. I looked at my husband. Again, I said, "He strangled her."

Slowly, Junius said, "I think you must be feverish, Lea. Come to bed. Please."

"I'm not feverish. Did he tell you anything of this? Of her? Anything at all?"

Something flashed in his eyes, a quick knowledge. He banked it quickly and glanced away, but I'd seen it there. "What do you know, Junius? And think carefully before you answer me."

"I don't know anything about any murder. I don't know what you're talking about. Who told you this? Bibi? She's half crazy."

"The mummy isn't ancient," I told him softly. "She's my mother. My father killed her and put her in the basket. He buried her. It's why his necklace was with her. It fell off when he strangled her."

"Your mother?" Junius looked so shocked and surprised that I knew he'd known nothing of it. "Are you joking? She can't be, Lea. She's ancient, anyone can see it. We'll cut into her. You'll see. We'll find the rags and herbs—"

Daniel's disbelieving laugh cut him off. "Are you mad?"

"She's been mummified. Deliberately. She's ancient. I'll prove it to you right now. Fetch me the saw, boy."

"Fetch it yourself. Listen to her, for Christ's sake. Look at her." Daniel stepped over, squatting beside me. "How do you know this, Lea?"

"In my dreams, I saw—"

"Your *dreams*?" Junius burst out laughing. "You're talking as crazy as the widow."

I ignored him. Daniel hadn't taken his gaze from me, and it was to him I spoke. "It's true. Lord Tom told me."

Junius looked at Lord Tom, who was tossing aside the soiled rags, rising. "What do you know of this, Tom?"

"It was before you came, *sikhs*. Teddy asked me for help to bury her, but I refused. She was dead already. I would not touch her. I did not know what he had done with her body until we found her. He said she was dangerous, that she'd come for her child and he did not want to give her up. But that was all he said. We never spoke of it after that day."

"And you've said nothing of it all this time?"

"It was not my secret to tell," Lord Tom said quietly. "She was not of my people, and I owed Teddy my life. He was afraid of her, and I was glad that he kept her from taking her child from us. So I said nothing."

"Her child," Daniel repeated. "Leonie?"

Lord Tom said, "I have always believed so."

"She was Nez Perce," I said dully, and I waited for Daniel to flinch, to look horrified, but before I could see his reaction, Junius made a sound—impatient, short, and I looked at him.

"This is all nonsense," he said. "Whoever that was, it wasn't the mummy. She's ancient, I tell you. Tom's mistaken."

"It was all a lie," I said to him. "My whole life has been a lie."

"You don't know what you're saying," Junius told me.

"It explains everything. The way I feel about things. What I know—"

"Leonie, don't jump to conclusions."

"What other conclusion can I make?"

Again, that little flinch, that slip away.

I rose. I grabbed his arm. "Junius, you know something. Tell me."

He pulled away.

"I need to know," I insisted. "Is it something about her?"

"I knew your mother was Indian. But that's all, Leonie. That's all I knew. I didn't know she came for you. Hell, I still don't believe he would have killed her."

"Even if she threatened to take me away?"

"He said she was a savage. She could never have taken you away. He didn't need to kill her." Junius frowned. "Don't you see? No one would have let her take you."

"He never said a word to me," I whispered. "He never told me." I looked at Daniel, whose expression was carefully blank, that actor in him, the way he knew to shield his emotions, to admit nothing, *to do whatever avails him*...I turned away. "He should have told me!"

Junius gave me an impatient look. "He couldn't tell you. It would have ruined the—"

Experiment.

The word burst into my brain, even as he hadn't spoken it. And it all settled into something I knew, every journal entry fallen into place.

I was the experiment. Papa's attempt to determine once and for all the question of blood and environment. His need to keep her silent, to keep me ignorant of my heritage, of everything I was.

It explained everything. Everything I'd ever thought. My father's fear over the way the Indian legends affected me. His pooh-poohing of my intrinsic knowledge of relics—the call of my mother's blood, how he'd hated that I loved it here, the place where my mother was buried...Who I was, what I was, all those things Papa had tried to deny. My fierceness and my passion and the way he and Junius saw them as primitive traits, the dominance of my Indian blood, and how anxious they'd been to overcome it, to turn me into the respectable, staid white woman they'd wanted me to be.

I looked at my husband in horror. "It was me, wasn't it? The experiment was me?"

He looked uncomfortable; he glanced away. "Don't be absurd—"

"You knew about it."

Now he looked at me again. He spread his hands. "No, of course not."

"You did, Junius." I advanced upon him, not knowing what I meant to do, to say. "The journals say it. He says he told you. That you promised to help him. How was that? What help did you offer?"

"Only to keep it secret. Only to observe."

I laughed bitterly. "You did much more than that. How could you have borne it? Marrying me knowing what I was?"

"Lea, please. I love you."

"But you think I'm a savage, don't you? How many times have you said it?"

"Not you," he insisted. He grabbed my hand, twisting his fingers hard into mine. "You were never that. It was remarkable, the influence your white blood had. We thought it might overcome the rest in time—with the right training. As long as there were no children, there was no reason for you to know."

His words brought Bibi's sharply to mind. I wanted to cry. I wrenched my hand from his. "How lucky it was, then, that there weren't any."

"Yes," he admitted.

"But how could you have known that? What would you have done if I'd conceived?"

Now Junius looked uncomfortable. "Your father cautioned me…"

I was crying.

Junius said, "It was better this way, Lea. I promise you—"

"Bibi says I'm with child," I managed.

Junius froze. "What?"

At the same moment Daniel said, "Lea?"

I could not bear to look at Daniel. To see the condemnation in his eyes, the disgust. I kept my gaze on Junius, who seemed to waver before me.

"You're *what*?" His voice was strangled. "You can't be."

"She seemed certain," I said.

"You *can't* be."

Daniel started toward me. "Is this true?"

But he never got to me. Junius grabbed Daniel by the collar. "Do you know what the hell you've done?" he shouted. "You stupid boy, do you have any idea?"

I grabbed Junius's arm. "Junius, please. Please, don't."

Junius shrugged me off in the same moment that Daniel pushed him away, his eyes blazing. "Don't touch me, old man."

Junius barely stepped back. He spat in Daniel's face, "You've ruined everything. From the day you first came here, you've done nothing but rile up things that should have been left alone."

"How inconvenient of me," Daniel said. "Too bad you couldn't just go on the way you had been, everyone doing what you wanted. You don't even know what you have. You're a selfish bastard. The thought of your blood polluting my veins makes me sick."

"Polluting." Junius's laugh was aborted and mean. "You're the one who's polluting. You couldn't keep her from getting with child, could you? And now you've ruined everything—"

"I don't know that it's his," I said, stepping forward, coming between them. "It could be yours. It could—"

"It's not mine," Junius snapped.

I stared at him, confused. "But—"

"It's not mine. I've spent twenty years being certain of it, for Christ's sake."

My ears began to buzz. The world went gray, the sound of the rain pounding against the house beat in time to my blood. I could not make sense of what he was saying. "I don't understand."

His anger was ugly. "I've done what I could to keep you from getting pregnant. Do you understand that?"

"But...but why?"

"Because your father asked me to. Because it was part of the promise I made him. The experiment. He was afraid of what you would discover. He was afraid the baby would look Indian." Junius looked at me, tense and miserable. He went on, "He told me you were a half-breed. He told me he'd originally meant to leave you with your mother, that he wanted nothing to do with a little savage. But you looked so white. You could pass. So he took you. He said your mother was...that she'd been a...temporary madness."

"A temporary madness," I repeated numbly, sinking onto the settee.

"He hated himself for it," Junius said. "But you...you were the answer to a question he'd spent his life debating. How much does blood matter? Would it trump a white upbringing? If he treated you as if you were white, would that overcome the Indian part of you? Were you even capable of learning, or would the stain of your mother corrupt you?"

I looked at Lord Tom, who watched stonily, and suddenly I realized that he had spent twenty years hearing these words, twenty years of silently bearing Junius and Papa and their ceaseless contempt for Lord Tom's people. I said to him, "How could you listen to this? How could you stay?"

Lord Tom met my gaze; I knew he understood. "For you, *okustee.*"

Junius let out his breath. He looked at Daniel, who stood there, his fists half-clenched, and said with such disgust it startled me, "And as for *you*...you've ruined nearly forty years' worth of work in a few months. A lifetime's study, gone."

Daniel shook his head. "It's not me who's ruined things, old man. It's you. You and her father. I'd feel sorry for you if I didn't find you so pathetic."

I stared at my husband. "This is why you married me, isn't it? Because Papa wanted you to continue the experiment?"

"One of the reasons," Junius said. "The others I've told you. I wanted you. I loved you."

"*Loved?*"

"Love," he said, and the truth of it was in his eyes. "I love you, Leonie. You know that. I'm willing to forget all this, to forgive you—"

"You love me, but you didn't want to have a child with me."

His gaze begged me to understand. "The research was too promising. You were everything we'd hoped for, Lea. It was nearly time to write the paper. Your father's experiment, my managing of it. I couldn't take the risk that the child would be Indian. I couldn't risk your knowing. I made a *promise.*"

A promise. A lifetime of promises. I looked at Daniel, and I heard what he'd said to me only this morning: *Promises to the dead. What if now that they're gone they realize they were wrong?*

"I have dedicated my *life* to this," Junius said, rising, stepping in front of me, blocking Daniel from my view. "You're a scientist, Lea, you know the value of this. Can you blame me? Have I not taken care of you? Have I not loved you?"

"You lied to her," Daniel said softly.

Junius turned to him. "And you didn't?"

Daniel laughed. "Well, I didn't take away her life, did I?"

"I *gave* her a life," Junius spat. "What would she have been without me? A savage. A *half-breed.* I made her what she is. My *wife.* She's *respected*, goddammit! Everything would have been fine if you'd stayed the hell in San Francisco. If not for the damned mummy—"

"She wanted me to know the truth, Junius," I said.

"She's a *relic*, Lea," he snapped. "For God's sake, why can't you see that? Do I have to show you the truth?" He pushed past me. "She's not what you think she is. She's just a goddamned mummy." He jerked open the door. The sound of rain, the rush of wind, the roar of the river. He was out on the porch, and for a moment I stood there, stunned. For a moment it didn't occur to me what he meant to do. And then I heard the thud of the trunk lid against the house; I remembered Daniel dropping the saw there beside it.

"No," I said, whispering in horror. "He's going to cut her apart." I rushed to the door, and Daniel was beside me. Junius was already bending over the trunk, the saw in his hand. Daniel pushed by me, lunging across the porch, grabbing Junius's arm to stop him.

"Drop it," he said.

Junius wrenched away. He looked past Daniel to me. "There won't be any viscera. You'll see—"

Daniel hit him. Junius staggered back, dropping the saw, and then recovered. He threw himself at Daniel, and then the two of them were falling against the porch rail, bouncing off, stumbling down the stairs. Daniel fell into the mud, into the puddles rapidly forming from the rain, and Junius was on top of him, slamming his fist into him, yelling something—the words swept away by rain.

I screamed, "Junius, no!" and started toward the stairs, but Lord Tom pulled me back, holding me. When I tried to break loose, his hands tightened.

Lord Tom said, "No, *okustee*. The river is rising."

I looked beyond Daniel and Junius. Lord Tom was right. The Querquelin was overfull and whitecapping, the wind whipping my hair around my head like the wild spirit of Yutilma, the water roaring and beyond that the darkness of the bay. I heard her voice in my head. *The tide.* Or perhaps it was only my own, but I knew it was the plus tide feeding too much water into a river already swollen. Too much water, and nothing could hold it all.

Daniel was up now, grappling with Junius, the two of them splashing away from the house, toward the river, through ankle-deep water, and suddenly I was horribly, terribly afraid.

I wrenched from Lord Tom, racing down the stairs, racing for them, and I wasn't more than a few steps before I realized it was more than just puddling. The yard was flooding. The river had already overflowed its banks and was moving higher while I stood there. Shin deep, the rain bashing and heavy, pounding, and then Lord Tom was there, pulling me back again.

I screamed, "Stop!" but my voice was lifted away by the wind. I shouted again, "Daniel!" and my voice whisked away like smoke. He didn't hear me, and I couldn't get closer. Lord Tom's hold on me was unbreakable; he hauled me back to the porch—the house should be safe, the house was safe. On a rise, and just as I had the thought I heard a terrible sound—like the falling of a giant tree—and then the barn shuddered and went down and the river currents took it, a huge dark shadow on the water, swirling and churning. Itcixyan, the most powerful of the Chinook water spirits, crumbling the boards and beams into splinters.

Daniel and Junius were thigh deep, closer to the river, below the rise.

I looked at Lord Tom. "You have to stop them! Stop them!"

"It is rising too quickly." He sounded worried. He jerked his head, and I followed the motion to see that the river was coming steadily on—already lapping against the porch stairs.

"The house will be safe," I said, but he shook his head.

"High ground, *okustee*," he said, dragging me with him down the stairs, into the water, into the pounding rain, toward the back of the yard, the trees rising from the salt marsh.

Lord Tom shoved me toward the woods. "Go. I'll get them."

The water was knee deep, the current dragging so I must fight it, but I didn't go until I saw him reach them. I saw him shout at them, but the wind stole his words. I saw him gesture to me, the paleness of Daniel's face in the darkness as he turned toward me, and then the three of them were struggling through the currents, and we made our way toward the trees, the greater rise that climbed to the hill behind the house. Once I was there, I fell against a cedar, my skirts sodden and heavy, my boots full of water, the rest of me wet with the pouring rain, the chill creeping into my bones.

Junius and Daniel and Lord Tom stumbled up behind me. Junius shouted, "We should be at the house! The river won't rise so far!"

I said, "It already has. Look!"

He turned to see. Water rising past the root cellar, lapping at the boards. "The bones," he said.

And I remembered her. The trunk on the porch.

"Oh dear God," I gasped, and when Junius strode to the edge of the rise, I was with him. "My mother."

Lord Tom said, "No, *okustee*. She belongs to the river. She would want you to be safe. For *tenas yaka tenas klootchman*."

Her granddaughter.

Daniel's daughter.

He was right, I knew. Junius shook his head. "It's not too late. I can get them all."

Daniel shouted, "Are you mad? Leave them. It's too dangerous."

Lord Tom grabbed Junius's arm. "The river will take back what it wants."

Junius jerked away. "I haven't spent the last months collecting those things to give them back to the river."

"You cannot go, *sikhs*."

I forgot my anger. I forgot the lies Junius had told me, the things he'd said. All I knew were twenty years of habit. Twenty years of loving him. I rushed to him. "Junius, he's right. Leave them!"

He looked at me, his face grim.

I clutched his arm. "You can't go!"

He looked over my head. "Get her off me, boy."

I dug my fingers into his arm. "I won't let you go."

He pulled himself loose and strode quickly toward the water, and I rushed after him, plunging in after him, and then suddenly there was Daniel, grabbing me, holding me.

"Don't let him go," I said desperately.

"You can't go after him." Daniel's voice was low and urgent, his arms like iron, holding me in place. The wind whipped his soaking hair into his face, which was pale with cold and wet, stark. I looked helplessly toward Junius, fighting his way through the river, hip deep.

"He'll die there."

Daniel dragged me back. He bent to look me in the eyes. "I'll go after him. I'll bring him back. But Lea, you have to stay. Promise you won't follow me, no matter what happens."

"He won't listen to you."

His smile was grim. "If he doesn't, he'll drown. And believe me, he won't let me win so easily."

"Daniel, no." I clutched at him.

"I promise I'll be back," he said. "We've things to talk about, you and I."

I could not release my grip on his shirt. He peeled away my fingers. He looked past me to Lord Tom. "Don't let her follow."

Then he raced after his father, and soon all I could see was the white of their shirts in the darkness, and then they were rounding the house and there was nothing to see at all.

The river was climbing, sucking everything into it, the plus tide and the storm and my own desires crashing and swallowing. Lord Tom came to stand beside me, his hand on my arm as if he meant at any moment to drag me back, as if it might become necessary to anchor me. I watched for any sign of them. I strained to see. There was only darkness and water, the faint light from the house. "Where are they?" I asked. "What's taking them so long?"

I did not take my eyes from the house, from the light glowing from the windows, my hope that I would see one of them within it, or that I would see them coming back, Junius persuaded, Daniel keeping his promise. I could see almost nothing beyond that, not through the crashing rain, the whip of the wind in the trees above my head, but I was watching so carefully it was a moment before I heard the sound. Thunder, a terrible creaking groan, an unappeased roar. It was a moment before I realized what it was, a moment before I comprehended the house rising as if it were being lifted in Itcixyan's palm, and then collapse as if he'd crushed it in his fingers.

I screamed out, "Daniel!" and lurched forward, and it was only Lord Tom's hold that kept me there. What was left of the house crumpled and broke, swirling in the currents of the river like toothpicks, swept away. The lie of my life washed away by the river, which had indeed taken back its own, and I didn't realize how I was struggling until Lord Tom pulled me hard into his arms and I went limp, staring blindly at the spot where the house had been, where I had last seen them.

"No," I whispered desperately. "No. No. You gave him to me."

Lord Tom said, "*Okustee,* the canoe."

I looked to where he pointed, where a dark shadow nudged the bank where we stood. The canoe, insistent and relentless as if to say *here I am. Let me save you.*

Lord Tom released me, leaning to grab the bow, pulling it up onto the bank, and I stopped him with a touch. "I need to find them if I can."

He nodded. "Get in."

And so we did. There was only one paddle, laying on the floor beneath our feet, the other washed away. I sat in the bow and Lord Tom pushed us off and took up the paddle. The current was hard and fast, buffeting us, and I wiped away my tears and looked past my despair, searching for them, for any sign in the darkness. She had brought him for me, why give him and take him back? But I saw nothing.

"He promised," I said desperately, to nothing, to her, who was gone now. "He promised." And there, suddenly, as if my desire had given birth to it, I saw something floating, a white shirt, Daniel clinging to what looked like the front door.

"There!" I shouted, unnecessarily, as Lord Tom had seen him at almost the same moment, and we were moving toward him, not fast enough, and then we reached him. He was white faced, his hair dark and plastered to his skull, and Tom and I hauled him in, and I cupped his cold face in my hands and kissed him hard, my tears mixing with the rain and my relief, and he wrapped his arms around me and said, "I pulled him out, Lea. I did what I promised. He's out here somewhere."

But it seemed forever until we found him. There, unconscious in the flood, half-buoyed by a piece of siding, floating out to the bay. I thought he was dead, but when Lord Tom and Daniel pulled him into the canoe, he was still breathing. There was something clutched in his hand, held hard as a death grip.

My notebook.

CHAPTER 29

I STOOD ON THE EDGE OF THE BANK AND WATCHED THE storm, the avenging spirit of the river rushing over my land, until Daniel came up beside me and drew me gently back into the nominal shelter of the trees. "You need to be warm," he said, though his own teeth were chattering, and he looked like some gaunt spirit of the cold himself with his pale face and his hair stringing dark and wet and lank.

But I went with him. My sorrow over Junius's lies, and my father's, was a heavy, dark and freezing thing, a regret I could not lose, and that neither had realized what they'd cost me was something I could not easily forgive. My life felt unformed and new and raw, something unmolded that I was uncertain I could recast. How did one come to terms with becoming something else?

I remembered Daniel's words—*I'm afraid of what you'll become if I leave you*, and my own, back to him, *Become? I am already* become.

But I was not, after all.

Daniel led me deeper into the woods. The branches creaked and groaned in the wind above our heads, but they kept off the worst of the rain. The canoe had been turned upside down next to a huge nurse log, which crumbled beneath its burden of ferns and moss, a dark fuzziness in the night. Lord Tom had found Edna, lowing piteously in the forest, and brought her back, tying her tether to a tree, and now she was quiet. Junius was there already, huddled beneath the canoe. He watched wordlessly as we came up, and Daniel released me, squeezing my hand before he stepped away, leaving me to face my husband alone.

Junius rose and came to me. He was bedraggled, pale, white with cold. "I tried to save your notebook," he said. "The translations. Your drawings. I grabbed it, but…"

"I have it," I said, touching my pocket, where I'd shoved it. It was heavy and wet; I wondered if the ink and pencil had melted away, but I hadn't had the time or the courage to look at it. "It was in your hand."

"I remembered to save it for you. It was the only thing I tried to save. Does that make a difference? It's not much, but we could use it to start over. You and me, Lea. We could leave this wretched place. Go north. You'll have the Bela Coola talked out of secret society masks in no time."

I said nothing. Silence stretched between us.

Junius said, "I've lost you, haven't I?"

"I trusted you," I said softly. "I loved you."

He sighed. The sadness in it hurt. The loss of hope. But I could not forgive him, and I don't think he really expected me to. He said in a quiet, stark voice, "I stayed, Lea. I didn't want to. I've never stayed this long anywhere. But I stayed for you. Doesn't that count for anything?"

"It was the experiment," I said. "You stayed for that."

He shook his head. "For *you*."

"I wish I could say it mattered," I said, equally softly. "I wish I could forgive you. But I can't, Junius. You and Papa…you took too much."

He took a deep breath, then gave me a quick nod. He glanced over his shoulder, to Daniel, who sat watching, tense and pale in the darkness. When Junius looked back at me, he smiled a little, but his mouth was stiff with cold; it was awkward and sweet. "Well. I love you, Lea. If you believe nothing else, believe that."

I didn't know that to say—that it was enough, that it wasn't. Both things were true. My vision blurred. I looked down at my feet.

He said, "Tell me not to go. Ask me to stay the way you always have."

But it was a useless plea, and I thought he knew it. My throat was too tight to speak.

"Well," he whispered. "Maybe I'll go north. See the Bela Coola for myself."

My tears came on full. I thought of everything we could have been, everything he and my father had taken from me, had given away. But before I could say anything, Junius said, "You'll be a good mother. I always thought so. Good-bye, Lea."

He left me without a touch, without a kiss. Just words, heavy with regret, that echoed in my ears. I looked up in surprise, but he was already moving into the darkness. I watched as he went to Lord Tom and murmured something I couldn't hear, and then he turned to Daniel, who stood.

"You be good to her, boy," he said.

And then he was gone, melting into the darkness and rain, into a forest loud with spirits, voices from a deep past, from my own, swallowing him as if he belonged there.

I might have stood there all night, but Daniel came to lead me over to the canoe, drawing me down beside him beneath its shelter, leaning back against the nurse log, wrapping his arms around me and cocooning me with his body the way he'd done the night I'd almost drowned.

He said to me, whispering against my ear, "When we were in the house, I heard…something. Some voice telling me to leave. Your voice."

"*Her* voice," I said.

He kissed my shoulder.

"There was a part of him that *was* good, Daniel," I said. "In spite of everything."

His arms tightened around me. I didn't feel sorrow in him, or regret, or relief. I felt only acceptance, and I was sad for him, for the man he'd never known, the one who had so easily left him, who had not bothered or cared to share himself with his only child. But Daniel said nothing. Not until minutes later, when his voice came to me, uncertain, a whisper, "Is it true? What Bibi said about the baby? Is it true?"

"I don't know. Would you be very disappointed?"

"I told you it didn't matter to me."

"I meant…if I *was* pregnant. Would you be disappointed?"

I held my breath, but he said without a pause, almost as if he were puzzled, "How could I be disappointed?"

"She would be…part Indian. You heard Junius. All his talk of…pollution, and…she might look…"

"*She?*" His voice was light with amusement.

I glanced to where Lord Tom stood, studiously ignoring us. "That's what Lord Tom thinks."

"Is that some Indian superstition? Or is he in direct contact with some all-knowing spirit?"

I laughed a little. "The latter, I think."

Daniel went quiet. "I love you, Lea. All of you. I can't separate one part from another. Whatever that must mean."

I looked out through the dark sentinels of the trees, shadows against shadows, listening to the rushing wind and the rain and the roar of the river. And I wondered how much of it I'd put into motion. Unknowingly. Blindly. How much had been only the action of my own desires, the blood I hadn't known was within me rising, making itself known? Had it truly been my mother's memories and my mother's dreams I'd seen, or some half memory of my own, something I'd fashioned from a scrap of cloth, something I'd somehow always known but never faced—these parts of me I denied and resisted, pushing past the walls of the life others had chosen, making themselves real until I could no longer look away?

And then I wondered, Did it matter how or why it had happened? Or only that it had?

His arms were hard and warm about me. The thing I craved that I'd never known I wanted. Beyond us, the river churned and swirled and sang. I heard it murmur in my ear. *Start over.*

Live.

CHAPTER 30

THE RIVER TOOK EVERYTHING. THE MUMMY, EVERY SKULL and bone. But I found a few relics in the mess, some ruined by the mud—a mask and a few horn spoons, and a coiled tangle of hiaqua, things spread here and there, doled out like bits of candy, but little more than that. My father's journals were gone, the Bela Coola masks, my collection. It wasn't until days later that I dared to open the notebook to see how well it had fared. The pages were wrinkled and stuck together in places, the ink and pencil blurred here and there but still legible. I opened it to the drawing of her, caught forever sleeping. More than a memory now, and from it and my dreams, I drew her portrait as I knew her. Alive and walking through prairie grass. Something to show our daughter.

Because she was a girl, just as Lord Tom had predicted. A girl with skin just this side of copper, and hair the color of molasses taffy, and eyes so blue they looked like the piece of sea glass I found deep within a pocket, lost in the lining of my coat. Sea glass the color of the sky tossed and polished by the waves. Her father's eyes. His father's.

"But you have my mother's hair," I found myself whispering to her. "Funny, isn't it, how things find their way down?"

The storm that night became a legend, the kind of thing that people talked about over bottles of whiskey on rainy, windy nights. The tide so high it flooded the streets of Bruceport and tossed boats onto the driftwood of the beach as if they were no more than toys. Waves that drowned two oystermen and a flooding river that washed away Junius Russell—("Though his wife married his son and they have a baby already. Indecent, if you ask me," which talk made Daniel laugh).

But none of that was what I remembered about that night. What I remembered was Junius disappearing into a wood dense with rain and spirits, an awkward, sweet smile. What I remembered was Daniel's warmth as he'd cradled me tightly against the storm, and the last time I'd looked upon the trunk, how I hadn't realized it would be the last time I saw her, how I hadn't said good-bye.

There were no more dreams after that night. No longer did I hear her voice. After a few months it all began to seem like something I'd imagined, a power I could not possibly have known. Until the hour I looked into my daughter's eyes for the first time and knew that I would reach through worlds for her.

It was only then I truly understood the gift my mother had given me. The gift of a life washed clean. Her hope for me manifest in rain and wind and a rising river, in a heron standing on the riverbank, in a pretty feather blown along a San Francisco street.

ACKNOWLEDGMENTS

Some books have a longer than usual incubation period, and *Bone River* was one of them. I'd like to thank Bruce Weilepp of the Pacific County Historical Society Museum, who spent a long and invaluable day with me several years ago, answering questions and providing numerous and valuable county records and oral histories. It paid off in the end! I'd also like to thank Melody Guy for her insightful and very helpful editorial guidance; Courtney Miller and everyone else at Amazon for their enthusiasm and hard work on my behalf; and Kim Witherspoon, Allison Hunter, and the staff at Inkwell Management for everything they do. Thanks also must go to Kristin Hannah, who has spent more hours talking with me about this book than can be reasonably expected of anyone, and who—as always—helped me find my out of a dark and swampy morass into the light. And finally, to Kany, Maggie and Cleo, whose support and love make it possible for me to tell stories for a living—I owe them more than I can say.

ABOUT THE AUTHOR

Born in Columbus, Ohio, and raised in Olympia, Washington, Megan Chance is the award-winning author of several novels, including *City of Ash*, *Prima Donna*, *The Spiritualist*, and *An Inconvenient Wife*. She lives in the Pacific Northwest with her husband, a criminal defense attorney, and their two daughters.